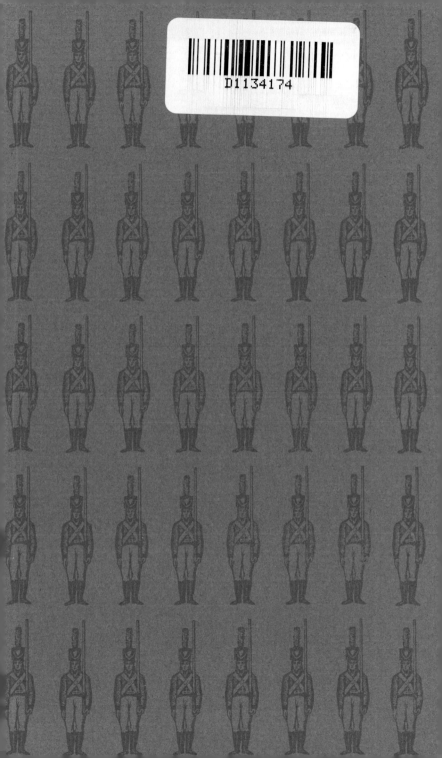

A Heron Books Collection

WAR AND PEACE

TOLSTOY

WAR AND PEACE

I

Illustrations by
Christian Wilhelm von Faber du Faur

HERON BOOKS
LONDON

The illustrations of Christian Wilhelm
von Faber du Faur were taken from the
collection of lithographies entitled
"Sheets from my portfolio sketched on
the spot during the campaign in Russia
of 1812", published at Stuttgart in 1845.

Published by arrangement with
J. M. Dent & Sons Ltd.

INTRODUCTION

By Vicomte de Vogüé

War and Peace presents us with a complete tableau of Russian society during the great Napoleonic wars from 1805 to 1815. The stage is immense and the actors are innumerable; among them are three emperors with their ministers, their marshals, and their generals, and a countless retinue of minor officers, soldiers, nobles, and peasants. We are transported by turns from the salons of St. Petersburg to the camps of war, from Moscow to the country districts. And all these diverse and varied scenes are joined together with a controlling purpose that brings everything into harmony. Each one of the prolonged series of constantly changing tableaux is of remarkable beauty and palpitating with life.

The interminable series of incidents, of portraits, of reflections which the author presents to us, unrolls itself around a few fictitious personages; but the true hero of the story is Russia in her desperate struggle against the foreigner, and the real personages, Alexander, Napoleon, Koutouzof, Speransky, occupy almost as prominent a position as the imaginary ones. Pleasure has to be purchased from the book much the same as from the ascent of mountains; the way is at times unpromising, the reader has to summon up his energy and take plenty of trouble; but when he reaches the summit and looks back, his recompense is a magnificent one, the landscape spreads out beneath him in all its immensity: he who has not made the ascent will never know the exact conformation of the province, the course of its rivers, and the position of its towns. In the same way the foreigner who had not read Tolstoy would vainly flatter himself with having a true knowledge of Russia in the nineteenth century, and he who wished to write a history of the country would uselessly overhaul all the archives and would produce only a dead work if he neglected to consult this inexhaustible repertory of the national existence.

It is easy to predict the impressions which readers of *War and Peace* will successively experience. At the beginning the mind will be out of its element, ignorant as to where it is being led, and will even feel somewhat bored.   But gradually it will be carried away captivated by the complex working of so many interests; it will feel at home amidst all these personages, will make friends with them, and become passionately interested in the secret of their destinies.   On closing the book one feels all the grief of a parting after years spent in an adopted family. We find in it a faithful picture of life, the experience as it were of the traveller thrown amidst fresh surroundings.   The first sensation of strangeness soon gives way to curiosity, which yields in its turn to a lasting attachment.

On beholding these camps, these soldiers, this court, these drawing-rooms which ape the court and which have scarcely changed during half a century—on beholding the inner workings of the hearts of men which never change, the reader cannot withhold his admiration and exclaims at every page, "How life-like this is!"   And those imperial battles, Austerlitz, Friedland, Borodino, pass before one in the course of these volumes.   They are not what we are in the habit of calling "battle pictures."   Tolstoy talks of war like a man who has gone through it, he knows that one never *sees* a battle.   The soldier, the officer, even the general himself whom the novelist introduces, never sees more than one point of the combat, but by the way that some men fight, think, speak, and die upon a particular spot, we can imagine all the remainder of the action and guess upon which side victory leans.

One must not expect classical conventionality from a realistic writer, an army breathing heroism from the example of its leaders, living solely for the great things which it accomplishes.   Tolstoy adheres to human truth, each soldier treating the sublime as a trade, the privates heedless and occupied with silly trifles, like the officers with their pleasures or their advancement, and the generals with their ambitions and their intrigues: all this world becomes accustomed and indifferent to that which appears to us so extraordinary and grandiose. With regard to the leaders of the Russian armies, Tolstoy is most severe; he conjures up the councils of war by the aid of contemporary reports: he ridicules the French and German strategists who surrounded Alexander; and his historical nihilism finds a voluptuous enjoyment in depicting this Babel of tongues and opinions.

What Count Tolstoy studies with most passion and felicity after war are the intrigues of the highest spheres of society and of their centre of gravitation, the court. As differences of race and country disappear in the same ratio as one rises in the social sphere, the novelist in this instance no longer confines himself to Russian types, he creates human types which are both universal and eternal. When writers of imagination undertake to depict the closed circle of a court we refuse them our confidence; we divine by means of a thousand false notes that they have listened at doors, seen through keyholes. The superiority of the Russian writer shows itself inasmuch as he is in his native element; he has seen both the court and the army, and has held a position at the one the same as in the other; he speaks of his peers in their own language and with their ideas. Enter the drawing-room of Anna Schérer, the old maid of honour; listen to the cackle of the *émigrés*, the judgments delivered by them; observe the manœuvres of the courtiers and "that accent of respectful sadness" with which the names of members of the imperial family are uttered; seat yourself at Speransky's table, in the home of that statesman "who laughs as one laughs on the stage"; follow the track of the sovereign at balls guided by that aurora which lights up every face directly he enters; above all draw nigh old Count Bésoukhow's death-bed, watch the tragedy which is being enacted behind the mask of etiquette, the quarrel of sordid interests around this speechless moribund, the agitation of all these minds. Here the sinister, as elsewhere the sublime, borrows a matchless energy from the sincerity, the simplicity of the picture, from the effort which good breeding imposes on utterances and looks alike.

Two figures stand out prominently from Count Tolstoy's grand canvas. The first is Maria Bolkonsky, Andrew's sister, the pious daughter who devotes herself to softening the declining days of a cross-grained father. Quite different is Natacha Rostow, the lively and seductive child, beloved by all, smitten with many; who moves through this serious work, leaving in her wake an odour of love. She is good, upright, severe, but a slave to her sensibility. Betrothed to Prince Andrew, the only man she really loves, Natacha falls a victim to a fatal passion for that good-for-nothing fellow Kouraguine. Undeceived in time, she finds Andrew dying of his wounds and nurses him with mournful despair. This portion of the work is a masterly study, inexorable like life with its sudden misfortunes.

The varying influence exercised on man by his surroundings

WAR AND PEACE

is one of those phenomena which have been the most closely observed by Count Tolstoy; he delights in successively plunging one of his characters in divers atmospheres, that of the army, that of the country, that of society, and in showing us the corresponding moral mutations. When an individual, after having acted for a time under the influence of strange thoughts and passions, is caught up and placed again in his habitual surroundings, his views on all things immediately undergo a change. Follow young Nicholas Rostow returning from the army to the paternal roof, or else starting to rejoin his squadron of hussars; he is no longer the same man, he has an existence for each occasion; in the post-chaise which brings him to Moscow or which takes him away, we behold him slowly casting off or reassuming his professional existence.

Count Tolstoy amuses himself in taking every part of the human puppet to pieces. A stranger enters a drawing-room; the author studies his gaze, his voice, his walk; he initiates us into the profoundest depths of the man's mind, he analyses a glance exchanged between two individuals engaged in conversation, he finds in it friendship, fear, the feeling of the superiority which one of them attributes to himself, all the shades of the intercourse between these two men. Never yielding to emotion, this doctor is at every minute of the day feeling the pulses of all whom he meets, and coldly noting the state of their moral health. He proceeds objectively; he scarcely ever tells us when presenting one of his creations—"This is a dissipated and ambitious man, a gambler"; but he causes him at once to act in a typical manner which reveals his habits. It is thus with old Count Rostow; we have not been told that he is dissipated; but when, after becoming aware of the embarrassed state of his affairs, we hear him asking his steward for freshly-coined roubles, we at once divine his real character.

The realistic writer has revived this fundamental precept of classic art in his anxiety to depict real life, wherein we divine the individuals by means of similar signs, without having been informed of their position and qualities. The fact is, there is much art in this apparent chaos, no end of selection in this formidable accumulation of details. Mark how, during a conversation, Tolstoy is careful always to bring the actors present to our eyes by noting some gesture, some twitching, by interrupting their speech to show us the direction of their glance: it is perpetually like a scene at a theatre.

Finally there is a large amount of wit pervading this grave

x

SELECT BIBLIOGRAPHY

style of Tolstoy's which never breaks into a smile; not wit such
as we ordinarily understand it, the flash and the sparkle, the
unexpected clash of antitheses; but what Pascal terms the wit
of subtlety.

BEFORE TILSIT

1805–1807

BOOK ONE

CHAPTER I

"WELL, prince, what did I tell you? Genoa and Lucca have become the property of the Bonapartes. Now, I give you fair warning, you will forfeit your position as my friend—as my faithful slave, as you choose to say—if you persist in disbelieving in war, and are still determined to defend all the horrors and atrocities perpetrated by this Antichrist—for that he is Antichrist I am convinced! Well, well, and how are you my dear friend? I see I have quite frightened you. Come, sit down and chat."

The time was July 1805, the place St. Petersburg, and the speaker Anna Paulovna Schérer, maid of honour to her majesty the empress-dowager of the Russias, and one of the more intimate court-circle. Her words were addressed to Prince Basil, a personage of official gravity, and the first to arrive at her soirée. Anna Paulovna had been coughing for some few days: it was influenza—a *grippe* she called it (*grippe* being at that time a new and fashionable word).

A footman in red livery—the court livery—had been round the town that morning carrying a number of notes each saying in the same terms and in French:

"If you have nothing better to do this evening, count, or prince, and are not too much alarmed at the prospect of spending it with a hapless invalid, I shall be delighted to see you between seven and ten. ANNA SCHÉRER."

"Mercy on us, what a terrible attack!" said the prince, not in the least upset by this reception. He wore a court uniform

1

embroidered with gold, and sparkling with orders, silk stockings, and buckled shoes; his flat face wore an affable smile; he spoke French—that elaborate French which to the Russians of a generation or two back was the language even of their thoughts—and his voice had the deliberate and patronising tones of a man influential at court and grown old in its atmosphere.

He came up to Anna Paulovna and kissed her hand, bending his bald and perfumed head over it; then he seated himself comfortably on the sofa.

"First of all let me entreat you to give me good news of your health. Reassure a friend," he said in a gallant tone, which nevertheless betrayed a shade of irony, not to say of indifference, under the formalities of politeness.

"How can I be well when my spirits are so ill at ease? Every feeling soul must suffer in these days—but you have come to spend the evening, I hope?"

"No, I regret to say. It is Wednesday; the English ambassador is giving a great ball, and I must show myself there. My daughter is coming to fetch me."

"I fancied the party had been put off; and I must confess that all these entertainments and fireworks are beginning to bore me dreadfully."

"If only your wish had been known, the reception would of course have been put off," replied the prince, mechanically, as if he were a well-regulated watch, and without the smallest expectation of being supposed to be in earnest.

"Come, now, do not tease me; and tell me, for you know everything, what is settled about the despatch from Novosiltzow?"

"What can I tell you?" said the prince, looking weary and bored. "You insist on knowing what they have concluded? Well, they have concluded that Bonaparte has burnt his ships, and we, it would seem, are about to do the same."

Prince Basil always talked with cool indifference, like an actor rehearsing an old part. Anna Paulovna, on the contrary, affected extreme sprightliness in spite of her forty years. She had made a social reputation for enthusiasm, and she sometimes worked herself up without any sense of excitement, simply in order not to disappoint her acquaintance. The half-suppressed smile that her face always wore was, to be sure, a little out of keeping with her worn features, but it expressed her consciousness of an amiable weakness, which, like a spoiled child, she could not or would not correct. The tone of this political dialogue had thoroughly provoked Anna Paulovna.

"Oh! do not talk to me about Austria. Of course I may know nothing about it, but I don't believe Austria wants, or ever has wanted, war! She is betraying us, and Russia will have to deliver Europe single-handed! Our benefactor fully realises his glorious mission, and he will prove equal to it. I believe it, I cling to it with all my soul! A splendid part lies before our good, kind, generous sovereign, and God will not abandon him! He will fulfil his mission and crush the hydra of revolution, which is more hideous than ever, if possible, under the mask of this monster, this assassin! It will be our fate to ransom the blood of the righteous! Whom can we trust, I ask you? England is too mercantile to understand the magnanimous soul of Alexander! She has refused to surrender Malta. She is waiting and looking for some selfish motive behind our actions. What did they say to Novosiltzow? Nothing. No, no; they do not understand the devotion of the emperor, who wants nothing for himself and cares only for the public good.— What have they promised? Nothing—and their promises are worth nothing. Has not Prussia declared that Bonaparte is invincible and that Europe is helpless to fight him! I do not believe in Hardenberg—no, nor in Haugwitz. Your famous Prussian neutrality is nothing but a snare. But I trust in God and in the high standing of our beloved emperor—the saviour of Europe!"

She suddenly broke off, smiling mockingly at her own excitement.

"What a pity that you are not in Wintzingerode's place," said Prince Basil with a smile. "Your eloquence would have taken the king of Prussia's consent by storm; but—will you give me some tea?"

"Directly. By the way," she added more calmly, "I expect two very interesting men this evening: the Vicomte de Mortemart, who is connected through the Rohans with the Montmorencys—one of the best families in France; he is one of the best of the emigrants, and genuine. The other is the Abbé Morio, one of the deepest thinkers.—The emperor, you know, received him. . . ."

"I shall be delighted!—But tell me," he went on with greater indifference than ever, as though the question on his lips had but this instant occurred to him, while it was in fact the chief object of his visit. "Is it true that her majesty the empress-dowager has asked for the appointment of Baron Funke to be first secretary at Vienna? The baron strikes me as quite second-rate!"

Prince Basil coveted the appointment for his son, and efforts were being made to obtain it for Baron Funke through the influence of the Empress Maria Féodorovna. Anna Paulovna's eyelids drooped till they were almost closed, to convey that neither she nor any one else could know what would or would not please the empress.

"Baron Funke was recommended to the empress-mother by her majesty's sister," she said drily but sadly; and as she spoke she put on an expression of deep and utter devotion with a tinge of pathos—an expression she always assumed when she pronounced the name of her august patroness; and her eyes drooped again as she added that her majesty had expressed a high opinion of Baron Funke.

The prince said nothing and looked completely indifferent; and yet Anna Paulovna, with her subtle woman's tact, had just given him a sharp little touch of her claws to punish him for having dared to express an opinion of a man who had been recommended to the empress's good offices. However, she hastened to console him.

"But tell me about your own people. Do you know that your daughter is the joy of all our hearts since you have brought her into society? She is thought as lovely as the day." The prince made a bow conveying his respect and thanks.

"How often I have been struck by the unfair distribution of happiness in this world!" the lady went on after a short pause. She settled herself a little closer to the prince, and smiling amiably at him, as if wishing to imply thereby that she had quitted the ground of politics and of drawing-room gossip for that of confidential chat. "I often think how unfairly distributed is happiness in life. Why, for instance, should you have been blessed with a family of charming children— excepting Anatole, your youngest? I do not like him," she added, raising her eyebrows, and with the decision of a verdict beyond appeal. "You do not in the least appreciate them, and do not deserve to possess them. . . ." She smiled her rapturous smile.

"What can I say?" asked the prince. "Lavater would certainly have found me devoid of the bump of philoprogeni-tiveness."

"But joking apart; I must really talk to you seriously. I am

greatly displeased with your youngest son, between you and me"
(and her face took on a sad expression). "They were speaking
of him in her majesty's presence the other day and pitying you."

Prince Basil said nothing; she waited, looking at him meaningly
in silence.

"I do not know what to do!" he said crossly. "I have
done what I could as their father to give them an education,
and they have both gone wrong. Hippolyte is a harmless idiot
at the worst, while Anatole is a turbulent idiot: that is the
only difference between them."

He smiled as he spoke more gaily and unnaturally than
ever, and there was a coarse unpleasant curl in the corners of
his wrinkled lips.

"Such men as you ought never to nave children; if you were
not a father I should not have a fault to find with you," said
Anna Paulovna with a pensive look.

"I am, as you know, your faithful slave, so you are the only
person I can confess to; my children are a heavy burthen and
the one cross I have to bear. That is how I explain it. What
more can I do?" he completed the sentence with a resigned shrug.

Anna Paulovna seemed to be thinking deeply.

"Have you never thought of a wife for your prodigal son?
Old maids, they say, have a passion for match-making; I do
not think it is a weakness of mine, and yet I have my eye on a
young girl who would do for him—a connection of ours: a
Princess Bolkonsky, who is miserable with her father."

Prince Basil said nothing, but a slight nodding of his head
suggested swift conclusions—the habitual swiftness of a man
of the world—and eagerness to stamp the fact on his memory.

"Do you know that this boy Anatole costs me forty thousand
roubles a year?" he sighed, giving way to his dismal reflections.
(He remained silent for a few moments.) "And what will he
come to five years hence if he goes on at this rate? These are
the joys of being a father! . . . Is your princess rich?"

"Her father is very rich and a great miser. He lives on his
estate in the country. He is that famous Prince Bolkonsky
whom they got to leave the service before the old emperor died,
and who was nicknamed "the Prince of Prussia." He is
extremely clever, but very eccentric—a difficult temper. The
poor girl is as miserable as she can be. She has only one
brother, who married Lisa Meinen a short time since; he is
Koutouzow's aide-de-camp; you will see him here presently."

"My dear Anna," exclaimed the prince, suddenly taking the

lady's hand and for no apparent reason drawing her down, "settle the matter for me and I am your slave for ever. If she is rich and of a good family she is the very thing I want."

And then, with the easy but elegant familiarity that stamped the man, he kissed her hand, waved it about, threw himself back in his seat and looked another way.

"Well then," said Anna Paulovna, considering in her mind, "I will speak about it this evening to Lisa (the wife of young Bolkonsky). Who knows but we may be able to arrange it. For the sake of your family I must begin my apprenticeship to the business of an old maid!"

CHAPTER II

ANNA PAULOVNA'S drawing-room gradually filled with the cream of St. Petersburg society. The gathering was composed, to be sure, of persons differing widely in age and character, but they were all of the same stratum. Prince Basil's daughter, the beautiful Princess Helen, came to carry off her father to the English Embassy. She was in her ball-dress, with the court order sparkling on her shoulder. Then there was the most fascinating woman in St. Petersburg, the very youthful, tiny, and engaging little Princess Bolkonsky. She had been married in the winter and, being *enceinte*, did not go out into the *great* world, but still went to *small* parties. There was Prince Hippolyte, Prince Basil's son, and with him Mortemart, whom he was introducing right and left; the Abbé Morio, and many more.

"Have you spoken to my aunt?" or: "Do you know my aunt?" said Anna Paulovna to all her guests, leading each in turn up to a little old lady, wearing a cap with enormous bows, who had just come into the room. Anna Paulovna slowly gazed first at her guests and then at her aunt as she effected the introduction, and then withdrew to bring up some one else. Every one had to go through the same ceremony with this obscure and quite useless old lady, for whom no one cared a straw, while Anna Paulovna listened approvingly to their exchange of civilities with a half-solemn half-melancholy look. The aunt always repeated the same formula, asking after her visitor's health, reporting on her own and on that of her majesty the empress-dowager, "which was better, thank God." The victim politely tried to betray no undue haste to escape, but took good care not to come near the old lady again during the rest of the evening.

Princess Bolkonsky had brought some needlework in a little velvet work-bag embroidered with gold. Her upper lip—a bewitching little lip, shaded with the faintest trace of down—could never be persuaded to close on her lower lip; but this little defect, which was quite original and peculiar, this half-open mouth, only made her more charming—a gift which is the exclusive privilege of a perfectly fascinating woman. Every one admired the young future mother so full of life and health, and so easily carrying off her condition. All men, whether young and bored or old and morose, after a few words of conversation with her, felt as though they had caught some of her charm, or at any rate had made themselves particularly agreeable, so infectious was the bright smile which showed her pearly teeth as she spoke.

The little princess made her way round the table with short tripping steps and slightly rocking gait; then, shaking out the folds of her dress, she sank into the sofa close to the silver *samovar*, with the air of a person whose only aim in life is to please herself and others.

"I brought my work," she said, opening her bag and addressing the circle generally. "Anna, I hope you are not going to play me false; you wrote 'to meet a few friends,' so you see how badly I am dressed . . ." and she held up her arms to display an elegant grey morning-dress trimmed with lace and fastened round the waist with a broad belt.

"Do not let that trouble you, Lisa, you will always be the prettiest whatever you wear."

"And do you know," Lisa went on in just the same tone, but turning to a general officer, "that my husband is going to desert me? He is going to get himself killed! What is the good of this horrible war?" she added to Prince Basil. But she did not wait for an answer, and went on talking to his daughter Helen.

"What a sweet little person it is!" said Prince Basil in a low voice to the mistress of the house.

A few minutes after the young princess a tall and burly young man with a closely cropped head was shown in. He wore spectacles, and was dressed in light-coloured trousers of fashionable cut, a brown coat and an immense shirt-frill. This was the natural son of Count Bésoukhow, a famous noble in the days of the Empress Catharine, and who, at this time, was ill—dying slowly—at Moscow. The young gentleman had as yet taken up no particular career, and had but lately returned from abroad, where he had been educated; this was his first appearance in St. Petersburg society.

Anna Paulovna received him with the degree of civility and warmth which she bestowed on her least important guests; nevertheless, and in spite of this very second-rate greeting—as she looked at Peter, a look of anxiety and alarm crossed her face: an expression of the feeling we experience in seeing some colossal object quite out of place. Peter was, no doubt, much taller than any other man in the room; but Anna Paulovna's feeling had another source; it was his shy but candid glance, at once keen and true, that startled his hostess, and distinguished him from the rest of her guests.

"It is more than kind of you, *Monsieur Pierre*, to come to see a poor invalid," she said, glancing uneasily at her aunt as she introduced him to the old lady.

Peter muttered some incoherent reply while his eyes wandered round the room as if in search of someone. Suddenly a bright smile lighted up his face, he nodded to the little princess as if they were the best friends, and approached "*ma tante.*" Indeed, Anna Paulovna had cause for her alarms, for he turned on his heel and left the aunt without even waiting for the end of her speech about the empress's health.

His frightened hostess stopped him.

"Do you know the Abbé Morio?" she asked. "He is a very interesting man."

"Yes, I have heard of his schemes for a perennial peace; it is very clever—but hardly practical."

"Do you think so?" said Anna Paulovna vaguely, in order to say something and free herself to attend to her duties as hostess. And Peter was guilty of a second blunder: he had quitted one lady before she could finish her sentence, and now he detained another who was wanting to be rid of him, bending over her, with his big feet apparently rooted to the floor, while he proceeded to explain why the Abbé Morio's dreams were Utopian.

"We will discuss it another time," said Anna Paulovna, smiling.

Having shaken off this young man who had no manners, she resumed her duties—listening, looking on, ready at any moment to strengthen a weak point and give fresh impetus to a flagging conversation. She worked like the overseer of a spinning-mill who walks up and down among the machinery noting every spindle that has stopped, or creaks, or rattles, and hastening to ease it or to stop it. Anna Schérer moved about her drawing-room, going first to a silent circle, and then to a group of too eager gossips: a word, or a skilful shifting of the figures, gave a fresh start to the talking-machine which then went on again at an even and easy pace. But her doubt and dread of Pierre were perceptible through it all, she kept her eye upon him and saw him first go to listen to what was going on round Mortemart, and then join the circle of which Morio was the centre. Peter himself, a total stranger, was going through his first experience of St. Petersburg society; he knew that all the intellect of the capital was assembled there, and he wandered wide-eyed from one group to another, so fearful was he lest he should miss something in the conversation that bore the hall-mark of talent. As he looked at all these faces, stamped with distinction and self-confidence, he expected every word to be profound or witty. The abbé's conversation finally attracted him, and he paused, awaiting an opportunity for giving his opinion. It is the weakness of all young people.

CHAPTER III

ANNA PAULOVNA's soirée was fairly started—all the spindles were twirling. Excepting "*ma tante*," who was sitting apart with another old lady with a tear-worn face that looked rather out of place in this gay circle, the company had fallen into three groups. The abbé was the centre of one, composed chiefly of men; the second, young for the most part, had gathered round the splendidly beautiful Helen and the fascinating little Princess Bolkonsky—who was so fresh and pretty, though rather too fat; the third had formed round Mortemart and Anna Paulovna.

The viscount, who had a gentle face and pleasing manner, looked as if he considered himself a celebrity but modestly allowed the company in which he found himself to make use of him. Anna Paulovna took every advantage of this, with the air of a *maître d'hôtel* who recommends a dish as particularly choice and elegant which, cooked by a less skilful hand, would have proved uneatable; she had served up the viscount first to her guests, to be followed by the abbé—two refined and delicate morsels.

Round Mortemart the conversation turned on the death of the Duke d'Enghien. The viscount maintained that the duke had died a victim to his own magnanimity, and that Bonaparte had a private and personal spite against him.

"Indeed—tell us all about it!" cried Anna Paulovna, happily feeling that there was something à la Louis XV in this phrase "contez-nous celá, Vicomte."

Mortemart smiled and bowed assent; Anna bid her company come to listen.

"The viscount," she whispered to her neighbour, "knew the duke intimately; the viscount," she repeated, turning to another, "tells a story delightfully; the viscount," she added, to a third, "has moved in the best society, that is evident at a glance."

And this was how the viscount was handed round and offered to the company as a rare treat, in the most graceful and tempting manner, as a piece of roast beef on a hot dish garnished with parsley; and he smiled subtly as he began his story.

"Come and sit down here, my dear Helen," said Anna to the fair girl who formed the centre of the other circle. Princess Helen rose, her face still lighted up by the smile it had worn ever since she came in, and which was the natural adjunct of her unrivalled beauty. As she moved across the room, her white dress with its garlands of ivy and moss lightly sweeping past the men who made way for her, she was a radiant vision of sparkling gems, shining hair and glistening shoulders—the living symbol of festivity. She did not look at any one but smiled on all, vouchsafing to them, as it were, the privilege of gazing at her splendid figure, and the dazzling fairness of her shoulders and throat fully displayed by her fashionably low dress. Helen was so surprisingly lovely that she could not have a grain of petty vanity; if she had felt awkwardly conscious of such perfect and triumphant beauty and had wished to mitigate its effect she could not have done it.

"What a beautiful creature!" was on every lip. The viscount shrugged his shoulders, and dropped his eyes as if some supernatural vision had struck his sight, when Helen took a seat near him and turned on him the charms of that perpetual smile.

"I feel quite shy," he said, bowing smilingly, "before such an audience."

Helen, leaning her pretty arm on the table, did not think it necessary to answer; she only smiled and waited. All the while the narrator was speaking she sat upright, looking sometimes at her dimpled arm, that had changed shape from the pressure of the table, or at her white bosom, adjusting her diamond necklace, patting the skirt of her dress, and turning at the more exciting parts to look at her hostess, whose expression she would for a moment copy and then relapse into that placid smile.

The little princess had come forward, too, from the tea-table.

"Wait a moment," she exclaimed, "till I get out my work. —Well, what are you about—what are you thinking of?" she added to Hippolyte. "Give me my bag, please."

Laughing and talking she made a general stir in the room.

"There, now I am quite comfortable," she added, seating herself and taking her bag from Prince Hippolyte, who drew a chair to her side and sat down.

The young prince—*le charmant Hippolyte*, as he was called— was strikingly like his sister, though she was "fair beyond compare," and he was decidedly ugly. Their features were alike; but in her they were transfigured by that perennial, brilliantly youthful, and self-satisfied smile, and by the classical proportions of her whole face and figure; while he looked almost idiotic and always sulky, his frame was feeble and unhealthy, his eyes, nose, mouth all lost their individuality in a sour and bored expression, while his hands and feet were twisted into impossible attitudes.

"Is it a ghost story?" he added, sticking his glass in his eye, as if that would help him to express himself.

"Nothing of the sort," replied the viscount, shrugging his shoulders, quite taken aback.

"Oh!—only I hate them," said Hippolyte; and it was clear from his manner that it was not till after he had spoken that he understood the full meaning of his words. Still, he had such complete assurance that it was always hard to tell whether he was clumsy or witty. He wore a dark-green frock-coat and inexpressibles of a pinkish-drab colour—"*cuisse de nymphe effrayée*" as he called it: "maiden's blush" to translate it freely —with stockings and buckled shoes.

The viscount told his story with much grace. The Duke d'Enghien, it was said, had come secretly to Paris to see Mademoiselle Georges, and had there met Napoleon, on whom the great actress also bestowed her favours. The consequence of this unlucky accident was one of those long fainting-fits to which Bonaparte was subject, and which put him in the power of the enemy. The duke had taken no advantage of his position, and Bonaparte had revenged himself for this magnanimous behaviour by having the duke assassinated. The story was dramatic, and particularly exciting at the point where the rivals recognised each other. The ladies were much moved.

"It is delightful!" said Anna Paulovna, trying to read the little princess's eyes.

"Quite charming!" said the little princess, taking up her work with renewed energy, to show that the interest of the narrative had made her forget it.

Mortemart fully appreciated the implied compliment and was going on with his story, when Anna Paulovna, who had kept one eye on Peter, perceived that he and the abbé were engaged in a sharp skirmish and flew to avert mischief. Peter had succeeded in getting the abbé into conversation on the subject of the balance of power, and the abbé, evidently enchanted by his listener's ingenuous ardour, was dilating at full length on his cherished scheme; both were talking loud with eager enthusiasm, and this had jarred on the maid of honour.

"By what means? Why by the balance of power in Europe and the rights of men," the abbé was saying. "A single empire, as powerful as Russia, with a reputation for barbarism, frankly setting herself at the head of an alliance with the avowed purpose of maintaining that balance—and the world would be saved!"

"But how will you establish that balance?" persisted Peter at the very moment when his hostess, with a look of stern reproof at him, asked the Italian how he bore the northern climate. The abbé's face changed at once; he put on the insultingly sweet and affected expression which he commonly wore when addressing a woman.

"I am too keenly alive to the charms of wit and culture, especially among the women of the society into which I have the honour of being admitted, to have had time to think of the climate," he said, while Anna Paulovna manœuvred to draw him and Peter into the general circle so as not to lose sight of them.

CHAPTER IV

AT this instant a new actor appeared on the scene; this was
Prince Andrew Bolkonsky, the little princess's husband, a
good-looking young man of middle height, with marked, hard
features. Everything about him, from his weary eyes to his
firm and measured step, was the very opposite of his wife, who
was vivacious and bustling. He knew everyone in the room
and was bored to death by them all—nay, he would have given
a handsome sum never to see or hear any one of them again,
his wife included. She, indeed, seemed more antipathetic to
him than anyone, and he turned away from her with a grimace
that disfigured his handsome features. He kissed Anna
Paulovna's hand, and looked round at the company with a frown.

"So you are preparing to fight, prince?" she said.

"General Koutouzow is kind enough to wish to have me as
his aide-de-camp," replied Bolkonsky.

"And your wife?"

"She will go into the country."

"I wonder you are not ashamed to deprive us of the fascinating
little woman?"

"Andrew," cried Lisa, just as coquettish with her husband
as with everyone else, "if only you had heard the pretty story
the viscount has just been telling us about Mademoiselle Georges
and Bonaparte."

Prince Andrew made a face again and turned away. Peter,
whose merry, kindly eyes had been watching him ever since his
entrance, now came up to him and took his hand. The prince's
frown did not vanish at the sight of the new-comer; but when,
a moment later, he recognised the frank face, his own lighted
up with a cordial smile.

"Ah! you here, afloat on the tide of fashion!"

"I knew I should meet you here. I will go home to supper
with you if I may?" He spoke low, not to interrupt Mortemart, who was still speaking.

"No, you may not, of course," said Andrew, laughing, and
wringing his hand to show how unnecessary the question was.
He was about to say more, when Prince Basil and his daughter
rose and there was a little stir to make way for them.

"Excuse our leaving you," said Prince Basil to the viscount,
not allowing him to rise; "this tiresome ball at the English
Embassy deprives us of a pleasure and compels us to interrupt

13

you. I am so sorry, my dear Anna Paulovna, to be obliged to quit your delightful party."

Helen made her way among the seats, holding up her gown with one hand and never ceasing to smile. Peter gazed at her dazzling loveliness in a rapture mingled with awe.

"She is very handsome," said Prince Andrew.

"Yes," was all Peter answered.

Prince Basil shook hands with him as he passed him.

"Take that young bear in hand and finish his education," he said, turning to Anna Paulovna. "He has been in my house for months and this is the first time I have seen him in company. Nothing forms a young man like the society of clever women."

CHAPTER V

THE lady smiled and promised to take Peter in hand, knowing that his father and Prince Basil were related. The old lady, who had remained by the aunt, now started up and pursued Prince Basil into the ante-room. Her kind, worn face had lost the expression of attentive interest that she had assumed; it betrayed anxiety and alarm.

"And what can you tell me, prince, of my Boris?" (She pronounced the name Boris with particular accentuation of the "o.") "I cannot stay in St. Petersburg any longer. Tell me, I entreat you, what news I may take to my poor boy."

In spite of Prince Basil's obvious displeasure and gross want of politeness in listening to her, she smiled in his face, and clung to his hand to detain him. "What effort would it cost you to say a word to the emperor and he would be admitted into the Guard at once."

"I assure you, princess, that I will do everything in my power, but there are difficulties in the way of my proffering such a request to his majesty. I advise you rather to get at Roumianzow through Galitzine. It would be more to the purpose."

The old lady was a Princess Droubetzkoï—one of the oldest names in Russia, but she was poor, and having lived out of the world for years, had lost all her former connections. She had now come to St. Petersburg solely with a view to gaining an appointment in the Imperial Guard for her only son; and it was in the hope of meeting Prince Basil that she had invited herself and come to Anna Paulovna's party. Prince Basil's words frightened her. Her face, which had once been handsome, betrayed some annoyance, but only for a moment; then she smiled again and clasped Prince Basil's arm.

"Listen, prince," she said. "I have never asked you for anything before, and I will never ask you for anything again; I have never taken any advantage of the friendship which once bound you to my father. But now, for God's sake, do this for my boy and you will be our providence. Nay, do not be angry, but just promise. I have asked Galitzine and he refused. Be a dear good fellow, as you used to be," she added, trying to smile while her eyes were full of tears.

"Papa, we shall be late," said Princess Helen, who was waiting at the door, and she turned her lovely face on her father.

Power is capital, and only to be used with economy. No one knew this better than Prince Basil: the surest way to get nothing for himself was to petition for all who applied to him —he had learnt that very early. Hence he rarely exerted his personal influence; but Princess Droubetzkoï's earnest prayers had stirred some faint remorse in the depths of his conscience. She had reminded him of the fact that it was to her father that he had owed his first introduction to a successful career. He had observed, too, that she was one of those women—of those mothers, who neither pause nor rest till the object of their desires is gained, and who, if the occasion requires it, are ready at any moment with fresh entreaties and recriminations. This last reflection turned the scale.

"My dear Anna Mikhaïlovna," he said in his usual bored tone and with his habitual familiarity, "it is next to impossible to do what you want; however, I will try, in token of my regard for you and my respect for your father's memory. Your son shall enter the Guard, here's my hand on it—now, are you satisfied?"

"My dear friend, you are my benefactor! I expected no less, for I know how good you are. Stop, one word," she cried, seeing him about to go. "When he is appointed . . ." but she paused in some confusion. "You are on the best terms with Koutouzow, I know—you will recommend Boris for the post of aide-de-camp? Then I shall be quite happy and never again . . ."

Prince Basil smiled.

"That I cannot promise. Since Koutouzow was appointed

to the chief command he has been stormed with applications. He told me himself that all the ladies in Moscow had offered him their sons as aides-de-camp."

"No, no; you must promise—my friend, my protector; promise, or I will not let you go."

"Papa," said the fair Helen in the same tone, "we shall be late."

"Good-bye—good-bye. You see—I cannot . . ."

"Then you will speak to the emperor to-morrow?"

"Without fail; but as to Koutouzow I promise nothing."

"My dear Basil . . ." persisted Anna Mikhaïlovna with a coquettishly persuasive smile, forgetting that these graces of a past date were now out of harmony with her worn features. She was not thinking of her age indeed, and was merely, without a thought, falling back on every feminine resource. But as soon as the prince had turned his back her face was cold and had resumed its expression of simulated interest.

She rejoined the circle who were still listening to the viscount, watching, now that her task was accomplished, for a favourable moment for disappearing from the scene.

CHAPTER VI

"AND what have you to say to the latest farce, the coronation at Milan?" asked Anna Paulovna. "With the people of Genoa and Lucca coming to do homage to Monsieur Bonaparte, Monsieur Bonaparte seated on a throne and accepting the homage of nations! It is delicious! It is enough to turn one's brain; the whole world must have gone mad together!" Prince Andrew looked at her and smiled:

"'God has given it me, beware of touching it,'" he said; they were Napoleon's words as he set the crown on his head. "They say he looked splendid as he spoke," he added, and he repeated the words in Italian: "*Dio mi la dona, guai a chi la tocca.*"

"I only hope," said Anna Paulovna, "that this will be the drop too much. Really and truly the sovereigns of Europe ought no longer to endure this man, who is a living threat to them all."

"The sovereigns!" echoed the viscount politely and hopelessly,

"I do not include Russia. The sovereigns of Europe? What did they do for Louis XVI, for the queen, for Madame Elizabeth? Nothing—and, believe me, they are suffering now for having betrayed the cause of the Bourbons. The sovereigns! Why, they send ambassadors to present their compliments to the usurper!" And he shifted his attitude with an exclamation of contempt.

Prince Hippolyte, who had not ceased gazing at Mortemart through his eye-glass, turned himself stiffly towards the little princess, of whom he requested a needle, with which he scratched the outline of the arms of the Condé family, and then he blazoned them with the utmost gravity, as if she had requested it:

"A baton and a bordure engrailed, gules on azure," he said.

She listened placidly.

"If Bonaparte remains a year longer on the throne of France," the viscount went on, like a man who is accustomed to follow out his own train of thought without heeding the reflections of others on a familiar subject, "things will only go too far. French society—good society, I mean—will be utterly disintegrated by intrigue, violence, exile, and sequestrations—and then . . ."

He threw up his hands with a shrug.

Peter was about to speak (he was interested in the conversation), but his hostess, who was watching him, anticipated him.

"The Emperor Alexander," she said, with her usual tone of melancholy reverence, "has declared that he will leave it to the French to choose their own form of government, and I am fully convinced that the whole nation, when once they are delivered from the usurper, will throw themselves into the arms of the legitimate monarch."

She was anxious, it will be seen, to flatter the royalist emigrant.

"That is not very likely," said Prince Andrew. "The viscount is right in thinking that matters have gone too far, and that it will be difficult to revert to the past."

"I have heard," said Peter, getting very red and coming forward, "that most of the nobles have gone over to Napoleon."

"The Bonapartists may say so," replied the viscount without looking at Peter. "It is impossible to know what public opinion in France really is."

"It was Napoleon, at any rate," replied Prince Andrew, satirically, for he did not like the viscount whose retorts were aimed at him, "who said, 'I showed them the path to glory and they would not tread it'—those are the words attributed to him—'I opened my ante-room, and they rushed in in crowds.' —I do not know how far he had a right to say so."

"He had none whatever," exclaimed Mortemart. "After the murder of the Duke d'Enghien the most enthusiastic ceased to regard him as a hero; and if ever he had seemed one to certain people," he continued, addressing Anna Paulovna, "after that there was a martyr the more in heaven and a hero the less on earth."

These last words had hardly been uttered, and rewarded with an approving smile, before Peter rushed into the arena, without giving Anna Paulovna, who apprehended something tremendous, time to prevent him.

"The execution of the duke," he began, "was a political necessity, and Napoleon showed his magnanimity by assuming the whole responsibility for the act."

"Good Heavens! Good Heavens!" murmured Anna Paulovna in dismay.

"What, Monsieur Peter, can you find any 'magnanimity' in a murder?" said the little princess, shaking up her work.

"Oh! oh!" said several.

"Capital!" said Prince Hippolyte in English, slapping his hand on his knee. The viscount merely shrugged his shoulders.

Peter looked at them over his spectacles.

"I say this," he went on, "because the Bourbons fled at the revolution, leaving the country a prey to anarchy. It was Napoleon who understood and quelled the revolution, and that is why, when public order was in danger, he could not pause to save the life of a single individual."

"Will you come to the other table?" suggested Anna Paulovna. But Peter, growing more excited, went on with his speech, without heeding her.

"Yes, Napoleon is great because he has risen superior to the revolution, has remedied its abuses and preserved what was good in it: the equality of citizens, and liberty of the press and of speech—that is how he gained his power."

"If he had restored the legitimate king to the throne, instead of taking advantage of his power to commit a murder, I should have called him a great man," said the viscount.

"That was out of his power. The nation had given him the throne on purpose that he might rid her of the Bourbons; she recognised him as a master-mind. The revolution was a great fact," continued Peter, betraying his extreme youthfulness by his persistency in trying to explain his views and uttering advanced and irritating ideas.

"The revolution and the regicide! After that—but will you not come to the other table?" repeated the hostess.

"*Le Contrat social* !" said Mortemart, with a resigned smile. "I do not allude to the regicide—I mean the idea."

"The idea of robbery, of murder, and of regicide!" said an ironical voice.

"Those are the extremes; but the real marrow of the idea is emancipation from prejudice and the equality of men, and Napoleon maintained it in its integrity."

"Liberty and equality!" retorted the viscount scornfully, for he was bent on proving to the young man the weakness of his argument. "Those high-sounding words have already lost their value. Who would not love the reality? The Saviour himself preached them! But have we been any happier since the revolution? On the contrary. We asked for liberty; Napoleon has confiscated it."

Prince Andrew stood smiling and looking first at Peter and the viscount and then at the mistress of the house, who, with all her experience of the world, had been shocked and alarmed at Peter's sallies; however, when she saw that these sacrilegious views did not make the Frenchman angry, and also that it was impossible to check them, she made common cause with the noble exile and, in her turn, fell upon the orator.

"But, my dear Monsieur Peter," she said, "how can you account for the conduct of a great man who has a duke—or the commonest man—put to death when the victim has committed no crime, and without even a trial?"

"And I should like, too, to ask you," said the viscount, "to account for the 18th Brumaire. Was it not an act of treason, or rather of trickery, utterly unlike any impulse of a great man?"

"And the prisoners in Africa that were massacred by his orders," cried the little princess. "It is perfectly fearful!"

"He is a low fellow, say what you will," Prince Hippolyte threw in.

Peter, having no answer ready, looked at them all and smiled—not a pinched, unmeaning smile, but a frank, sincere smile which lent his usually stern and rather morose face an expression of kindly candour, like that of a child who pleads to be forgiven.

The viscount, who had never seen him before, understood at

once that this Jacobin was less terrible than his words. There was a brief silence.

"How is he to answer you all at once?" said Prince Andrew, suddenly. "Is there no difference between the actions of a private gentleman and a statesman—a general or a ruler? To me, at any rate, there seems to be a great difference."

"Why, certainly," said Peter, delighted at this unexpected support.

"Napoleon on the bridge at Arcola or giving his hand to his plague-stricken soldiers in the hospital in Jaffa is great as a man, and it is impossible to refuse to recognise it; but there are other things, it is true, which can hardly be justified," continued Prince Andrew, who was evidently bent on making up for Peter's blundering and who, as he spoke, rose, thus giving his wife a hint to take leave.

Prince Hippolyte did the same, but with a wave of his hand seemed to beg the rest to remain seated.

"By the way," he began eagerly, "I heard a delightful Russian story to-day—I really must tell it you. Excuse me, viscount, but I must tell it in Russian; it would lose all its point. . . ." And he began his anecdote in Russian with the accent of a Frenchman who has only lived a year in Russia.

All paused: with such interest and insistence did Hippolyte require attention to his story.

"In Moscow there lives a grand lady who is extremely stingy and who wanted to drive with two tall footmen behind her carriage—it was her whim. Well, this lady had a tall waiting-maid . . ." At this point Prince Hippolyte stopped to think, as if he had some difficulty in going on with his story. "So she said to her—yes, she said to her: 'Girl, dress up in livery and stand up behind the carriage, I am going to pay some calls.'"

Here Prince Hippolyte burst out laughing, much before his audience, and thereby produced an unfavourable impression for his story. A few, however, managed to smile, among them the old lady and Anna Paulovna.

"So they set out. But suddenly the wind rose; the girl's hat blew off, and her long hair came down . . ." Then, unable to control himself any longer, he fell into such a fit of laughing as almost choked him. "Yes, yes," he said, rolling in his seat, "all her hair came down, and the whole town knew it."

This was the end of the story. No one could see the point of it or why it had to be told in Russian; but Anna Paulovna and some others were grateful to the narrator for having so happily interrupted Peter's unpleasant and tiresome harangues. The conversation was diverted into more trivial channels—remarks on balls past and to come, and on the theatres with fifty questions as to when and where they might meet again.

CHAPTER VII

AFTER this the company thanked their hostess for a delightful evening and withdrew in detachments.

Peter, besides being unusually tall, square-shouldered, and awkward, had, among other physical blemishes, very large red hands; he had no idea of how to come into a room and still less of how to get out of it with a proper modicum of polite speeches. In his utter absence of mind, when he rose to leave, he took up, instead of his own hat, the cocked and plumed hat of a general officer, which he stood twisting in his hands till the owner, in some alarm, succeeded in rescuing it. Still, it must be said, all this clumsiness and blundering were atoned for by his thorough good-nature, frankness, and modesty.

Anna Paulovna bade him good night with an air of forgiveness bestowed as became a Christian.

"I hope," she said, "that I may have the pleasure of seeing you here again; but I also hope that before then you will have amended your opinions."

He made no reply, but as he bowed, his honest, simple smile seemed to say: "Well, after all, an opinion is but an opinion, and you see I am a thorough good fellow." Which was so true that everyone, including Anna Paulovna, felt it instinctively.

Prince Andrew, in the ante-room while the footman was putting his cloak on his shoulders, listened indifferently to the chatter of his wife and Hippolyte, who had followed them. Prince Hippolyte stood near the pretty *enceinte* woman and stared at her fixedly through his glass.

"Go into the drawing-room, Anna," said the little lady, "you will take cold . . . It is quite understood!" she added in an undertone.

Anna Paulovna had found an opportunity for speaking to Lisa of the marriage she was scheming between her sister-in-law and Anatole.

"I rely on you," she replied, also in a whisper. "You will write her a line, and then you must let me know what her father

21

thinks of it. Good night . . ." And she disappeared. Prince Hippolyte came up to the princess, and leaning over her, stood chattering in her ear. Two menservants—his carrying an officer's cloak, and hers holding a shawl—were waiting till they should have finished their *tête-à-tête* in French which the servants appeared to be listening to, though it was unintelligible to them —nay, and to understand without showing it. The little princess was talking, smiling, laughing, all in a breath.

"I am so glad I did not go to the English embassy," said Hippolyte. "It would have been such a bore, and we have had such a delightful evening. Delightful, hasn't it been?"

"But they say it is to be a splendid ball," said the princess with a curl of that downy lip, "and all the pretty women in St. Petersburg are there."

"Not all, since you are not," said the prince, laughing. Then, taking the shawl out of the footman's hands and pushing him aside, he wrapped it round the princess. His hands fumbled with it for some little time round her throat, and he almost seemed to embrace her—was it intentional or mere clumsiness? No one could have decided. She drew back a little, still smiling, and looked up at her husband whose eyes were shut and who looked tired and half-asleep.

"Are you ready?" he said, with a side-glance at his wife. Prince Hippolyte hastily flung on his cloak, which being in the latest fashion fell below his heels, and stumbling and struggling with it he rushed forward to help the princess into her carriage.

"*Au revoir*, princess," he said, his tongue as clumsy as his feet. The princess picked up her dress and settled herself in the dark corner of the carriage; her husband was taking up his sword. Prince Hippolyte, who seemed to be helping them, was only in the way.

"I beg your pardon . . ." said Prince Andrew in a dry, sharp tone and in Russian, for Hippolyte stood in his path. "Now, Peter, you will follow us," he added warmly.

The postilion started and the carriage rolled clattering away.

Hippolyte, standing on the step, giggled uncomfortably; he was waiting for the viscount, whom he had promised to take home.

"Well, my dear fellow, your little princess is very nice, very nice indeed," said Mortemart as he seated himself in the carriage, "very nice indeed, and quite French!" and he kissed the tips of his fingers. Hippolyte chuckled complacently.

"And you, do you know you are dangerous with your innocent ways? I pity the poor husband—a little officer who gives himself as many airs as a sovereign prince."

Hippolyte went into fits of laughter.

"And you said that Russian women were nowhere, as compared with French women!" he spluttered. "You must know how to take them, that is all."

Peter, having reached the house first, went straight into Prince Andrew's private room as an intimate in the house; he stretched himself on a sofa, as was his wont, and took up a book—it happened to be *Cæsar's Commentaries*—which he opened in the middle.

"What have you been doing at Anna Paulovna's?" said Prince Andrew. "You will really make her ill." He came in rubbing his hands, which were small and white.

Peter turned over, all at once, making the sofa groan under his weight; and looking up at his friend with his bright, eager face, he said with an indifferent shrug:

"That abbé is really a very interesting man, only he has got hold of the wrong end of the matter. . . . I have not a doubt that a permanent peace is quite possible, but I cannot see my way to it; not by a balance of power at any rate. . . ."

Prince Andrew, who did not look like a man to trouble himself about abstract questions, interrupted him:

"My dear fellow, the thing that is absolutely impossible is that we should everywhere and at all times say exactly what we think. Now, have you made up your mind? will you be a Chevalier Guardsman or a diplomatist?"

"Would you believe that I really do not know yet? Neither prospect smiles upon me," said Peter, sitting up on his heels.

"Still, you must come to some decision; your father is waiting."

Peter had been sent abroad at the age of ten with an abbé for a tutor; he had remained absent till he was twenty. On his return his father had dismissed the abbé, and said to the young man:

"Now, go to St. Petersburg, inquire for yourself and choose. I will agree to anything you wish. Here is a letter to Prince Basil, and here is money. Write to me and rely on my doing what I can for you."

Since then for three months Peter had been looking about him and doing nothing. It was of this choice of a career that Prince Andrew was speaking.

23

He passed his hand over his forehead: "He must be a free-mason?" he said, alluding to the Italian abbé.

"That is all nonsense," said Prince Andrew. "I want to talk about your affairs. Did you go to see the Horse Guards?"

"No, I did not go. But I thought over one thing which I meant to tell you. We are at war with Napoleon; if we were fighting for liberty I should be the first to join, but when it means helping England and Austria to crush the greatest man now living, I do not see my way to it."

Prince Andrew raised his shoulders at this childish sally; he appeared to scorn to answer it seriously, but in reality this simple question was difficult to answer any other way than that chosen by Prince Andrew, and only said:

"If we only fought for our convictions there would be an end of war."

"Nothing could be better," retorted Peter.

"Possibly, but it will never come to pass," said Andrew, smiling.

"But, come now, what are we going to war about?"

"I have not the faintest idea. We must; and what is more, I am going to the front . . ." he paused, "because the life I lead here . . . does not suit me."

CHAPTER VIII

THE rustle of a dress was audible in the adjoining room. The sound seemed to bring Prince Andrew to himself; he drew himself up and put on the expression his face had worn all the evening at Anna Paulovna's. Peter slipped his feet off the couch. The princess came in; she had changed the dress she had been wearing for a loose gown, equally fresh and elegant; her husband rose and politely pushed forward an easy chair.

"I often wonder," she began, seating herself briskly, "why Anna never married. You are very foolish, you men, not to have asked her. Begging your pardon, you really know nothing about women. What a wrangler you are, Monsieur Peter."

"I wrangle with your husband, too, for I cannot understand why he is going to fight," said Peter, addressing her without any sign of the embarrassment which is sometimes perceptible in a young man with a young woman. She shuddered slightly; Peter's remark had touched her to the quick.

"That is just what I tell him, too. I cannot conceive why men cannot live without fighting. Why do we wish for nothing, ask nothing—we women? Now, I appeal to you. I am always telling him that his position here as my uncle's aide-de-camp is all he could wish; every one knows him, every one values him. Only the other day at the Apraxines' I heard a lady say: 'That is the famous Prince Andrew'—on my word she did." And she laughed. "And it is the same wherever he goes; he can be aide-de-camp to the emperor any day he pleases—for the emperor, you know, has spoken most graciously to him. We were talking it over just now, Anna and I—it would be so easy to manage. What do you think?"

Peter looked at Andrew, and seeing that his friend looked annoyed he made no reply.

"When do you start?" he asked.

"Oh! do not talk of his starting; I will not hear a word about it," exclaimed the princess, with that odd mixture of waywardness and light-heartedness that she had shown to Prince Hippolyte, and which was strangely discordant in the intimacy of home, of which Peter was, as it were, a member. "To-day, as I thought that I should have to break off all these dear connections—and besides—Andrew," and she threw her husband a look fraught with meaning, with a little shiver, "I am afraid."

Her husband looked at her in a bewildered way, as if he had only just become aware of her presence; he answered her with cold politeness:

"What are you afraid of, Lisa? I do not understand."

"How like a man! Selfish—they are all selfish! He has taken this fancy into his head, so he deserts me, God knows why, and shuts me up all alone, in the country."

"With my father and sister, remember," he said quietly.

"It comes to the same thing; I shall be alone, away from my own friends—and then he expects me to be satisfied!"

She spoke petulantly and her short upper lip no longer gave her face a smiling expression, but, on the contrary, a look that suggested some vicious little rodent. But she was silent, not liking to assign the real reason of her terrors before Peter.

"I cannot imagine what you have to fear," her husband went on, fixing his eyes on her. She coloured, and with a little

25

desperate shrug she exclaimed: "Andrew, Andrew, why are you so changed?"

"Your doctor tells you not to sit up late; you ought to go to bed."

The princess made no reply, but her lips quivered; her husband shrugged his shoulders, rose, and began to walk up and down the room. Peter, frankly astonished, watched them alternately over his spectacles; at last he was about to go, but he stopped.

"What do I care whether Monsieur Peter is present or not!" exclaimed Lisa, her face puckered up like that of a child just going to cry. "I have been meaning to ask you for a long time, Andrew, why you are quite different to me from what you once were. What harm have I done? You are going off to the army; you have no pity for me—why?"

"Lisa!" said Prince Andrew. The word conveyed an entreaty, a threat, and a warning that she would presently regret her speech. But she went recklessly on:

"You treat me like an invalid or a child. I can see . . . it was not so six months ago!"

"Lisa, be silent, I beg," said her husband, raising his voice.

Peter, whose painful excitement had gradually increased during this dialogue, rose and went up to the young woman. He could not bear to see her tears, and seemed almost ready to cry, too.

"Be calm, princess," he said. "These are fancies—I know, I have felt the same kind of thing. And I assure you—excuse me, I am in the way, a stranger. But, pray be calm. Good night."

Prince Andrew detained him.

"No, stay; the princess is too kind to deprive me of the pleasure of an evening in your society."

"Yes, he thinks of no one but himself," she muttered, unable to control her tears of vexation.

"Lisa," repeated Prince Andrew, his hard stern tone showing plainly that his patience was wearing thin. Suddenly her pretty little face—like that of a squirrel in a rage—took a quite different expression: the cowed doubtful look of a dog with its tail down wagging it noiselessly on the floor.

"Oh dear! oh dear!" she sighed, then, gathering up her dress, she went up to him and kissed his forehead.

"Good night," he said, and he rose and kissed her hand as if she had been a stranger.

26

BEFORE TILSIT

CHAPTER IX

THE friends were silent; neither of them could make up his mind to speak. Peter stole a glance at Prince Andrew, who was rubbing his forehead slowly with his slim hand.

"Come to supper," he said, leading the way. They went into a splendid dining-room recently redecorated; the glass, plate, china, and damask all were unmistakably new—the sign of a recently-established household. In the middle of supper Prince Andrew put his elbows on the table, and began talking with a nervous irritability which was new to Peter; like a man who has had something on his mind for a long time, and has determined at last to make a clean breast of it.

"My dear fellow, do not marry till you have done everything in life that you care to do, till you have ceased to love the woman you mean to marry, and have studied her thoroughly: if you do, you will make a fatal and irreparable mistake. Better wait till you are old and good for nothing else; then you will not run the risk of wasting everything good and noble in your soul. Yes, it all gets frittered away in small change! It is so, I assure you; you need not look so astonished. If you ever hoped and believed that you would do anything worth doing, you will feel at every turn that it is all at an end; that every door is closed but those into drawing-rooms, where you stand on the same boards with court footmen and idiots.—But what is the use . . .?" He let his hand fall heavily on the table.

Peter took off his spectacles, and this, which completely altered his face, revealed still more plainly his amiability and his astonishment.

"My wife," Prince Andrew went on, "is a good little wife, a woman in whose hands her husband's honour is perfectly safe. But what would I not give at this moment, great heavens, not to be married! You are the first and only soul to whom I have confessed it—for I love you."

As he spoke Andrew was less and less like the Prince Bolkonsky who had sprawled in his chair at Anna Paulovna's, firing off short sentences in French, in a low tone and with his eyes half-shut. Every muscle of his thin, keen face quivered with feverish excitement, and his eyes, in which the fire seemed always dead, shone and sparkled vividly. It was easy to guess that he would be violent in his short bursts of morbid irritation in proportion to his habitual apathy and nervelessness.

27

"You do not understand! and yet it is the story of a whole life. You talk of Bonaparte and his career," he went on, though Peter had not breathed a syllable, "but Bonaparte while he toiled was making straight for his goal, step by step; he was free; he had but one object in view, and he gained it. But once tie yourself to a woman and you are chained like a galley-slave. Every impulse and aspiration, the very forces within you, only crush you and fill you with regret. Drawing-room gossip, balls, vanities, meannesses—these are the charmed circle that fence you in. I am starting to help in this war—one of the most tremendous wars ever waged—and I know nothing, am fit for nothing. To make up for it I am most amiable, most satirical, at Anna Paulovna's they hang on my lips! Then think of that dull society which my wife cannot bear to do without! If only you could know what all these fine ladies—nay, all women—are worth. My father is right: Egoism, vanity, folly, utter mediocrity—that is the essence of woman when she shows her real self. When you see them in the world you might fancy there was something better in them; but no—nothing, nothing! My dear fellow, never marry. . . ."

Prince Andrew finished with these words.

"But what, to me, seems strange," said Peter, "is that you, of all men, should think yourself incapable and a failure, when the future is before you, and . . ."

His very voice showed how highly he thought of his friend and how much he expected of him.

"What right has he to talk so?" thought Peter, to whom Prince Andrew was the type of perfection, precisely because he felt that the prince possessed the qualities which he himself most lacked: Force and Will. He had always admired the ease and equanimity of his friend's demeanour towards others in every rank of life, his wonderful memory, his varied knowledge — for he read or made note of everything—and his powers of work and study. And if Peter had ever been struck at finding in Andrew no taste for speculative philosophy, which was his own particular weakness, he regarded it not as a deficiency, but as a proof of strength. In all the relations of life, however intimate, friendly and simple, flattery and praise are as indispensable as the oil which greases a machine and makes it work.

"I—I am done for; do not talk about me but about yourself," said the prince presently, smiling at having hit on so happy a diversion.

"About me?" said Peter, and his face reflected his friend's

look in a broad, merry, boylike smile. "But there is nothing to be said about me. After all, what am I? A bastard! . . ." And he coloured deeply, for it had been a great effort to bring out the word. "Without a name, without money, and—and yet free and happy, for the present at any rate. Only I may honestly confess that I do not know what I had better set to work to do, and I really want your advice on the subject."

Andrew looked at him with kindly benevolence, but it was a benevolence which betrayed a consciousness of superiority.

"I have a great affection for you, because you are the only living soul in all our circle of acquaintance; you are happy, you say—well, choose as you please; the choice matters little. You will get on anywhere. But I do beg you to break with the Kouraguines; give up that side of your life; this debauched, devil-may-care existence does not in the least become you."

"What is to be done, my dear fellow?" said Peter, shrugging his shoulders; "the women, you know, the women!"

"I do not admit it," said Andrew. "Women of good breeding, yes—but not such women as take up with Koura-guine. Women and wine—that I don't understand."

Peter was living with Prince Basil and led the same dissipated life as his youngest son Anatole—the very man who was to be married to Prince Andrew's sister in the hope of reforming him.

"Do you know," said Peter, as if he had had a sudden inspiration, "I have been thinking of it seriously for a long time. It is owing to that sort of life that I am unable to think or decide on anything—that I have headaches, and no money. He asked me again this evening, but I will not go."

"Give me your word of honour that you will give it up."

"On my word, I will."

CHAPTER X

IT was past one o'clock when Peter left his friend. It was a June night—a northern night of luminous twilight; he got into a hackney-carriage, firmly intending to go home. But as he drove along he felt that sleep was out of the question on such a night as this, which was more like the evening or dawn of a fine day. He looked down the long perspective of the empty streets. Then he remembered that the club of gamblers were to meet to-night at Anatole Kouraguine's;

after cards they drank, ending with one of Peter's favourite amusements.

"Supposing I were to go?" he said to himself, and then he remembered the promise he had just made to Prince Andrew.

At the same time such a wild desire came over him—as it does in men of no determination—to enjoy, just once more, that dissipated life which he knew only too well, that he made up his mind to go to Anatole's rooms, persuading himself that his word was not binding, since he had promised Anatole one thing before he had promised Andrew another; that, take them for all in all, such pledges were merely conventional and had no definite meaning; that, after all, no one could be sure of to-morrow, or know whether some extraordinary accident might not sweep honour and dishonour, with life, into the grave. This habit of arguing with himself often upset what seemed to be his most deliberate purpose.

Peter gave way, and went to Kouraguine's. He drew up at the front steps of a large house standing close to the barracks of the Horse Guards, went up and into the door which stood wide open. There was no one in the hall. The place smelt of wine; empty bottles, cloaks, and overshoes were strewed about, and the noise of shouts and talking came from some upper room.

Cards and supper were over, but the company had not separated. Peter, having flung off his cloak, went up into the first room where the remains of the supper were to be seen, and a footman, thinking himself unseen, was secretly drinking the sips of wine left in the glasses. Farther on, in another room, above the general hubbub of laughter and shouting, the growls of a bear were audible. Eight young men were crowding eagerly round an open window; three of them were playing with a bear-cub which one was dragging about by a chain and stirring up to frighten his companions.

"I will back Stevens for a hundred!" cried one.

"But you must not help him," said a second.

"I am for Dologhow," cried a third.

"Kouraguine, come and part them . . ."

"No, no, Mishka; leave the bear alone, here's a bit."

"He must do it at one pull or it does not count!" said a fourth.

"James, bring a bottle," said the master of the house at the top of his voice. He was a tall handsome fellow who had taken his coat off, and his shirt was open on his breast.

"Stay—wait a minute, gentlemen," he exclaimed. "Here is our dearly beloved Pétroucha," and he turned to Peter.

A man of middle height, with pale-blue eyes, whose calm and sober voice contrasted strangely with the vinous tones of the rest of the party, called to him from the window:

"Come here—part the hands!"

This was Dologhow, an officer of Séménovsky's regiment, a well-known duellist and gambler, who lived with Anatole. Peter looked about him smiling brightly:

"What is going on? I do not understand."

"Stop a minute—he is sober!" exclaimed Anatole. "Bring some wine; make haste," and taking a glass from the table he went up to him. "First of all you must drink."

Peter swallowed glass after glass, but this did not prevent his listening to what was going on, and glancing out of the corner of his eye at the company who were all tipsy and crowding round the window. Anatole poured out the wine for him, and told him meanwhile how the wager stood between Dologhow and Stevens, an Englishman in the navy. The Russian had backed himself to drink off a bottle of rum, sitting on the sill of the window of the third story with his legs hanging outside.

"Here, finish it off," said Anatole, offering Peter the last glass. "I will not let you off."

"No, I don't want any more," said Peter, pushing away his friend and going to the window.

Dologhow held the Englishman by the hand and clearly and distinctly repeated the terms of the wager, addressing himself chiefly to Anatole and Peter.

Dologhow, a young man of about five-and-twenty, was of middle height with curly hair and blue eyes. He, like all infantry officers at that time, wore no moustache, and his mouth, which was his most striking feature, was therefore visible. It was singularly well shaped and fine, with the upper lip something in the shape of a wedge closing energetically on the prim lower lip; the corners were marked by a perpetual smile—by two perpetual smiles, one on each side, as it were; and this, added to his look of intelligence and insolence, commanded attention. He had no fortune and no connections; he lived with Anatole Kouraguine, who spent tens of thousands of roubles, and in spite of everything contrived to be far more respected by their acquaintance than Anatole himself. He played every kind of game, always won, and however much he drank, never lost his head. He and Kouraguine were at that time celebrities among the rakes and spendthrifts of St. Petersburg.

A bottle of rum was brought in; two servants, evidently rather scared by the shouts and orders that pelted them from all sides, hastened to break away the sash-frame, which prevented a man from sitting on the high outer sill of the window. Anatole came up with his swaggering air; he longed to break something, and pushing away the servants he pulled the sash inwards. It was too strong to give way, but the panes flew to pieces.

"Now it is your turn, Hercules," he said to Peter.

Peter took hold of the frame, gave it a wrench, and the woodwork, which was oak, came away with a crash.

"Break it all away or you might fancy I clung to it," said Dologhow.

"The Englishman is bragging," said Anatole.

"Well done!" said Peter, keeping his eye on Dologhow, who, with the bottle of rum in his hand, went towards the window where morning and evening light were beginning to meet. He sprang upon the low ledge with the bottle in one hand.

"Listen," he said, standing in the embrasure with his face to the room. Everyone was silent. "I wager"—in order that the Englishman might understand him he spoke French, and very badly, too—"I wager fifty imperials—or shall I say a hundred?"—to the Englishman.

"No, fifty," said the Englishman.

"Very well, fifty imperials, that I will drink the whole of this bottle of rum, without taking my lips from the bottle; and that I will drink it there"—and he pointed to the sloping stone sill—"sitting on that, and holding on to nothing. Is that it?"

"Quite right," said the Englishman.

Anatole, holding Stevens by a button and looking down at him, for Stevens was a little man, repeated the terms of the bet in English.

"And that is not all," Dologhow went on, rapping the bottle against the woodwork to command attention. "That is not all. Kouraguine—listen! If anyone else does the same I will give him a hundred imperials. Do you all understand?" The Englishman bowed, without explaining whether or no he accepted this second wager. Anatole still held him fast and translated Dologhow's words in spite of Stevens's repeated nods of intelligence and assent. A young hussar who had been out of luck all the evening pulled himself up to the high window and leaned out to look down.

"Oh, ho!" he muttered doubtfully, as he measured the height from the pavement with his eye.

"Silence," cried Dologhow; he pulled back the young officer, who, being hampered by his spurs, leaped awkwardly into the room.

The bottle was placed within reach; Dologhow slowly and carefully got astride on the window-sill, and placing a hand on each side of it, he seemed to be measuring the width. Then he gently seated himself, left hold, leaned a little this way and that, and took up the bottle. Anatole brought a pair of candles and placed them in the bay, though it was now broad daylight. Dologhow's back as he sat in his shirt, and his crisp hair, were thus lighted on either side. They all stood round the window, the Englishman in front, Peter smiling and silent. Suddenly one of the party, alarmed and shocked, slipped forward, intending to take hold of Dologhow's shirt.

"This is madness; he will kill himself!" said the man—wiser, beyond a doubt, than his companions.

Anatole held him back.

"Do not touch him; you will startle him and he will fall, and what then? Eh?"

Dologhow, resting on his hands and feeling his balance, looked back.

"If anyone interferes again I will have him down there in no time. Do you hear?" he said, speaking slowly and pinching his lips tight. Then he sat straight, put the bottle to his lips, and threw back his head, raising his free hand to balance himself. One of the servants who was clearing the broken glass stood motionless and never took his eyes off Dologhow's head.

The Englishman looked another way, his mouth tightly shut, and the Russian who had tried to prevent this insane piece of folly had flung himself on a divan in a corner of the room with his face to the wall. Peter covered his eyes with his hand, a ghastly smile of horror and fright parting his lips. There was solemn silence.

Peter presently looked to see what was happening. Dologhow was in the same position, excepting that his head was so far thrown back that his hair rested on his shirt collar, while his right arm, holding the bottle, was slowly rising higher—higher—and trembling a little with the strain. The bottle was evidently nearly empty.

"What a long time it takes!" thought Peter—it seemed

33

like half an hour. Dologhow suddenly threw himself farther back, and his arm shook more. Sitting, as he was, on a sloping ledge, this tremulous action was enough to make him slip. In fact, he seemed to slip, his arm and head shook still more; he instinctively raised the other hand to clutch the woodwork, but he did not touch it. Peter shut his eyes again, vowing that he would open them no more; but a general stir a moment after made him look up, and he saw Dologhow standing in the bay, pale but triumphant.

"It is empty!" And he flung the bottle at Stevens, who caught it flying. Dologhow sprang into the room; he smelt strongly of the rum.

"Capital! well done! That is something like a bet!" they all shouted at once.

The Englishman had pulled out his purse, and was paying the bet to Dologhow, who had turned silent and sullen. Peter rushed to the window.

"Who will bet that I do not do the same thing," he cried— "or even without a bet? Quick, a bottle, and I will do it."

"Pooh!" said Dologhow, with a smile.

"Are you mad? What next! You are not to do it—do you hear? You, who turn giddy on a ladder!" said several.

"I will do it; make haste, a bottle!" cried Peter, thumping on the table with drunken vehemence, and he got astride on the window-sill. One of his companions seized his hands, but Peter was so strong that he flung them off.

"No, you will never succeed like that," said Anatole. "Stop, I will manage him. Listen to me, I will take the bet, but not till to-morrow—Come away, now let us be off."

"All right, let us be off, Michka and I the foremost!" He put his arms round the bear-cub, and lifting it off the ground, waltzed round the room with it.

CHAPTER XI

PRINCE BASIL had not forgotten his promise to Princess Drou-betzkoï the evening of Anna Schérer's party. The request had been preferred to the emperor, and Boris was privileged to enter the Imperial Guard as sub-lieutenant in Séménovsky's regiment; but in spite of all his mother's efforts, he was not appointed aide-de-camp to Koutouzow. Some little time after, the princess returned to Moscow, on a visit to her rich relations the Rostows, with whom she often stopped, and where her darling Boris, just promoted to a sub-lieutenancy in the ordinary army and immediately transferred to the Guards, had spent the chief part of his childhood. The Guards had left St. Petersburg on the 10th of August, and Boris, who was detained at Moscow while his outfit was getting ready, was to join at Radzivilow.

It was a high day at the Rostows'. Both mother and younger daughter were named Natalia, and their fête, or name day, was being kept. A stream of carriages had never ceased all day from setting down a crowd of friends at the great house in the Povarskaïa street, eager to offer compliments and congratulations. The countess and her eldest daughter, a handsome young girl, were receiving them in the drawing-room, where fresh arrivals constantly poured in.

The countess was a woman of about five-and-forty, and of rather an Eastern type, with a thin face, and the weary look of a mother of twelve children. Her deliberate speech and movements, which were the result of weak health, gave her a certain dignity that commanded respect. With her was the Princess Droubetzkoï, who, as one of the family, was helping to receive the company and keep up the talk.

The younger members of the family, who did not care for this business-like reception, were in the other rooms. The count went forward to meet his friends, and put them into their carriages again; and each and all he begged to return to dinner.

"I am so truly obliged to you, my dear friend," he said to everyone, high or low.

"Thank you so much for my dear wife. You will be sure to come to dinner? I shall really be hurt if you fail. I sincerely beg you to come to dinner in the name of my whole family. . . ." He repeated the same formula to all alike, with exactly the same cordial expression on his full, cheerful, clean-shaven face, pressing their hands and bowing. After seeing off those who were departing he came back to those who had not yet taken their leave, pulled forward a chair in which he seated himself, and placing his feet squarely before him and his hands on his knees, he rocked from side to side, expressing his opinions on the weather, on health and events, sometimes in Russian and sometimes in French, though he spoke it badly, but always with the readiness of a man of the world. Tired as he was he was alert to bow his friends out, like a man determined to do his duty to the utmost, and repeated his invitations; and all the time he smoothed his few remaining hairs over his bald skull. Now and then, on his way back to the drawing-room, he crossed the hall and the conservatory, and went into a large room with plaster walls, where tables were being laid for eighty guests. After glancing round at the servants who were bringing in the crockery and plate, and folding the damask napkins, he would call a certain Dmitri Vassiliévitch—a man of good family —who officiated as steward.

"I say, Mitenka, try and have everything in good order; yes, that is right, that is right. . . ." And looking with immense satisfaction at an enormous table, on to which a piece was being added, he said: "The waiting, that is the chief thing—the waiting, you understand . . ." and he went gleefully back into the drawing-room.

"Maria Luovna Karaguine and daughter," announced the countess's footman in a deep voice as he threw open the door.

"Mercy, I am dead! Well, this is the last—and she is so full of airs! Oh! show her up," she said wearily, and she took a pinch of snuff out of a gold snuff-box with a portrait of her husband painted on it.

A tall, stout woman, with a haughty air, followed by a round-faced, merry-looking girl, came into the room, heralded by the rustle of their long full dresses.

"My dear countess . . . it is such an age . . . she has been in bed, poor child . . . at the Razoumovskys' ball, and Countess Apraxine's . . . I enjoyed it so much."

These fragmentary phrases were drowned in the fuss of silk trains and of moving chairs. Then the conversation would be carried on with more or less interest till a pause offered an opportunity for rising to take leave, when, after a repetition of: "I am delighted . . . my mother's health . . . Countess Apraxine . . ." etc., etc., the ladies would make their way back to the ante-room, put on pelisses and cloaks, and take their departure.

The illness of old Count Bésoukhow, one of the handsomest men at the court of Catharine, was the chief subject of interest and, of course, of conversation, and even his natural son Peter —the same who had blundered through the evening at Anna Schérer's—was under discussion.

"I really pity the poor count," said Mrs. Karaguine. "His health is wretched, and to have a son who gives him so much anxiety."

"Why, what anxiety can he give him?" said the countess, pretending ignorance, though she had heard it at least fifteen times.

"This is the result of the education that is the fashion nowadays. The young man was left to be his own master when he was abroad, and now they say he does such things at St. Petersburg that he has been ordered out of the city by the police."

"Indeed?" said the countess.

"He got into bad company," said Princess Droubetzkoï, "and with Prince Basil's son and a fellow named Dologhow, he has been playing horrible pranks. Dologhow has been degraded to private, and Bésoukhow's son has been sent to Moscow. As to Anatole, his father has managed to hush up the affair; however, he has been desired to quit the capital."

"But what did they do?" asked the countess.

"They are perfect brigands, Dologhow especially: and he is Maria Dologhow's son—such an excellent woman! Would you believe that the three had got hold of a bear-cub, I do not know where, and took it in a carriage to some actress's house! The police tried to arrest them, and then, what did they take into their heads? They seized the police officer, and after tying him on the bear's back, they flung them into the Moika, the bear swimming with the man on his back."

"Oh, my dear, what a fool the man must have looked!" cried the count, rolling with laughter.

"But it is horrible. There is nothing to laugh at," exclaimed Mrs. Karaguine, though, in spite of herself, she, too, was in fits of laughing.

"They had the greatest difficulty in rescuing the poor wretch . . . and to think that a son of Count Bésoukhow's should find any amusement in such mad tricks! He is said to be intelligent and well educated, too; but this is the consequence of a foreign education. I only hope no one will receive him in spite of his fine fortune. They wanted to bring him to my house, but I declined the honour—I have daughters."

"But who says he is so rich?" asked the countess, leaning over to Mrs. Karaguine and turning her back on the young ladies, who immediately pretended not to hear. "The old count has none but natural children, and Peter, I think, is one of them." Mrs. Karaguine threw up her hands.

"There are a score of them, I believe," she said.

Princess Droubetzkoï, burning to parade her intimacy with

the minutest details of everybody's life, now threw in her word, saying in a low, emphatic tone:

"The truth is that Bésoukhow's reputation is notorious—he has so many that he has lost count of them; but Peter is his favourite."

"And what a splendid old man he was, no longer ago than last year," said the countess. "He was the handsomest man I ever saw."

"Ah! he is very much altered now. By the way, I was going to tell you that the heir-at-law to all his fortune is Prince Basil, through his wife; but the old man is very fond of Peter; he has spent a great deal on his education, and has written to the emperor about him. No one has the slightest idea which of them will come in for the money, and he may die at any moment. Dr. Lorrain has also come from St. Petersburg. The count's fortune is something colossal—forty thousand souls,[1] and millions of roubles in the funds. I know it for a fact, for Prince Basil himself told me. I am myself distantly connected with old Bésoukhow through his mother, and he is godfather to Boris," she added, as though she considered these facts quite unimportant.

"Prince Basil arrived in Moscow last evening," said the visitor. "He has come to make some inspection, I believe."

"Oh! but that is a mere pretext, between ourselves," said the princess. "He has come only to see Count Cyril Vladimirovitch, because he heard he was dying."

"It is a delicious story all the same," said the count, who, as the older ladies paid no heed to him, had addressed himself to the girls. "How funny the man must have looked!" And he went through a little performance of the gestures and attitudes of the police officer, chuckling in his deep bass—the noisy, thick chuckle of a man who loves good eating and drinking, and more particularly drinking. His whole burly frame shook.

"You will come back and dine?" he added to Mrs. Karaguine.

---

[1] Serfs on estates were at that time property, saleable and devisable with the land.

38

CHAPTER XII

THE words were followed by a silence; the countess smiled pleasantly on her visitor, making no concealment of the satisfaction she would feel at seeing her go. The daughter glanced inquiringly at her mother, and arranged the folds of her skirt, when suddenly there was a noise as of several persons running across the adjoining room; then a chair was upset, and immediately after a young girl of thirteen rushed into the room holding up the skirt of her muslin frock, in which she had something hidden. She stopped short; it was clear that in her headlong flight she had come farther than she had intended. She was instantly followed by a college student with a purple collar to his coat, a young guardsman, a girl of about fifteen, and a little boy in a round frock, with a bright rosy face.

The count rose and put his arms round the first-comer. "Ah ha! Here she is!" he exclaimed. "It is her fête, too, to-day; my dear, it is her fête."

"There is a time for all things," said the countess, trying to seem stern. "You always spoil her, Elias."

"How do you do, my dear; many happy returns of the day. What a darling!" said Mrs. Karaguine, turning to the mother.

The little girl with her black eyes and wide mouth was plain rather than pretty, but to make up for it she was amazingly full of life; her shoulders were still throbbing in her low frock from her breathless run; her black curls, all in disorder, were thrown off her face; her bare arms were thin; she still wore long trousers trimmed with lace, and had low shoes on her little feet. She was at the age, in short, when a little girl has ceased to be a child, but when the child is not yet a conscious maiden. She slipped away from her father and threw herself against her mother, without heeding her reproof; then, hiding her blushing face in the lace flounces of the countess's wrap, she went into fits of laughter, and began a long, incoherent story about her doll, which she took out of the skirt of her frock.

"You see, it is only a doll—it is Mimi, you see. . . ." And Natacha, leaning on her mother's knee, laughed so infectiously that Mrs. Karaguine could not help laughing too.

"Come, come; run away with that hideous object," said the countess, gently pushing her away. "She is my youngest daughter," she explained to her visitor.

Natacha, looking up for a moment from her mother's flounces, glanced at the stranger through tears of laughter, and then hid her face again. Mrs. Karaguine, feeling herself bound to admire this family scene, tried to take part in it.

"Tell me, dear," she said, "who is Mimi?—Is she your little girl?" But Natacha, not liking her condescending tone, turned suddenly grave, and only looked at her without speaking.

Meanwhile the younger members of the party: Boris — the young officer, the Princess Droubetzkoï's Boris; Nicholas— the student, and the eldest son of the Rostows; Sonia—the count's niece, a girl of fifteen; and Pétroucha, the youngest of the family, had collected in a group, making conspicuous efforts to control their glee and excitement within the bounds of propriety. Only to look at them, plainly showed that in the back rooms, from whence they had so rashly appeared on the scene, the entertainment had been of a more lively character than here in the drawing-room, and that they had talked of something besides the gossip of the town, the weather, the Countess Apraxine. They glanced at each other with merry meaning, and had the greatest difficulty in checking their impulse to laugh.

The two lads, the student and the officer, who had been companions all their life, were of the same age, both good-looking, but as different as possible. Boris was tall and fair, with regular, placid features. Nicholas had a curly head; he was short, and his expression was frank and simple. His upper lip showed the dark shade of an infant moustache. Every look and gesture was eager and enthusiastic; he had coloured crimson when he found himself in the drawing-room, and could not find a word to say. Boris, on the other hand, recovered himself at once, and said with some humour that he had had the honour of Miss Mimi's acquaintance some five years, but that lately she had grown very old and was undoubtedly cracked! As he spoke he stole a glance at Natacha, who looked at her little brother; Pétroucha, with his eyes almost shut, stood shaking with a convulsion of noiseless laughter, and his sister, feeling she could not control herself any longer, started up, and flew out of the room as fast as her little feet could carry her.

Boris did not stir: "Mamma, do not you want the carriage ordered to go out?" he said with a smile.

"Yes, go and order it," said his mother. And he left the room without hurrying himself, to follow Natacha, while the little boy, vexed at their desertion, trotted off after them.

CHAPTER XIII

Of younger members of the party, only Nicholas and Sonia remained, with Miss Karaguine and the Rostows' eldest daughter, who was four years older than Natacha, and considered as one of the "grown-ups."

Sonia was a sweet little brunette, with soft eyes and long dark lashes; the olive tint of her complexion was more marked round her throat, and on her small, slender hands, and a thick plait of black hair was bound twice round her head. The smooth grace of her movements, and her softness and roundness generally, with a rather shy manner, reminded one of a kitten growing up into a beautiful cat. She smiled, to look as if she took an interest in the conversation; but her eyes, which, under their silky lashes, constantly stole a glance at the student cousin, who was soon to be off to his regiment, so frankly expressed the adoring admiration peculiar to very young girls, that her smile could deceive no one. It was quite evident that though the kitten had curled itself up for a moment, the instant she was out of the drawing-room after Boris and Natacha, she would jump and play again with this charming cousin.

"Yes, my dear," said the count, pointing to Nicholas, "his friend Boris has been appointed to the Guards, and he insists on going with him to join the army—he will desert me, and leave college, and be a soldier—and to think that a place in the Archives is waiting for him! That is what I call devotion."

"And war is declared, they say."

"They said so long since, and they will say so again, and then we shall hear no more of it. Yes, my dear, real devotion, if I know what friendship means. He is going into the Hussars."

Mrs. Karaguine, not knowing what to say, nodded assent.

"It is not out of friendship at all!" exclaimed Nicholas, turning crimson, and defending himself as if he were accused of a crime; "simply because I feel a call to a military vocation." He glanced at his cousin and at the younger guest, and both girls looked their approval.

"Schubert, the colonel of the Pavlograd Hussar regiment, is to dine with us to-night; he is here on leave, and will take Nicholas back with him. What can I say?" and the count shrugged his shoulders, and tried to take the matter lightly, though it had in fact occasioned him no small pain.

"I have told you, papa, again and again, that if you forbid

my going, I will stay. But I cannot be anything but a soldier, I know; for a diplomatist or an official is bound to conceal his opinions and feelings, and I do not know how . . ." and he sent a killing glance at the young ladies, while the little kitten kept her eyes fixed on his, and seemed only to be waiting for an opportunity to be at her tricks and games.

"Very good, very good," said the count. "He fires up at once! Bonaparte has turned all their heads, and they all want to find out how, from being a lieutenant, he has become an emperor. Well, well. I wish them good luck," he added, not noticing Mrs. Karaguine's scornful smile.

Then they began to talk of Napoleon, and Julia Karaguine turned to Nicholas Rostow:

"I am sorry you were not at the Argharows' on Thursday— I was so dull without you," she murmured softly.

The young man, greatly flattered, went closer to her, and they carried on a coquettish dialogue "aside," he entirely forgetting Sonia, while she, poor child, scarlet and quivering with jealousy, tried to force a smile. In the middle of this he turned to look at her, and Sonia, flashing a look of love and anger out of her dark eyes, walked out of the room, with difficulty restraining her tears.

Nicholas suddenly ceased his lively flirtation, and availing himself of the first favourable interruption, he went off in search of her, visibly disturbed.

"The young folks' secrets are kept in a glass case," said Princess Droubetzkoï, looking after them. "Cousins are dangerous neighbours."

"Yes," said the countess, as all the light and life of the party finally disappeared. And then she went on answering a question which no one had asked her, but which was ever present to her mind: "How much anxiety, how much suffering we go through before happiness for them is our return! . . . and even now I am more fearful than happy. It is the most perilous age for girls as well as boys!"

"Everything depends on education."

"You are quite right, I have always been the friend of my children, thank God!" said the countess, who, like many parents, cherished this illusion, and believed she knew all her children's secrets. "My daughters, I know, tell me every-thing! and if Nicholas commits some follies—every boy must, more or less—at any rate, he will not behave like those young gentlemen at St. Petersburg."

"They are dear good children," said the count, whose way of settling any knotty point was to believe that everything was perfect. "What is to be done? He insisted on being a soldier. . . . What would you have, my dear?"

"What a delightful child your Natacha is."

"Yes, she is just like me," said the count innocently. "And with such a voice! Though she is my own child, I must say it. She will be quite first-rate, a second Salomoni! She is taking lessons from an Italian master."

"But is it not too soon? At her age it might spoil her voice."

"Why should it be too soon? Our mothers married at twelve or thirteen."

"And do you know, she is desperately in love with Boris. What do you think of that?" said the countess with a meaning smile at Arna Mikhaïlovna. Then she went on again, as if she were arguing with herself: "If I were strict with her, if I forbade her to see him, God knows what might come of it" (she meant perhaps that they would meet and kiss in secret); "while, as it is, I know everything they say; she comes to tell me every evening. I spoil her, perhaps, but believe me it is the best plan; my eldest daughter was very strictly brought up."

"Yes, indeed, I was educated quite differently," said Countess Vera, smiling. But her smile unluckily did not improve her, for it gave her face an unpleasant and affected expression. Still she was handsome, fairly intelligent, and well taught; her voice was pleasant, and what she said was perfectly true, and yet it made her audience look from one to another in awkward surprise.

"We always want to do wonders with our elder children," said Mrs. Karaguine.

"It must be confessed," said the count, "that my wife wanted to make a miracle of Vera—but after all, she succeeded," he added with an approving glance at his daughter.

Mrs. Karaguine at last made up her mind to depart, promising to return to dinner.

"What a nuisance!" cried the countess, after seeing her to the door. "I thought she was never going."

CHAPTER XIV

NATACHA had paused in her flight at the door of the conservatory: there she waited for Boris, keeping one ear open to catch the conversation in the drawing-room. At last, out of all patience, she stamped her foot and was on the verge of tears, when she heard the young man's step as he came across the room in no sort of hurry. She had just time to hide behind the tubs of evergreens. Boris, having entered the conservatory, looked about him, and flicking some dust off the sleeve of his coat, he went to a mirror to contemplate his pretty face.

Natacha watched him with much curiosity; she saw him smile, and make his way towards the opposite door. She thought she would call him. "No," she said to herself, "let him look for me."

He had hardly disappeared when Sonia, with flaming cheeks and streaming eyes, rushed into the conservatory. Natacha was on the point of springing to meet her, but the delight of being invisible and seeing others—just like a fairy-tale—kept her quiet. Sonia was speaking to herself in a low tone with her eyes fixed on the drawing-room door. In a minute Nicholas followed her.

"Sonia, what is the matter? How can you . . . ." he began.

"Nothing, leave me alone!" and she melted into sobs.

"No, no—I know what it is."

"Well then, if you know, so much the better for you. You had better go back to her."

"Sonia, one word! How can you torment yourself and torment me so for a mere whim, a fancy!" he said, taking her hand.

Sonia stopped crying, but did not draw her hand away. Natacha, riveted to her place, held her breath; her eyes were sparkling: "What is going to happen?" she wondered.

"Sonia, the whole world is nothing to me; you are everything, and I will prove it to you."

"I do not like you to talk so . . ."

"Well, I won't, only forgive me." And drawing her to him, he kissed her.

"Ah! well done!" said Natacha to herself.

Nicholas and Sonia went away; she followed them at a little distance to the door, and called Boris.

"Boris, come here," she said with a look of mysterious

44

importance. "I have something to say to you. Here—just here." And she led him to her hiding-place among the flowers. Boris followed her smiling:

"What have you to say to me?"

She coloured and looked about her anxiously; then, seeing her doll, which was lying on one of the tubs, she snatched it up and held it out to him: "Kiss my doll," she said.

Boris looked down at her eager little face.

"You will not? Then come this way. . . ." She dragged him into a thicker clump and tossed away the doll. "Come close, come closer . . ." and she pulled his coat; then, scarlet with excitement and on the point of tears, she said in a low voice:

"Now, will you kiss me?"

Boris coloured.

"What a strange child you are!" he said, bending over her, but undecided.

With one spring she was standing on the edge of one of the tubs, she threw her little bare arms round her companion's neck, and tossing back her hair she kissed his lips; then slipping down again she hastily escaped and stood still on the farther side of the wooden tub, her head hanging.

"Natacha, I love you, you know it, but . . ."

"Are you in love with me?"

"Yes, I am. But pray, pray do not do that again. In four years—then I will ask to marry you. . . ."

Natacha stood thinking. "Thirteen, fourteen, fifteen, sixteen," she said, counting on her fingers. "That is a promise," and her face lighted up with happy confidence.

"Yes, a promise," said Boris.

"For ever and ever, in life and death," the child went on, and she took his arm and led him into the drawing-room, quite happy and satisfied.

CHAPTER XV

THE countess was tired; she had at last said she could see no one, and desired the servant to ask anyone else who came to call to return to dinner. She wanted also to have a few minutes' chat with Princess Droubetzkoï, who had only lately returned from St. Petersburg, and who had been her friend from childhood.

"I will be frank with you," the princess began, drawing her chair closer to the countess. "We have so few old friends left that your regard is doubly dear to me." Then, glancing at Vera, she was silent. The countess pressed her hand.

"Vera, you might understand, I think"—it was quite clear that she was not fond of her daughter. "Do you not see that you are not wanted here? Go and join the others."

"If you had told me sooner, mamma," replied the handsome Vera with a scornful accent, but not seeming offended, "I should have been gone by this time."

And she went into the next room. There she discovered two couples, each seated in one of the windows, the counterpart of each other.

She paused, looking at them with a satirical expression. Nicholas, sitting by Sonia, was writing out some verses, his first attempt at composition. Boris and Natacha were whispering together, but were silent as soon as Vera came in. The two little girls had a radiant and conscious look that betrayed their feelings; it was both pretty and comical. But Vera did not see that it was either pretty or comical.

"How often have I desired you not to touch anything of mine? You have a room to yourselves," she said, and she took the inkstand from Nicholas.

"One minute—just one minute," said Nicholas, dipping his pen.

"You always do the wrong thing.—Just now you came tearing into the drawing-room like mad creatures, startling and upsetting everyone."

In spite—or perhaps in consequence of the truth of her remark, no one spoke a word, but the four guilty ones looked at each other. Vera, with her inkstand in her hand, did not go.

"And what secrets can you have at your age? It is ridiculous, mere silly nonsense."

"But what does it matter to you, Vera?" said Natacha gently, being the peacemaker.

"It is monstrous, and I blush for you! What are your secrets, pray?"

"Everyone has his own, and we leave you and Berg in peace," said Natacha hotly.

"There is no reason why you should not, we never do anything we are ashamed of; but as for you, I will tell mamma how you behave to Boris."

"Natalia Ilinischna behaves very well to me, I have nothing to complain of."

46

BEFORE TILSIT

"Be quiet, Boris, you are a perfect 'diplomat'!" exclaimed Natacha, hurt and offended. (This word, which the children were very fond of using, was to them full of peculiar meaning.) "It is intolerable! why does she attack me? You will never understand, for you never loved anyone in your life. You have no heart; you are Madame de Genlis"—this nickname, which Nicholas had found for Vera, was supposed to be particularly abusive. "Your only pleasure is to annoy others. You can flirt with Berg as much as you please."

"Well, at any rate I do not run after a man into a room full of company . . ."

"There, you have done what you wanted," cried Nicholas. "You have upset us all with your nonsense; let us go into the schoolroom." And they all four made their escape like a covey of frightened birds.

"It is you, on the contrary, who have been talking nonsense," exclaimed Vera, while outside the four voices sang merrily in chorus: "Madame de Genlis, Madame de Genlis!"

Vera, who succeeded in irritating everybody and leaving behind an unpleasant impression, paying no heed, went to the glass to arrange her sash and her hair, and the sight of her own pretty face restored her equanimity.

In the drawing-room the two friends had been discussing their most private affairs.

"Ah! my dear!" said the countess, "everything is not rose-coloured in a life like mine. I see quite plainly that if we go on at this rate our money will not last much longer. It is his liberality—and his club. Even in the country we have no peace: entertainments, hunting, shooting, what not! But what is the use of talking? Tell me what you have been doing. Really, I admire your energy; how you can go posting about at your time of life! Moscow—St. Petersburg—this minister —that big-wig! And you manage and persuade everybody! How in the world do you do it? It is marvellous, and I cannot understand it."

"Oh! my dear friend, may Heaven preserve you from ever knowing what it is to be a widow and alone with a son you adore. One puts up with anything for his sake. My lawsuit has been a hard school! When I wanted to see some great man I first wrote to him; then I went myself, in a hired carriage, once, twice, four times, as often as was necessary, till I had got what I wanted, and I did not care in the least what they thought of me."

"And who did you apply to about Boris, for after all, here he is an officer in the Imperial Guard, while Nicholas is no more than a 'Junker.' No one took any trouble about him. To whom did you go?"

"To Prince Basil, and he was most kind. He promised at once to speak to the emperor," she added eagerly, forgetting the snubbing she had received.

"And is Prince Basil much older? I have not seen him since the days of the theatricals at the Roumiantzows'; he has probably forgotten me, though in those days he made himself very agreeable to me!"

"He is just the same as ever, polite and courtly; his grandeur has not turned his head. 'I am only sorry, my dear princess,' he said, 'that it should cost me so little trouble; you have only to command.' He really is a kind man and a worthy relation. You know, Natacha, how devoted I am to my boy; there is nothing I would not do to secure his happiness. But my situation is really a cruel one, a most painful one; and it gets worse and worse," she went on, lowering her voice. "That miserable lawsuit makes no progress, and is ruining me. I have not ten kopeks in my pocket, and I assure you I do not know how I am going to get Boris his outfit." She drew out her handkerchief and began to weep. "I shall want five hundred roubles and I have only a note for twenty-five roubles in the world. I am in the most miserable straits; my only hope is in Count Bésoukhow. If he will not come forward to help his godson, all my pains will be lost."

The countess's eyes were sympathetically moist, and she seemed lost in meditation.

"I often think of Count Bésoukhow and his lonely existence," the princess went on, "and of his enormous fortune, and I cannot help wondering—it is a sin perhaps—why he is allowed to live on. Life is a burthen to him, while Boris is young. . . ."

"He will be sure to leave him something," said the countess.

"I doubt it, my dear; these enormously rich men are so egoistical. However, I mean to go there and to explain to the count how matters stand. Let people think of me what they like. It is now two," she said, rising, "and you dine at four— I shall have plenty of time."

The princess sent for her son: "Then we meet again presently.

Wish me good luck," she whispered so that her son should not hear.

"You are going to see Count Cyril Vladimirovitch?" cried the count, coming out of the dining-room. "If he is better, ask Peter to come to dinner; he used to be here often, and dance with the children. Make him promise to come. We shall see if Tarass does himself credit; he assures me that Count Orlow never gave such a dinner as he has had prepared for this evening."

CHAPTER XVI

"My dear Boris," said the princess, as the carriage that the countess had placed at her disposal rolled over the straw-covered street and into the courtyard of Count Bésoukhow's house: "My dear Boris," she repeated, and she put out her hand from under her shabby cloak, and laid it with a shy caress on her son's, "be amiable and judicious. He is your godfather and your future prospects depend on him, do not forget that. Be nice, as you can be when you like."

"I should have been glad, I must own, to feel sure that I should get anything out of it but humiliation," he said coldly. "However, I promised you, and I will do it for your sake."

The princess refused to be announced by servant. She and her son went into the entrance-hall where two rows of statues stood in the niches. The porter eyed the mother and son from head to foot, taking note of the lady's threadbare mantle; then he asked if their call was for the count or for the young princesses. "For the count," and he assured them that his excellency saw no one, he was much too ill.

"Then we may as well go," said Boris in French.

"My dear," said his mother, lightly touching his arm, as if her touch had a magic power to excite or soothe him. Boris said no more, and his mother went on in a plaintive tone to the manservant: "I know that the count is very ill and that is why I came to call; I am a relation of his—but I will not disturb him; I only want to see Prince Basil; he is here I know, pray have the goodness to send my name up."

The porter angrily pulled the bell.

"Princess Droubetzkoï, for Prince Basil," he called up to the footman, who put his head over the stair-rail.

The princess shook out the folds of her dyed silk gown, looking at herself as she passed in a large Venetian mirror that was framed into the wall, and boldly set her shabby shoe on the carpeted steps.

"You have promised, remember," she said, lightly stroking her son's hand to encourage him.

Boris followed her calmly with downcast eyes, and they were ushered into a room through which they must pass to that of Prince Basil. An elderly manservant rose to meet them, and they were on the point of repeating their wishes, when one of several doors was opened, and Prince Basil came out in a loose velvet coat trimmed with fur and with only one order, which, in him, was a sign of a hasty toilet. He was showing out a handsome young man with very black hair. This man was the celebrated St. Petersburg doctor, Lorrain.

"It is final, then?" he said.

"*Errare humanum est*, prince," replied Dr. Lorrain, pronouncing the Latin with a strong French accent.

"Thank you, thank you," said Prince Basil, who, having caught sight of the princess and her son, dismissed the physician with a bow. He then came forward to meet them with a look of inquiry. Boris saw his mother's face put on an expression of deep regret, and he turned away to hide a smile.

"We meet again under very sad circumstances," she began, ignoring the cold and offensive eye that the prince fixed upon her. "How is our dear invalid?"

Prince Basil looked at her and at Boris in silence, not attempting to conceal his astonishment at their presence there; without even returning Boris's bow he answered her inquiry with a contraction of his lips and a shake of his head, conveying that there was no hope for the count.

"It is true then!" she exclaimed. "Oh! it is terrible, terrible to think of! This is my son," she added, "he was anxious to thank you in person." Boris bowed again. "Believe me, prince, a mother's heart can never forget all you have done for her son."

"I am very glad, Anna Mikhaïlovna, to have been able to oblige you," said the prince, twitching his shirt frill. But his tone and manner were far more patronising than at the soirée at Anna Schérer's. "Do your duty to the best of your ability and try to prove yourself deserving. I am delighted—charmed— are you on leave?" All with an air of absolute indifference.

"I am waiting for orders, your excellency, before joining

my regiment," said Boris, without betraying the smallest annoyance at his dry tone or any wish to carry on the conversation. The prince was struck by his quiet reticence, and looked at him with more attention.

"Do you live with your mother?"

"I live with Countess Rostow, your excellency."

"With Elias Rostow, whose wife was Natacha Schinchine," explained Anna Mikhaïlovna.

"I know, I know," said the prince with cold monotony. "I never could understand Natacha. How she could marry that unlicked cub! A dull, absurd creature, and a gambler, they say, into the bargain."

"Yes, but a very kind soul, prince," said the princess, with a smile expressing her concurrence in his opinion, though she defended the poor count. "And what do the doctors say?" she went on, once more assuming a look of deep dejection.

"There is very little hope."

"I should so much have liked to see *uncle* once more, to thank him for all his kindness to Boris. Boris is his godson," she added with consequential emphasis, as though the fact must impress Prince Basil. But the prince said nothing and scowled. She, understanding at once that he considered her a dangerous competitor for the inheritance, hastened to reassure him.

"But for my sincere affection and devotion to my uncle"— and she let the words "my uncle" drop with a sort of careless effrontery—"I know his noble nature.—And he has no one with him but the princesses; they are very young." Then, looking down, she went on: "Has he fulfilled his religious duties? Every moment is precious. He cannot be worse, and it is indispensable that he should be prepared. We women," and she smiled sweetly, "can always manage these things best. I really must see him, painful as such an interview must be to me; but I am accustomed to sorrow."

Prince Basil understood, and saw as he had seen that evening at Anna Schérer's, that there would be no getting rid of the lady.

"I am afraid it would do him harm, my dear princess," he said. "Wait till the evening at any rate, the doctors think there may be a crisis."

"Wait! but his hours are numbered. His salvation hangs in the balance. The last duties of a Christian soul are a terrible ordeal."

At this moment a door, leading into another suite of rooms, opened and one of the princesses made her appearance. She had a crabbed, hard face and an enormously long waist, out of all proportion to the rest of her person.

"Well, how is he?" asked Prince Basil.

"Just the same—and how can he be otherwise with all this noise?" said the lady, staring at Anna Mikhaïlovna as though she were a stranger.

"Ah! my dear, I did not recognise you," exclaimed Princess Droubetzkoï, ambling forward. "I have only just arrived from St. Petersburg, and I came at once to help you to nurse my uncle. What you must have gone through!" and she raised her eyes to heaven. The young princess turned on her heel and left the room without a word.

Anna Mikhaïlovna drew off her gloves and settling herself in an arm-chair, as though she had captured an entrenchment, she signed to the prince to sit down by her.

"Boris, I will go in to see the count—my uncle; you can pay a call on Peter and give him the Rostows' invitation. They want him to dine there, you know. But I suppose he will not go," she added, turning to Prince Basil.

"Why not?" asked the prince, evidently much annoyed. "I shall be only too glad to get rid of him. He has made himself at home here, and the count has not once asked for him."

He shrugged his shoulders, and rang the bell. A footman came in, and was desired to take Boris to see Peter Kirilovitch through another part of the house.

CHAPTER XVII

PETER had not had time to decide on what he would do when he had been warned to leave St. Petersburg, in consequence of his disorderly absurdities. The story as told at the Rostows' was accurate: he and his madcap associates had tied the police officer on to the bear's back. He had now been in Moscow for some days, and had put up, as usual, at his father's house. Of course, he understood that the story of his adventure would be known, and expected the womankind of the house, who were always inimical, to be more than ever hostile. He nevertheless went up the first day to his father's room, pausing on his way to pay his respects to the three princesses. Two of

52

them were doing needlework at a large frame, while the third, the eldest, read aloud. Her appearance was severely neat with her odd-looking long waist; the two younger ones were both very pretty and wonderfully alike, excepting that one of them had a mole just above her lip which was thought particularly bewitching.

Peter was received like a leper. The eldest ceased reading and looked at him with horror and amazement; the second—the one who had not a mole over her lip—did the same; the third, who had some sense of fun, bent over her work to hide a smile at the scene which she foresaw was about to take place. She stuck her needle into the canvas and pretended to be studying the pattern while she was smothering a fit of laughter.

"Good morning, cousin," said Peter. "You do not seem to know me."

"I know you only too well—too well!"

"How is the count? Can I see him?" asked Peter with his usual abruptness, but not in the least discomposed.

"The count is suffering both in mind and body, and you have taken care to add to his mental trouble."

"Can I see him?" repeated Peter.

"Oh! if you want to kill him—to kill him outright, of course you can. Olga, go and see if my uncle's broth is ready—it is time," she added, to show Peter that they had no thought but for their uncle, while he evidently was only bent on displeasing him. Olga left the room. Peter waited a minute, and then, looking keenly at the two sisters, he said with a bow:

"If that is the case, I will go back to my own rooms, and you will let me know when I can see him."

He went away, the youngest princess laughing, ringing but not loud laughter, as he retreated.

Next day Prince Basil arrived, and took up his quarters in the house. He sent for Peter.

"My good fellow," he said, "if you go on here as you have been doing in St. Petersburg you will come to a bad end; that is all I have to say to you. The count is dangerously ill; there is no use in your seeing him."

From that moment Peter was forgotten, and spent his days in solitude in his rooms on the second floor.

When Boris went in Peter was pacing his room, which was spacious, stopping at the corners and shaking his fist at the walls as if he longed to run a sword through some invisible enemy, flashing wrathful glances over his spectacles, and then

53

walking on again, shrugging his shoulders, flourishing his arms, and haranguing to himself.

"England's day is over!" he said, frowning sternly, and pointing his finger at some imaginary auditor. "Mr. Pitt—a traitor to his country and to the rights of man, is condemned to . . ."

But he had not time to utter the verdict pronounced by Napoleon, whom he was representing; he had only crossed the Channel and taken London by storm when a handsome and well-dressed young officer came into the room. He stopped short. Boris was but fourteen when Peter had seen him last, and he did not recognise him; prompted however by his friendly instincts he held out his hand with a pleasant smile.

"You have not forgotten me?" said Boris, answering the smile. "I came with my mother to see the count, but they say he is too ill."

"Yes, so they say; but they do not give him a minute's peace," said Peter, wondering who his visitor might be.

Boris saw that he did not know him, but he thought it unnecessary to enlighten him, not feeling in the least awkward himself, and he looked him full in the face.

"Count Rostow begs you will dine with him to-day," he said after a long silence, which Peter was beginning to find very uncomfortable.

"Ah! Count Rostow!" exclaimed Peter joyfully. "Then you are his son Elias! Would you believe that I did not know you again? Do you remember our walks together, with Madame Jacquot, ages ago?"

"You are under a mistake," said Boris deliberately, with a cool, satirical smile. "I am Boris, the Princess Droubetzkoï's son. Count Rostow's name is Elias, but his son's name is Nicholas, and I never saw Madame Jacquot."

Peter shook his head and waved his hands, as if he were waving off a swarm of gnats or bees.

"Good heavens! Is it possible? I must have mixed it all up. I have so many relations in Moscow. You are Boris—to be sure . . . now I know all about it. Well, and what do you think of Napoleon's expedition to Boulogne? The English will have their hands full if Napoleon can only cross the Straits. I think it quite possible, if only Villeneuve is to be depended on."

Boris, who never read the papers, knew nothing about the expedition, and had never before heard the name of Villeneuve.

"Here, at Moscow, dinners and gossip occupy our minds

more than politics," he replied, with his ironical smile. "I know nothing whatever about them, and I never think. You and the count are the only subjects of conversation."

Peter's face lighted up with his frank, kind smile, though he seemed to fear lest his visitor should say something injudicious or unpleasant; but Boris spoke coolly and dryly, and kept his eyes fixed on Peter.

"Moscow has nothing else to think about," he went on. "Everyone wonders who will be the count's heir; and who knows whether he will not live to bury us all? I am sure I wish he may with all my heart."

"Yes, it is very sad, very sad indeed," stammered Peter, still feeling that the subject was an awkward one.

"And you, of course, must think," Boris said, colouring a little, but not losing his self-possession, "that all alike are hoping for a handful of gold from the millionaire . . ."

"Now for it," thought Peter.

"And I am most anxious to explain to you, that we may perfectly understand each other, that you would be quite mistaken if you included my mother and me among the number. Your father is very rich, and we are very poor; for that very reason I have never thought of him as a relation. Neither my mother nor I will ever ask or accept anything from the count."

Peter did not immediately take this in; but suddenly seizing Boris eagerly and clumsily by the hand, while he blushed with confusion, he began:

"Is it possible! Can it be supposed that I . . . or that anyone . . . ?"

"I am glad I told you; you must excuse me," said Boris, in a soothing tone. "I did not mean to offend you. I make it my principle to be perfectly frank.—But what answer am I to take? Will you come to dinner?"

And Boris having thus shifted the onus and burthen of a false position on to the shoulders of another person, could be as charming as usual.

"Do you know," said Peter, calming down, "that you are a wonderful man? You have just done a very noble thing. You do not know me—how should you? We have not met since we were children—and of course you might have supposed . . . I understand perfectly; but I should never have done it, I should not have had the courage . . . it is really admirable. I am delighted to have made your acquaintance.

It is very odd," he went on, after a short silence, "you really thought that I . . ." and he began to laugh. "But we shall know each other better, I hope and beg," and he grasped his hand. "Do you know I have not seen the count; he has not asked for me—it pains me, as a man; but there is nothing to be done."

"And do you really think that Napoleon will have time to get all his army across?" said Boris.

And Peter, seeing that Boris wanted to change the subject of conversation, went on enlarging on the advantages and the difficulties of the Boulogne expedition. He was still in the middle of the subject, when a servant came to tell Boris that his mother was going; Boris took leave of Peter, who shook hands warmly, and promised to dine with the Rostows.

When Boris was gone, he continued his walk round his room, but he no longer sparred with spectral foes. He smiled with the sense of a sudden warm affection for this intelligent and sympathetic new friend—the result no doubt of his own isolation —and quite made up his mind to improve the acquaintance.

Prince Basil accompanied the princess to her carriage; she came down weeping, her face hidden in her handkerchief.

"It is frightful, quite frightful," she murmured. "But I will do my duty to the end. I will come back and sit with him; he cannot be left in this state; every minute is precious. I do not know what his nieces are waiting for. God willing, I may perhaps find an opportunity for preparing him. Good-bye, prince, and may God support and comfort you."

"Good-bye, my dear," said Prince Basil indifferently.

"Oh! he is in a terrible state," said the mother to her son, as soon as they were in the carriage; "he knows no one."

"I cannot understand what is his position with regard to Peter?" asked the son.

"His will will explain everything; and our fate, too, will depend upon it," said the princess.

"But what makes you think that he will leave us anything?"

"Oh! my dear, he is so rich, and we are so poor!"

"That does not seem to me a sufficient reason, I must confess, mamma. . . ."

"Good God! How ill he is!" exclaimed his mother.

CHAPTER XVIII

WHEN Anna Mikhaïlovna and her son had set out to pay their visit, they had left the countess alone, lost in thought, and now and then wiping away a tear. At last she rang the bell.

The maid was long in answering the summons. Her mistress's nerves were all on edge; her friend's anxieties and squalid poverty had quite upset her, and she was very cross. "It strikes me," she said to the girl, "that you do not choose to do your work—just as you please. I can find another place for you." The girl apologised penitently. "Well, go and beg the count to come to me."

The count immediately obeyed; he waddled into the room, and came shyly up to his wife.

"Ah, ha! little countess," he said, "what a dish of partridges with Madeira we are going to have! I know—I have tasted it, my dear. Well, I have paid a thousand roubles for Tarass; and he is well worth it."

He sat down by her, passing one hand through his hair, and laying the other on his knee with an air of triumph. "And what do you want, little countess?"

"I will tell you. But what is this stain?" said she, pointing to a spot on his waistcoat. "The stewed partridges, no doubt?" and she smiled. "Well, my dear, I want some money." And her face wore a sad look.

"Really?" he said. "But, my dear little countess . . ." and he hastened to take out his pocket-book.

"Yes, a great deal of money. I want five hundred roubles," and as she spoke she rubbed the stain on his waistcoat with her cambric handkerchief.

"Certainly, at once. Hi! is there anyone there?" he shouted with the decision of a man who knows that he will be obeyed, and that crouching servants will appear at his call. "Ask Mitenka to come here."

Mitenka was the gentleman's son, whom the count had brought up, and then trusted with the stewardship of all his affairs; he came with a slow and measured step, and stood respectfully before his master.

"Listen to me, my dear fellow; bring me"—he paused. "Bring me seven hundred roubles—yes, seven hundred; and mind the notes are not all dirty and torn like the last. I want new ones; they are for the countess."

"Yes, Mitenka; let them be clean ones, pray," said the countess, with a sigh.

"When does your excellency wish to have them? for you know . . . However, be quite easy," added Mitenka hurriedly, as he saw the hard, quick breathing which in the count was the unfailing sign of a burst of rage. "I forgot—you shall have them."

"Very well. Bring them to the countess. What a treasure that fellow is!" said the count, looking after him; "he never says a thing is impossible, and that is just what I like; in fact, just as it ought to be."

"Oh! money, money! How many ills it causes in this world; and this will be of the greatest use to me, my dear."

"Everyone knows how extravagant you are, my little countess," said her husband; he kissed her hand, and left her.

A packet of crisp new notes was presently brought to the countess, who laid them in her lap, and covered them carefully with her pocket-handkerchief. In a few minutes Princess Droubetzkoï came in.

The countess saw that Princess Droubetzkoï was very worried.

"Well, my dear?" asked the countess.

"Oh! the most fearful state of things. You would not know him, and he is so ill! I only stayed a minute, and did not say two words."

"Anna, if you love me, do not refuse to do me a favour," said the countess, quite inconsistently, and with a bashful look that was oddly out of place on her worn and rather stern features. She snatched up her handkerchief, and presented the packet to Anna Mikhaïlovna. The princess guessed what it was at once, and leaned over, ready to clasp her friend in her arms.

"It is to fit out Boris."

This was the moment for effusiveness; the princess embraced Natacha with a burst of tears. Why should they both weep? Was it because they were reduced to consider the money question—a sordid matter between such devoted friends; or were they thinking of their youth, of the days of childhood when they had first loved each other? Be that as it may, their tears flowed freely, and were tears of entire satisfaction.

BEFORE TILSIT

CHAPTER XIX

Countess Rostow was in the drawing-room with her daughters and a crowd of ladies. Her husband had taken the men into his private room, and was displaying a fine collection of pipes; now and again he came into the drawing-room to see whether Maria Dmitrievna Afrossimow had come.

Maria Dmitrievna — nicknamed the "Dreadful Dragon" — had neither fortune nor title, but she was strictly honest and frank, and her manners were natural and unaffected. She was known to the imperial family, and the best society of both capitals was to be seen at her house. People might laugh in their sleeves at her free-and-easy ways, and tell wonderful stories of her eccentricities; she was feared and respected all the same.

In the count's room they were smoking and talking over the war, which had just been declared and publicly announced in a manifesto on the recruiting question. None of those present had read it yet, but it was known that it had been published. The count, seated on a divan between two of his guests, who were talking and smoking, said not a word, but turned from one to the other, listening to each with evident satisfaction.

One of them was a civilian; his wrinkled, yellow, lean, and close-shaven face betrayed his advanced age, though he was dressed in the latest fashion; he sat with his feet curled up on the divan in the attitude of a man who felt himself at home, and he was smoking a chibouque, sucking the amber mouth-piece with noisy deep inspirations, and a variety of contortions. Schinchine was an old bachelor, a connection of the countess's, and regarded in every drawing-room in Moscow as a spiteful gossip. He always talked as if he thought he was conferring an honour on his auditor. The other man was a young officer in the Imperial Guard, fresh, rosy-cheeked and curly; elaborately got up, and as smart as a new pin. He held his chibouque daintily between his cherry lips, and puffed off the smoke in light spiral clouds. This was Lieutenant Berg of the Sémé-novsky Regiment, which he and Boris were about to join; and it was to him that Natacha had alluded as "Vera's Berg."

The count sat listening attentively, for his chief joys in life were playing Boston,[1] and absorbing the conversation of

---

[1] A game of cards said to have been invented by officers of the French army in America during the time of the Revolutionary war.

two steady talkers when he was so fortunate as to get two together.

"And how do you mean to manage that, my dear and highly-respected Alphonse Karlovitch?" asked Schinchine sarcastically. He had a way of mixing colloquial Russian vulgarisms with the most elaborate French phrases, that gave a quaint originality to his conversation. "Do you propose to invest your capital in the state funds and draw a handsome interest?"

"No, Peter Nicolaïévitch, I only aim at proving that the advantages of serving in the cavalry are much smaller than in the infantry. But you will see what I mean. . . ." Berg always spoke very quietly, precisely and politely; he never talked of anything but himself, but when a conversation happened to have no personal interest, he could sit silent for an indefinite length of time without seeming awkward or making anyone else uncomfortable, though, the moment an opportunity offered, he would come to the front with evident satisfaction.

"This is how matters stand," he went on. "In the cavalry, even as a lieutenant, I should not have more than 200 roubles every four months; now, as it is I have 230 . . ." and Berg smiled at Schinchine and the count with the happiest confidence that his career and his interests must be of the highest importance to his audience. "Then, I am seen and known, and vacancies occur more frequently. Of course I could not go on for ever on 230 roubles, for I save some money, and send it to my father," Berg added, puffing out a cloud of smoke.

"The calculation is a close one, 'a German can grind his corn on the back of his hatchet,' says the proverb. . . ."

And Schinchine shifted his pipe to the other corner of his mouth, with a side glance at the count, who laughed heartily. The rest of the company, seeing that Schinchine was in the vein, gathered round them, while Berg, who never perceived that he was being laughed at, proceeded to enumerate all the advantages he had gained by exchanging into the Guard: a rise in rank to begin with; then, in war-time, the officer in command might be killed, and he, as senior, would be all the more likely to be appointed in his stead, as he was a favourite in the regiment, and his papa was very proud of him. He told all his little stories with the greatest enjoyment, never seeming to suspect that there could be any more important interests in the world than his own; and there was something

BEFORE TILSIT

so ingenuous in his innocent and youthful egoism that his
hearers were disarmed.

"Ah well, my boy, you will get on whether in the cavalry or
the infantry, I will answer for that," said Schinchine, patting
him on the shoulder as he put down his feet. Berg smiled
self-satisfied, and followed the count, who led the way, into the
drawing-room.

It was just before dinner was announced, the moment when
no one cares to begin a conversation in expectation of the
zakouska.[1] Politeness, however, demands at any rate a pretence of talk, if only as a cover to hide one's impatience. The
host and hostess keep an eye on the dining-room door, and
exchange uneasy glances; the guests on their part, catching
these hints of despair, rack their brains to guess why or for
whom they are kept waiting—is it some influential relation, or
is it the soup?

Peter had only just come in, and had seated himself, clumsily
as usual, in the first arm-chair he saw, in the very middle of
the room. The countess was doing her best to make him talk,
but could only extract monosyllables, while he sat staring
about him through his spectacles as if he were looking for
someone. He was, no doubt, very much in the way, but he
was the only person who failed to perceive it. Everyone had
heard something of the history of the bear, so this big, burly,
stalwart young fellow was an object of general curiosity; people
wondered how such a heavy, indolent creature could have
played such a trick on a police officer.

"You have only just come?" asked the countess.

"Yes, madam," and he looked to the left.

"You have not seen my husband?"

"No, madam," and he smiled vaguely.

"You were in Paris not long since; it must be an interesting
place."

"Very interesting."

The countess cast a beseeching glance at Anna Mikhaïlovna,
who, catching this silent entreaty on the wing, as it were, came
forward, to put a little life, if possible, into the conversation.
She spoke to Peter of his father, but with no better success;
he could only answer in monosyllables.

The rest of the company were gossiping languidly; one heard

[1] Caviar or pickled fish served with brandy before dinner to whet the
appetite.

61

such phrases as: "The Razoumovskys—quite delightful.—How kind you are.—Countess Apraxine . . ." when the countess suddenly moved across the room, "Maria Dmitrievna?"

"Her very self," added a rather harsh voice, and Maria Dmitrievna came in.

Excepting the old ladies, all, whether girls or married women, rose to receive her. She paused in the doorway. She was tall, masculine and erect, a woman of fifty with iron-grey curls; and while she affected to be deliberately patting down her cuffs, she cast a searching glance round at all the company. Maria Dmitrievna always spoke Russian.

"Health and happiness to the lady we are met to honour— to her and to all her children!" she said in her full voice, which sounded above every other. "And what are you doing with yourself in Moscow, old sinner?" she went on to the count, who kissed her hand. "You are bored to death here, confess it; there is nowhere to give a dog a good run. What is to be done, my good man? As these little birds grow up"—and she waved a hand towards the girls—"they must have husbands found for them, whether or no. And you, my little Cossack"— so she always called Natacha, and she stroked her hair while the child merrily kissed her hand without the least shyness. "This child is an elf, I know, but I am very fond of her." She took out of a vast handbag a pair of onyx ear-rings, pear-shaped drops of fine gems, and gave them to the little girl who beamed with delight; then, turning to Peter, she added in a tone that she meant to be insinuating: "Ho, ho! my good friend, come here, come to me," and she turned back her wide sleeves with a threatening gesture.

"Come here, come close. I was the only person to tell the truth to your father when occasion required it, and I am not going to spare you. It is my mission from God."

She paused and everyone listened for what would follow this thunder of a coming storm: "Well, you are a pretty fellow, I must say. . . . While your father is lying on a bed of sickness you can amuse yourself with lashing a police officer on to a bear's back! It is indecent, positively indecent, boy! You had better have gone to the war."

She turned her back on him, and giving her hand to the count: "Well, to dinner!" she exclaimed, "it is ready, I believe!"

The count led the way with Maria Dmitrievna; the countess followed with the colonel of Hussars, who was a guest to be made much of as Nicholas was to go with him to join his regiment. Anna Mikhaïlovna went with Schinchine; Berg took Vera, Nicholas took Julia Karaguine, all smiles, and the rest of the party came in couples along the great dining-room, the procession closing with the governess and tutors, each leading one of the children. The servants rushed to push in the chairs with much noise, a band struck up in the gallery, and everyone sat down. The music was soon drowned in the clatter of knives and forks, the voices of the company, and the bustle of the servants. The countess sat at one end of the table with Maria Dmitrievna at her right, and Anna Mikhaïlovna on her left; the count, at the other end, was between Schinchine and the colonel; the rest of the gentlemen placed themselves as they pleased; in the middle, on one side, Vera with Berg, Peter and Boris faced the children and their guardians on the other. The count kept glancing at his wife and her towering cap with blue ribands, which he could see between the decanters, bottles, and high dishes of fruit which stood between them, and devoted himself to offering wine to his neighbours, not forgetting himself. The countess, peeping over the crowns of the pine-apples, responded to her husband's glances; his rubicund forehead, framed in scanty grey hair, was a conspicuous object.

At the ladies' end there was a buzz of voices in unison; at the men's end, tones by degrees grew louder, and the colonel's voice particularly, for he ate and drank so much and so heartily that his face had grown purple, while the count held him up as an example to his other guests. Berg, with a tender smile, was explaining to Vera that love was a gift from Heaven and not a product of this world. Boris was naming the persons present to his new friend Peter, and sending meaning glances at Natacha, who sat opposite to him. Peter spoke little; he was studying the faces he did not know, and eating with a will. Of two soups that had been offered him he had chosen turtle, and from the kouliabiaka [1] to the birds basted with Madeira he had not let a single dish pass, or refused a single wine of all the variety offered by the butler, who stood majestically behind him and muttered in his ears: "Dry Madeira, Hungarian wine, Rhine wine."

He drank indiscriminately out of any of his glasses—four, with the count's arms engraved on them, were placed by every guest—and he felt a flow of general benevolence towards all his neighbours which grew with each bumper that he swallowed. Natacha sat gazing at Boris as none but a very young girl can

[1] Kouliabiaka is a popular Russian dish.

63

when she is first in love, and especially when she has just had a kiss. Peter did not trouble himself about her, but as he caught sight of the strange little person, with her eyes glowing with passion, he felt a weak disposition to laugh.

Nicholas, who was a long way from Sonia, by the side of Julia Karaguine, chatted gaily with his neighbour. Sonia, too, could smile, but jealousy was gnawing at her heart; she turned red and pale alternately, and racked her brain to guess what they could be saying to each other. The governess sat looking pugnacious, as if prepared to turn and rend anyone who should speak to the children; the German tutor was trying to take mental note of all the dishes and wines that were passed round, so as to give a full description of them in his next letter home, and he was deeply hurt because the butler never offered him wine. He swallowed his humiliation as best he could, making believe that he did not wish for any, and trying to persuade himself that if he had taken any it would have been merely from motives of scientific curiosity.

CHAPTER XX

THE conversation among the gentlemen was growing loud and eager. The colonel said that the manifesto declaring war was already issued in St. Petersburg, and that he had seen a copy which a courier had just brought to the commander-in-chief.

"What evil star is leading us to fight against Napoleon?" cried Schinchine. "He has succeeded already in teaching Austria to hold her tongue; now I am afraid it will be our turn."

The colonel, who was a German, stalwart and ruddy, a good officer, and a staunch Russian, in spite of his foreign birth, fired up at these words.

"An evil star!" he exclaimed, with his barbarous accent. "When it is the czar, sir, who knows why! He says in his manifesto that he cannot remain indifferent to the danger that threatens Russia, and that the safety of the empire and the sacred dignity of his *alliances* . . ." and he emphasised the word as if it contained all the marrow of the matter.

Then, with the facility of a man who has had long practice in remembering official edicts, he proceeded to quote the opening clause of the manifesto: "'The emperor's sole and constant wish and aim being the establishment of a permanent peace in Europe, he has determined, in the hope of attaining that end, to send a portion of the army across the frontier.'—There, sir, that is the reason," and he slowly emptied his glass, looking round at the count for approbation.

"You know the saying: 'Jeremiah, Jeremiah, stay at home and mind the spindle,'"[1] retorted Schinchine, sarcastically. "It fits us like a glove. When we remember that even Souvorow was beaten hollow—and where is there a Souvorow nowadays, let me ask?" he said, dropping from Russian into French.

"We ought to fight to the last drop of our blood!" exclaimed the officer, striking the table with his fist, "and be ready to die for the emperor! That is what we must do, and argue as little as possible," he added, as he addressed the count. "That is the form of argument that goes down with us old hussars.— And you, young man, and young hussar, how do you argue?" and he turned to Nicholas, who was neglecting his fair neighbour, to listen.

"I entirely agree with you," he said, turning as red as a poppy, twisting his plate round and fidgeting with his glass till he was like to break it. "I am convinced that the thing for us Russians is to conquer or to die. . . ." He had hardly finished his sentence when its absurdity struck him; it was pompous and declamatory, and quite beside the question.

"That is splendid!" murmured Julia Karaguine. Sonia, quivering with excitement, had coloured up, too, while Peter expressed his admiration of the colonel's speech.

"That is something like!" he said.

"You are a true hussar, young man!" cried the colonel, and again he thumped the table.

"Hey day! What is all that noise about?" It was Maria Dmitrievna who asked. "Why such a thumping? Who are you fighting with? Why, you are as furious as if you were charging the French. . . ."

"I am speaking the truth!" retorted the officer.

"We are talking about the war, Maria Dmitrievna," said the count. "Do you know I have a son who is going into the army?"

"Well, I have four in the army, and I do not complain.

[1] Anglice: "Cobbler, cobbler, stick to your last."

The will of God governs all. One may die lying on one's stove,[1] or come safe out of a battle," said Maria Dmitrievna, her loud voice ringing across the table.

"That is so."

Then the conversation again was among the women, on one side, and the men on the other.

"I tell you, you will not do it," said Pétroucha to Natacha in a whisper. "You will not dare to ask."

"I tell you I will," said Natacha; and half rising from her seat, her face crimson with mischief and audacity, she challenged Peter's attention with a glance: "Mamma," she said, in her clear, childish voice.

"What is it?" said the countess in alarm; for she suspected some monkey's trick from the little girl's face, and held up a warning finger, shaking her head in displeasure.

There was a sudden silence.

"Mamma, what sweet dish is coming?" Natacha went on without hesitating a moment.

Her mother vainly tried to frown.

"Ah! Cossack!" said Maria Dmitrievna, raising a threatening forefinger. The company looked at each other; the elders doubting how to take the interruption.

"Naughty child!" chided the countess.

"Mamma, tell me what sweets?" repeated Natacha, not at all uneasy as to the result of her prank. Sonia and the fat Pétroucha were in fits of suppressed laughter.

"There, you see—I did ask," said Natacha, turning to her little brother and Peter, at whom she again threw a glance.

"Ices and you will not be allowed any," said Maria Dmitrievna.

Natacha, seeing that she had nothing more to fear, even from this imposing personage, answered her boldly. "What ice?— I do not like cream ice."

"Carrot ice then?"

"No, no—what ice, Maria Dmitrievna, what ice? I want to know."

The countess laughed, and everyone laughed with her; not so much at Maria Dmitrievna's retort as at the child's audacity and tact in daring to hold her own.

Natacha was told pine-apple ice, and she quieted down. Then champagne was taken round, the band struck up again;

[1] In Russia the peasants' houses are fitted with stoves on which they can sleep in the winter.

the count kissed his "little countess," and all the guests rose to pledge them and drink their health, touching glasses with their hosts, with their *vis-à-vis*, with their neighbours, and with the children. The servants drew back the chairs and all the company, a little heated with dinner and wine, filed out in couples as they had come in, and returned to the drawing-room in the same order.

CHAPTER XXI

THE card-tables were placed ready; sets were formed for games at Boston, and the company dispersed in two drawing-rooms, the reception-room and the library. The count sat gazing at a pack of cards spread out before him like a fan. At this hour he was accustomed to take a nap, and he was doing his best to conquer his disposition to sleep, and laughing at everything that was said to him. The young people, following the mistress of the house, had gathered round the piano and the harp. Julia, yielding to a general request, performed an air with variations on this instrument, and then joined the rest of the party in begging Natacha and Nicholas, whose musical talents were known to all, to sing something. Natacha, though much flattered at being treated like a grown-up person, was rather alarmed.

"What are we to sing?" she asked.

"*La Source*," said Nicholas.

"Well, let us begin. Where is Sonia? Come, Boris." And seeing that her cousin was not in the room, Natacha flew off in search of her. She ran to Sonia's room, but it was deserted; in the schoolroom—no one. Then it struck her that Sonia would be sitting on the bench in the corridor. This seat was the spot consecrated to the griefs of the young ladies of the family; there, no doubt, Sonia would be found. And there she was, flung upon the seat, crying bitterly, in her gauzy pink dress, which she was crumpling cruelly without heeding it; her bare shoulders throbbed convulsively with her sobs, and her face, covered with her hands, was hidden in a dirty striped cushion that belonged to her old nurse. Natacha's face, till this moment so radiant, lost its festal expression—her eyes grew rounder, the veins of her throat swelled, and the corners of her mouth drooped.

"Sonia, what has happened, what is the matter? Oh dear, oh dear!" And at the sight of Sonia's distress she, too, melted into tears. Sonia tried to look up and tell her, but it was too much for her; she buried her head more deeply in the pillow. Natacha sat down by her and threw her arms round her, and at length, controlling herself a little, Sonia half raised herself and wiped her eyes.

"Nicholas is going in a week," she sobbed. "The order is out, he told me so himself. But I should not have cried for that . . ." she added, and she showed Natacha a paper she held, on which Nicholas had written some verses. "But you cannot understand me—and no one knows how good and noble he is!" And she began to cry again because he was so good and noble. "You are happy—and I am sure I do not grudge it you, for I love you and Boris, too; he is a nice, dear fellow, and nothing need come between you; but Nicholas is my cousin and the bishop himself . . . or else it is impossible. And then if mamma" (for Sonia always thought of the countess as her mother) "were to think I was a hindrance or a check on his future prospects, she would say I was ungrateful and heartless; but God is my witness, I love him so much, and her too, and all of you—except Vera; what have I done to her that she . . .? Yes, and I am so truly grateful that I would make any sacrifice . . . but I have nothing, nothing. . . ."

And Sonia, unable to control herself, hid her face again in the cushion. It was clear from the earnestness of Natacha's efforts at consolation that she understood how deeply her friend was wounded.

"Sonia!" she said. Suddenly the truth had dawned on her. "I will bet that Vera has been talking to you since dinner?"

"But it was Nicholas who wrote these verses, and I had copied the others, and she found them on my table and says she will show them to mamma. . . . And she says I am ungrateful, and that mamma will never let me marry him— that he will marry Julia Karaguine, and you see how he has devoted himself to her all day: oh, Natacha, why is it?" and her tears flowed again.

Natacha drew her to her, kissing her and smiling at her through her own tears.

"Sonia, do not believe her. Remember what we were saying, you and I and Nicholas, after supper the other evening. We settled it all—I forget exactly how, but I know it all came right and was quite possible. Uncle Schinchine's brother married his first cousin and we are much farther off. And even Boris said there would be no difficulty; I told him all about it, he is so clever and so kind. Do not cry, Sonia, my pet, my darling. . . ."

And she laughed and covered her with kisses. "Vera is so spiteful; but let her be, and it will all come right. And she will not tell mamma; Nicholas will tell her himself. He does not care for Julia."

She kissed Sonia again, and the girl started up, her eyes bright with joy and hope. She really was a sweet kitten that seemed only to be on the lookout for the moment when it might drop softly on its paws and spring after the ball that, like others of its kind, it could play so skilfully.

"You think so? You are sure? You swear it?" she exclaimed eagerly, as she shook out her skirts and smoothed down her hair.

"I swear it," said Natacha, fastening up a strand of hair that had fallen away from her long plaits.

"Well, then, come along, and we will sing *La Source*," they exclaimed, laughing together.

"Do you know, that big Peter who sat opposite to me is immensely funny," said Natacha, stopping suddenly. "Oh, what fun it all is!" and she danced away. Sonia shook off the down that had clung to her dress, slipped the verses inside her bodice, and followed her hastily, with glowing cheeks.

The quartette, as may be supposed, was a great success. Then Nicholas sang a new song:

> Phoebe is shining in the night,
> Of thee I dream, my leal heart's flight
> Thy heart doth seek, my worshipped one;
> In dreams I see thy fingers fair
> Draw forth the gilded harp's sweet tone . . .
> But what avails each tender air
> From my dear love, each fond appeal,
> If still my burning lips beneath
> Her kisses thrill not, ere they feel
> The icy, frozen kiss of death?

He had no sooner finished than the band in the gallery struck up a dance tune and all the young people rushed in.

Schinchine had taken possession of Peter, whom he regarded as a choice morsel freshly imported for his benefit, and he was starting a tiresome political discussion, in which some others joined, when Natacha came into the drawing-room again, and walking straight up to Peter said with a laugh and a blush:

"Mamma desires me to ask you to come and dance."

"But I am afraid I shall put all the figures into confusion," said Peter; "however, if you will be my guide . . ." and he offered the little girl his hand.

While the couples were taking their places and the instruments were tuning up, Peter took a seat by his little lady's side, and she could hardly contain herself for joy at the mere idea of dancing with a grown-up man, just come from abroad, and of talking to him like a grown-up person. She sat flirting a fan that someone had given her to hold, and with an air of perfect ease, picked up God knows where or how, she chatted and laughed with her partner.

"Look at her—do look at her!" said the countess, as she crossed the room.

Natacha coloured, but did not lose her self-possession: "Mamma, how can you like . . .? What is there extraordinary in me?"

They were dancing the third set when the count and Maria Dmitrievna, who had been playing cards, pushed back their chairs and came into the ball-room, followed by some elderly folks, stretching their limbs after sitting still for so long and slipping their purses back into their pockets. Maria Dmitrievna and her partner were in the best of humours; the count offered the lady his hand like a ballet dancer, with a curved arm in a style of comically theatrical politeness, and she graciously laid her fingers on it. The master of the house, drawing himself up with great spirit and liveliness, waited till the set was over; then he clapped his hands, and turning to the leader of the band: "Semione," he said, "play *Daniel Cooper*—you know."

This was his favourite dance, the dance of his youth, one of the figures of the "*Anglaise*."

"Oh, do look at papa!" cried Natacha at the top of her voice; and, forgetting that she was dancing with a grown-up man, she bent over her knees, laughing heartily.

Indeed the whole room was amused with watching the action and attitudes of the jolly old gentleman and his imposing partner, who was taller than he was. With his elbows curved, his shoulders held in, and his toes turned out, he stood beating time with his foot on the floor. The radiant smile on his face gave warning of what was coming, and at the first notes of the irresistible tune of *Daniel Cooper*, which always reminded him of the "*trépak*"—the national dance of Russia—every door was filled with men on one side and women on the other: these were the servants, who had assembled to enjoy the sight of their master's merry freak.

"Our dear little father!" cried the old nurse, "what an eagle he is!"

The count's dancing was a work of art, and he was proud of it—as to the lady, she never had tried even to dance well.

She gave her handbag into the countess's keeping and stood upright and immovable, looking quite a giantess. Her large hands hung down by the side of her large person, and a fixed smile, with a slight quivering of the nostrils, gave the only sign of animation to her features, which were well-cut though stern. If the gentleman charmed all hearts by the briskness and grace of his steps and capers, the smallest movement on the lady's part excited no less enthusiasm. Maria Dmitrievna, as she "set" to her partner, or gave him her hand for a half-turn, or merely moved her shoulders, was very dignified in spite of her large size, and was greatly admired; her habitual severe reserve made it all the more wonderful. The dance grew more lively, the other couples were forgotten; all eyes were centred on the two older folks. Natacha kept pulling the dresses of everyone near her to bid them look at her father, and heaven knows they needed no telling.

In the intervals of the figure the count stopped for breath, fanned himself with his handkerchief, and shouted to the musicians to play faster. Then he began again, hopping round his partner, now on his toes, and now on his heels. At last, quite carried away by his childlike excitement, after conducting the lady to her seat and bowing gallantly, he concluded his terpsichorean performance by lifting one leg in the air and spinning a splendid pirouette, amid the applause and laughter of all the spectators, and to Natacha's great delight.

The two dancers were quite out of breath and perspiring with heat.

"Ah! my dear, that is how we used to dance when I was young!" exclaimed the count.

"Hurrah for *Daniel Cooper*!" said Maria Dmitrievna, and she turned up her cuffs.

CHAPTER XXII

WHILE at the Rostows' the sixth set was being danced—the band playing out of tune from sheer fatigue, and the servants, almost worn out, were preparing supper—Count Bésoukhow was struck by a sixth stroke. The physicians having pronounced him past all hope, the form of absolution was read over the dying man, the Sacrament was administered, and arrangements were made for performing the rites of extreme unction.

All the bustle and expectancy inevitable on such occasions had gathered round the rich man's death-bed. Undertakers' agents, scenting a magnificent funeral, crowded round the front door, dodging to hide themselves behind the carriages that drove up to make inquiries. The military governor of Moscow, who had sent his aides-de-camp several times to ask how the invalid was progressing, came this evening in person to bid a last farewell to this famous noble of Catharine's reign. The state reception-room was full of people. All rose respectfully as the general came out after spending half an hour with the dying man; he bowed right and left as he hurried through the room, an object of universal attention.

Prince Basil came out with him, speaking to him in a low voice. The prince was pale, and had grown thinner; as he returned from escorting the governor to his carriage he stopped in the great room and dropped into a chair, covering his eyes with his hands. He soon rose, however, and making his way with a look of anxious haste towards a passage which led to the rooms of the eldest princess, he disappeared.

The visitors who remained in the dimly-lighted drawing-room whispered together or relapsed into sudden silence, casting eager and inquisitive glances at the door whenever it opened for anyone going into or coming out of the sick-room.

"There is a limit to life—a limit that cannot be passed," said an old priest to a lady who was listening with profound respect.

"Is it not too late for extreme unction?" asked the lady, affecting ignorance on the point.

"It is a very solemn sacrament," replied the minister of the Church, as he gently passed his hand over his bald head to stroke forward a few locks of grey hair.

"Who was it? The commandant?" asked someone at the other end of the room. "How young he looks!"

"He is very nearly seventy.—They say the count is quite

72

unconscious. . . . They are going to administer extreme unction. . . ."

"Oh! I knew a person who received it seven times!"

Count Bésoukhow's second niece had just come out of his room; her eyes were red. She seated herself by the side of Dr. Lorrain, who had placed himself in a graceful attitude under the portrait of the Empress Catharine.

"It is lovely weather, princess, really lovely," said the doctor . . . "and in Moscow one seems to be in the country. . . ."

"Yes, quite . . ." said the princess with a sigh. "May I give him something to drink?"

Lorrain seemed to be considering.

"He has had his medicine?"

"Yes."

He looked at his watch. "Then a glass of water that has been boiled, and put in a pinch—just a pinch, of cream of tartar." And he illustrated the pinch with his slender fingers.

"I never knew a case of a man living on after the third stroke," said a German doctor, with his heavy accent, to an aide-de-camp.

"He was a wonderfully strong man," said the officer. "Who will inherit all his money?" he added, in a low voice.

"Someone will be found to accept it," said the German, with a broad smile.

The door opened again; it was the young princess, who, having prepared the draught, was going into her uncle's room.

The German went to Dr. Lorrain. "He may hang on till the morning," he said.

Lorrain puckered up his lips and solemnly shook his forefinger.

"To-night, at latest," he said, and he smiled at his own superior knowledge which enabled him to prognosticate so precisely his patient's end.

Prince Basil opened the door of the eldest princess's room. It was almost dark there: two little lamps were burning before images of saints and exhaling a faint scent of flowers and incense. A quantity of small furniture — little tables and cabinets—filled up the room, and a very high bed was only half hidden by a screen. A little dog barked as the prince went in.

"Oh! it is you, cousin." She rose, smoothing down the bands of her hair, which were always so faultlessly tidy and shining that they might have been varnished to her skull.

"What is the matter?" she said. "You startled me."

"Nothing new—just the same. But I came to talk business

with you, Catiche." And he seated himself wearily in the chair from which she had risen.

"How hot you have made your room! Well, sit down there, and let us talk."

"I thought something must have happened."

She sat down facing him, ready to listen, as cold and hard as ever. "I was trying to sleep, but I could not."

"Well, my dear?"—Prince Basil took her hand and then slowly dropped it in his usual manner. His three words were intended to cover a multitude of meanings, for they had understood each other without speaking. The princess slowly turned her expressionless, prominent grey eyes and fixed them on him; then she shook her head and gazed at the images with a sigh. The gesture might convey grief and resignation, or it might imply fatigue and the hope of an early respite. Prince Basil took it to mean this.

"And do you suppose I do not feel the same? I am as done up as a post-horse. But we will talk all the same, and seriously, if you will have the goodness. . . ."

He ceased, and his cheeks fell in with a disagreeable expression, very different from that which his features usually wore in company. Impudence and fear were legible in his face.

The princess, holding her little dog on her lap with her lean bony hands, looked at him steadily in the silence, fully determined not to be the first to break it if it were to last all night.

"You see, my dear cousin and princess, Catherine Sémenovna," Prince Basil began again with a visible effort, "on these occasions we must think of everything; we must think of the future—of your future. I love you all three as my own daughters, as you know . . .?"

As the princess sat unmoved and impenetrable, he went on without looking at her, and giving the little table at his side an angry push: "And I must also think of my own family. You know, Catiche, that you three sisters Mamontoff and my wife are the only legal heirs. I quite understand how painful the subject must be to you—and to me too, I can assure you; but, my dear, I am past fifty, and we must think of everything. Do you know I have had to send for Peter? The count ordered it by pointing to his portrait. . . ."

And Prince Basil looked up at her; but nothing in her face indicated that she had heard him—she might have been thinking of nothing.

"I never cease putting up fervent prayers to God, cousin,

that he may be saved, and that his noble soul may take its flight without too much suffering."

"Yes, yes, of course!" said the prince, and he dragged the hapless table back again with an impulse of rage. "But, after all, the marrow of the matter—you know very well—the count, last winter, made a will, by which he left everything to Peter, setting aside his legitimate heirs."

"Oh! he has made so many wills," said the niece, quite calmly. "And at any rate, he cannot make Peter his heir, for Peter is his natural son."

"But what should we do," exclaimed Prince Basil, clutching the little table tightly enough to break it, "what could we do if the count had left a letter to the emperor, petitioning him to legitimise this son? In consideration of the count's services, it might perhaps be done."

The lady smiled, and her smile seemed to say that she was better advised in the matter than her visitor.

"I can tell you more," continued Prince Basil, seizing her hand, "such a letter is written, but not yet sent, but the emperor knows of it. The point now is to ascertain whether it has been destroyed; if, on the contrary, it is still in existence—then—when all is over," and the prince sighed to explain what he meant by "all"—"the count's papers will be searched for the will, it will be delivered to the emperor with the letter, this petition will be granted, and Peter will be heir-at-law to everything."

"And what of our share?" said the princess with a distinctly sarcastic accent, fully convinced that there was nothing to fear.

"Why, my poor Catiche, it is as clear as day. He will be sole heir, you will not get a kopek. . . . Now you ought to know whether the will and the letter have been destroyed. If he has forgotten them, where are they? In that case we must take possession of them for . . ."

"That would be the crowning stroke!" she said, interrupting him with the same emphasis and expression. "I am only a woman, and I know you think us all fools. But I am sure that a bastard can inherit nothing. A bastard!" she repeated, as if the word contained in itself the refutation of all her opponent's arguments.

"You do not choose to understand, Catiche, for you are sensible enough. If the count succeeds in legitimising him, Peter will be Count Bésoukhow, and all the estate will be his by right. If that will and letter are in existence, all that you

75

will get will be the comfort of having been dutiful, devoted, etc., etc.,—that is perfectly certain."

"I know that the will does exist; but I also know that it is illegal, and I really think you must take me for an idiot," replied the princess, convinced that she had been severely sharp.

"My dear Princess Catherine," said her cousin with undisguised annoyance, "I did not come to offend you, but to talk to you in your own interest. You are a very friendly and amiable relation, and for the tenth time I assure you, that if the will and the letter are found among the count's papers, you and your sisters cease to inherit. If you do not believe me, ask some expert. I have just been talking it over with Dmitri Onoufrievitch, the count's man of business, and he said the same thing."

Light suddenly flashed on the princess's brain. Her thin lips turned white, but her eyes remained fixed, though her voice, which she could no longer control, betrayed her by unexpected bursts.

"That will be delightful! I never asked for anything and I will accept nothing!" she exclaimed, dropping the lapdog on the floor and patting down her skirts. "That is his gratitude and affection for those who have sacrificed everything to him. Bravo! it is perfect in its way! Happily I want nothing, prince!"

"But you are not alone, your sisters . . ."

"Oh, yes!" she went on without listening to him, "I have known it a long time, but I had forgotten it; envy, duplicity, intrigue, the blackest ingratitude—that was what I might have looked for in this house."

"Do you or don't you know where this will is?" asked Prince Basil, with his cheeks twitching more than ever.

"I was foolish, I still believed in people and loved them and sacrificed myself. But only those who are mean-souled and bad succeed. I know whose intrigues are responsible for this." The princess wanted to rise, but the prince held her down. She had the appearance of a person suddenly disenchanted in the whole human race; she looked fiercely at her companion.

"There is still time, my friend. You will remember, Catiche, that all this was done by mistake, in a minute of anger, of illness, and then forgotten. It is our duty, my dear, to put right this mistake, ease his last moments, not to allow him to commit this injustice, to die with the knowledge that he has made unhappy those people . . ."

"Those people who have sacrificed all for him," interrupted the princess, again attempting to rise, but the prince would not let her, "which he never valued. No, cousin," she added with a sigh, "I will remember that one must not expect any reward in this world; in this world there is neither honour nor justice. In this world one must be scheming and evil."

"Come, calm yourself; I know your kind heart."

"No, I have a wicked heart."

"I know your heart," repeated the prince, "I value your friendship and would wish you to have the same opinion of me. Calm yourself and let us talk this over reasonably while there is yet time—perhaps twenty-four hours, perhaps an hour; tell me all that you know of this will, particularly, where it is; you must know. We will take it at once and show it to the count. He has probably forgotten it and would wish to destroy it. You understand that my one wish is religiously to carry out his wishes; that is why I came here. I am here only in order to help you."

"Now I quite understand; I know whom to thank for all this intriguing."

"But that is beside the mark, my dear . . ."

"It is your protégée, that charming Princess Droubetzkoï, whom I would not take for a waiting-maid—a base, wicked creature!"

"Come, come; we are losing time."

"Ah! let me be! She came sneaking in here during the winter, and told the count all sorts of horrible things, shameful things about us all, and about Sophie especially. I could not possibly repeat them. . . . They made the count quite ill, and he would not let us go into his room for a fortnight. It was then that he wrote that horrid paper, which I believed to be worthless."

"That is the point. But why did you not let me know? Where is it?"

"It is in an inlaid note-case that he always keeps under his pillow. . . . Yes, it was her doing; and if I have a heavy sin on my conscience it is my hatred for that woman. Why did she come sneaking in here! Oh! the day will come yet when I shall speak my mind to her!" cried the princess, quite beside herself.

CHAPTER XXIII

WHILE all these conversations were going on, the carriage was returning from the Rostows' with Peter and Princess Droubetzkoï, who had thought proper to accompany him. When the wheels became noiseless as they rolled over the straw spread in front of the Hôtel Bésoukhow, she turned to her companion with some cut-and-dried speech of condolence, but, to her great surprise, Peter was asleep; she roused him, and as he followed her, the idea struck him for the first time that he was about to see his father on his death-bed. The carriage had stopped at one of the back entrances: as he got out, two men in black shrank hastily into the shadow of the wall; there were others about who seemed anxious to hide themselves. No one took any notice of them. "I suppose it is all right," said Peter to himself, and he went after the princess, who hurried up the servants' staircase. He wondered why she had chosen this back way in, why she had come to see the count, and what could be the use of it; but his guide's confident and rapid movements forced him again to the conclusion that "it was all right."

Half-way up they ran against some servants who were running downstairs with pails of water, and who stood back against the wall to let them pass, but who did not seem surprised to see them there.

"This way, is it not, to the princesses' rooms?" asked Anna Mikhaïlovna.

"Yes," said the man to whom she had spoken; and he answered in a loud voice, as if the time had come when it did not matter what liberties were taken. "It is the door on the left."

"Perhaps the count did not ask for me," said Peter when they stopped on the landing. "I would rather go straight to my own room."

Anna Mikhaïlovna stood waiting for him: "My dear friend," she said, lightly stroking his hand, as a few hours since she had stroked her son's. "Believe me, I am suffering as much as you are. But be a man!"

"Really, I had better go to my own room." And Peter looked at her affectionately over his spectacles.

"My dear boy, forget all the wrong that has been done you— remember only that he is your father, and dying," and she sighed. "I love you like a son; trust in me and I will guard your interests."

Peter did not in the least understand, but he said to himself once more: "It is all right, no doubt," and followed her.

The princess opened a door and went into a little ante-room. An old manservant attending on the princesses was sitting in a corner, knitting a stocking. Peter had never been in this part of the house before, he never even suspected its existence. Anna Mikhaïlovna inquired of a maid—on whom she lavished "my good girl" and "my child"—how the ladies were. The girl, who was carrying a bottle of water on a tray, went on down a paved passage, and the princess followed at her heels. The first door on the left was that of the Princess Catharine's room. In her haste (everything was being done in haste in the house at that time) the maid left the door ajar as she went in, and Peter and his guide, involuntarily looking in, discovered the lady and Prince Basil talking together. As he caught sight of the new arrivals the prince threw himself back in his chair, evidently much provoked, while Princess Catiche flew at the door and slammed it in their faces. This burst of rage, so unlike her usual calm demeanour, and the dismay and vexation betrayed by Prince Basil, were so strange that Peter stopped short, and looked inquiringly at his companion; the worthy lady, who did not share in his astonishment, answered with a sigh and a smile:

"Be a man, my dear boy; I will guard your interests," and Anna Mikhaïlovna went on faster.

"I will guard your interests." What did she mean? Peter could not imagine. "But it is all right, no doubt," he thought.

The corridor opened into the great dim drawing-room adjoining the count's bedroom, which Peter knew from having crossed it whenever he came in by the front staircase. This room, though splendid, was gloomy. A bath had been left there and forgotten; the water was leaking out of it drop by drop, and soaking into the carpet. A servant, and a sacristan carrying a censer came towards the new-comers, whom they did not notice. On one side another room—not the one with the bath—opened on to a conservatory, on the other it was lighted by two enormous French windows; a marble bust and a full-length portrait of the Empress Catharine were its chief adornments. The persons we have already seen there were still whispering and muttering together in the same attitudes.

As Anna Mikhaïlovna went in all were silent and turned to

look at her pale, tear-stained face, and at tall, burly Peter, who followed her with his head down. She knew that the critical moment had come, and her face plainly showed that she knew it. She stood the fire of their inquisitive eyes with the calm assurance of a St. Petersburger, hardened to the pressure of circumstances. She was protected in fact by the presence of her companion, since the count had asked for him. Without an instant's hesitation she went straight up to the count's confessor, and bowing her head without any excess of humility, she respectfully craved his blessing; then, with equal reverence, she turned to the other priest.

"Thank God we are in time! We all, the count's relatives . . . were so much afraid. . . . It is the count's son. What a fearful moment!" she murmured, and then she turned to the doctor:

"Dear doctor, this is Count Bésoukhow's son: is there any hope?"

The doctor cast up his eyes to heaven and shrugged his shoulders. Anna Mikhaïlovna imitated his gestures and covered her face with her hand; then, turning from him with a deep sigh, she approached Peter, her face expressing a significant combination of respect, affection, and pathos.

"Put your trust in His mercies!" she said, and she pointed to a little sofa where she desired him to be seated; then she noiselessly went to the mysterious door, which was the centre of attention, opened it softly and vanished.

Peter, who had made up his mind to obey her implicitly, sat down on the little sofa, and noted with some surprise that he was an object of curiosity rather than interest. He was pointed at and whispered about, and the cause, it would seem, of some alarm, with a certain servility. He was treated with a degree of respect to which he was not accustomed, and the unknown lady who was talking to the two priests rose to offer him her seat; an aide-de-camp picked up his glove, which he had dropped, and handed it to him; the doctors were silent and made way for him to pass. His first impulse was to refuse the seat for fear of disturbing the lady, to pick up his own glove, to keep out of the doctors' way—not that they were in his; but then it struck him that it might not be the right thing: that he had suddenly become a person of importance, that something was expected of him in the course of this mysterious and melancholy night, and that he was bound to accept the services offered to him. So he silently took the glove from the aide-de-camp, and seated himself in the lady's place, laying his hands square on his knees with the simple formality of an Egyptian statue; fully determined to follow the guiding of other people's wills rather than his own impulses, so as not to compromise himself in any way.

Not two minutes later Prince Basil came in, his head erect, in his long frock-coat, with three stars blazing on his breast, a majestic personage. He seemed to have grown suddenly thin; his eyes opened wide at the sight of Peter. He took his hand—which he had never done before—and slowly dropped it as if he were testing its power of resistance.

"Courage, courage, my boy. . . . He asked for you, and that is well."

And he was leaving him when Peter thought he ought to make some inquiry: "How is he—how is . . ." and he paused in confusion, not knowing how to call the count his father.

"He had another stroke half an hour since. Be brave, my dear fellow."

Peter's mind was so utterly dazed that he fancied that the dying man had been hit by someone, and he stared at Prince Basil in dismay; then he realised that the word "stroke" referred to an illness. Prince Basil said a few words in passing to Dr. Lorrain and entered the door on tiptoe. He did not know how to walk on tiptoe and his whole body bounded clumsily forward. He was followed by the Princess Catharine, by the priests and the servants of the household. There was a stir in the chamber of death and Anna Mikhaïlovna, pale but resolute in the performance of a duty, came out to fetch Peter.

"The mercies of the Lord are without end," she said. "The sacrament of extreme unction is about to be administered. Come."

He rose and noticed that the strange lady and the aide-de-camp, and also somebody from among the servants, followed him into the bedroom.

CHAPTER XXIV

PETER was well acquainted with this great bedroom. An alcove was divided by columns and an arch and hung with Persian carpets. Within the columns stood an immense and very high mahogany bedstead with heavy curtains, and opposite was a niche, with glass over it, containing the holy images, and lighted up like a chapel for the sacred ceremony. In front

81

of this niche, in a large, deep arm-chair, lay, rather than sat, Count Bésoukhow, a stately and majestic figure, covered to the waist with a bright green quilt, and propped on snowy pillows. A mass of strong grey hair, like a lion's mane, and the deep wrinkles of his face, threw his noble and handsome features, now as pale as wax, into high relief. His hands, which were large and powerful, lay lifeless on the coverlet; between his right finger and thumb a taper had been placed which was held upright by an old servant who leaned over his master's chair. The priests and deacons, with their long hair falling over their shoulders, and their rich vestments, were deliberately fulfilling their functions, carrying lighted tapers in their hands. In the background stood the princesses, the two younger ones with their handkerchiefs to their eyes, a little in front of them Catiche with an angry and determined expression, who seemed to fear that if she once took her eyes from the holy images she could no longer be mistress of her feelings. Princess Droubetzkoï's face wore an expression of calm sorrow and unbounded forgiveness as she stood leaning against the door, by the side of the strange lady. Prince Basil, who was opposite to her and quite close to the dying man, held a taper in his left hand, leaning his elbows on the back of a carved chair covered with velvet, and he cast up his eyes to heaven every time he crossed his forehead with his right. His expression was one of pious resignation and utter submission to the will of the Almighty: "Woe unto you who cannot rise to the height of my sentiments!" he seemed to say.

Behind him stood the medical attendants and all the household, the men on one side and the women on the other, as if they were in church, all silent and crossing themselves diligently. There was not a sound but the hum of the officiating priests and the steady chant of the choir. Now and then some one sighed or moved a little.

Suddenly Princess Droubetzkoï crossed the room, and with the resolute manner of a woman who knows very well what she is about, she handed a taper to Peter. He took it, lighted it, and then, absorbed in his own reflections, crossed himself with the hand in which he held it.

Sophia, the youngest of the princesses, the one with the "beauty-spot," watched him and smiled. Then she hid her face again in her handkerchief and stood so for some minutes; but after glancing again at Peter, she felt she could no longer keep her countenance, and crept away behind one of the columns.

BEFORE TILSIT

In the middle of the service there was a sudden pause; the priests whispered together; the old man who held up the count's taper straightened himself and turned to the ladies. Anna Mikhaïlovna went forward at once, and leaning over the sufferer she beckoned to Dr. Lorrain without looking up at him. The doctor was standing with his back to a column in an attitude of reverent attention that conveyed his appreciation of the importance of the sacrament in spite of his foreign birth and difference of creed; he came softly to the count's side, and with his slender fingers raised the hand that lay on the coverlet; he felt the pulse and seemed lost in calculations. There was a little bustle, the dying man's lips were moistened with a cordial, then all returned to their places and the ceremony proceeded. During this interruption Peter had been watching Prince Basil, and he saw him leave his chair and go up to Princess Catiche; then, both together, had gone to the back of the alcove, round by the head of the big bed, and out of a little door in the wall.

Before the service was ended they were in their places again.

This manœuvre did not excite Peter's curiosity, for he had made up his mind that everything that might happen was but natural and a matter of course.

The chanting ceased, and the drone of the priest who was offering respectful congratulations to the dying man—but he lay there speechless and motionless. Then the stir began again: steps and whispering, and above all the rest the loud whisper of Anna Mikhaïlovna. Peter heard her say: "He must positively be put into bed again, or else . . ."

The doctors, princesses, and servants were crowding round the count and hid him from Peter, but that sallow face with its tangle of hair was still before his eyes, as it had been ever since he came in. He understood that they were carefully lifting the count to carry him to bed. "Here, take hold of my arm, you will let him fall!" exclaimed a servant in alarm.

"His feet—make haste!—one more!" said another.

And from their hard breathing and shuffling steps it was easy to guess what a weight they had to carry. Those who carried him, among them Anna Mikhaïlovna, pushed by the young man, and for an instant, in the middle of the group of bent heads, he caught sight of the sufferer's broad deep chest, his shoulders, off which the clothes had slipped, and his leonine head with its mane of curls. The face, with its unusually wide brow, strong cheek-bones, well-cut lips, and cold, impressive gaze, was not yet disfigured by death; it was the same that

Peter had seen three months ago, when his father had sent him to St. Petersburg. But now it rolled heavily as the men walked with an unequal step, and the fixed eyes had no speculation.

After a few minutes' bustle round the bed the servants withdrew. Anna Mikhaïlovna lightly touched Peter: "Come," she said.

He obeyed. The sick man, propped half-sitting on a pile of pillows, had been placed in a formal attitude in honour of the sacrament that had just been administered. His hands were spread out on the green silk counterpane, and he stared in front of him with that vague, far-seeing look which no one can follow or understand; had he nothing, or had he everything to say? Peter stood still, not knowing what to do; he turned to his companion who, by an almost imperceptible gesture, suggested to him that he should kiss the dying man's hand. Peter bent very gently over the bed so as not to touch the coverlet, and his lips touched the count's broad, heavy hand.

Not a muscle of it quivered, not a sign was visible on the face; nothing—nothing responded to this light contact. Peter, still doubtful, again referred to the princess, who signed to him to sit down in the arm-chair at the foot of the bed. He sat down, still watching her face, and she nodded that that was right. He resumed the Egyptian attitude, evidently hampered by his own clumsiness, and making every effort to fill as small a space as possible, while he kept his eyes on the face of the dying count. The count looked fixedly at the spot where Peter's face had been when he was standing. Anna Mikhaïlovna also watched him narrowly, with an appearance of being aware of the importance of this last, pathetic meeting of father and son.

Two minutes, which seemed to Peter an age, had hardly elapsed when the count's face was suddenly distorted by a convulsion, his mouth was drawn on one side and his breathing became stertorous and difficult. To Peter this was the first omen of approaching death; Princess Droubetzkoï watched the sufferer's eyes to guess what his wishes might be. She pointed in turn to Peter, to the cup of tisane, to Prince Basil, to the counterpane . . . all in vain, and a flash of irritation lighted up the dim eyes, which seemed to want to attract the attention of the valet, who was standing motionless at the foot of the bed.

"He wants to be turned over," said the man, proceeding to move his master. Peter helped him, and they had succeeded in turning him when one of his hands fell back heavily in spite of his efforts to raise it. Did he see the look of dismay that passed into Peter's troubled face at the sight of the paralysed limb, or did some other idea dawn on his brain? Who can tell? He looked first at the helpless arm and then at his son's awed face, and a dull, lifeless smile, appalling at such a moment, fluttered over his lips. It was as though he were retorting with ironical pity on the gradual and growing extinction of all his powers.

This unlooked-for smile was a shock of pain to Peter, he had a sharp cramp about his heart, his throat swelled, and the tears started to his eyes. The sick man, who had been laid down with his face to the wall, sighed deeply.

"He is asleep," said Anna Mikhaïlovna seeing one of the nieces return to her watch. "Come. . . ."

And Peter followed her.

CHAPTER XXV

THERE was no one now in the drawing-room but Prince Basil and Princess Catiche, sitting under the portrait of the empress, and talking eagerly; they broke off suddenly as Peter and his companion went in, and he could not help seeing that Princess Catiche seemed to be hiding something.

"I cannot meet that woman," she murmured, as she saw Princess Droubetzkoï.

"Catiche has had tea brought up into the little drawing-room," said Prince Basil to Anna Mikhaïlovna. "Go, go, my poor friend, and eat a mouthful or you will break down. . . ." And he gave Peter's arm a silent and affectionate pressure. Peter and Anna Mikhaïlovna went into the little drawing-room.

"There is nothing so reviving as a cup of this capital Russian tea after a wakeful night," said Dr. Lorrain, slowly sipping the hot liquid from a cup of old Oriental china. He was standing in the middle of the little drawing-room, in front of a table on which tea and some cold refreshments had been laid out.

All those who had spent the night in the house were now collected in this room, where the walls were almost entirely covered by mirrors, and the furniture was chiefly gilded *consoles*. This had been Peter's favourite nook on the occasions of the count's grand balls, for he could not dance, and he liked to sit

85

in here alone and take note of the ladies, who would come in their elegant freshness, all sparkling with diamonds and pearls, to see their dazzling figures reflected in the looking-glasses. At this moment the room was barely lighted by two wax-candles; on a table set all askew was a disorderly array of plates and cups; and there were no ball-dresses, but strangely mixed groups of persons of every degree stood talking in undertones, while every word, every gesture, betrayed that the one subject of their thoughts was the solemn mystery that was going forward in the alcove of that state-room. Peter was hungry, but he would not eat. He looked round for his companion, and saw her steal away into the big drawing-room, where they had left Prince Basil and the eldest princess. Thinking he ought to follow her he did so, and found her and the elder princess whispering excitedly both at once.

"Allow me, madam, to decide what is and what is not necessary," said Catiche, in a tone of irritation which was a survival of the wrath in which she had slammed the door.

"Dear princess," said Anna Mikhaïlovna sweetly, but standing in her path, "it would, I am afraid, be too painful to your uncle; at this moment he is so much in need of rest . . . and to discuss worldly matters when his soul has been prepared . . ."

Prince Basil, buried in an arm-chair with his legs crossed as usual, seemed to be paying very little attention to this colloquy, but the quivering of his cheeks, which twitched incessantly, betrayed some strongly-controlled emotion.

"Come, my good princess, let Catiche do as she likes. The count is so fond of her, you see. . . ."

"I do not even know what is in it," Catiche went on, turning to Prince Basil, and holding up the inlaid note-case, which she held with a nervous clutch. "All I know is that his will is in his desk. There is nothing in this but some papers that he has forgotten. . . ." And she tried to pass Anna Mikhaïlovna who, with a spring, again stood before her.

"I know that, my dear, good princess," she said, and she grabbed at the note-case, with a grasp that showed her firm determination not to let go. "My dear princess, I entreat you be judicious with him." The two ladies fairly wrestled for the possession of the note-case. Catiche simply held on without a word; but it was very evident that a flood of abuse was pent behind her tightly-set lips, while her enemy's tones were as calm and sugared as ever, in spite of the obstinacy of the struggle.

"Peter, my dear, come here," cried Anna Mikhaïlovna. "He will not be in the way in this family council, will he, prince? . . ."

"Why, cousin, do you not answer?" cried Catiche so loudly that those in the drawing-room heard her, and were startled by her voice. "Why are you so silent, when God only knows who comes meddling in our private affairs, not even respecting the chamber of death? . . . Intriguing creature!" she added in a low growl, and she gave the note-case a sharp pull.

The violence of the action staggered Anna Mikhaïlovna, who was dragged forward; but she did not relax her hold.

"Oh!" groaned Prince Basil reprovingly, and he rose.

"Come, this is preposterous," he said. "Leave go I tell you."

Catiche obeyed; but her adversary still kept the object of dispute. "Do you give it up too," he added. "I will take the whole responsibility—I will ask him.—Will that satisfy you?"

"But surely, after such a solemn sacrament, you will give him a moment's respite?" said Anna Mikhaïlovna. "What do you think?" she added, turning to Peter, who was gazing in dismay at Catiche's flaming face, and Prince Basil's twitching lips.

"Remember that you are responsible for the consequences," said Prince Basil, "you know not what you are doing."

"Odious wretch!" cried Catiche, suddenly flying at her, and snatching away the note-case. The prince hung his head, and his arms fell by his side.

At this instant, the mysterious door which had so often been opened and shut with noiseless care in the course of this long night was flung open, and the count's second niece rushed into the midst of them, her hands clasped.

"What are you about?" she cried desperately; "he is dying, and you leave me alone with him!"

Catiche dropped the note-case; the princess threw herself upon it, picked it up and fled into the bedroom. Prince Basil and Catiche, when they had got over their amazement, followed her. Catiche came out again in a minute or two; her face was white, her features set, and her underlip very pinched. As she caught sight of Peter, her spite broke out:

"Oh yes! play the farce out. . . . It is what you expected. . . ."
But sobs checked her utterance; she covered her face and went away.

Presently Prince Basil also returned. He made his way to the sofa, where Peter was sitting, and had hardly reached it when he dropped on it as if he were going to faint; his face was ghastly, his jaw trembled, and his teeth chattered as if he had an ague.

"Oh! my dear fellow!" he exclaimed, and he seized Peter by the arm. Peter was startled by the earnest ring of sincerity in his voice, which was faint and weak; it was quite a new thing in the prince. "We sin, we cheat, and all for what? I am past fifty, my dear boy . . . and death is the end of it all. . . . Death! horrible, horrible!" And he burst into tears.

Anna Mikhaïlovna soon made her appearance too; she came slowly and solemnly up to Peter.

"Peter!" she murmured. He looked up at her; she bent down and kissed his forehead, wetting it with her tears:

"He is dead!" but Peter only looked at her over his spectacles.

"Come—I will take you away. But try to shed tears, nothing gives so much comfort."

She led him away into a dark room, and as he went in Peter felt the immense relief of finding himself no longer an object of curiosity. Anna Mikhaïlovna left him there, and when she came back to look for him, she found him fast asleep, with his head on his hand.

Next day she said to him:

"Ah, my dear friend, it is a terrible loss for us all. I am not speaking of you; God will give you strength; you are young, and the master of a colossal fortune. The will has not yet been opened, but I know you well enough to feel sure that this will not turn your head: but you will have new duties to fulfil, and you must be a man."

Peter said nothing. "One day, perhaps—by and by, I will tell you the whole story. . . . In short, if I had not been there, God knows what might have happened! My uncle had promised me, only the day before, not to forget Boris, but then he had no time to attend to that. I hope, my dear friend, that you will carry out your father's wishes."

Peter, who had no idea of what she was driving at, did not answer, but coloured deeply, and looked awkward.

After the old count's death, Princess Droubetzkoï returned to the Rostows' house to rest a little after her fatigues. No sooner was she up again next day than she related to all her friends and acquaintances the minutest details of that eventful night.

The count, she said, had died as she herself hoped to die. . . . His end was most edifying, and the last interview between the father and son so touching that she could not think of it without emotion. She really did not know which of the two had been the more admirable during those solemn moments of parting—the father, who had a word for everyone, and who was so pathetically tender to his son, or the son who, though overwhelmed and broken with grief, had struggled to master his feelings before his dying father. . . . "Such scenes wring one's heart, but they do it good: It elevates the soul to see such men as those suffer!" she added. Then she reported and criticised the proceedings of Prince Basil and Princess Catiche, but in a whisper, in her listener's ear, and under the seal of absolute secrecy.

CHAPTER XXVI

AT Lissy-Gory, the residence of Prince Nicholas Andréévitch Bolkonsky, young Prince Andrew and his wife were daily expected; but this did not in any way affect the plan of life laid down by the old prince, who had been nicknamed by some who knew him well "the King of Prussia." He had been commander-in-chief under the Emperor Paul, but was banished by him to his estate of Lissy-Gory, where he had led a secluded life ever since, with his daughter Maria, and her paid companion, Mademoiselle Bourrienne. The accession of a new emperor had unlocked the gates of exile, and left him free to live in either of the capitals; but he obstinately refused to leave his own domain, declaring, to all who cared to hear it, that those who wanted to see him could very well travel the one hundred and fifty versts that divided him from Moscow, but that for his part he wanted nothing and nobody.

The vices of the human race, he asserted, had their origin solely in two causes: in idleness and in superstition; and he recognised only two virtues: energy and intelligence, and he himself undertook his daughter's education with a view to developing these two qualities in her, to the utmost. Up to the age of twenty she had studied geometry and algebra under his tuition, and her day had always been methodically spent in regular and consistent employment.

He himself was writing his memoirs, he solved mathematical problems, turned snuff-boxes on a lathe, worked in his garden, and superintended the construction of the buildings on his estate; and this gave him plenty to do, for the property was extensive, and building was always going on; and as the chief condition of activity is order, order in his life was carried to the utmost.

His appearance in the dining-room was always at the same hour, or rather at the same minute. He was sharp and exacting to the last degree with everyone he had to do with, including his daughter; thus, without being cruel, he commanded an amount of submission and fear that a really brutal man would have found it difficult to obtain. Notwithstanding his being retired, and though he had no official interest, all the dignitaries of the province in which he resided made it a point of duty to pay their respects to him, and carried their deference so far as to await his appearance in the great hall, as his daughter did too, with the gardener and the builder. And the same mixed feeling of respect and fear came over them all when the heavy door of his private room slowly opened, and the little old man came out, with his powdered wig, his slender withered hands, and his thick grizzled eyebrows, which sometimes seemed to soften the keen glitter of eyes that still were almost youthful.

On the morning of the day when the young couple were expected, Princess Maria crossed the hall, according to invariable rule, to go and bid her father good morning; and, as usual, at that critical moment she could not help feeling a pang of agitation, so to give herself courage she crossed herself and put up a little prayer that their meeting might pass off without squalls. The old, powdered manservant, who always sat in the hall, rose at her approach, and said in a subdued voice: "Have the goodness to go in."

The steady whir of a turning-lathe was audible within; the princess timidly opened the door, which made no noise on its hinges, and stood still in the doorway; the prince was at work. He looked round at her, and then went on again.

The room was full of furniture and articles of daily use. A large table was piled with maps and books; there were cupboards with glass doors and keys in the locks, a tall desk for standing at to write, on which lay an open copy-book, and a lathe with its various tools; shavings were scattered on the floor; everything revealed habits of constant and various industry. The regular tread of his foot in its Tartar boot of soft leather, and the firm, steady pressure of his sinewy hand revealed an amazing fund of tenacity of will in this vigorous specimen of a green old age. After continuing his work for a few seconds he took his foot from the treadle, wiped the tool, and dropped it into a leather bag that was nailed to the bench, and came to the table. He was not in the habit of giving his children a blessing, but he always offered them a cheek to kiss—innocent generally of the razor. This ceremony being over, he looked closely at his daughter, and said roughly, but not without a touch of affection:

"You are well, quite well? . . . Sit down there." And taking up a copy-book of geometrical problems written out with his own hand, he reached out a leg and drew an arm-chair towards himself.

"This is for to-morrow," he said, and he marked the passage with his nail. Princess Maria leaned over to note it.

"By the way, here is a letter for you," he said suddenly, and taking a letter addressed in a woman's hand from a pocket-bag that hung against the wall, he tossed it to her.

At the sight of it Princess Maria's face coloured in patches; she took it up and looked at it.

"Is it from your Héloïse?" asked her father, with an icy smile which showed his teeth, yellow but sound.

"Yes, it is from Julia," she said timidly.

"I will let two more letters pass, but I shall read the third; you write all sorts of nonsense, I will be bound—I shall read the third."

"But, father, read this one. . . ." And blushing she held it out to him.

"I said the third, and I mean the third," cried the old man, pushing back the letter and taking up the geometry book. "Well, young lady . . ." and he bent over his daughter, with one hand on the back of the chair in which she had seated herself, and where she felt all round her the peculiar sour smell, mingled with the fumes of tobacco—the stuffy atmosphere of old age to which she was so long accustomed.

"Well, these triangles are equal; you see the angle ABC . . ."

The princess gazed with terror into her father's keen eyes, her cheeks tingled with a scarlet flush, and fear deprived her of the faculty of thought or of understanding her master's explanations, clear as they were. This little scene recurred every day—but whose fault was it? The teacher's or the pupil's—who at last could see nothing clearly and hear nothing distinctly? Her father's face was close to hers, his acrid breath was the air she breathed, she could think of nothing but making her escape as soon as possible to her own room where she might solve the problem in peace and liberty. He, on his part, got angry—pushed away his chair, dragged it back with a clatter—trying all the while to control himself; then again he would break out and storm, and wish the whole thing to the devil.

As ill-luck would have it, to-day again his daughter answered at random and wrongly.

"What an idiot!" he exclaimed, flinging down the book. Then he rose, walked up and down, came back and stroked his daughter's hair, sat down again, and began his explanation once more.

"It does not do, princess, it does not do," he said, seeing her rise to leave him with the book in her hand. "Mathematics is a noble science, and I do not want you to be just like all the silly young ladies one meets. Persevere and you will learn to like the work, and the dullness will be knocked out of your brain." And he patted her cheek.

She was going, but he signed to her to stop; he took from his desk a book he had just received and held it out to her.

"Here, your Héloïse has sent you some *Key to the Mystery*—a religious work it would seem. I do not trouble my head about anybody's beliefs, but I have looked it through. Take it, and be off." And patting her this time on the shoulder he closed the door behind her.

Maria returned to her room. The scared expression her plain, sickly face habitually wore, made it even less attractive than nature had intended. She sat down at her writing-table, on which stood a few miniatures in frames, and which was loaded with books and papers in utter disorder—for she was as untidy as her father was precise—and eagerly broke the seal of the letter which was from the favourite friend of her childhood, that Julia Karaguine whom we have met at the Rostows.

It was as follows:

"DEAR AND BEST FRIEND—How terrible a thing is absence! It is in vain that I say to myself that half my life and happiness is bound up in you; that, in spite of the miles that part us, our hearts are linked inseparably—mine rebels against fate, and notwithstanding all the pleasures and amusements that surround me, I cannot get over the sadness that has lurked at the bottom of my heart ever since we parted. Oh! why are we not side by side as we were in the summer, on the blue sofa in your sitting-room—the confidential sofa! And why may I not now—as I did three months since—refresh my moral strength by looking into your soft, calm deep eyes—the eyes I love so much, and can fancy I see while I write!"

At this point Princess Maria sighed deeply, and turned to look at herself in a long mirror which reflected the whole of her graceless figure and pinched features, while her eyes, as they met their own image in the glass, seemed to have grown more melancholy than ever. "She is flattering me," she said to herself as she went on with the letter.

But Julia was quite truthful; Maria's eyes were large and deep, and lightened up occasionally with a flash that made them startlingly beautiful and transfigured the face they lighted up with a soft and loving gleam. But she herself knew nothing of this look that came into her eyes whenever she forgot herself to think of others; the ruthless mirror only showed her a sharp and unattractive face. She went on with the letter:

"All Moscow is talking of war. One of my brothers is already across the frontier; the other is marching to the front with the Guards. Our beloved emperor has left St. Petersburg, and is, they say, preparing to expose his precious person to the risks of war. God grant that the Corsican monster who has wrecked the peace of Europe may be crushed by the angelic being that the Almighty has mercifully sent to rule over us. Not to mention my brothers, the war has bereft me of one of those who are dearest to me: young Nicholas Rostow, who, fired by enthusiasm, could not bear to remain inactive, and has left college to join the army. Yes, my dear Maria, in spite of his extreme youth, I will own to you that his departure has been a bitter grief to me. I spoke to you of this young man when I was with you; he is so high-minded, and has so much of the genuine youthfulness which is so rare in these days when every lad of twenty is an old man—above all he is so freshly frank, so purely poetical, that my intimacy with him, brief as it has been, is one of the great joys of my heart, which has suffered so bitterly. Some day I will tell you all about our parting and what passed between us; at present it is all too recent.

"Ah, my dear, you are happy in your ignorance of these joys and acute pangs—yes, you are happy, for the pain is generally the keenest. I know of course that Count Nicholas is too young ever to be anything more to me than a friend; but this kind of friendship, these poetical ties, are a real need of my heart. However, no more of that. The great news in Moscow and the talk of the day is the death of Count Bésoukhow, and the reading of his will. Just fancy, the princesses get very little, and Prince Basil nothing; it is Peter who inherits everything. His legitimacy has been established into the bargain, so he is Count Bésoukhow and the owner of the largest fortune in Russia. They say that Prince Basil played a very disgraceful part in the whole business, and has gone off to St. Petersburg looking very foolish. For my part I do not understand all the details of will and bequests. All I know is that this young man, who was no more than Mr. Peter to us all, is now Count Bésoukhow and one of the richest men in Russia. It amuses me immensely to watch the altered tone and manner of the mammas burdened with daughters to marry—nay, of the daughters themselves, towards this individual, who, between you and me, always seemed to me a poor specimen. As, for the last two years, the world has amused itself by making matches for me—generally with men I do not even know—of course I am now designated as the future countess. But I need not tell you that I have no ambition of that kind.

"Apropos—do you know that quite lately Anna Mikhaïlovna, 'aunt in general,' whispered to me as a most solemn secret a plan for marrying you. Neither more nor less than to Prince Basil's son Anatole, whom they want to settle by marrying him to a damsel of wealth and rank; and you are the object of his relations' choice. I do not know what view you may take of the matter, but I thought it my duty to warn you. He is said to be very handsome and a great scamp, and that is all I have been able to find out about him. Now, this is gossip enough; I am at the end of my second sheet, and mamma is calling me to go to dine with the Apraxines. Read the book I am sending you. It is mystical and the rage here; and though there are many things in it which are hard of apprehension to weak human minds, it is a beautiful work and soothes and edifies the soul. Farewell. Give my respects to your father and remembrances to Mademoiselle Bourrienne. I embrace you fondly. "JULIA.

"P.S.—Let me have news of your brother and his fascinating little wife."

On reading this effusion Princess Maria remained sunk in a pleasing reverie; she sat thinking and smiling, and her face, lighted up by her beautiful eyes, was transfigured. Then she suddenly rose, crossed the room with an air of determination, and settling herself to write she rapidly penned the following reply:

"MY DEAR, BEST FRIEND—Your letter of the 13th has given

94

me the greatest pleasure. So you still care for me, my poetic Julia, and absence, which you rail at, has not had its usual effect on you. You complain of parting! What then could I say, if I dare to complain, bereft as I am of all who are dear to me? Ah, if we had not religion to comfort us, life would indeed be dreary.—And why do you fancy I shall look stern as I read of your regard for your young friend? In such matters I am lenient to all but myself. I quite understand such feelings in others, and if I cannot actually approve them, never having experienced them, I cannot condemn them. Only it seems to me that Christian love—the love of our neighbours, the love of our enemies—is more worthy and more tender than the feelings roused in a romantic and sentimental girl like you by a young man's fine eyes.

"The news of Count Bésoukhow's death had reached us before your letter, and affected my father deeply; he was—he says—the last representative but one of the good old times, and now it is his turn, but he intends to postpone it as long as possible. God preserve us indeed from such a misfortune! I cannot agree with you in your opinion of Peter, whom I knew as a child. He always seemed to me thoroughly good-hearted, and that is the quality I most value. As to the property, and Prince Basil's conduct in the matter, it is most sad for both. Indeed, my dear friend, our Lord's saying that 'it is easier for a camel to go through the eye of a needle than for a rich man to enter the kingdom of God' is terribly true! I pity Prince Basil, but I pity Peter even more. So young, and so loaded with wealth, what temptations he must be exposed to. If I were asked what I most wish in this world it would be to be poorer than the poorest beggar.

"Many thanks, my dear, for the book, which you tell me is the rage with you. At the same time, as you say that among many good things there are others which the weakness of our understanding can scarcely attain to, it seems to me useless to spend time in reading what is incomprehensible and therefore can bear no good fruit. I never could understand the mania that some people have for bewildering their judgment by devoting themselves to the study of mystical works which only raise doubts in their minds, while they excite their imagination and lend it an inflated exaggeration quite contrary to true Christian simplicity. Let us read the Apostles and the Gospels, and not try to penetrate the mysteries they contain; how can we, miserable sinners as we are, presume to inquire into the holy and awful secrets of Providence so long as we wear the burden of this flesh which forms an impenetrable veil between our spirits and the Almighty? Let us be content to study the sublime principles which our Saviour has given us for guidance on earth; let us try to conform to them and live by them, convincing ourselves that the less we give the reins to our puny human intellect the more pleasing it will be in the eyes of God, who contemns all knowledge that is not of Himself—that the less we strive to search out those matters which He has thought fit to hide from our ken, the sooner He will vouchsafe us knowledge through His Divine Spirit.

"My father has said nothing to me of any suitor; he only told me that he had had a letter and expected a visit from Prince Basil. With regard to the plan for my marriage, I may say to you, my dear kind friend, that marriage is in my opinion a divine institution to which we are bound to conform. However painful it may be, if the Almighty should ever require me to undertake the duties of a wife and mother I will try to fulfil them as faithfully as I can, without puzzling myself by analysing my feelings towards the man whom He appoints to be my husband. I have had a letter from my brother announcing his arrival here with his wife. It will be but a brief happiness, since he is off at once to this miserable war into which we have been dragged God knows how or why. It is not only at Moscow, in the whirl of the busy world, that war is the sole topic; but here as well, in the heart of the country, amid field-labourers and that peace which townsfolk always attribute to rural scenes, the rumours of war are heard, and cruelly felt. My father talks of nothing but marches and countermarches, which I do not understand; and the day before yesterday, as I took my usual walk down the village street, I saw a scene that went to my heart: a squad of recruits just enlisted here and being drafted off to join the army. You should have seen the state the women were in—mothers, wives, and children of the men who were starting—you should have heard their sobbing and crying! It really would seem as if human beings had altogether forgotten the precepts of the divine Saviour who preached forgiveness and love, and thought that their greatest merit lay in their skill in killing each other.

"Farewell, my dear good friend. May the Saviour and His Blessed Mother have you in their holy keeping!   "MARIA."

"Oh! princess, you are sending off the courier; I have written to my poor mother," cried Mademoiselle Bourrienne, in her full, sweet voice and strongly Parisian French. Her brisk appearance contrasted strangely with the gloomy, solitary, and melancholy atmosphere that hung round the princess.

"I must warn you," she added in a lower tone. "The prince has had a squabble"—(she said "altercation"—squabble —with special emphasis, apparently hearing herself say it with particular pleasure)—"with Michael Ivanow; he is in a very bad temper—very savage. . . . Be careful . . . you know . . ."

"Oh, my dear friend, I have often begged you not to make remarks to me about my father's bad temper. I never allow myself to pass judgment on it, and I expect others to follow my example," replied Maria, looking at her watch, and perceiving with alarm that it was five minutes after the time when she was required to practise on the piano, she hurried into the drawing-room. While the prince took a siesta from noon till two, his daughter was to exercise her fingers; this was the immutable rule of the house.

CHAPTER XXVII

THE grey-haired manservant was nodding in his chair, to the sound of his master's regular snore as he took his midday nap in his study, and of the remoter tinkle of the piano on which the difficult passages of a sonata by Dreyschock were being repeated as often as twenty times.

A chaise and britzska drew up at the front entrance; Prince Andrew got out first and then gave his hand to his wife. Old Tikhon, in a wig, who had softly stolen out of the ante-room and closed the door behind him, explained in a low voice that the prince was asleep; not even the advent of the son of the house, not any event, however extraordinary, could be allowed to interrupt the order of the day. Prince Andrew knew this as well as he did, for he looked at his watch to assure himself that no change had occurred in his father's habits.

"He will not wake for the next twenty minutes," he said to his wife; "we will go to Maria."

The little princess had grown stouter, but on her short downy upper lip and in her eyes there was the same bright and attractive smile.

"But this is a palace!" she exclaimed, expressing her admiration as if she had been complimenting her host on the success of a ball. "Come along, quick—quick!" And she smiled at her husband, at old Tikhon, and at the manservant who led the way. "Hark! Maria is practising. Let us go gently and surprise her." Prince Andrew followed gloomily.

"You are growing older, Tikhon!" he said to the man who kissed his hand.

Just as they were going into the room where they heard the piano a side door opened, and a pretty young Frenchwoman came out; this was the fair Mademoiselle Bourrienne, who looked delighted at seeing them.

"Oh! how glad Princess Maria will be!" she exclaimed. "I must go and tell her."

"No, no—I beg you not! You are Mademoiselle Bourrienne: I know of you already as my sister-in-law's friend," said the princess, kissing her. "She does not expect us yet, I fancy."

They were at the door now, while within, the same passages went on again and again, unceasingly. Prince Andrew frowned as if he were prepared to feel some painful sensation. His wife went in first; the music suddenly ceased. There was a little cry—a sound of kisses—and Prince Andrew saw his wife and sister, who had only met once before on the occasion of his marriage, fondly clasped in each other's arms, kissing each other upon the cheek effusively and at random, while Mademoiselle Bourrienne looked on, her hand on her heart, and ready to cry and laugh in a breath.

He shrugged his shoulders and knit his brows, like a musician who hears a false note. The two young ladies having stood apart and looked at each other, once more met in a close embrace. Finally, to his great consternation, they melted into tears. Mademoiselle Bourrienne also began to cry. Prince Andrew was most uncomfortable, but his wife and sister seemed to think it quite a matter of course that their first meeting should not take place without tears.

"Ah! my dear!" "Ah, Maria!" they kept saying, and laughing at the same time.

"Do you know I dreamed of you last night?"

"And you did not expect us? But, Maria, you are much thinner!"

"And you are stouter!"

"I recognised Madame la Princess immediately," Mademoiselle Bourrienne threw in.

"And I was not thinking of your coming so soon.—Oh, Andrew—and I did not see you!"

Prince Andrew kissed his sister.

"What a baby you are!" he said, as she looked up at him with her lovely eyes dim with tears, trying to look into his with a bright, tender gaze. His little wife never ceased chattering. That short upper lip danced up and down, lightly touching the lower one then curling in a radiant smile that showed off her small, gleaming teeth, and the brightness of her merry eyes.

"They had had an accident . . ." she rattled on, "and it might have been serious—at Spasskaïa-Gora. And she had left all her dresses at St. Petersburg; she had not a thing to put on . . . and Andrew had altered—and Kitty Odirrtzow had married such a queer old man—and she had found a husband for Princess Maria—yes, a husband in earnest. . . . But we will discuss that by and by," she added.

Maria stood looking at her brother; her eyes were full of love and sadness. She had ceased to attend to the pretty little sister-in-law's prattle, and even broke into a description of one of the late fêtes at St. Petersburg to ask her brother whether he had really decided on joining the army.

"Yes—and I must start to-morrow."

Lisa sighed. "He deserts me," she exclaimed, "and God knows why, when he might have taken his promotion. . . ."

Maria did not heed her; she glanced significantly at her sister-in-law and at her brother. "And I am frightened," added Lisa. She turned pale, her lips puckered, and leaning her cheek against her sister-in-law's, she melted into tears again.

"She needs rest," said her husband, with some displeasure. "Do not you, Lisa? Take her with you, Maria, while I go to see my father. . . . Tell me—he is the same as ever?"

"Yes—so far as I am concerned," said his sister.

"The same hours, the same walks, and then the turning-lathe. . . ." And Prince Andrew's almost imperceptible smile showed that, in spite of filial respect, he quite appreciated his father's weaknesses.

"Yes—the same hours, the same turning, the lessons in geometry and mathematics," she said, laughing, as if those hours of study were the joy of her life.

When the final twenty minutes of the old prince's nap were over, old Tikhon came to call Prince Andrew; his father did him the honour of so far changing the order of his day as to receive him while his toilet was going on. Prince Bolkonsky always had his hair powdered for dinner, and put on an old-fashioned frock-coat. When his son went into his dressing-room he was sitting in his leather arm-chair, covered with a white wrapper, and his head under the hands of the faithful Tikhon. Prince Andrew went forward eagerly; the peevish expression which was habitual with him had vanished; he looked as bright as we have seen him when walking with Peter.

"Ha! here you are, my brave soldier! So you are going to conquer Bonaparte," cried the old man, shaking his powdered head, so far as he could, while Tikhon plaited his pigtail. "Very good, very good—go by all means, forward, march! Or we may be numbered among his subjects before we know where we are. And you are quite well?"

He offered his son his cheek. His nap had put him into a good humour; indeed, he was wont to say, "Sleep before dinner is golden; sleep after dinner is silver." He glanced at his son with immense satisfaction out of the corner of his eye from under his bushy brows, while Andrew kissed the cheek presented to him, and made no reply to his inexhaustible jests about the military men of the day, and Napoleon especially.

"Yes, here I am, father. And I have brought you my wife at an interesting crisis. . . . And you, are you quite well?"

"My dear boy, only idiots or rakes ever need be ill, and you know what I am—I work from morning till night, and I keep sober, so I am perfectly well."

"Thank God for that," said his son.

"God has nothing to do with it! Come . . ." and he returned to his hobby. "Tell me how the Germans teach us to beat Napoleon by the rules of this new game they call Tactics."

'Give me breathing time, my dear father," said the son, smiling, for he loved and respected him, in spite of his crotchets. "I have not even seen my room yet."

"Nonsense, nonsense, all that is nonsense," said the old man, feeling his pigtail to make sure that it was firmly plaited. He took his son's hand: "The rooms for your wife are quite ready. Maria will take her there and show them to her, and they will chatter three basketfuls . . . that is all women's work. I am very glad to have her here. Now, sit down there and talk. I understand the force under Michelson and the army under Tolstoï: they will work together; but the army in the south—what is that to do? Prussia remains neutral I know; but Austria and Sweden, what of them?" And he got up and paced about the room, Tikhon following him and handing him his various articles of clothing. "How are we to get across Pomerania?"

His father was so persevering in his inquiries that Prince Andrew began, unwillingly at first, but with increasing interest, to explain, changing in the middle of his story from Russian to French through force of habit, the plan of the campaign, which was beginning. He explained that an army of 90,000 men were to threaten Prussia and force her to abandon her position as a neutral power; that part of these troops would join the Swedes at Stralsund; that 220,000 Austrians and 100,000 Russians would meanwhile manœuvre in Italy and on the Rhine; that 50,000 English and 50,000 Russians would be landed at Naples, and that the total force of 500,000 men would thus attack Napoleon at several points at once.

The old prince did not seem to take the smallest interest in this long story; in fact he might have not been listening, for he thrice interrupted it as he walked about the room and went on with his dressing. The first time he exclaimed: "The white one, the white one," which arose from old Tikhon having handed him the wrong waistcoat.

The second time he asked when his daughter-in-law's baby was expected, and shook his head reproachfully, saying: "That's a pity, that's a pity! Go on."

And the third time, while his son was finishing his explanation, he began singing in a cracked tuneless voice: "*Marlbrouck s'en va-t-en guerre. . . .*"

"I am not telling you that I approve of this scheme," said his son with a faint smile, "I have stated it as it is now planned; Napoleon will certainly have one of his own at least as good as ours."

"There is nothing new—nothing new whatever, in all that; that is all I have to say to it," and the old man went on in a meditative undertone: '*Dieu sait quand reviendra. . .*' Now go into the dining-room."

101

CHAPTER XXVIII

At the appointed hour when Prince Bolkonsky, shaved and powdered, came into the dining-room, there his daughter-in-law, his daughter, and Mademoiselle Bourrienne were waiting for him, and with them his architect, or clerk of the works, who was admitted to dine with him, though his subordinate position gave him no claim to such an honour. The old prince, who rode a very high horse on points of etiquette and rank, rarely invited the provincial bigwigs to his table, but it amused him to demonstrate the equality of all men in the person of this architect, who shyly blew his nose on a checked pocket-handkerchief. He not unfrequently represented to his daughter that Michael Ivanovitch, as a man, was as good as they were, and he almost always addressed his conversation to him during meals.

Behind each chair in the spacious dining-room stood a servant; and the butler, with a napkin over his arm, cast a last anxious look from the table to the footman—from the big clock to the door, which was about to open for his master. Prince Andrew was studying a pedigree of the family, which hung, in a gilt frame, opposite a large picture infamously painted by an amateur, and representing the head of the Bolkonsky clan, a descendant of Rurik, as a sovereign prince with a crown on his head. Andrew could not help smiling as he looked at the family-tree and smiled as one smiles at a portrait that is comically like the original.

"How like him to have such a thing; that is the man, all over!" he exclaimed.

Princess Maria, who had just come in, gazed at him in surprise, not understanding what he could find to laugh at: she had a sort of religious reverence for everything relating to her father which no criticism could touch.

"Well, every man has his Achilles' heel," Andrew went on. "So clever as he is, and to make himself so ridiculous!"

Princess Maria, who did not approve of such audacious remarks, was on the point of answering, when the steps they were waiting for with so much impatience were heard approaching. The old man's brisk, light gait, and his quick, sharp ways were in such strange contrast to the austere and precise order of the house, that he might have been suspected of intentional mystification.

One hall clock had just struck two, and the drawing-room

was giving a melancholy echo, when the prince made his appearance; his keen undimmed eyes, under the penthouse of their shaggy grey brows, fell on one and another of the persons present, and rested finally on the little princess, who at once felt for her father-in-law the respect mingled with fear which is felt by courtiers when the king appears and which he inspired in all who came near him. He softly stroked her hair, and clumsily patted her on the back of her neck.

"I am very glad—very glad . . ." he said. And after staring her in the face for a few seconds, he seated himself at the table: "Sit down—sit down, Michael Ivanovitch."

He pointed out a chair by his side to his daughter-in-law, and the servant pushed it forward for her.

"Hum!" said the prince, as she took her seat; he looked at her plumpness: "You've been in a hurry. That's bad!" and he laughed a dry, unpleasant laugh, as he always laughed, with the mouth only, not with the eyes. "You must walk about, take plenty of exercise," he said.

Lisa did not hear, or pretended not to hear; she sat uncomfortable and silent till the prince asked after her father and some old acquaintances; then she recovered herself, and smiled again, and told him all the small gossip of St. Petersburg.

"Poor Countess Apraxine has lost her husband, and quite cried her eyes out. . . ."

But the more lively she became the more sternly did the prince look at her; suddenly he turned abruptly away, as if he had heard all he wanted to know.

"Well, Michael Ivanovitch," he exclaimed, "your friend Napoleon will come to grief. Prince Andrew"—he always spoke so of his son—"has explained it all to me. A tremendous force is being brought against him. . . . And to think that we —you and I—have always thought him a poor creature!"

Michael Ivanovitch was well aware that he had never thought anything of the kind, or in such good company; however, he understood that he was addressed simply as an opening to the discussion, and he looked up at Prince Andrew somewhat puzzled, and not very clear as to what was coming next.

"Oh, he is great at tactics!" said the prince to his son, meaning the architect; and then he dilated on his favourite themes: the war, Napoleon, the commanders and statesmen of the day. By his account the men at the head of affairs were mere schoolboys, ignorant of the first elements of war or of administration: Bonaparte was a trumpery little Frenchman whose success was entirely due to there being no Potemkins and Souvorows to oppose him. Europe was involved in no complications, and as to the war, it was not a serious matter, but a farce played by puppets in the hands of the ruling jobber to cheat the public.

Prince Andrew answered all his sallies in a gay vein, and even incited his father to go on.

"Ah! the past is always better than the present; and yet Souvorow let himself be caught in the trap laid by Moreau; he could not outwit him."

"Who told you that, who told you that?" cried the prince. "Souvorow . . ." And he tossed his plate into the air; old Tikhon was quick enough to catch it before it fell.

"Frederick and Souvorow were a pair; but Moreau! Moreau would have been a prisoner if Souvorow had only been free to act. But he was saddled with the Hofkriegswurstsrath [1] whom the devil himself could not have shaken off. You will see—oh! yes, you will see what a Hofkriegswurstsrath is like. And if Souvorow could not make elbow room Michael Koutouzow is not the man to do it. No, no, my friend. Your generals will not serve your turn; you must have French generals, men who turn and rend each other to fight Napoleon. Pahlen, who is a German, has been sent already to New York to seek out Moreau," he went on, alluding to the overtures made to Moreau to go over to Russia. "It is monstrous. Potemkin, Souvorow, Orlow, were they Germans, I ask you? Take my word, either they have lost their heads or I have lost mine. I wish you good luck—but we shall see.—Bonaparte a great general? Ha, ha!"

"I am far from thinking our organisation perfect, but I confess I do not see things quite as you do; you may laugh at Bonaparte as much as you like; that will not alter the fact that he is a great general."

"Michael Ivanovitch," cried the old prince, "do you hear that?"

Michael Ivanovitch, who was giving his mind to his dinner, had hoped that he was forgotten.

"Do you hear? I always maintained that Bonaparte was a great strategist—well, and he thinks so too."

"Why, of course, your excellency," murmured Michael Ivanovitch, while the prince laughed shortly.

"Bonaparte was born under a lucky star, his soldiers are first-rate; and then he was so fortunate as to fight the Germans

[1] As in the original—a farcical sham title.

first and beat them: only a helpless idiot could escape beating them; since the world began they have always been thrashed, and they have never been able to thrash anyone. Well, yes, they have thrashed each other, but that does not count. Well, he owes all his glory to them." And he began a list of all the mistakes Napoleon had made—in his opinion.

His son listened in silence, but no argument could shake his convictions which were as firmly rooted as his father's; still, he wondered how a solitary old man, living in retirement in the country, had managed so thoroughly to master the military and political situation of Europe, down to the smallest details.

"You fancy I know nothing about it because I am old? Well, you see. . . . It works in my brain and keeps me awake at night. . . . Show me what your great commander has done; where and how has he proved his skill?"

"It would be too long to explain."

"Well, well, go and join your Bonaparte! Mademoiselle Bourrienne, here's another admirer of your blackguard emperor" exclaimed the old man.

"Nay, you know I am no Bonapartist, mon Prince."

"*Dieu sait quand reviendra*," hummed the old prince in a cracked voice, and he laughed grimly as he rose from table.

All through this discussion the little princess had sat scared and speechless, looking by turns at her sister-in-law and the old man. As soon as dinner was over she put her hand through Maria's arm, pulling her away into the next room:

"How clever your father is!" she exclaimed. "That is the reason I am so much afraid of him, I think."

"But he is so kind," said Maria.

CHAPTER XXIX

PRINCE Andrew was to start next evening. The old prince had made no alteration in his habits, and had retired to his room after dinner. His daughter-in-law was with Princess Maria, while his son, having exchanged his uniform for an undress surtout without epaulettes, was making the last preparations for his departure with the help of his valet. He went in person to inspect his travelling-chaise and trunks, and ordered the horses to be put to. Nothing remained in his room but various small objects of constant use; a dressing-case, a canteen with silver fittings, a pair of pistols, and a Turkish sabre which his father had seized at the assault on Otchakow, and had given to him; and everything was cleaned and repaired, put into perfect order, and sheathed in cloth covers strongly fastened and strapped. If a man is at all inclined to reflection, he is almost always in a serious frame of mind on the eve of a parting or of some serious change in his life: he glances back on the past, and forms some plans for the future. Prince Andrew was anxious and saddened; he walked up and down his room with his hands behind his back, nodding his head now and again, and staring before him with an absent gaze. Was he uneasy as to the issue of the war, or was he regretting his wife? A little of both perhaps; but he evidently had no wish to be detected in this sentimental mood, for, hearing steps in the adjoining room, he hastily went up to the table, and pretended to be busy arranging his dressing-case, putting on his usual calm and inscrutable expression.

Princess Maria came running in quite out of breath.

"They told me you had ordered the carriage round, and I wanted to speak to you alone, for God knows how long it may be before we meet again. . . . It does not vex you to have me here? . . . You are very much altered, Andrioucha," she added, as if to explain her question. She could not help smiling as she called him by this pet name; it was strange to her that this handsome young fellow, with his austere manner, could be the Andrioucha of her childhood, the companion of her games, the mischievous slip of a boy of a not very remote past.

"And where is Lisa?" he said, answering her question by a smile.

"She is gone to sleep on my sofa, quite tired out. Ah, Andrew! what a treasure of a wife you have found! A perfect child: gay, lively—I love her dearly."

Andrew had seated himself by his sister's side; a slightly ironical smile parted his lips; she observed it and went on:

"You must not be too hard on her little weaknesses. . . . Who is there that has none? She has been brought up in the middle of the gay world, her position is a painful one. . . . You must put yourself in her place: to understand the difficulties of others is to forgive. You must admit that it is very hard for her, under the circumstances, to be parted from her husband, left alone in the country—yes, really very hard."

Prince Andrew listened as a man listens to anyone whom he knows thoroughly.

106

"But you live in the country," he said. "Do you find this life so intolerable?"

"I! oh, that is quite different! I know nothing else, I cannot wish for another life; but for a young woman who is used to a wider world, it is burying all her best years in a hermitage, for my father, as you know, is always engaged, and I—what company can I be for her?—She has always lived in the best society. So there is no one but Mademoiselle Bourrienne. . . ."

"I do not like your Bourrienne."

"But I assure you she is very kind, and very nice, and most forlorn—she has no one in the world. To tell you the truth, she is in my way more often than she is of use; I have always been a rustic, and I prefer being alone. My father likes her, and is always kind to her and to Michael Ivanovitch—you, know, as Sterne says, 'we like people in proportion to the good we do them, and not to the good they do us.' My father took her in as an orphan from the streets, and she is really a very good soul. He likes her way of reading, and she reads aloud to him every evening."

"But come, Maria, you must suffer cruelly sometimes from my father's temper?"

Maria, astounded at the question, could only stammer out: "I . . . suffer?"

"He was always stern, and now he must be desperately hard to get on with," Andrew went on to try his sister.

"You are good, Andrew, very good, but you sin in pride," she said, answering her own thoughts, as it were. "How can you allow yourself to judge in such a way, or suppose that I could ever feel anything but reverence for my father? I am quite happy and contented with him, and I am only sorry that all the world cannot share my lot."

Her brother shook his head incredulously. "One thing only," she went on, "to be perfectly honest, worries and distresses me: his notions about religion. I cannot understand how so clever a man can be so perverse and blind as to discuss questions that are as clear as day. That is, really and truly, my only trouble. At the same time I fancy that lately I have observed some slight improvement; his satire is a little less biting, and he even consented to see a monk, with whom he had a long interview."

"Oh, oh! I am very much afraid that on such points you and your monk may save your breath to cool your porridge."

"Well, my dear, I pray with all my heart, and I hope God will hear me. . . . Andrew," she added kindly. "I want to ask you something."

"What can I do for you?"

"Promise me that you will consent—it will give you no trouble: it is nothing unworthy of you, you may be sure, and it will be the greatest comfort to me. Promise me, Andrioucha," and putting her hand into her bag she took out some small object which she held hidden in her hand as not daring to show it to him till he had answered explicitly. She looked at her brother anxiously and pleadingly.

"Even if it cost me a real sacrifice I would. . . ."

"You must think what you choose, you are just like my father, but I cannot help that. Promise me, I beg and pray: our grandfather wore it in all the battles he fought in, and you will wear it—will you not?"

"Certainly, but what is it that I am to wear?"

"Andrew, this little image, with my blessing—and promise me that you will never take it off."

"Simply to please you, I will promise that, if it is not heavy enough to break my neck," replied Andrew; but seeing his sister's grieved look at this ill-timed jest, he changed his tone: "To be sure, my dearest," he said, "I will accept it with pleasure."

"He will conquer your obduracy; He will save and pardon you and lead you to Himself, for He alone is truth and peace!" she said in a voice tremulous with emotion, and with an action of devout solemnity she held up over her brother's head a small medallion blackened by time and wear. It was an oval image of the Redeemer mounted in silver and with a little silver chain. She crossed herself, kissed the medallion, and held it to him: "Do it for my sake," she said.

Her fine eyes shone with a softened light, and her pale thin face was transfigured. Andrew put out his hand for the sacred amulet, but she drew it back. He understood and kissed it, crossing himself at the same time with a mixture of pathos and irony.

"Thank you, my dearest," she said, and she sat down again. "Be kind and generous, Andrew, do not judge Lisa too hardly . . . she is very sweet and gentle, and her position is a very painful one."

"But I cannot see what fault I have found or hinted at in my wife, Maria. Why do you take this tone about it?"

108

Maria coloured, but had no explanation to offer.

"But granting that I have said nothing," he went on, "some-one else I see has been making remarks, and I am sorry for that."

The colour mounted in patches to her face and throat, and she tried in vain to find something to say, for her brother had guessed rightly. The little princess had been crying, and telling her of all her terrors: she should die, she was sure, when her child was born, and she was very miserable and very much to be pitied—she complained of her lot, of her father-in-law, of her husband; and then, having exhausted herself with weeping, she had fallen asleep.

Prince Andrew was sorry for his sister.

"Listen, Maria," he said, "I have nothing to blame my wife for—I never have said, and never shall say, a word against her. I, on my part, have never done her a wrong, and I will try never to do one. But if you want to know the truth, to know whether I am happy . . . no, I am not. Nor is she; but why I know not." He turned and kissed his sister, but he did not see the loving light in her eyes, for his own were fixed on the door she had left ajar.

"We must go to her, Maria; I must bid her good-bye; or rather, if you will go in and wake her I will follow you. Petroucha," he said to the servant, "here, carry down all these things: put this on the right-hand side and this under the seat."

Maria went, but she stopped half-way:

"Andrew, if only you had faith you would have turned to God and implored him to give you the love you do not feel; He would have heard your prayer."

"Ah, yes! to be sure—perhaps. Go on, Maria, I am coming."

A few minutes after, as Prince Andrew was passing along the corridor which joined the wing, where his wife was to be lodged, to the main building, he met Mademoiselle Bourrienne, crisp and smiling; it was the third time that day that she had crossed his path.

"Oh! I thought you were in your own rooms," she said, blushing and looking down. Prince Andrew looked excessively annoyed, and his only answer was a glance of such supreme contempt that she stopped quite abashed and vanished at once.

As he went towards his sister's room he could hear Lisa's sprightly tones; she was awake, and prattling as if she were bound to make up for lost time.

"Just picture to yourself, Maria," she was saying with fits

of laughter, "old Countess Zoubow, with her false curls and her mouth full of false teeth, as if she could defy old age . . . ha, ha, ha!"

It was at least the fifth time that Andrew had heard her tell the same story. He went in softly and found her quite refreshed, with a bright colour on her cheeks, and comfortably seated in a deep arm-chair doing some needlework, while she poured out her unconnected reminiscences of St. Petersburg. He affectionately stroked her hair and asked her if she felt better.

"Yes, yes," she said, and went on with her story.

The travelling-carriage with six horses was waiting at the door. The intense darkness of an autumn night threw its shroud over even the nearest objects: the coachman could hardly see the pole of the coach round which the servants were busy with their lanterns. The house was lighted up inside, and broad beams of light were shed from the huge front windows. All the household had gathered in the hall to take leave of the young master, while a little party of intimates had assembled in the great drawing-room. Everyone was waiting for Prince Andrew, who had gone into his father's room, the old prince having sent for him to speak with him alone.

Andrew, on going in, had found his father seated at his table writing, with his spectacles on, and wrapped in a white dressing-gown—a costume in which, as a rule, he never allowed himself to be seen. He looked up at his son.

"You are off then?" he said, and he began to write again.

"Yes—I have come to say good-bye."

"Kiss me," and he offered him a cheek. . . . "Thank you, and again thank you."

"What for?"

"For not stopping at home tied to your wife's apron-strings. The service before all things—so thank you."

And again he began writing, but he was so nervous that his pen creaked and spluttered in every direction. "If you have anything you want to say I am listening. . . . These two things I can do at the same time. . . ."

"My wife—I am vexed to leave her here in this way, a burden on your hands."

"Speak the truth! What is it you want?"

"When the time draws near send to Moscow for a doctor; let him be here in time. . . ."

The old man looked at his son in stern astonishment.

"Of course, I know that nothing can be done if nature rebels against science," Andrew went on, not without some emotion; "and I know that out of a million such cases not more than one perhaps goes wrong, but it is her fancy, and mine too. She has been crammed with all sorts of notions in consequence of a dream."

"Hm"—murmured the old man between his teeth. "Well, well, I will see to it," then he signed his name with a determined flourish. "It is a bad business, heh?" he added with a smile.

"What is a bad business?"

"Your wife," said the old man bluntly.

"I do not understand you."

"Well, my boy, you see they are all alike, and you cannot get unmarried. Do not be afraid, I will tell no one, but you know it as well as I do—it is the truth." His lean, bony fingers grasped his son's hand and wrung it firmly while his piercing eye seemed to look through him. Prince Andrew's answer was a sigh—a wordless confession.

The old prince folded and sealed his letters in no time.

"Well, there is no help for it, and she is very pretty. Be easy, everything shall be done," he said briefly.

Andrew said no more; he was distressed, but at the same time glad to have been understood.

"Do not worry yourself about her; all that is possible shall be done. Now, here is a letter for Michael Illarionovitch; I have asked him to give you good chances and not to keep you as his aide-de-camp too long. It's a worthless sort of job. You must tell him that I remember him with faithful regard, and let me know how he receives you. If you are satisfied, stay with him and do your best; if not, leave him. Nicholas Bolkonsky's son cannot remain with a chief on sufferance. Come here." He had been speaking very rapidly and swallowing half his words, but his son understood him; he followed him to the desk which the old man opened, and then took out a note-book, closely written in a big and long but cramped hand but quite legible. "I shall probably die before you; this is a memorandum to be sent to the emperor after my death; and this is a letter and a cheque. It is a prize that I intend to offer for a history of Souvorow's campaigns. Send these to the Academy; I have made some notes—you can read them when I am gone; they may be of use to you."

Andrew feeling that there would be a sort of indelicacy in bidding his father look forward to a long life, simply said:

"Your wishes shall be implicitly fulfilled."

"And now good-bye," said the old prince, giving his son his hand to kiss. "Remember, Prince Andrew, that if death overtakes you my old heart must bleed;" he broke off suddenly and all at once his voice was very high-pitched, "and if I were to hear," he added, looking him full in the face, "that Nicholas Bolkonsky's son had failed in his duty, I should be ashamed—you understand." He hissed out the last words.

"You might have saved yourself the trouble of telling me that," said Andrew smiling. "I, too, have a request to make: if I should fall, and if a son should be born to me, keep him with you, have him brought up here, I beseech you."

"And not give him into your wife's care?" said the old man laughing. They stood opposite each other in silence. The old man's quick eyes were fixed on the eyes of his son. The lower part of his face suddenly quivered.

"Now, go . . ." he said, loudly and angrily as he opened the door, and pushed his son out of the room.

"What is the matter, what has happened?" exclaimed the two ladies, seeing the old prince in his dressing-gown, without his wig and with his spectacles on; but he instandly disappeared.

Prince Andrew sighed: "Well?" he said to his wife, in a cold, slightly sarcastic tone, as if he were bidding her carry on her usual little airs.

"Andrew, already!" The little princess turned pale with terrors and agitation: he bent over her and kissed her; she gave a cry and fainted away. He raised her head, which dropped on his shoulder, and gently placed her in the arm-chair.

"Good-bye, Maria," he said in a low voice; their hands clasped warmly, he kissed her and hurried away. Mademoiselle Bourrienne was chafing the princess's temples, while Maria held her up and sent a last glance of love and blessing after her brother, from eyes full of tears. The old prince, in his study, was blowing his nose so often and with so much vehemence that it sounded like a succession of ferocious pistol-shots. Suddenly he put his head into the room:

"He is gone. Come, it is just as well. . . ." Then, seeing the little woman unconscious, he shook his head reproachfully, and went quickly into his own room again, slamming the door after him.

BOOK TWO

CHAPTER XXX

In October, 1805, the Russian army was quartered in certain towns and villages in Austria. Every day fresh regiments were coming in, and their presence there was a heavy burden on the country and the inhabitants. These troops, constantly increasing in number, were being concentrated round the fortress of Braunau, the headquarters of Koutouzow, the commander-in-chief.

It was the 11th of October, and a regiment of infantry that had just arrived had stopped at about half a mile from the town. It had borrowed nothing that could affect its appearance from the country which formed a background to the scene; in the midst of orchards, stone walls, and tiled roofs, with more distant mountains on the horizon, it was an essentially Russian crowd of soldiers, preparing to be inspected by the commandant.

The order to make ready for this inspection had been forwarded the day before to the last encampment; but as there was something inexact in the announcement, the officer in command of the regiment had called a little council of officers to decide on the details. Were they to appear in marching order, or in parade dress? That was the question. Votes were in favour of the latter: too great zeal would be better than too little. The soldiers set to work, and though they had marched thirty versts that day, not one closed an eye that night; everything was cleaned, mended, and furbished up. The aides-de-camp and captains called the roll of their men, and when day broke their satisfied eyes rested on a compact mass of 2000 men, all drawn up in close order, where last night there had been a slovenly mob. Each one was at his post and knew what he had to do; not a button or a strap was wanting; everything shone and glittered in the sunshine.

All was in readiness, and the general might inspect or examine any man in the ranks, for every shirt was clean and every knapsack contained the regulation kit. One detail only was not wholly satisfactory; more than half the men had their boots in ribbons; the regiment, to be sure, had marched a thousand versts, and the Austrian commissariat turned a deaf ear to the repeated applications sent up by the officer in command of the regiment for a supply of the necessary materials. This officer was a burly general of advanced age and sanguine temperament; bigger from chest to back than from shoulder to shoulder, with grizzled whiskers and eyebrows. His uniform was new and splendid, though it bore the inevitable traces of its long sojourn in a valise; the heavy epaulettes raised his shoulders to the sky. He marched up and down in front of the ranks with an important waddle, leaning forward a little, and looking like a man who is happily conscious of having fulfilled a solemn function. He was proud of his regiment, to which he was devoted heart and soul; his gait, however, betrayed perhaps some other absorbing cares, for, besides his military responsibilities, the interests of the world at large, and of the fair sex in particular, filled a large place in his thoughts.

"Well, my dear Michael Dmitriévitch," he said to a major who came towards him with an equally satisfied smile. . . . "A hard night's work, heh? Our regiment makes not a bad show . . . not one of the worst, heh?" The major seemed to relish his superior's jest and laughed.

"Certainly not. We should not be turned away even from the Champ de Mars." [1]

"What is it?" cried the general, catching sight of two horsemen, an aide-de-camp and a Cossack, riding towards him down the high road from the town, along which foot-soldiers were posted at intervals as scouts. The officer, who had been sent from headquarters to explain the order issued the day before, announced that the commander-in-chief wished to inspect the regiment in marching order, and without any preparation or display: a member of the council of war had arrived from Vienna the day before to desire Koutouzow to join the army under Archduke Frederick and Mack as soon as possible: this did not at all meet Koutouzow's views, and to support his objections he was anxious that the Austrian himself should be able to report on the miserable state of the Russian troops after their long march.

The aide-de-camp, however, did not know this; he could only explain that the commander-in-chief would be greatly annoyed not to find the men in marching order. The poor

[1] The parade ground in St. Petersburg.

114

general hung his head, shrugged his shoulders, and wrung his hands in despair.

"That is just the way. Did not I say so, Michael Dmitriévitch? Marching order, in great-coats," he added, turning angrily to the major. "Good God! gentlemen—sergeants-major!" . . . he exclaimed in a voice accustomed to command, and he advanced a step. "Will his excellency be here soon?" he asked the aide-de-camp, with respectful deference.

"In about an hour, I fancy."

"Shall we have time to get into marching order?"

"I do not know. . . ." The commanding officer went forward and gave his orders. The majors trotted off, sergeants-major bestirred themselves, and in an instant the compact squares, till then silent and motionless, broke up and dispersed; the soldiers rushed about in every direction, strapping their knapsacks on to their shoulders, flinging up their capotes and getting their arms into them as fast as they could. In half an hour everything was in order again, only that the black squares were now grey. The general again approached his regiment and examined it from a distance.

"What is that? What is that?" cried the general. "Captain of the third company?"

"Third company. The general wants the captain of the third company," was repeated by several, and an aide-de-camp flew to hurry up the delinquent. In the frenzy of zeal and general scare some had even called out: "The company wants the general!" when finally the outcry reached the ears of the absentee, a man of middle age. He could not run, but he was coming along at a sort of short trot, on the tip of his rather tottering feet. It was plain that the elderly captain was as uneasy as a schoolboy who foresees a question he cannot answer. His nose was purple and spotted with traces of intemperance; his lips quivered with nervousness; he panted and slackened his pace as he came up to the general, who scanned him from head to foot.

"You make your men wear fancy dress, do you? What is the meaning of that?" he asked, pointing to a soldier of the third company, whose military coat was a glaring contrast in colour to the rest of his dress. "Where were you hiding; the commander-in-chief is expected, and you are not at your post, heh? I will teach you to dress your men like that for a review."

The captain never took his eyes off his chief, while more and more discomfited, he held two fingers to the peak of his shako as if the salute might be the saving of him.

"Well, why do not you answer? And that one—dressed up as a Hungarian—who is he?"

"Your excellency. . . ."

"Well, what then? You may go on repeating 'your excellency' in every key—what next? What is the meaning of 'your excellency?' tell me that."

"Your excellency, that is Dologhow, the man who was degraded," stammered the captain.

"Degraded! Then he is not a field-marshal, that he should take such liberties. He is a private, and a private should be dressed according to regulations."

"But you yourself authorised him to dress so while on the march."

"Authorised, authorised! That is always the way with you youngsters," said the general, quieting down a little; "we give an inch, and you take . . . what next!" and he fired up afresh. "Dress your men properly!"

Then he turned to Koutouzow's envoy, and went on with his inspection, satisfied with his little explosion, and seeking an excuse for another. An officer's stock came under suspicion, and he blew the wearer up smartly; then the front rank of the third company not being accurately dressed, he called out in agitated tones to Dologhow, who wore a bluish-grey capote:

"Where is your foot?—where is your foot?"

Dologhow deliberately drew it back, fixing a keen, bold eye on the general.

"And why that blue cloak? Take it off! Sergeant-major, undress this man."

"It is my duty, general, to obey orders," said Dologhow, interrupting him, "but I am not forced to submit. . . ."

"Not a word in the ranks—not a word!"

"I am not forced to submit to insult," Dologhow went on in a loud voice. And he looked straight into the eyes of his commanding officer. The general stopped, and pulled at his scarf.

"Have the goodness to change your dress," he said, furiously; and he turned away.

CHAPTER XXXI

"HE is coming!" cried one of the outposts; and the general, crimson with excitement, ran to his horse, seized the bridle with a trembling hand, jumped into the saddle, and drew his sword with triumphant determination; then he sat with his mouth open ready to give the word of command. A wave, as it were, ran through the mass of soldiers; then they were perfectly still.

"Attention!" cried the general, in a ringing voice, in which satisfaction and command were curiously mingled with deference, for the chief was drawing near. A high Vienna chariot, hung on springs, and painted blue, was coming down the wide country road, shaded by trees, with a mounted escort, and a company of Croats. The Austrian general's white uniform, as he sat by the side of Koutouzow, was conspicuous in contrast to the dark Russian uniforms. The carriage stopped, the two generals were talking quietly, and Koutouzow got out, slowly and heavily, without seeming to pay any heed to the two thousand men, whose eyes were fixed on him, and on their general. At the word of command the regiment started like one man, and presented arms. The voice of the commander-in-chief was audible in the death-like silence that ensued, then a shout of "Long live your excellency!" rang out in response to his salute, and silence fell again.

Koutouzow, who had stood waiting while the regiment had gone through this little commotion, walked down the ranks with the Austrian general. The way in which the inferior general had received his chief, and now followed him with his head bent, watching his every movement, and pricking up his ears at the least word, plainly showed that the duty was congenial to him. Thanks to his strict discipline and good care his regiment was in fact in far better order than any that had lately arrived at Braunau: only 217 men were missing, sick or laggards, and everything was in good trim, excepting of course, shoe-leather.

Koutouzow stopped now and then to speak a few words to the officers and soldiers he had known in the campaign in Turkey. Looking at their boots he shook his head sadly, and pointed them out to his companion with a look which implied much, and saved him the trouble of making any direct comments; each time he did this the commander of the regiment rushed forward, as if to catch the observations he expected him to make. A score of officers forming the great man's suite, followed a few paces behind with one ear open while they talked and laughed among themselves. An aide-de-camp, a handsome young fellow, walked close to Koutouzow; this was Prince Andrew Bolkonsky. At his side came the tall and stalwart Nesvitsky, a staff-officer, with a good-natured, smiling face, and kindly eyes. Nesvitsky was doing his best to suppress a fit of laughter caused by the antics of one of his companions, a dark-complexioned hussar, who, with his eyes fixed on the back of the regiment's commander, was repeating every one of his gestures with imperturbable gravity. Nesvitsky coughed and nudged the others in order that they should notice the fun.

Koutouzow walked with leisurely indifference in front of the thousand eyes that seemed ready to start from their sockets to see him better.

"Ah! Timokhine!" he exclaimed, recognising the ruddy-nosed captain.

Timokhine, who seemed to have drawn himself up to his utmost height during the general's scolding, managed nevertheless to pull himself up a little higher still when the commander-in-chief addressed him, till it really seemed that the tension, if prolonged, might prove fatal. Koutouzow detected this, and to relieve him turned away, while a faint smile wandered over his scarred features.

"Another comrade in arms at Ismail," he said. "A brave officer. Are you satisfied with him?"

He spoke to the commander of the regiment, who, never suspecting that an invisible double, in the person of the swarthy hussar, was repeating him from head to foot, started and stepped forward, saying, "Quite satisfied, your excellency."

"Every man has his weak point, and he, I fancy, is a son of Bacchus," added Koutouzow, as he moved away. Fearful lest he should be held responsible, the hapless general made no reply. Meanwhile the young hussar, who had been struck by the appearance of the worthy son of Bacchus, with his red nose and his strained erectness, imitated him so exactly, that Nesvitsky exploded with laughter. Koutouzow turned round, but the mimic had a perfect command of countenance, and his grimaces turned, as if by magic, to an expression of respectful gravity.

The third company was the last. Koutouzow paused meditating, evidently trying to remember something. Prince

Andrew stepped forward, and said to him in French and in an undertone:

"You desired me to remind you of Dologhow—the man who was degraded . . . ."

"Where is Dologhow?" said the commander promptly.

Dologhow, now wearing a soldier's regulation grey coat, came forward at once, stepping from the rank and presenting arms; he was a fine-looking soldier, no doubt, well built, fair haired, with clear blue eyes.

"A complaint?" said Koutouzow, frowning slightly.

"No—this is Dologhow," said Prince Andrew.

"Ah! Well, I hope you will profit by this lesson; do your duty in the service. The emperor is merciful, and I will not forget you either if you deserve well."

Dologhow's keen blue eyes looked as boldly into Koutouzow's as they had into those of his superior officer; their expression seemed to ignore the gulf of etiquette which divides a private from a commander-in-chief.

"I only ask one thing, your excellency," he said in his steady ringing voice: "Give me the opportunity of wiping out the record, and of proving my devotion to the emperor and my country."

Koutouzow turned away, the same smile in his eyes passed over his face as when he turned from Timokhine, and went to his carriage with sullen dissatisfaction, as if these commonplace phrases, always the same, bored and wearied him.

"What is the use," he said to himself, "of answers in this strain, of saying the same thing over and over again?"

The regiment broke up into companies, and marched forward towards Braunau to find quarters, to renew its outfit, to get shoes, and the rest.

"You are not vexed with me, I hope, Prokhor Ignatovitch," said the general in command to the captain of the third company as he rode past. His face was radiant with satisfaction at having got through the inspection so well.

"In the emperor's service, you know. . . . And then one is afraid of disgracing oneself in the face of the whole regiment; but I am always the first to apologise . . ." and he held out his hand.

"Indeed, general, how could I for a moment think. . . ." The captain's nose turned plum-colour with joy, and his mouth, widening to a grin, displayed his irregular teeth—two of his front teeth having been broken out in the attack on Ismail.

"Tell Mr. Dologhow, too, that I will not forget him—to be quite easy. How does he behave, by the way?"

"He is punctual in his duty, your excellency, but temper. . . ."

"What about his temper?"

"He has fits of it. Some days he is quiet, intelligent, well-informed; at other times he is a perfect wild beast. Quite lately you know he was within an ace of killing a Jew in Poland—you heard of it?"

"Yes, yes . . ." said the general. "But he has been very unfortunate—he is much to be pitied . . . he has influential friends; you will be wise to. . . ."

"Exactly so, your excellency," and the captain's smile showed that he had quite understood the hint.

"You may win your epaulettes in the first fight!" cried the general, aiming the words at Dologhow as he marched past. Dologhow looked round with a sarcastic smile, but said nothing.

"Good, very good!" the general went on, so as to be heard by all the men. "An allowance of brandy for each of you, and I thank you each and all—God be praised!" And he rode off to the next company.

"He is a capital fellow; after all, one can manage to serve under him!" said the red-nosed captain to a subaltern officer.

"In short 'the King of Hearts,'" said the subaltern, laughing as he quoted the nickname given to the old general. The happy issue of the inspection had put the officers into a good temper, which soon spread among the soldiers. They marched briskly onward, talking as they went.

"Who invented the story that Koutouzow was blind of one eye?"

"For the matter of that, so he is."

"For the matter of that, not a bit of it; he quickly noticed the state of our boots."

"What a fright I was in when he looked at mine!"

"And the other one—the Austrian. What do you think of him? A lump of chalk—a sack of flour. What a job it must be to whiten all that!"

"I say, you—you were in front. When did they say we should come to fighting? We certainly heard that Napoleon was here, at Braunau."

"Napoleon here! What nonsense! You idiot, don't you know that the Prussian has turned tail, and the Austrian must

The regiment broke into companies and marched forward to find quarters

walk over him—then, when he has thrashed him, he will begin to fight Bonaparte. Here? Tell that to the marines! Bonaparte at Braunau! what a ninny you must be! Keep your ears open, gaby."

"Plague take these quartermasters! There! the fifth company has turned off into the village, and the pot will be boiling before we get there!"

"Come, give me a crust at any rate."

"And I gave you some tobacco last night—come, didn't I? Well, take your crust—here."

"If they would only let us stop—not a bit of it; five versts more to carry an empty stomach."

"Ah! what would just suit you would be a lift in one of these Germans' carriages: that would be something like, heh?"

"And the people hereabout—did you notice? Not the same as ours; the Poles at any rate were our emperor's people, but here there are Germans and nothing else wherever you go."

"Singers to the front!" shouted an officer, and a score or so of soldiers stepped out of the ranks. The drummer who led the singing faced about, and started a song, beginning:

"It is the morning drum, the sun has risen."

And ending with the words:

"And we shall have our fill of glory under our father Kamensky."

This song, composed in Turkey, now rang out on Austrian soil; the only change was that the name of Koutouzow was substituted for that of Kamensky. When he had boldly given out these last words, the drummer, who was a handsome fellow of about forty, and of wiry build, looked at his comrades with a searching frown, while his hands jerked to right and left, and seemed to fling some invisible object on the ground. Having made quite sure that they were all watching him, he gently raised his arms, and held them for some seconds steadily above his head, as if he were carrying this precious and invisible treasure with the greatest care. Suddenly throwing it down, he gave out: "My home, my home," and twenty voices took it up in chorus. Then another soldier rushed forward, and without seeming in the least embarrassed by the weight of his kit, began to jump and dance, going backwards all the time in front of the rest, wriggling his shoulders and flourishing a couple of spoons. The rest marched in quick time.

Behind them came a sound of wheels and horses—Koutouzow and his suite returning to the town. He gave a sign that the soldiers were to march on without stopping on his account. His face and the faces of his suite shone with pleasure at the sound of the songs, the sight of the dancing soldier, and the briskly-marching soldiers. In the second rank of the right-hand file, which the high chariot passed close to, Dologhow, the blue-eyed private, was a conspicuous figure; his light measured gait, at once graceful and bold, his audacious, mocking glance, which seemed a challenge to the riders who passed him by, expressed his pity for those who could not go on foot like himself and his jolly comrades. Gerkow, the sub-lieutenant of hussars who had amused himself by mimicking the general, reined in his horse to get within speaking distance of Dologhow, though he had been one of the fast young fellows among whom Dologhow had been the ringleader—till this moment he had prudently refrained from betraying his acquaintance with a man who had been degraded; but Koutouzow's words had led him to change his tactics and it was with an affectation of eager pleasure that he said:

"Well, and how are you getting on, my dear fellow?"

"As you see," said Dologhow coldly.

The gay brisk tune of the soldier's song was a singular accompaniment to Gerkow's odd familiarity, and his ex-friend's icy replies.

"And you get on with your chiefs?"

"Oh, yes—well enough; they are very good fellows. And you have squeezed your way into a staff appointment?"

"Yes, I am atached—on duty."

Then they were both silent: "The hawk is thrown off from the right hand!" the song went on, and the mere sound of it seemed to revive confidence and determination. Their conversation would undoubtedly have taken a different turn but for that lively accompaniment.

"Are the Austrians really beaten? Is it true?" asked Dologhow.

"So they say, but who the devil can tell?"

"So much the better," said Dologhow shortly, to the time of the song.

"Come into our place this evening, will you? We shall have a faro table."

"You have plenty of money then?"

"Come, at any rate."

"Impossible. I have vowed neither to play nor drink till I have regained my rank."

"Very well; after the first fight then."

"Very well; we will see."

"But look in all the same: if you want anything the staff will help you."

Dologhow smiled.

"Do not trouble yourself about me; I shall ask for nothing. What I want I shall take."

"All right—I only just meant. . . ."

"Exactly—and I only just meant. . . ."

"Good-bye."

"Good-bye!"

And louder but more distant the song rang out: "At home, in the fatherland," as Gerkow spurred his horse. And the horse, covered with foam and galloping to the measure of the music, soon outstripped the infantry and fell into place near the chariot.

CHAPTER XXXII

KOUTOUZOW, as soon as he reached home, went to his private room; there he made his aide-de-camp give him various papers relating to the state of the troops and some letters received from Archduke Ferdinand, in command of the advanced army. Prince Andrew Bolkonsky entered the room with the papers. A map lay on the table, in front of which the commander-in-chief was sitting with a member of the Austrian supreme council of war. While he took the papers from Bolkonsky's hand and signed to him to remain in the room, he went on with his conversation in French, speaking slowly and with a polish of phraseology and inflection which were extremely pleasing; nay, he evidently took pleasure in listening to himself.

"You have my only answer, general," he said. "If the matter in question had concerned no one but myself, his majesty the Emperor Francis should have been instantly obeyed, and I would have joined the archduke at once. Pray believe me when I say, that I would gladly have resigned the command of our army and the heavy responsibility that has been laid upon me, to place it in the hands of one of the distinguished and capable generals who swarm in the Austrian army, and to whom I am so entirely inferior; but our actions are often fettered by circumstances."

The smile with which he spoke the last words fully justified the Austrian officer's visible incredulity. As to Koutouzow he was sure of not being contradicted to his face, and that, to him, was the chief point; he cared little for anything beyond. His companion had no choice but to adopt the same tone; but his voice betrayed his ill humour in whimsical contrast to the flattering speeches brought out with an effort.

"On the contrary: the emperor highly appreciates all that your excellency has done for our common interests; the only thing is that the slowness of your advance prevents your brave Russian soldiers and their leaders from winning the laurels they are accustomed to reap."

Koutouzow bowed, still with that ironical smile.

"I cannot share your opinion; I am quite certain on the contrary from the letter that Archduke Ferdinand has done me the honour of writing to me, that the Austrian army, under the command of so experienced a leader as General Mack, is at this moment triumphant, and that you have no further need of our assistance."

The Austrian found some difficulty in containing his rage; Koutouzow's observation was not, in fact, in harmony with the rumours which were rife of an Austrian defeat, only too probable indeed under the circumstances. The speech had the colour of a jest, and yet the commander-in-chief, calm and smiling, had every right to assume the facts, since Mack's last despatch spoke of an impending victory, and praised in high terms the position held by his army, from a strategical point of view.

"Hand me the letter," he said to Prince Andrew. "Listen to this . . ." and he read:

"The strength of our army—about 70,000 men—enables us to attack and defeat the enemy if he attempts to pass the Lech. On the other hand, as we hold Ulm, we remain masters of both banks of the Danube: we can cross it if necessary, fall on the enemy, cut off his communications, and recross the river lower down, and so finally prevent his turning the main body of his forces against our faithful allies. Thus we can bravely await the moment when the Imperial troops of Russia are ready to join us in inflicting on the enemy the fate he deserves." As he ended this elaborate rhodomontade, Koutouzow looked up and sighed.

"Your excellency must be aware that a wise man is prepared for the worst," replied his interlocutor, anxious to put an end

Half an hour later aides-de-camp riding in every direction were bearing the orders, which, within a short time, would release the Russian forces from their inaction and send them forward to meet the enemy.

Prince Andrew was one of those exceptional staff-officers whose whole interest is centred on the general scheme of military operations. Mack's arrival here, and the details of his defeat, enabled him to understand that the Russian army was now in a critical position, and that the first half of the campaign was a failure. His fancy pictured the part about to be played by the Russian army, and his own share in it; and he could not help feeling a thrill of exultant satisfaction as he reflected that Austria's pride was humbled, and that within a week he would be assisting in an inevitable struggle between the French and the Russians, the first since Souvorow's day. Still he feared that Napoleon's genius would prove too strong for all the valour of his adversaries, while, on the other hand, he could not bear that his hero should meet with a check.

Prince Andrew, over-excited by the working of his brain, went to his own rooms to write his daily letter to his father. On his way he met Nesvitsky, with whom he shared his quarters, and with him Gerkow; both were in fits of laughter.

"Why are you so dismal?" asked Nesvitsky, seeing his pale face and sparkling eyes.

"There is nothing to be gay about," replied Bolkonsky.

As they spoke they saw at the further end of the corridor a member of the Hofkriegsrath with the Austrian General Strauch, who was attached to Koutouzow's staff as head of the commissariat in charge of the supplies for the Russian forces. The member of the Hofkriegsrath had only arrived the day before. The passage was a wide one and there was no need for the three young men to stand aside, but Gerkow, giving Nesvitsky a push, exclaimed in breathless haste: "They are coming —they are coming this way; make way, pray."

The two generals seemed anxious to avoid any demonstration of respect; Gerkow, however, with a broad smile of silly complacency stepped forward:

"Your excellency," he said in German, and addressing the Austrian, "I have the honour of congratulating you . . ." And he bowed, scraping first one foot and then the other, like a schoolboy learning to dance. The war-councillor looked stern, but he was struck by the simplicity of Gerkow's broad, stupid smile, and could not refuse to listen.

"I have the honour of congratulating you," Gerkow repeated. "General Mack has arrived, safe and sound all but a slight cut here," and he raised his hand to his head with a triumphant expression. The general frowned and turned away:

"Good Heavens, what an idiot!" he exclaimed and went on.

Nesvitsky, quite enchanted threw his arms round Prince Andrew, but he, paler than ever, pushed him roughly aside and turned to Gerkow. The painful excitement produced by seeing Mack, by hearing his news, and by his own reflections on the situation of the Russian army, at last found an outlet over this ill-timed jest.

"If you, sir," he said in cutting tones, and his chin trembled, "choose to set up for a buffoon, I, of course, cannot prevent it; but I warn you that if you ever again venture to play the fool so grossly in my presence, I will give you a lesson in manners."

Nesvitsky and Gerkow, astounded at this outbreak, looked at each other in silence.

"What do you mean? I congratulated him, that was all," said Gerkow.

"I am not in jest—hold your tongue," said Bolkonsky, and taking Nesvitsky's arm he walked off; Gerkow found nothing to answer.

"Come, come; what ails you?" said Nesvitsky, wishing to soothe him.

"What ails me? Don't you understand? Are we officers in the service of our czar and country, proud of success and miserable at defeat, or are we hired servants who take no interest in our master's concerns? Forty thousand men killed, our ally's army cut to pieces . . . and can you see anything to jest at!" And he spoke the last words excitedly, and in French, as if that would give them added weight. "It is all very well for an empty-headed fellow like that Gerkow, of whom you have made a friend, but not for you, not for you. It is sport for a street-boy perhaps. . . ."

Noticing that Gerkow could hear what he was saying, he paused to see if he would answer, but the lieutenant turned on his heel and left the corridor.

BEFORE TILSIT

CHAPTER XXXIII

THE Pavlograd Regiment of Hussars was encamped at about two miles from Braunau. The squadron in which Nicholas Rostow was *junker* was quartered in the village of Saltzeneck, and the best house in the place had been given up to the officer in command: Captain Denissow, known in the division as Vaska Denissow. Since joining his regiment Rostow had always shared his captain's quarters. On this particular day, the 11th of October, when at headquarters everything was in utter confusion in consequence of Mack's defeat, the squadron was leading its regular camp life just as usual. Dennissow, who had been gambling all night, had not come in when Rostow, in his subaltern's uniform came riding home from his early morning's duty of seeking and distributing forage. He pulled up at the front steps, and throwing up his right leg with boyish agility, he stood for a moment in the stirrup as though he regretted having to dismount; then he sprang to the ground and called the orderly, who hurried forward to hold his horse:

"Here, Bonedareneko, walk him about for a little while," he said, with the good-natured familiarity which comes naturally to kindly souls when they are happy.

"All right, your excellency," said the man, a native of Little Russia.

"Mind, walk him about well."

Another soldier had run up at the same time, but Bonedareneko had seized the horse's bridle; it was clear that the *junker* paid well and was worth serving. Rostow, after patting his steed, stopped on the steps to admire him.

"He will make a fine horse!" he said to himself; then picking up his sabre, he went in, jingling his spurs as he walked.

The German to whom the house belonged was visible, in a flannel shirt and cotton night-cap, at the door of his stable, where he was turning over the manure-heap with a pitchfork. His face lighted up with a jolly smile as he saw Rostow.

"Good day, good day," he said, returning his bow with evident pleasure.

"At work already!" said Rostow, smiling too. "Hurrah for Austria! Hurrah for the Russians! Hurrah for the Emperor Alexander!" he added. These were the German's favourite watchwords. The man came towards him, waved

129

his cotton night-cap in the air with a laugh, and shouted: "Hurrah for all the world!"

Rostow repeated his cry; and yet they had no reason for all this vehement rejoicing, neither the Austrian, who was cleaning his stable, nor Rostow who had had far to ride with his fatigue-party. When they had thus given free vent to their fraternal feelings, the good man returned to his work, and Rostow went indoors.

"Where is your master?" he asked Lavrouchka, Denissow's servant, a cunning rascal, whose character was well known in the regiment.

"He has not been in since last evening; he has been losing most likely," replied Lavrouchka. "I know him well; when he has won he comes in early to boast of it; when he does not come in all night it is because he is out of luck, and then he is in a devil of a temper. Are you ready for coffee?"

"Yes—and make haste."

In ten minutes the man brought the coffee.

"He is coming," he said, "look out for the shell."

Denissow, in fact, now made his appearance. He was a little man, with a flushed face, bright black eyes, and black hair and moustache, in great disorder. His pelisse was unfastened, his wide trousers hardly held up, and his shako was stuck on the back of his head. He came in looking gloomy and tired, hanging his head.

"Lavrouchka," he called out angrily. "Here, idiot, take this off."

"Well, I am taking it off!"

"What, you are up!" he added, as he entered the room.

"And high time, too. I have been to find forage, and I have seen Fraulein Mathilda."

"Ha, ha! And I, my dear boy, have let myself in like a double-distilled dunce.—The devil's luck! A run against me from the moment when you left. . . . Here, bring me some tea," he called crossly. He spoke without pronouncing the "r." Then he smiled—a sort of snarl that showed his small square teeth, and pushed his fingers through his hair that stood all on end. "The devil himself drove me to the Rat's hole"—the Rat was a nickname given to one of the officers. "Just fancy, I had not a card—not one. . . ."

And Denissow, after knocking the ashes out of his pipe, flung it on the floor, where it broke into a hundred pieces. He paused for half a second, looking at Rostow with a merry twinkle in his bright black eyes. "If there were any women here! But there is nothing to do but to drink! . . . When shall we get to fighting? . . . Hallo! Who is there?" he called out, hearing a noise of heavy boots and spurs outside the door, with a respectful little cough.

"The quartermaster," Lavrouchka announced.

"It is a bad job!" said Denissow, and he flung his purse, containing a few gold pieces, across to Rostow. "Just be so good as to count what is left, would you; and then put my purse under my pillow." And he went out.

Rostow amused himself with piling the gold pieces in little piles of the old and the new, while Denissow's voice was audible in the next room.

"Ah! Télianine, good morning; I ruined myself last night."

"Where?"

"At Bykow's."

"At the Rat's—I knew it," said a second voice, sweet and piping; and Lieutenant Télianine, another officer of the same company, came into the room where Rostow was sitting. Rostow hastily thrust the purse under Denissow's pillow, and shook the small damp hand that was offered him. Télianine had been dismissed from the Guards some little time before the campaign; his conduct was now blameless, but he was not liked. Rostow especially could neither conquer nor conceal his antipathy.

"Well, my young horseman, are you satisfied with my little Crow?" (the name of the horse he had sold to Rostow). Télianine never looked the man he addressed straight in the face; his eyes were always wandering from one object to another; "I saw you riding just now."

"He is a good horse," said Rostow, who was well aware that he had paid 700 roubles for a beast that was worth about half. "He is a little lame of the near foreleg."

"The hoof cracked perhaps; that is nothing; I can show you how to rivet it."

"Yes, show me."

"Oh; it is quite simple and no secret. You will thank me for that horse, I am sure."

"I will have him brought round," said Rostow to get rid of Télianine, and he went away.

In the outer room Denissow, seated on the ground with his legs crossed and a pipe in his mouth, was listening to the quartermaster's report. As Rostow came through he made a face, and

131

pointing with his thumb over his shoulder with an expression of disgust: "I do not like that fellow," he said, regardless of the presence of his inferior. Rostow shrugged his shoulders as much as to say: "Nor I either, but what is to be done!"

Having given his orders he returned to Télianine, who stood idly rubbing his little white hands.

"To think that some faces should be so strangely antipathetic!" thought Rostow.

"Well, have you sent for the horse?" asked Télianine, looking about him with an indifferent stare.

"He will be here in a minute."

"Very well—I came only to ask Denissow whether he had received to-day's orders—have you, Denissow?"

"Not yet. Where are you going?"

"I am going to show our young friend how to shoe a horse."

They went off together and Télianine, having done the job, presently returned to his own quarters.

Denissow, sitting at a table with a bottle of vodka and a large sausage before him, was writing, his pen creaking and spluttering on the paper, when Rostow came in; he looked up with a gloomy gaze.

"I am writing to her. . . ." and resting his elbow on the table, without laying down his pen, he poured forth in speech the gist of his letter, as if he were only too glad of an opportunity of saying aloud all he wanted to write:

"You see, my dear fellow, a man does not live, he is only torpid, when he is not in love. We are creatures of dust, but when we love we are gods, we are pure again as on the first day of creation! . . . Who is there? Send him to the devil, I have no time. . . ."

But Lavrouchka came up to him quite coolly.

"It is nobody," he said. "Only the quartermaster, who is come for the money as you told him."

Denissow controlled an impatient gesture.

"It is a bad job," he growled. "I say, Rostow, how much is there in my purse?"

"Seven new pieces and three old ones."

"A bad job! What are you about, standing there like a post? Go and fetch the quartermaster."

"Denissow, let me beg you to take some of my money," cried Rostow, colouring. "You know I have plenty."

"I do not like borrowing of my friends—I cannot bear it."

"If you do not treat me as a comrade I shall be seriously hurt; I have plenty I assure you," repeated Rostow.

"No, I tell you. . . ."

Denissow went to his bed to find the purse.

"Where have you hidden it?"

"Under the bottom pillow."

"It is not here." And Denissow tossed both pillows on to the floor.

"It is very odd!"

"You must have thrown it out, stop a minute," said Rostow, shaking the pillows and throwing back the bed clothes . . . "Not here! Can I have forgotten it? No. I am sure I did not, for I remember thinking that you kept it under your pillow as if it were a treasure. I certainly put it there; where can it be?" he added turning to Lavrouchka.

"It must be where you put it, for I have not been in."

"I tell you it is not where I put it."

"It is the old story. You always forget where you have put a thing. Look in your pockets."

"No, no, I tell you; I said that to myself about the treasure. I perfectly remember putting it there."

Lavrouchka entirely unmade the bed, looked everywhere, hunted every corner, and at last stood still in the middle of the room with his hands spread out, at his wits' end. Denissow, who had been watching him in silence, now turned to Rostow.

"Come," he said, "have done with this fooling."

Rostow, feeling his friend's stern gaze, looked up at him, but immediately looked down. His face crimsoned, and he breathed hard.

"Nobody has been in here but the lieutenant and you two," said Lavrouchka, "so it must be here."

"Very well, then, helpless idiot, stir, search, hunt!" cried Denissow, red with anger, and threatening the man with his fist. "It has to be found, or I will give you a horsewhipping —I will horsewhip you all."

Rostow buttoned up his jacket, tightened his belt, and took up his cap.

"Find it, I tell you," Denissow went on, shaking the man, and pushing him hard against the wall.

"Let him go, Denissow; I know who has taken it." And Rostow, still looking at the floor, made his way towards the door.

Denissow, suddenly understanding what he meant, seized his hand.

"What nonsense!" he exclaimed; the veins in his throat and forehead stood out like cords. "You are out of your mind I believe. I will flay this rascal, and the purse will be found."

"I know who has taken it," Rostow repeated in a choked voice.

"And I forbid you, I tell you . . .!" cried Denissow.

Rostow wrenched himself free from his grasp.

"Do you not understand?" he said, looking straight into his eyes. "Do you not understand what you are saying? No one has been here but myself, so if it is not he—the other—it must be . . ." and he rushed out of the room without finishing his sentence.

"Devil take you and all the rest! . . ."

These were the last words Rostow heard; a few minutes later he reached Télianine's lodgings.

"My master is out," said the servant, "he is gone to head-quarters. Has anything happened?" he added, seeing the young man's disturbed look.

"No, nothing."

"You have only just missed him."

Rostow, without going indoors, mounted his horse and rode to headquarters, which was at about three versts from Saltzeneck; there was a little eating-house there where the officers were wont to meet. At the door he saw Télianine's horse tied up; the lieutenant was at table in an inner room, with a plate of sausages and a bottle of wine before him.

"You too, youngster!" he said, smiling and raising his brows.

"Yes—" said Rostow, with an effort, and he sat down at a neighbouring table. In the room were two Germans and a Russian officer.

No one was talking; the only sound was the chink of knives. When he had finished his breakfast, Télianine drew a long purse out of his pocket, slipped up the rings between his white fingers, which turned up at the tips, took out a gold coin, and offered it to the waiter.

"Make haste," he said. The coin he gave was a new one.

"Allow me to look at that purse," said Rostow, in a low voice, and Télianine, whose eyes were wandering as usual, handed it to him.

"It is pretty, is it not?" he said, turning paler. "Look at it."

Rostow glanced from the purse to the lieutenant.

"All that money will be left at Vienna if we ever get there, for here, in these wretched little holes, there is nothing to spend one's money on," said Télianine, with forced gaiety. "Give it back to me, I am going." Rostow said nothing. "Are you not going to have some breakfast? The food here is pretty good; but, come, give it back . . ." and he put out his hand and took hold of the purse.

Rostow let go and the lieutenant slipped it quietly into the pocket of his trousers; he raised his brows with a devil-may-care expression, and his lips parted as though he would say: "Yes, it is my purse; it goes into my pocket as a matter of course, and no one can have anything to say to that. . . ."

"Well!" he said aloud, and their eyes met with a flash.

"Come this way," said Rostow, drawing Télianine into the window. "This money is Denissow's. You took it," he whispered in his ear.

"What! How dare you?" But these broken words were evidently nothing more than a desperate appeal and prayer for pardon. They dissipated the last doubts that weighed with fearful oppression on Rostow's soul. He felt joy at the immense relief, but at the same time deep pity for the hapless wretch. But once begun the matter had to be carried through.

"There are other men here, God knows what they may fancy," murmured Télianine, taking up his cap, and going towards an empty room beyond, "we must come to some explanation."

"I knew it, and can prove it," answered Rostow. The guilty man's pale and terrified face was convulsed; his eyes wandered right and left, but still gazed at the floor; he dared not raise them. Some hoarse and inarticulate noises broke from him: "I entreat you, count . . . do not ruin me; here is the money, take it. My father is old, my mother. . . ."

He threw the purse on to the table. Rostow took possession of it, and went to the door without looking back at Télianine; but on the threshold he turned round and returned.

"Good God!" he said, in a tone of anguish, and there were tears in his eyes. "How could you do it?"

"Count. . . ." And Télianine came towards him.

"Do not touch me," exclaimed Rostow, drawing back. "Well, if you are in want of it, take it—here." He flung down the purse and ran out of the room.

CHAPTER XXXIV

THAT same evening an animated conversation took place in Denissow's room, among the officers of the squadron.

"You ought to make an apology to the colonel, I tell you," said Captain Kirsten, the second-in-command; he had iron-grey hair, an enormous moustache, strongly-marked features, and deeply wrinkled; he had twice been degraded to the ranks for affairs of honour, but had always succeeded in recovering his commission.

"I will allow no one to say that I lie!" cried Rostow, his face flushed while he trembled with excitement. "He said I had lied, and I told him it was he that had lied, and there the matter rests. They may put me on extra duty every day, or place me under arrest; but as to an apology that is another matter, for if the colonel thinks it beneath him to give me satisfaction. . . ."

"Come, come, listen to me," said Kirsten, interrupting him in his bass tones as he coolly stroked his long moustache. "You told him before several officers that one of their fellow-officers had committed a theft?"

"It was not my fault that there happened to be witnesses. I was wrong so far, perhaps, for I am not diplomatic; it was for that very reason that I joined the Hussars, believing that such superfine discretion would not be needed—and then he gives me the lie direct! Well then, let him answer for it."

"That is all very fine; no one doubts your courage, but that is not the question. Just ask Denissow if a subaltern like you can demand satisfaction of the colonel of your regiment."

Denissow sat, sullenly gnawing his moustache and taking no part in the discussion, but he shook his head in negation to Kirsten's question.

"You spoke to the colonel of this piece of rascality before other officers? Then Bogdanitch (they called the colonel Bogdanitch) was quite right in calling you to order."

"He did not call me to order. He said I was not speaking the truth."

"Just so, and you talked all sorts of nonsense in reply, so you owe him an apology."

"Certainly not."

"I did not expect this from you," said the captain gravely, "for you are in the wrong, not merely as regards him, but as regards all the regiment. If you had only taken time to reflect, if you had asked advice before acting—but no, you broke out at once and before other officers. What could the colonel do but put the man you accused on his trial; it was bringing disgrace on his regiment and putting it to shame for a miserable rascal. This in your eyes would have been justice, but we do not see it in that light, and Bogdanitch was quite right to say you were not speaking the truth. You are aggrieved, but it is your own fault; you sought the quarrel; and now that everyone wants to hush the matter up you insist on noising it abroad—and your self-conceit will not allow you to make an apology to such an old and respected officer as our colonel! Much you care, I suppose? It is nothing to you that the regiment should be disgraced"—and Kirsten's voice shook a little. "You have only been in the regiment a short while . . . It's nothing to you if they say 'There are thieves among the Pavlograd officers!' But it is a great deal to us if it is said that there are thieves in the Pavlograd Hussars!—What do you say, Denissow?"

Denissow, motionless and silent, looked up now and then at Rostow.

"Your silly pride won't allow you to apologise, but we old soldiers," Kirsten went on, "who have grown up with the regiment and hope to die in it, we have its honour at heart, and Bogdanitch knows it. It is wrong, quite wrong; you may be angry if you choose, I have never minced the truth to anyone."

"He is right, damn it all!" cried Denissow. "Well, Rostow, what next?"

Rostow, turning red and white, looked from one to the other.

"No, indeed, gentlemen, do not suppose—do not think me capable . . . I have the honour of the regiment at heart too, and I will prove it, and the honour of our flag . . . Yes, I was wrong, altogether wrong; what more can I say?" and the tears started to his eyes.

"Well done, count," said Kirsten, patting him on the shoulder with his big hand.

"I told you so," said Denissow, "his heart is in the right place."

"Yes, that is right; well done, count," repeated the old soldier, giving the boy his title in acknowledgment of his candour. "Come, go and offer your apologies."

"Gentlemen, I will do anything you like, and never say

another word about the matter; but as to apologising, it is impossible, I do assure you. I should look like a schoolboy begging to be let off."

Denissow burst out laughing. "So much the worse for you! Bogdanitch is not forgiving, and you will pay dear for your obstinacy," said Kirsten.

"I declare it is not obstinacy, I cannot explain my feeling . . . but I simply cannot do it."

"Very well, please yourself. And where is the miserable wretch? Where has he hidden himself?" asked Kirsten of Denissow.

"He is pretending to be ill; he is to be dismissed in to-morrow's orders."

"Well; it is an illness: there is no other way of accounting for it."

"Illness or not, he had better keep out of my way, I should kill him," said Denissow furiously.

At this instant Gerkow came in.

"You!" exclaimed the three men.

"We are off, gentlemen. Mack and his army have surrendered."

"Not true?"

"I saw him—saw him with my own eyes."

"What, you saw Mack alive, in the flesh?"

"And we are off? Let us have a bottle in honour of the news! But what brought you here?"

"I am in disgrace again, and all by reason of that wretched Mack. The Austrian general complained because I congratulated him on the arrival of his superior officer. But what is the matter with you, Rostow? You look as if you had just had a hot bath."

"Oh! my dear fellow, everything has been in such a mess here these last two days!"

The regimental aide-de-camp now came in and confirmed Gerkow's news. The regiment was to march next morning.

"So we are off, gentlemen! Thank God! no more idleness."

CHAPTER XXXV

KOUTOUZOW was falling back on Vienna after destroying the bridges over the Inn at Braunau and over the Traun at Lintz. In the course of the 23rd of October the troops crossed the river Enns. The baggage-waggons, artillery, and columns of infantry went through the little town of Enns, forming in files on each side of the bridge. It was a mild, showery autumn day. The wide landscape which spread before the eye from the heights where the Russian batteries had been posted to defend the bridge, was veiled now and again by a curtain of fine rain that filled the air with slanting lines, and then at intervals showed a more remote horizon when a gleam of sunshine lighted up the distance and made every object glitter as if it had been varnished. The little town, with its white, red - tiled houses, its cathedral, and its bridge—where, on both sides, the Russian army was pouring past in dense masses—was situated at the foot of the hill. In a reach formed by the junction of the Danube and the Enns lay boats, and, on an island, a country-house and park surrounded by the waters of the two rivers; on the rocky left shore of the Danube rose a mysterious distance of grassy mountains, with the ravines clothed with wild and impenetrable pine forests, beyond which the turrets of a convent were visible; and farther off still, on a height, the enemy's outposts could be discerned.

In front of the Russian battery the general in command of the rear division, attended by a staff-officer, was examining the position through a field-glass; a few paces off Nesvitsky, who had been sent to the rear by the commander-in-chief, sat perched on a gun-carriage and doing the honours of some little pies which he was offering to his fellow-officers with genuine Riga Kümmel to wash them down.[1] The Cossack who served him handed the flask and the canteen, while the officers crowded round, some kneeling and some squatting on the wet grass.

"Not a bad notion of the Austrian prince's, to build himself a house here! What a delightful situation! Well, gentlemen, have you lost your appetites?"

"Thank you very much, prince," said one of them, who greatly appreciated the pleasure of chatting with such a big-wig of the staff as Prince Nesvitsky. "Yes, the place is nice. We walked round the park and saw two deer, and what a fine house!"

[1] Kümmel is a liqueur flavoured with carraway, for which Riga is famous.

"Do you see, prince," said another, who being ashamed to eat another pie diverted his mind by studying the landscape, "look—our infantry have got in already. Down there, behind the village, in that little meadow, three men are dragging something along. They will soon clear the house out," he added, with an approving smile.

"Yes, that they will," said Nesvitsky, putting a pie into his large handsome mouth with its dewy lips. "For my part I want to get in there," he went on, pointing to the turrets of the convent on the hill and half closing his sparkling eyes. "That would be something like, gentlemen; come, confess! To have a chance of frightening those little nuns I would have given, faith! five years of my life. Italians, they say, and some of them quite young."

"And bored to death into the bargain," an officer, more bold than the rest, ventured to throw in.

Meanwhile the aide-de-camp was pointing out something to the general, who examined it carefully with his field-glass.

"Just so, just so!" said the general, with much annoyance, as he laid down the glass with a shrug. "They are going to fire on our men.—How they dawdle!"

Even with the naked eye the enemy's battery could be seen; a puff of light white smoke rose up, followed by a dull report, and the Russian troops hurried forward to cross the river. Nesvitsky rose, fanning himself, and went up to the general with a smile.

"Will not your excellency take something to eat?"

"It will not do," said the general, not answering his invitation, "our men are behindhand."

"Shall I run down to them?"

"Yes—do go—I wish you would;" and the general repeated the orders he had previously given: "Say that the hussars are to cross last and burn the bridge according to orders, and make sure that all the combustibles are properly placed."

"Very good," said Nesvitsky. He beckoned to the Cossack to bring up his horse and pack up his canteen, then he lightly lifted his large person into the saddle. "My word! but I will pay the little nuns a visit as I pass," he said to the other officers, as he spurred his horse along the winding path that led down the slope.

"Now then, captain," said the general, turning to the artillery officer: "Fire. Luck will guide the shell, you may have a little fun."

"Fire!"

"Forward to serve the guns!" shouted the officer, and in a moment the gunners contentedly quitted their bivouac fires to load the pieces.

"Number one!" and number one rushed madly into space. There was a deafening metallic roar; the shell sang as it flew over the heads of the Russians, and fell far in front of the foe; a light cloud of smoke showed where it had fallen and burst. Officers and soldiers grew gay at all the noise, and watched with intense interest the march of the Russians at the foot of the hill, and the advance of the enemy. Everything was plainly visible. The echoes of this single shot, and the broad radiance of the sun piercing its veil of clouds mingled in a common impression of life and stir.

CHAPTER XXXVI

Two of the enemy's balls had fallen across the bridge, and the bridge was now crowded. Half-way across, leaning against the parapet, stood Prince Nesvitsky, laughing and looking at his Cossack who, a few feet off, was holding the horses. He tried once or twice to proceed, but the soldiers and waggons forced him back against the parapet and again he smiled.

"Look out, there!" said the Cossack to a soldier who was driving a waggon, and pushing his way through the foot-soldiers that were packed round the wheels. "Look out! wait a minute, make way for the general."

But the driver, paying no heed whatever to the title of general, only shouted to the men who blocked the road.

"Now then lads to the left—look out!" But the "lads," shoulder to shoulder with their bayonets almost interlocked, marched on in a dense mass. Nesvitsky, looking down, could see the little, babbling waves of the rapid Enns, running after each other, mingling and breaking in white foam under the arch of the bridge; looking round him he saw the living waves of soldiers, in endless succession like those below—waves of shakos with their covers on, of knapsacks, of guns with their spiky bayonets, of faces with high cheek-bones—hollow-jawed, weary, but untroubled—and of trampling feet over the muddy beams of the wooden bridge. And now and then an officer in his cloak forced his way through the stream like the crests of white foam that rode on the waters of the Enns. Here and there, carried along by the mass of soldiers, came a dismounted hussar, an officer's servant, or a native of the town, like chips borne down by the current; or again, an officer's or a company's baggage-waggon covered with leather floated slowly past above the surface of the stream, like a log going down the river.

"It is like a flood through a broken dyke," said the Cossack, unable to stir. "I say—are there many more to come?"

"A million all but one!" retorted a wag in the ranks in a ragged cloak. Next to him came a solemn old soldier, who was saying to his neighbour:

"Now that he (the enemy) is going to warm the bridge, we cannot stop to scratch ourselves. . . ." And they passed on.

Behind them came a waggon, with a military servant fumbling under the tilt and exclaiming:

"Where the devil have they hidden the patches for boots?" and that, too, went on its way. After these came a party of soldiers in high spirits, having a few drops of brandy on their conscience.

"He drove the butt end of his gun well into his teeth, poor dear!" said one of them with a giggle; with his coat well tucked up, he gesticulated vehemently.

"It was well done for such a molly-coddle," said the other laughing; and they went by, so that Nesvitsky never knew who had been struck with the gun-stock, or to whom the word molly-coddle applied.

"What is the hurry? Because the enemy has burnt a charge of powder, they think they are all going to be killed!" growled a corporal.

"When I heard the ball whistle past me, do you know, old Daddy, I quite lost my breath; what a fright I was in! Good God!" said a young soldier, laughing from ear to ear, as if he were proud of having been frightened. And he, too, tramped by.

Next came a vehicle quite unlike any that had preceded it; it was a German cart with two horses, driven by a countryman and carrying a mountain of household goods. A fine piebald cow was tied up to follow it; on a heap of eiderdown quilts sat a woman nursing a baby, an old granny, and a handsome, rosy-cheeked girl. The party had no doubt obtained a special permit. The two young women had attracted the attention of the soldiers who, as the cart went slowly forward, did not spare their jests:

"Look at the great German sausage moving her goods . . ."

"I will buy the little wife if she is for sale," said another to the German who hurried on, scared and savage, with his head down.

"Isn't she smart? The little hussies! It would just suit you to lodge with them, Fédotow?"

"Where are you going?" asked an infantry officer, smiling up at the girl; he was eating an apple. The German signed that they none of them understood.

"Would you like it? You may have it," said the officer, handing the apple to the girl who took it and smiled. Every eye, including Nesvitsky's, was fixed on the women as they passed on; then came the endless files of soldiers again, with the same cross-fire of words till presently all once more came to a standstill, because a horse in one of the baggage-waggons had got entangled in the harness, a not uncommon accident on the down-slope of a bridge.

"Now then, what are we waiting for? What confusion! Don't push! Devil take it, don't hurry! It will be worse than this when they fire the timbers . . . That officer is being squeezed to a jelly!" These and other cries rose from the mass of soldiers, who looked at each other or pressed forward.

Suddenly Nesvitsky heard a sound that was new to his experience; something flew straight towards him—a large object, that fell into the water with a heavy splash.

"I say, look where that came to!" said a soldier very seriously, as he looked round.

"Well, it is to encourage us to trot a little faster," said another with some uneasiness. And Nesvitsky understood that the object in question was a shell.

"Here, Cossack! My horse!" he said. "And make way there, do you hear? Make way."

It was not without a struggle that he got on his horse, and made his way against the crowd shouting to the right and left. The soldiers squeezed a little closer to let him pass, but they were thrown back by the outer ranks, and his leg was caught and nipped as if in a vice.

"Nesvitsky, Nesvitsky, you are the very man. . . ."

Nesvitsky turned at this address spoken in a hoarse voice, and saw, only a few paces distant, but parted from him by the rolling sea of marching men, Vaska Denissow, with his hair on end, his cap pushed back and his pelisse flung over his shoulder.

"Just tell those creatures to make way for us," cried Denissow, brandishing his sheathed sabre in his small hand, which was as red as his face.

143

"Ah! Vaska," cried Nesvitsky, delighted. "What are you doing here?"

"The squadron cannot get through," said Denissow, spurring his fine black Arab, whose ears were quivering as he felt the accidental touch of the bayonets, while, flecked with foam, he pawed the beams of the bridge, and was ready to leave the parapet if his rider had not held him well in hand. "Good Heavens! What sheep—nothing on earth but sheep. Stand back, make way! You, beyond that waggon, stop!—stand still, or I will cut you all down!"

He drew his sabre, and flourished it ominously. The intimidated soldiers packed closer, and Denissow succeeded in joining Nesvitsky.

"So you are sober to-day?" said Nesvitsky.

"Have I time to drink? All day long the regiment is being sent this way and that. If we are to fight, well and good; let us fight. But, as it is, the devil only knows what we are at."

"And you are so elegant;" added Nesvitsky, glancing at his pelisse and at his horse's saddle-cloth. Denissow smiled, and pulling his perfumed handkerchief out of his sabretasche, he held it under his friend's nose.

"Of course," he said, "we may have to fight. Shaved, scented, teeth well brushed! . . ."

Nesvitsky's imposing presence, followed by his Cossack, and added to Denissow's determination, produced an effect. They got across the bridge, and now it was their turn to stop the infantry; Nesvitsky, having found the colonel, delivered the orders of which he was the bearer, and retraced his steps.

The road once cleared, Denissow took up his position at one end of the bridge, and lightly holding his stallion that stood pawing the ground, he watched his men pass by, four abreast, the officers leading the way: while the foot-soldiers drawn up and standing in the mud looked on at the proud, smart hussars with that ironical glance which is peculiar to soldiers of different corps when they happen to meet.

"Very pretty fellows! Fit to be seen in the Podnovinsky.[1] There is no work to be got out of them; they are all for show!"

"Now, you infantry-men, do not kick up the dust," said a hussar, laughing, as his horse splashed a foot-soldier with mud.

"Ah, if they had made you march two stages with a knapsack on your back, your gold lace would not look so new! . . .

[1] A promenade at Moscow.

144

A man! Why you are a bird on horseback," and the infantry-man wiped his face on his sleeve.

"Right you are, Zikine. If you were on horseback how nice you would look!" said a corporal to a poor little soldier bending under the weight of his kit.

"Put a stick between your legs and ride a cock-horse," retorted the hussar.

CHAPTER XXXVII

THE rest of the infantry were being rapidly hurried across; the waggons were safely over; the crush was less, and the last battalion were on the bridge. Denissow's hussars, drawn up on the other side, could not yet see the enemy, who were however plainly visible from the opposite heights. The horizon, from the plain below, was cut off by a hill about a third of a mile off. In the foreground was a plot of common where the Cossack outposts were moving about.

Suddenly, on the crown of the hill just above them, some artillery and blue capotes came into view—the French! The Cossack patrols trotted away down the hill. The officers and soldiers of Denissow's squadron, though they tried to talk of indifferent subjects and to look about them, could really think of nothing but of what was going forward on the opposite ridge, and involuntarily they looked up at the black objects that stood out against the sky, for they knew that those black objects were the foe.

It was now past noon, and the weather had cleared; a brilliant sun was moving westward over the Danube and the surrounding hills; the air was windless, rent now and then by the bugle call and the shouts of the enemy. There was nothing now between the squadron and the enemy but some patrols. An empty space of some three hundred fathoms divided them from each other. The enemy had ceased firing, and all the more one felt that ominous, insurmountable and indefinite barrier that lies between two hostile armies. "One step beyond the boundary on either side lies something that suggests that other boundary which divides the dead from the living. What is it? Is it the dread Unknown of suffering and death? What is it? just beyond that field, on the other side of that tree, of that roof on which the sun is shining? Who can tell, and who does

145

not wish to know? The soldier fears and yet longs to cross the line, for he feels that, sooner or later, he must, and that then he will know what lies beyond as surely as he will know what lies beyond this life. He is full of exuberant vigour, of health, spirits, and courage, and those around him are just as eager, just as brave as himself. . . ."

These are the sensations, if not actually the thoughts of every man in front of the enemy; and they lend a singular vividness, an indescribable distinctness and precision, to every incident that takes place during those few minutes.

A puff of smoke rose from the hill, and a ball whistled over the heads of the hussars. The officers, who had been talking in a knot, returned each to his post; the men pulled their horses into line. Perfect silence reigned in the ranks, and every eye was turned from the foe in front to the officer in command, watching for the word of command. A second and third ball came singing through the air; they were evidently aimed at them, but they flew too far, and were lost beyond and behind the squadron. The men never looked round, but as the long-drawn whistle passed over them they held their breath and rose slightly in their stirrups, and each one, without turning his head, cast a side glance at his neighbour to see what effect it had on him. From Denissow down to the bugler every face showed a slight quiver of the lips and chin, betraying an internal spasm of excitement and irritation. The quartermaster, a surly-looking fellow, looked at the men as though he were intending to punish them. A young subaltern, named Mironow, bent his head under each ball; Rostow, posted on the left, and sitting his sleek "Crow," looked as happy as a schoolboy who feels sure of distinguishing himself in a public examination before a crowded audience. He looked round at his comrades radiant and fearless, as if to call them to witness that he was cool under the enemy's fire; but even on his face an involuntary frown was graven by this new and solemn experience.

"Who is that bowing? Hallo, Mironow, that will not do—look at me!" cried Denissow, who was too restless to keep quiet, and was trotting his horse up and down the line. The little man looked just the same as usual, snub-nosed and black-haired. He grasped the hilt of his drawn sword in his small, hairy, strong hand with its short fingers: it was the Denissow of every day—or rather of every evening after emptying two bottles. His face was rather ruddier than usual; he tossed back his curly head as a bird does after drinking, he spurred his Arab unmercifully, he galloped down to the left flank, and, in a hoarse voice, ordered the men to see to the loading of their pistols. Then he turned to meet Kirsten, who came riding up on a heavy, peaceable-looking mare.

"What, what?" said the captain, grave as usual, but with a bright light in his eyes. "What, what! We shall not come to blows, you will see. We shall retire."

"The devil only knows what they are at," growled Denissow. "Ah! Rostow!'" he exclaimed, catching sight of the *junker's* smiling face. "So you are at the fête!"

Rostow felt perfectly happy. At this instant a general was seen on the bridge. Denissow rushed forward.

"Your excellency, let us attack them; I will upset them completely."

"Attack them indeed!" said the general, frowning, as if to get rid of a troublesome fly. "What are you doing here? The scouts are retiring. Take your men back."

The first and second squadrons of horse recrossed the bridge, got beyond the enemy's range, and rode up the hill without losing a single man. The last of the Cossacks retired from the bank.

On the hither side of the bridge Colonel Karl Bogdanitch Schubert came up with Dennisow's division, but did not go beyond a foot-pace, riding almost by the side of Rostow; however, he took no notice of the young subaltern whom he now saw for the first time since their dispute about Télianine. Rostow, riding in his place, felt himself in the power of his superior, towards whom he felt he was guilty; he never took his eyes off his broad back, his red neck, and his light, short hair. He thought that Bogdanitch was pretending not to see him, that he wanted to test his courage—and the lad drew himself up and looked boldly about him. He fancied that Bogdanitch kept close to him on purpose to make a display of his coolness; or again, that in order to revenge himself on Rostow, he would send the division into some desperate skirmish, and he dreamed of his coming, after it was over, to meet him— Rostow, wounded, and to give him his hand in token of reconciliation.

Gerkow, whose square shoulders were well known to the Pavlograd Hussars, now came up to the colonel. Gerkow was sent by the staff-officers; he had not stayed in the regiment, he was not such a fool, as he had said to himself, when by getting attached to any staff he could have nothing to do and a chance for promotion. He had, in fact, succeeded in getting himself appointed as an orderly to Prince Bagration, and he now had come to deliver a message from the colonel of the rear division to his former chief.

"Colonel," he said with gloomy gravity to Rostow's enemy, "you are ordered to stop and burn the bridge."

"Who?—I am ordered!" said the colonel surlily.

"Ah! that I do not know. Who? You are ordered!" replied Gerkow with no less gravity. "The prince merely sent me to tell you to bring back your hussars and burn the bridge."

At this moment a staff-officer rode up, bringing the same orders and followed closely by Prince Nesvitsky, riding as hard as his Cossack horse would carry him.

"Colonel, I told you that you were to burn the bridge. . . . There has been some misunderstanding.—Everyone has lost his head and makes some blunder!"

The colonel quite deliberately made his men halt, and then turning to Nesvitsky he said:

"You only mentioned combustibles; as to burning the bridge, you never told me a word about it."

"What, little father, I never told you?" said Nesvitsky, taking off his cap and pushing his fingers through his hair, which was quite wet with perspiration; "when I told about the combustibles?"

"In the first place I am not your 'little father,'[1] I would have you to know, though you are a staff-officer; and you did not tell me to burn the bridge. I know my duty, and I am in the habit of carrying out the orders I receive to the letter. You said: 'The bridge is to be burnt,' and how could I guess, unless by direct inspiration, who was to burn it?"

"It is always the way," said Nesvitsky, with an impatient gesture. "And you—what are you doing here?" he added to Gerkow.

"I came on the same errand. Why you are as wet as a sponge! Shall I wring you out?"

"What you said to me," the colonel began once more in an offended tone.

"Now, colonel, make haste," cried the officer, interrupting him, "or the enemy will fire into us."

Bogdanitch looked from one to another with a scowl.

---

[1] "Little father," "little uncle," "my children," and other words of endearment are terms of respectful familiarity often used in Russia. On the other hand formal titles of address, such as "highness," or "your nobleness," and so on, are freely given to superiors in rank, irrespective of birth.

He fancied that in order to revenge himself he would send the division into some desperate skirmish

"I will burn the bridge," he said solemnly, as if to testify that he would do his duty in spite of all the difficulties placed in his way. He struck his spurs into his horse with two vigorous kicks of his long shanks, as though the poor beast were in fault, and rode forward to order Denissow's squadron to go back to the bridge.

"That is it," thought Rostow, "he wants to try me."

His heart beat quicker and his temples throbbed. "Well, he may look! He shall see if I am a coward!"

The pinched look that the men's eager faces had worn when the balls whistled past came back again now. Rostow never took his eyes off his enemy the colonel, trying to read in his face some confirmation of his suspicions; but the colonel never even looked at him, but sat inspecting the men with stern solemnity.

He gave the word of command.

"Quick, quick," he heard them shout close to him. The men's swords caught in the harness and their spurs rattled as they dismounted, not knowing what was coming next. Some crossed themselves. Rostow had ceased to gaze at his chief; he had no time for that. His fear was lest he should be left behind; his hand shook as he flung his horse's reins to the soldier who was to be left in charge, and he could hear his heart beat. Denissow, leaning back, said a few words to him as he rode past. Rostow saw nothing but the hussars who were running on, hampered by their spurs, and their sabres clattering by their sides.

"A litter!" shouted a voice behind him, but the words conveyed no meaning to Rostow. He ran on to keep in front, but as he put his foot on the bridge he stumbled and fell with his hands in the deep greasy mud. The others got ahead.

"On both sides, captain!" shouted the colonel, who was sitting on his horse, not far from the bridge, with a radiant and triumphant expression.

Rostow scrambled up and wiped his hands on his cavalry trousers; then, glancing at Bogdanitch, he again rushed forward, thinking that the farther he went the better it would be; but the colonel called him back without recognising him.

"Who is that running on the middle of the bridge? *Junker*, come back!" he cried in a rage, and he added to Denissow, who, out of sheer foolhardiness, had ridden on to the bridge:

"Why do you run such a risk, captain? Get off your horse sir!"

Denissow, turning in his saddle, muttered: "He has always some fault to find."

Meanwhile Nesvitsky, Gerkow and the staff-officer, being out of range of the enemy's fire, were watching first the little group of men in dark-green laced jackets, yellow shakos, and blue trousers who were bustling about the bridge, and then the blue coats that were marching onwards followed by horses and artillery.

Will they burn the bridge or will they not? Which will gain the day—they, or the French who are firing into them? Every man in that vast mass of troops concentrated on a single spot is asking himself this question as he watches the progress of the scene, now lighted up by the setting sun.

"Oh!" cried Nesvitsky. "Our hussars will catch it now; they are within range of the guns."

"He took too many men," said the staff-officer.

"To be sure he did; a couple of steady fellows would have done the job," said Nesvitsky.

"Oh! Your excellency, how can you say so!" remarked Gerkow, still watching the hussars. He spoke with that odd mixture of simplicity and irony which left it doubtful whether or no he were in earnest. "What an idea! Two men; how should the rest of us get our crosses or the ribbon at our button-holes? . . . Let them catch it—then the regiment will be reported, and everyone may hope to gain his order: the colonel knows very well what he is about."

"Here comes the grape-shot!" said the officer, pointing to the enemy's guns, which were being unlimbered. A cloud of smoke rose into the air, then a second and a third almost together, and the fourth shot went off by the time the report of the first had reached them.

"Oh!" groaned Nesvitsky, as if he felt some acute and sudden pain, and he grasped his companion's hand.

"Look—one fell—one is down . . ."

"Two, I think."

"If I were a monarch, I would never make war!" cried Nesvitsky, turning away.

The French pieces were briskly served, and smoke rose again from several points. The blue-coated infantry rushed down towards the bridge, on which the grape-shot fell rattling like a storm of hail. But Nesvitsky saw no more. A thick smoke shrouded the scene; the Russians had succeeded in setting the timbers in a blaze, and the French batteries were no longer firing to prevent them, but because the guns were loaded and there was no one else to fire at.

The French had delivered three charges by the time the hussars had got back to their horses; two had been badly directed and had gone over the heads of the Russians, but the third was sent into the middle of a party of soldiers and three were hit.

Rostow, thinking of nothing but his relations with the colonel, had stopped short in the middle of the bridge, not knowing what to do. There was no one there to cut down. Cutting down had always been his one idea of a battle, and as he had no wisp of burning straw like the others he could not help to set the bridge on fire. So there he stood, undecided, when he heard a noise on the timbers like a pelt of walnuts, and a hussar fell near him with a groan. Rostow ran to help; men were called up with litters, and the wounded man was raised and placed upon one.

"Oh! let me be, for God's sake!" moaned the soldier; but they took him up and carried him away.

Rostow turned away; he gazed into the distance; he might have been trying to discover something there; then he looked at the river, at the sky, at the sun. How blue the sky looked, how deep and restful! How bright and glorious was the setting sun! How the waves of the Danube danced and sparkled in the distance! And far away in the background lay the blue mountains with their mysterious recesses, the convent, the pine forests veiled by a transparent haze. . . . All was peace there —peace and happiness!

"Ah! if I might have lived there I could have wished for nothing more," thought the lad—"nothing!—I feel so much that could have made me happy, in myself and in that bright sun . . . while here . . . shrieks of pain, terror, confusion, hurry . . . more cries and everyone pushes back, and I am running like the rest . . . and there it is again: Death! close over me! One second more perhaps, and I shall never again see the sun, and the river, and the mountains! . . ."

The sun was veiled in clouds; they were carrying litters past him. The dread of death and of a litter, the love of life and sunshine, were all mixed up in one feeling of anguish and pain.

"Oh, God in heaven keep me, pardon me, and protect me!" murmured Rostow.

The hussars were remounting, the voices round him became less confused, the litters had vanished.

"Well, my boy, so you have smelt powder?" said Denissow, close to his ear.

"It is all over, and I am a coward—a coward!" thought Rostow as he sprang into his saddle.

"That was grape-shot?" he asked Denissow.

"I believe you, and a heavy peppering too! We have worked pretty hard. It was a hot corner! An attack is one thing, but to be fired at as a mark is another . . ."

And Denissow moved off to join a group formed of Nesvitsky and his companions.

"I believe no one noticed it," Rostow said to himself; and this was the truth, for each one knew the feeling of the first "baptism of fire."

"By Heaven, there will be a splendid despatch! Perhaps they will give me a lieutenancy!" said Gerkow.

"Let the prince know that I fired the bridge," said the colonel triumphantly.

"And if he asks about the loss?"

"Not worth mentioning," said Bogdanitch in his heavy bass. "Two hussars wounded and one stark dead," and he did not try to conceal a satisfied smile; he even seemed to smack his lips over so happy a phrase as "stark dead."

CHAPTER XXXVIII

KOUTOUZOW'S 35,000 men, opposed by a French army of 100,000 men with Bonaparte at their head, met with hostile feeling throughout the country. They had lost confidence in their allies, they lacked provisions, and now, being forced into action under circumstances unforeseen by any rules of war, they were beating a retreat in all haste. They made their way down the Danube, stopping to show fight to the enemy whom they kept off by skirmishes in the rear, though they fought no more than was necessary to effect their retreat without losing their baggage. Engagements had taken place at Lambach, at Amstetten and at Melck; but, notwithstanding the steadiness and courage of the Russians, to which their adversaries did full justice, it was not the less a retreat—a genuine retreat. The Austrians who had escaped at the surrender of Ulm and joined Koutouzow at Braunau had again left him with his enfeebled forces. It was no longer possible to defend Vienna, for, in spite of the scheme of offensive warfare so scientifically elaborated by the new-fangled laws of strategy and placed in Koutouzow's hands by the Austrian supreme council of war, his only, almost impossible, chance of not sacrificing his army, as Mack had done, was to effect a junction with the troops arriving from Russia.

It was on the 28th of October that Koutouzow crossed to the left bank of the Danube, and there halted for the first time, having placed the river between himself and the main body of the French army; on the 30th he attacked Mortier, who was also on the left bank, and defeated him. The trophies of this battle were two guns, a flag, and two generals; for the first time in a retreat of fifteen days the Russians made a stand, harried the French, and remained masters of the field. In spite of the exhausted state of the troops, whose clothes were in rags, and who had lost a third of their number in stragglers, sick, dead, and wounded, who had been left behind with a letter from Koutouzow recommending them to the tender mercies of their foes—in spite of many more wounded in this fight, which the regular hospitals and the houses turned into infirmaries could not receive—in spite of every adverse circumstance, this pause at Krems and the defeat of Mortier had done much to raise the spirits of the Russians. News of the most satisfactory character, but absolutely untrue, was rumoured in the army and among the staff: Russian reinforcements were near at hand: the Austrians had won a victory: Bonaparte had beaten a hasty retreat.

During this fight Prince Andrew had been by the side of the Austrian General Schmidt when he was killed; he himself had had his horse wounded under him and his hand grazed by a bullet. As a mark of favour the commander-in-chief despatched him to bear the news of the victory to Brünn, where the Imperial Court had been in residence ever since the menacing proximity of the French army had forced it to quit Vienna. In the evening after the battle Bolkonsky, excited but not weary— for, in spite of his delicate appearance, he could bear physical fatigue better than many robust men—mounted his horse to carry Doktourow's report to Koutouzow, who at once sent him off with it as his special messenger, a certain augury of speedy promotion.

The night was moonless, the sky starry, the road was visible as a black riband through the snow which had been falling during the fight. Prince Andrew, carried swiftly along in his post-chaise, thought over all the impressions and feelings that filled his brain: his reminiscences of the struggle, the happy effect that the news of their victory would produce, and the parting words of Koutouzow and of his fellow-officers. He was exulting with the secret joy of a man who, after long patience, sees the first glimmer of the success he has longed for. Whenever he shut his eyes the rattle of musketry and thunder of cannon filled his ears, mixed up with the rumble of the wheels and the details of the battle. He dreamed that the Russians were flying, that he himself was killed; then he woke to the happy consciousness that nothing of this had happened, that, on the contrary, it was the French who had run away. Again he remembered all the details of the battle, his own cool courage, and having grown calm, dozed off once more. A brilliant morning at length dawned on this gloomy night; the snow was melting, the horses flew along, on each side of the way spread woods, fields, and villages.

At one of the post-houses he came up with a party of wounded; the officer-in-command was abusing a soldier. The wounded men, unwashed, pale, and bandaged in bloodstained rags, were crowded into large waggons and jolted over the stony road; some were talking (he could hear the Russian language), others eating their dry bread, while the worst gazed with calm and frank curiosity after the courier as he outstripped them. Prince Andrew stopped his chaise and asked the men when and where they had been wounded.

"The day before yesterday, by the Danube," replied one of them, and Prince Andrew took out his purse and gave them three gold pieces:

"For all of them," he said to an officer who came up. "Get well again, my lads, there will be plenty to do yet."

"What is the news, sir?" asked the officer, evidently glad to find someone to speak to.

"Good news! Go on!" he cried to the driver.

It was quite dark by the time Prince Andrew got into Brünn, and found himself among tall houses, shops lighted up, street lamps, and handsome carriages rattling over the pavement— the busy atmosphere, in short, of a large town which is so delightful to a soldier fresh from camp-life. Notwithstanding his hurried journey and an almost sleepless night, he felt even more excited than on the day before. As he approached the palace his eyes sparkled with fevered fire and his thoughts flowed with astonishing clearness. Every detail of the battle

The troops were exhausted, the clothes of the men in rags

had come out of the confusion and presented itself to his mind in the form of a concise statement—such a report as he could give to the Emperor Francis. He could hear the questions that would be asked and his own replies. He felt sure that he should at once be led into the emperor's presence; but at the main entrance of the palace he was met by a functionary in civil uniform, who, recognising that he was a special messenger, led him to another door, saying: "The passage to the right, if you please, *Hochgeboren* (High born sir); you will there find the aide-de-camp on duty who will take you to the minister."

The said aide-de-camp begged Prince Andrew to wait, and went to inform the minister of war of his arrival. He returned in a few minutes, and, bowing with marked politeness, he made the prince lead the way along the corridor and showed him into the room where the minister was sitting. The Austrian's excessive politeness seemed to imply that he wished to raise a barrier between them that would protect him against every approach to familiarity on the part of the Russian aide-de-camp. As Prince Andrew came more immediately within reach of the high official he gradually lost the exultant feeling he had so lately enjoyed, and acquired a vivid impression of offended pride, and this impression, in spite of himself, by degrees took the shape of a vague sort of contempt. His alert brain at once suggested all the causes that might give him a right to scorn this aide-de-camp and this minister: "It seems to them a mighty easy thing to win a victory, but they never smelt powder. . . ." This was the burden of his thoughts, and he went into the minister's room with an affectation of deliberateness. His smouldering annoyance increased when he saw the minister, who sat bending over a table, between two wax-candles, supporting his bald head with its fringe of grey hair on his hand, and taking notes; he paid no attention to his visitor.

"Take this," he said to the aide-de-camp, holding out papers and not noticing Bolkonsky.

"Either," said the prince to himself, "of all the business he has in hand the progress of Koutouzow's army is what interests him least, or he wants to make me think so."

When he had carefully arranged his papers with great precision the minister looked up, showing a face full of intelligence, character, and determination; but as he addressed Prince Andrew he put on the regulation manner—a silly, smiling affectation which becomes habitual to a man who daily receives a great number of applicants.

"From General Prince Koutouzow!—Good news, I hope? An engagement with Mortier . . . a victory; it was high time!" and he read the despatch. "Ah! Mein Gott, Schmidt! what a loss, what a loss!" he said in German; and when he had read it he laid it on the table and looked up anxiously, "What a sad loss! You say the action was decisive? But Mortier was not taken. . . ." Then, after a moment's silence, he added: "I am very glad to have your good news, though we have paid dear for it by the death of Schmidt. His majesty will no doubt wish to see you, but not just now. I am much obliged to you. Now go and rest, and to-morrow try to be on the spot as his majesty comes in from parade: but I will send you word. Good-day. His majesty will certainly want to see you," he added, as he bowed him out.

As Prince Andrew quitted the palace he felt as though he had left behind him, in the hands of a supercilious minister and his obsequious aide-de-camp, all the excitement and triumph of the victory. His frame of mind had totally changed, and the battle now wore the aspect only of a distant—a very distant memory.

CHAPTER XXXIX

PRINCE ANDREW betook himself to the house of a Russian acquaintance at Brünn, the diplomat Bilibine. "My dear prince, nothing could give me greater pleasure," said his friend, coming out to meet him. "Franz, take the prince's luggage into my room," he added to the servant who had admitted his visitor. "You bring news of a victory, nothing could be better. For my part, I am not well, as you see."

After changing his dress Prince Andrew joined his friend in an elegant study, where he sat down to the dinner that had been got ready for him, while Bilibine sat by the fire. It was with great satisfaction that Prince Andrew found himself once more surrounded by the element of comfort and luxury to which he had been accustomed from his childhood, and of which he had lately so often felt the lack. It was pleasant, too, after his reception by the Austrian, to be able to talk, not, indeed, in Russian, for they spoke French, but with a Russian who might be supposed to share the very lively aversion felt for the Austrians at this juncture.

156

Bilibine was a man of about five-and-thirty, a bachelor, and familiar with Prince Andrew's circle of friends. Having known each other in St. Petersburg, they had been thrown together and had become intimate during Bolkonsky's sojourn at Vienna in Koutouzow's suite. Each was gifted with the qualities best fitted to insure him, in his own line, a rapid and brilliant career. Bilibine, though still a young man, was not young in diplomacy, for he had been an attaché from the age of sixteen; after serving at Paris and at Copenhagen, he had come to Vienna, where he held an important position. The chancellor and the Russian ambassador at Vienna both thought highly of his talents. He was by no means one of those gentlemen of the Foreign Office whose qualities are purely negative, and whose whole art consists in never compromising themselves and in speaking French; he loved work, and in spite of a certain natural indolence he had often been known to spend the whole night at the office. The matter in hand made no difference; what he cared for was not the *why* but the *how* of his work, and he took a special pleasure in drawing up with ingenious and elegant skill any kind of note, memorandum, or report. Besides doing such good service with his pen he had an acknowledged talent for conduct and appropriate speech in the highest circles of society.

Bilibine did not care for any conversation that did not afford the opportunity of saying something noteworthy, and of throwing in those brilliant and original touches, those subtle and keen remarks which, after being elaborated beforehand in the alembic of his mind, were so easy to remember that they remained graven on the hardest brain. Bilibine's sayings were passed on round Vienna drawing-rooms, and sometimes were not without influence on events.

His face was yellow, lean and worn, and furrowed with lines —lines that looked so elaborately washed that he had the wrinkled look of a washerwoman's fingers after long soaking; the expression of his face lay in the perpetual play of these lines. Sometimes it was his forehead that wrinkled, sometimes his eyebrows that were raised or knit, or again his cheeks that puckered. His deep-set eyes had always a gay, straightforward look.

"Well, tell me of your exploits."

Bolkonsky at once, with much modesty, told him the history of the battle and of his reception by the minister: "I and my news were made as welcome as a dog at a game of skittles."

Bilibine smiled, and his wrinkles relaxed.

"At the same time, my dear fellow," he said, gazing at

his nails, while his left eye puckered into a wink, "and notwithstanding the high estimation in which I hold the arms of orthodox Russia, your victory does not seem to be a remarkably victorious one."

He spoke French, only using a Russian word now and then, when he wished to give it scornful emphasis. "You fell with all your weight on that wretched Mortier, who had only one division, and Mortier has slipped between your fingers. . . . Where is the victory?"

"But without boasting, you will allow that it is better than Ulm?"

"Why could you not take one marshal prisoner, one single marshal?"

"Because events do not fall out according to our wishes, and cannot be arranged beforehand like a review. We hoped to put them to rout by seven in the morning, and we did not succeed in doing it till five in the evening."

"And why did you not succeed at seven in the morning? You ought to have succeeded."

"Why did you not give Napoleon a hint through some diplomatist that he had better abandon Genoa?" retorted Prince Andrew, in the same mocking tone.

"Oh, yes! I know!" said Bilibine. "As you sit by your fire you say to yourself that it is easy enough to capture marshals, and so it is—but you have not done it. Why not? You need not wonder if the emperor and King Franz, following the minister's lead, are not overwhelmingly grateful over this victory. I myself, a humble secretary to the Russian embassy, feel no irresistible impulse to air my enthusiasm by giving my servant a thaler and leave to take a walk in the Prater with his 'Liebchen'—but I forgot, there is no Prater here." He looked at Prince Andrew, and his brow suddenly smoothed.

"Now, my friend, it is my turn to ask why," said Bolkonsky, "for, to tell you the truth, I do not understand it all. Perhaps there are some subtle diplomatic mysteries at work which are beyond my feeble comprehension, but it is all dark to me. Mack has sacrificed a whole army, while the Archdukes Charles and Ferdinand give no sign of life and commit blunder after blunder. Koutouzow is the only man who honestly gains a battle, and breaks the French spell, and the minister of war does not even care to know the details of the fight."

"That is the very reason. Don't you see, my good fellow? Hurrah for the czar, for Russia, for the Faith! That is all very fine, but what do we care—I mean, what does the Court of Austria care—for all your victories? Bring us news now of the success of an archduke—Charles or Ferdinand—they are, as you know, one as good as the other—a victory, let us say, even over a company of Bonaparte's firemen, and it will be quite another thing; it will be proclaimed with a flourish of trumpets, but this can only annoy us. What! Archduke Charles does nothing, Archduke Ferdinand covers himself with disgrace; you leave Vienna defenceless, as much as to say God is on our side, but as for you and your capital, God help you! Then you let Schmidt get killed—a general beloved by us—and you congratulate us on a victory? You could not invent anything more aggravating if you tried. It is as if you had done it on purpose—on purpose! Besides, even if you had really achieved a brilliant success, even if Archduke Charles could do the same on his side, would that make any difference in the march of events? It is too late now; Vienna is occupied by the French."

"Occupied! Vienna is occupied?"

"Not merely occupied, but Bonaparte is at Schoenbrunn, and our amiable friend Count Urbna is going there to take his orders."

Partly from fatigue, and partly from the confused impressions left on his mind by his journey and his reception by the minister, but chiefly from the effects of his dinner, Bolkonsky was beginning to be aware that he but dimly understood the gravity of this news.

"Count Lichtenfeld, whom I saw this morning," Bilibine went on, "showed me a letter containing full details of a review of the French troops at Vienna, with an account of Prince Murat and all his following. You see your victory is nothing much to boast of, and you are not likely to be hailed as a deliverer."

"As far as I am concerned, I assure you I do not care a straw," said Prince Andrew, who was beginning to understand how trivial the affair of Krems was in comparison with such an event as the occupation of the capital. "What—Vienna occupied! And what about the famous *tête-de-pont*, and Prince Auersperg, who was charged with the defence of Vienna?"

"Prince Auersperg is on this side of the river to defend us, and does it pretty badly, while Vienna is on the other side. As to the bridge, it has not been taken, and I hope will not be. It is undermined, and is to be blown up in case of need. But for that we should be in the wilds of Bohemia by this time, and you and your army would have a hot half-hour between two fires."

"But this does not mean, after all, that the campaign is at an end?" said Prince Andrew.

"Well, I believe it is. And our bigwigs here think the same, but dare not say so. It will be just as I foretold from the first. Your skirmish at Diernstein will not settle the question! No, nor gunpowder—but those who invented gunpowder." This was one of Bilibine's sayings; he paused over it for a second, then, with a satisfied look, he went on: "The upshot of it all depends on the meeting of the czar and the King of Prussia at Berlin. If Prussia joins the alliance Austria's hand is forced: there must be war; if not there is nothing for it, they have only to fix a place of rendezvous where they can arrange the preliminaries of a second Campo-Formio."

"What a genius he is! What luck he has!" exclaimed Bolkonsky, striking the table with his fist.

"Bonaparte?" said Bilibine, knitting his brows—the forerunner of a witticism. "Buonaparte!" he added, accenting the *u*. "But it strikes me that now he sits at Schoenbrunn dictating to Austria, he may be let off that *u*; I, at any rate, shall drop it and call him Bonaparte for the future."

"But come, joking apart, do you really think the campaign is over?"

"This is what I think: Austria for once has been the dupe in the game; this she is not used to, and she will be revenged. She has been the dupe; in the first place her provinces are ruined—orthodox Russia, is, as you know, the very devil at pillage—her army destroyed, and her capital taken, and all for the gratification of the King of Sardinia; in the second place, my dear fellow, between ourselves, I feel instinctively that we are being taken in. There is a scent in the air of treaties and peace with France—a secret peace, separately agreed on."

"Impossible! It would be too base!"

"Those who live will learn," replied Bilibine, again smoothing his brow to intimate that the discussion was at an end.

Prince Andrew went to bed, a room had been made ready for him. Once stretched between the fresh white sheets, with his head on downy and perfumed pillows, he soon felt, in spite of himself, that the battle of which he had brought the news was swiftly fading to a vague remembrance. He could think of nothing now but the Prussian alliance, of the treachery of Austria, of Bonaparte's latest triumph, of the review on the morrow, and of his own reception by the emperor. He closed his eyes, but instantly the roar of cannon, musketry, and wheels sounded in his ears. He saw files of soldiers coming down the hill-sides, he heard the French firing, he was there, in the front with Schmidt by his side, bullets whistling merrily about him; and his heart thrilled and swelled with a wild exultation in life, such as he had never felt since his boyhood. He woke with a start.

"Yes, yes, that was how it was!" Then he went to sleep again with a childlike smile, and slept as only youth can sleep.

CHAPTER XL

HE did not wake till late next morning, and collecting his thoughts, he remembered, in the first place, that he was to wait on the Emperor Francis; all the impressions of the previous evening—his interview with the minister, the extravagant politeness of the aide-de-camp, and his conversation with Bilibine crowded into his mind. He put on full-dress uniform which he had not worn for a long time, to go to the palace; and, with his hand in a sling, in the best possible spirits, he went into his host's sitting-room where four young attachés were already met, and among them Hippolyte Kouraguine, secretary now to the Russian embassy, who was known to Bolkonsky. The others, introduced by Bilibine, were young men of fashion, rich, well-dressed, and pleasure-loving, who here, as at Vienna, formed a select little circle, of which Bilibine was the leader and of whom he always spoke as "our set." This circle, consisting almost exclusively of diplomats, had other interests at heart besides war and politics. The doings of the fashionable world, their intimacies with certain ladies, and their duties in attendance filled up all their leisure hours. These young gentlemen did Prince Andrew the exceptional honour of receiving him eagerly, and as one of themselves; out of politeness, and as a preliminary, they condescended to ask a few questions with regard to the army and the battle, after which they went on with their gay and discursive talk, brightened by light sallies and superficial criticism.

"And this is the crowning detail!" cried one of them who was relating the discomfiture of a colleague, "the chancellor actually told him to his face that his transfer to London was promotion, and that he ought to regard it so. Can you see his face when he heard it?"

"And I, gentlemen, must inform against Kouraguine, that terrible Don Juan who will profit by the misfortune of others."

Prince Hippolyte had spread himself out in an arm-chair, with his legs thrown over the arms: "Come, come! What are you talking about!" he exclaimed, laughing.

Groans of "Oh, Don Juan! Oh, wily serpent!" from several of the party.

"You probably are not aware, Bolkonsky," Bilibine went on, "that all the atrocities committed by the French army—by the Russian army, I was on the point of saying—are as nothing in comparison with the ravages committed by this man among the ladies here."

"Woman is the helpmeet for man," said Prince Hippolyte, looking at his feet through his eyeglass. Bilibine and the "set" went into fits of laughter; and Prince Andrew perceived that this youth, of whom he had, it must be owned, so nearly been jealous, was the butt of his circle.

"I must draw out this Kouraguine for your benefit," whispered Bilibine. "He is delightful when he discourses on politics: you will see the important manner . . ." and turning to Hippolyte, with a furrowed brow, he began a discussion on the events of the day, which at once attracted general attention.

"The Berlin Cabinet cannot put forward any idea of an alliance," Hippolyte began, looking round at his audience with great composure, "without expressing, as in its last note, you know, you understand . . . And then, if his majesty the emperor maintains his principles, our alliance . . . stop, I have not done. . . ." He seized Prince Andrew by the hand—"I fancy that intervention will prove stronger than non-intervention, and the non-receipt of our despatch of the 28th of November cannot be charged as intentional; that is how it will all end," and he released Prince Andrew.

"Demosthenes, I know thee by the pebble hidden in thy mouth of gold!" cried Bilibine, who had shaken his mane of hair over his forehead, as it seemed to give more emphatic expression to his satisfaction. Hippolyte laughed louder and longer than any of them, but he did not appear quite comfortable in spite of this forced laugh which distorted his generally apathetic countenance.

"Now, gentlemen," said Bilibine, "Bolkonsky is my guest, and I am bent on his enjoying all the pleasures of Brünn so far as lies in my power. If we were at Vienna there would be far less difficulty, but here, in this horrible Moravian hole, I claim your assistance; we must do the honours of Brünn. If you will undertake the theatres, I will find him society. As for you, Hippolyte, you are best qualified in the matter of the fair sex."

"He must be introduced to the bewitching Amelia," said one of the "set," and he kissed the tips of his fingers.

"To be sure; the bloodthirsty soldier must be taught to feel some human sentiments," said Bilibine.

"Unfortunately," said Bolkonsky, "I cannot take advantage of your kind plans on my behalf. It is time for me to go out."

"Why, where are you going?"

"I am going to the emperor."

"Oh! indeed—then good-bye for the present."

"Yes, good-bye for the present; but come back and dine with us, and we will look after you."

"Listen to me," said Bilibine, in the ante-room, as he went to see Bolkonsky out. "In speaking to the emperor, you had better say a few words in praise of the commissariat, of the distribution of food, and the arrangement of halting-places."

"I could not even if I wished it," said Bolkonsky.

"Well, at any rate, talk for both; he has a passion for personal receptions, and never has a word to say, as you will find out."

CHAPTER XLI

PRINCE ANDREW found a place among the Austrian officers, where the emperor was to pass, and achieved the honour of attracting his notice and receiving a bow of his long narrow head. The ceremony ended, the aide-de-camp he had seen the day before came to express to Bolkonsky his majesty's wish to speak with him. The Emperor Francis received him standing, in his private room, and Prince Andrew was struck by his awkwardness; he blushed and hesitated and did not seem to know how to express himself.

"Tell me at what hour the battle began," he said hurriedly, and Prince Andrew, having replied to this question, was immediately required to answer a number of others no less childish.

"How is Koutouzow? When did he leave Krems?" and so forth.

The emperor's sole idea seemed to be to ask questions; the answers did not interest him.

"What o'clock was it when the fighting began?"

"I cannot tell your majesty the precise time when it began in front, for I was at Diernstein. There the first collison took place at six in the evening," said Bolkonsky eagerly, for he was prepared to give the emperor an exact description of all he had seen and heard.

The emperor, however, interrupted him by asking with a smile:

"How many miles is it?"

"From whence and to where, sire?"

"From Diernstein to Krems."

"Three and a half, sire."

"And have the French abandoned the left bank?"

"According to the reports of our scouts the French all crossed on rafts that same night."

"Is there plenty of forage at Krems?"

"Not enough. . . .'

The emperor again interrupted him. "At what hour was General Schmidt killed?"

"It must have been about seven."

"At seven? How sad—how very sad!"

And then, thanking him, he dismissed him. Prince Andrew retired and found himself immediately surrounded by courtiers. Every one had a polite speech ready, and he was the centre of approving glances; the aide-de-camp reproached him for not taking up his abode at the palace, and even offered him his own rooms. The minister of war complimented him on having won the order of Maria Theresa, of the third class, which his majesty had just conferred on him; the empress's chamberlain begged him to visit her majesty; the grand duchess also wished to see him, it would seem. He did not know what to say, and stood trying to collect his ideas, when the Russian ambassador touched him on the shoulder and led him away to a window to talk to him.

Notwithstanding Bilibine's evil augury, the news of which Bolkonsky was the bearer was hailed with joy; a *Te Deum* was to be performed by command. Koutouzow had received the grand cross of the order of Maria Theresa, and all the army was rewarded. Invitations showered in on Prince Andrew, who was obliged to devote his whole day to paying visits to the Austrian magnates.

Having fulfilled this duty, he was returning to Bilibine's at about five in the afternoon, composing in his head, as he went along, a letter, which he intended sending to his father, with an account of the battle and his journey to Brünn, when he perceived in front of the steps a britzska, more than half full of luggage and packages, while Franz, Bilibine's servant, was struggling to cram in another trunk. Prince Andrew had gone into a bookseller's on his way, and was rather late.

"What is the meaning of this?" he asked.

"Oh, your excellency," cried Franz. "We are moving on again: the villain is at our heels once more."

"But, what on earth is happening?" repeated Bolkonsky, just as Bilibine came out to meet him; his face, though always calm, betrayed some agitation.

"This is a pretty business this crossing of the bridge at Thabor. There was not a blow struck!" Prince Andrew did not understand.

"Where on earth have you come from that you do not know what every cab-driver knows?"

"I have come last from the archduchess'—I heard nothing there."

"And have you not seen that everyone is packing up?"

"I have seen nothing. But what is it all about after all?" he added impatiently.

"What is it about? Why, the French have crossed the bridge that Auersperg was to defend; he did not blow it up; Murat is coming full gallop down upon Brünn, and if they are not here to-day they will be to-morrow."

"Here! But if the bridge was mined why was it not blown up?"

"Why, indeed? I might as well ask you, for no one will ever know, not even Bonaparte himself."

Bolkonsky shrugged his shoulders: "But if they have crossed the bridge the army is lost, it will be cut off."

"There lies the hitch. . . . Listen to the facts: The French had occupied Vienna—very good; but the next day—that is to say, yesterday evening—Marshals Murat, Lannes, and Belliard [1] set out on horseback to reconnoitre the bridge. Mark, three Gascons! 'Gentlemen,' says one of them, 'the bridge, as you know, is mined, and countermined, it is guarded by that famous *tête-de-pont* of which we have heard so much, and 15,000 men are charged to fire it and stop our way; but, as it would suit our emperor and master far better to have possession, let

[1] This is a mistake on the part of the author: Belliard was never a marshal.

us go, us three, and take possession of it.' 'Let us go,' say the other two. So away they go; they take the bridge, they cross it, and all the army cross after them—across the Danube, straight down on us and on you, and cut off your communications."

"Do not jest," said Prince Andrew, "the subject is a grave one, and a sad one."

At the same time, in spite of the distress he ought to have felt at this disastrous news, he was conscious of a secret satisfaction. Since he had heard of the desperate situation of the Russian army he believed himself destined to extricate it: this was to be his Toulon; this would distinguish him above the obscure crowd of his fellow-soldiers and open his path to glory. Even while listening to Bilibine he pictured himself arriving at the camp, giving his advice at the council of war, and suggesting some plan—the only plan for saving the army. Of course, the execution would be entrusted to him.

"I am not jesting," said Bilibine, "nothing could be more true or more serious. These gentlemen rode on to the bridge and waved their white handkerchiefs, they asserted that an armistice had been agreed to, that they were going to confer with Prince Auersperg; the officer on guard let them pass into the outworks. They crammed him with no end of rhodomontade: the war was at an end, the Emperor Francis was going to receive Bonaparte, they were going to see Prince Auersperg—and fifty more monstrous lies. The officer sends for Auersperg. The Frenchmen embrace their enemies, laugh and joke with them, ride a-cock-horse on the cannon, and meanwhile a French battalion quietly walks across the bridge and throws all the combustibles into the water. . . . Then—at last, the lieutenant-general, our dearly-beloved Prince Auersperg von Nautern, appears on the scene: 'Our dear enemy, the flower of Austrian soldiery, hero of the Turkish campaigns, a truce to our hostility; we may now shake hands, the Emperor Napoleon is dying to make the acquaintance of Prince Auersperg!' In short, these gentlemen, who are not Gascons for nothing, threw so much dust in his eyes with their fine words, while he, on his part, was so supremely honoured by this sudden intimacy with the French marshals, and so dazzled by Murat's cloak and ostrich-feathers, that he was blinded by the blaze, and quite forgot that he ought to be blazing at them." And, in spite of the vehemence of his narrative, Bilibine paused that Prince Andrew might have time to take in the joke.

"The French soldiers make their way into the *tête-de-pont*, spike the guns, and the bridge is theirs. But the best of the story is to come," he went on, trusting to his delight in telling it to qualify his excitement. "The sergeant in charge of the cannon which was to give the signal for exploding the mine, seeing the French approach, was on the point of firing when Lannes stopped his hand. The sergeant, who was sharper than his master, went up to Auersperg and said, 'Prince, you are sold—the French are down on us!'—or to that effect. Murat, fearing that if the man said anything more the job would fall through, turned to Auersperg, like the Gascon that he is, and pretended to be surprised. 'Is this your boasted Austrian discipline?' said he. 'What!' do you allow an inferior to address you in this way?' What a stroke of genius! Prince Auersperg, who piques himself on such matters, had the sergeant put under arrest.

"Don't you think that a nice story altogether, this taking of the bridge? It is not stupidity nor cowardice . . ."

"But treason, perhaps!" cried Prince Andrew, thinking of the grey-coats, the gunpowder reek, the cannonade, and the glory he was expecting.

"Not a bit of it. This puts the Court into a very silly position. No, it is neither treason, nor stupidity, nor cowardice; it is Ulm over again, it is . . ." he paused for a word, "it is Mack—we are *Macked*," he said, quite pleased at having hit on a perfectly new word which was certain to be repeated; his brow unbent, and he contemplated his nails with a smile on his lips.

"Where are you going?" he asked Prince Andrew.

"I am off."

"Where to?"

"Why, to join the army, of course."

"But you meant to stay two days longer?"

"Impossible, I must start immediately."

And Bolkonsky gave his orders and went to his own room.

"My dear fellow," said Bilibine, following him, "what are you going for?"

Prince Andrew looked at him inquiringly, but did not answer.

"Yes, I say what are you going for? I know, you fancy it is your duty to join the army now that it is in peril; I quite understand; it is heroic."

"Not in the very least."

"Yes, you are a philosopher—but be so completely. If you only look at things from the other side you will see that your first duty, on the contrary, is to keep out of danger. Let those who are good for nothing else throw themselves into the gulf; you have had no orders to return, and we, here, will not let you go. You may as well remain and follow us whither our miserable fate may lead us. We are bound for Olmütz, they say—it is a pretty town, and we shall have a pleasant drive there in my carriage."

"For God's sake, Bilibine, cease jesting."

"I am speaking quite seriously, and as your friend. Judge for yourself: Why should you go when you can stop here? One of two things is certain: either peace will be concluded before you can reach the army, or there will be a mad stampede and you will share the disgrace of Koutouzow's army. . . ." And Bilibine looked satisfied that the dilemma was final.

"I cannot judge," said Bolkonsky coldly. And at the bottom of his heart the thought was: "I must go to save the army."

"My dear fellow, you are a hero," said Bilibine.

CHAPTER XLII

AFTER taking leave of the minister of war, Bolkonsky set out that night, intending to join the army, but not knowing where to find it, and fearing that he might fall into the hands of the French. All the Court was preparing to quit Brünn, and the heavy baggage was already forwarded to Olmütz.

On reaching the neighbourhood of Etzelsdorf, Prince Andrew unexpectedly came across the Russian army, which was retiring in great haste and utter disorder; vehicles crowded the road and intercepted the progress of his chaise. The prince, having begged a horse and a man from the captain of the Cossacks, though he was tired and almost dying of hunger, soon outrode the baggage-waggons, in search of the commander-in-chief. Dismal reports reached his ears as he went on, and the confusion all round him only too surely confirmed them.

"As for the Russian troops, which England's gold has tempted from the ends of the earth, they shall meet the same fate" (the fate of Ulm), Napoleon had said in his general orders at the beginning of the campaign. These words suddenly recurred to Bolkonsky's memory, and filled him with admiration for the man's genius, mingled with a sense of wounded pride, across which flashed a hope of imminent revenge. "And if there is nothing left but to die?" thought he. "Well, I shall know how to die, and no worse than another, if I must."

He looked round him contemptuously at the endless files of carts, of artillery, getting entangled and locked, and farther back more and still more carts and carriages of every form trying to outstrip each other, running foul of each other, and getting in each other's way as they toiled, three or four deep, along the miry road. In front and behind, as far as the ear could catch a sound, there was a rumbling of the wheels of vehicles and gun-carriages, the tramp of horses, the shouts of drivers urging on their teams, and the oaths of the soldiers, of servants and of officers. Lying by the road were the carcasses of dead horses, some of them flayed already, and broken-down carts; soldiers of every description poured out of the various villages, dragging sheep, fowls, hay, and sacks crammed to the brim; on every slope, up or down, the crowd packed closer, and their various cries mingled in an incessant roar. Some soldiers, up to the knees in mud, held up the wheels of the gun-carriages and waggons; whips whistled and cracked, horses slipped, harness gave way, and the shouting seemed enough to burst the men's lungs. The officers superintending the march rode backwards and forwards; their harassed faces betrayed their inability to restore order, and the word of command was lost in the general uproar of this sea of humanity.

"This is our precious orthodox army!" said Bolkonsky to himself, recalling Bilibine's words, as he made his way up to a waggon to inquire for the commander-in-chief.

An oddly-shaped vehicle, drawn by one horse, a sort of cross between a cart, a phaeton, and a gig, evidently of make-shift construction from heterogeneous materials, caught his eye. It was a little way behind him, driven by a soldier, and under the hood and leather apron a woman could be seen wrapped in a heap of shawls. Just as he was about to make his inquiry, Prince Andrew was interrupted by this woman's shrieks of despair. The officer who rode at the head of this file of vehicles was beating her driver for trying to get ahead of the others, and the blows of his whip lashed the apron of the carriage. Seeing Prince Andrew, the woman put out her head, and signing to him energetically with her hand, she called out: "Monsieur l'aide-de-camp, pity, mercy, defend me, protect me! What will become of me? I am the doctor's wife, the doctor of the

169

7th Chasseurs—and they will not let us go on. We have been
left behind and have lost our party!"

"Keep back, or I will thrash you as flat as a pancake," cried
the officer, fairly in a rage. "Keep back, you and your hussy!"

"Protect me! Monsieur l'aide-de-camp. What are they
going to do with me?"

"Let this carriage pass, do you not see that there is a woman
in it?" said Andrew to the officer, who looked at him but made
no answer, and turned to the soldier once more.

"So I should think, let you pass indeed! Back, I say,
hound!"

"Let him pass, I tell you," repeated Prince Andrew.

"And who are you, I should like to know," said the officer,
insolently. "Are you the master here? I am master here,
and you, do you hear? you there, go back, I say, or I will
beat you as flat as a pancake . . ." the expression had evidently
hit his fancy.

"Well done, the little aide-de-camp!" said a voice in the
crowd.

The officer had reached the pitch of rage when a man is
hardly aware of his actions, and Prince Andrew, felt for an
instant, that his interference was verging on the ridiculous—
the thing that, above all others, he dreaded; but his instinct
suddenly surging up, he too felt an impulse of mad rage; he went
up to the officer and said with a look of fury, raising his whip:

"Have the goodness to make way."

The officer hastened to draw back, though with an angry
gesture: "It always is the fault of the staff-officers; they make
all the confusion and turmoil," he muttered. "Very well,
go your own way."

Prince Andrew also made haste; without looking at the
surgeon's wife—who called him her deliverer, but thinking
over the details of this absurd scene, he cantered on to the
village where, as he was told, the commander-in-chief was to be
found. There he got off his horse, intending to get something to
eat, and to rest a little while, so as to recover from the painful,
agitation of his mind and feelings. "It is a troop of banditti,
it is not an army," he was saying to himself, when a familiar
voice called him by name. He turned round, and at a little
window perceived Nesvitsky, who was munching something and
gesticulating energetically:

"Bolkonsky, don't you hear me? Come, here, come quickly."

He went into the house, where he found Nesvitsky, and

another aide-de-camp at breakfast; they hastened to inquire, with much alarm, whether he had brought any news.

"Where is that commander-in-chief?" asked Bolkonsky.

"There, in that house," said the aide-de-camp.

"Well, and is it true about the peace and capitulation?" asked Nesvitsky.

"You must tell me that, I know nothing about it. I have had the greatest difficulty in joining you."

"Ah! my dear fellow, what is going on is absolutely frightful —I cry *mea culpa*—we laughed at Mack, but our plight is worse than his. Sit down and eat some breakfast," added Nesvitsky.

"It is quite impossible, prince, that you should now be able to discover your baggage-waggon and effects. As to your man Peter, God knows what has become of him!"

"Where, then, are the headquarters?"

"We are to sleep at Znaïm."

"I," said Nesvitsky, "have loaded two horses with everything I most needed, and have had capital pack-saddles made which will stand even a journey in the mountain roads of Bohemia.—It is a bad business, my good friend. Are you ill? You are shivering, I fancy."

"No, there is nothing the matter with me," replied Prince Andrew. At that moment he recalled his meeting with the surgeon's wife, and the officer in command of the train. "And what is the commander-in-chief doing here?"

"I have no idea," replied Nesvitsky.

"And I have only one; which is that the whole business is deplorable," said Prince Andrew.

He went to see Koutouzow; as he went he noticed his carriage and the horses of his staff, tired out, and dead beat, surrounded by servants and Cossacks, all talking at the top of their voices. Koutouzow was sitting with Bagration and Weirother, the Austrian general, who now filled Schmidt's place. In the hall, little Koslovsky, looking wan from late hours, was sitting on his heels and dictating some instructions to a secretary, who hastily wrote them down, using a tub for a table. Koslovsky glanced up at the new-comer, but could not spare time to bow.

"Next line—have you written? The regiment of Kiew Grenadiers; the regiment of. . . ."

"Impossible to keep up with your highness," said the secretary in a cross tone.

At this moment the eager and dissatisfied voice of the

commander-in-chief was audible through the door, answered by another, which was quite unknown to Bolkonsky. The noisiness of the discussion, Koslovsky's indifference, the incivility of the weary amanuensis, evidently quite exhausted, this strange scene with the tub for a writing table close to the commander-in-chief, the uproarious laughter of the Cossacks just outside the window—all these details forced upon Prince Andrew's mind the reality of some grave disaster. He besieged the aide-de-camp with questions.

"Directly, prince," said the officer, "Bagration is in command of the troops."

"And the capitulation?"

"There is none; we are preparing for battle."

Just as Prince Andrew was about to enter the adjoining room, Koutouzow, with his aquiline nose and burly figure, appeared at the door. Prince Andrew was in the front of him, but the commander-in-chief looked at him without recognition; the vague expression of his one eye showed that he was so absorbed by anxiety and worry as to be totally absent-minded as to the outer world around him. "Is it done?" he asked Koslovsky.

"In a moment, your excellency."

Bagration had followed the commander-in-chief; he was a small wiry man, still young, and his face, which was Oriental in character, commanded notice by its calm and firm expression.

"Your excellency. . . ." and Prince Andrew held out a packet to Koutouzow.

"Ah! from Vienna; very good, later on, later on . . ." He left the room with Bagration; and they went out and stood on the steps.

"Good-bye then, prince," he said to Bagration. "May the Lord have you in his keeping. Take my blessing on this great enterprise!"

His voice broke and his eyes were full of tears. He drew Bagration to him with his left hand, while with his right he made the sign of the cross—a gesture he was wont to make use of; then he offered him his cheek, but Bagration threw his arms round his neck.

"The Lord be with you!" said Koutouzow, and he got into his carriage. "Come with me," he added to Bolkonsky.

"Your excellency, I could wish to be of use here. If you would allow me to remain under the orders of Prince Bagration. . . ."

"Get in," said Koutouzow, seeing his hesitancy. "I, too, want good officers. If the tenth part of his division comes back to-morrow evening, we may thank God!" he added, as if speaking to himself.

Prince Andrew involuntarily looked round for a moment at Koutouzow's sightless eye and the scar on his temple, a double memorial of a Turkish bullet.

"Aye," said he to himself, "he has a right to talk so coolly of the death of so many men."

"That is the reason," he said aloud, "why I begged you to send me with them."

Koutouzow made no reply; he sat sunk in thought, and seemed to have forgotten what he had just said. Cradled on the cushions of his carriage, in five minutes he turned to Prince Andrew a passive face in which it would have been vain to look for any trace of emotion, and with a great deal of subtle irony he incited Bolkonsky to tell him the history of his interview with the emperor, the gossip of the Court as to the fight at Krems, and even questioned him about some ladies with whom they were both acquainted.

CHAPTER XLIII

On the 1st of November, Koutouzow had received information from one of his spies, which led him to believe that his army was in a position of almost checkmate. The French, said this reporter, after crossing the bridge, were marching on in considerable strength to intercept his junction with the reinforcements coming from Russia. If Koutouzow decided on remaining at Krems, Napoleon's 150,000 men would cut off his communications by surrounding his exhausted force of about 40,000, and he would be in the same predicament as Mack at Ulm; if, on the other hand, he abandoned his hold on the main road of communication with Russia, his only resource was to retreat, constantly defending his rear, into the barren and unknown highlands of Bohemia, giving up all hope of effecting a junction with Buchshoevden. If, finally, he made up his mind to fall back from Krems on Olmütz and meet the reinforcements, he ran the risk of being intercepted by the French, and forced to fight in the middle of his march, with all his baggage at his heels, against an enemy three times as strong, who could attack him on both flanks. This, however, was the alternative he accepted. He now heard that the French were making forced marches towards Znaïm, which was on the line of his retreat some 100 versts [1] ahead—to get there first meant a possibility of saving his army; to allow the French to beat him in this race would mean a certain disgrace, like that of Ulm, or a general disaster. But it was impossible to do this with a mass of 40,000 men; the road from Vienna to Znaïm was better and less circuitous than that Koutouzow had before him from Krems.

On hearing this news he had sent off Bagration across the hills with a vanguard of 4000 men to occupy the road from Vienna to Znaïm. Bagration was charged to effect this without a halt, and place himself with Vienna in front of him, and Znaïm behind; and if his good star prevailed, and he reached the spot first, he was to delay the enemy as long as he could, while Koutouzow and the main force made their way to Znaïm. Bagration having marched over thirty miles of mountainous country devoid of roads, through a dark and stormy night, losing a third of his men in stragglers, brought out his famished and ill-shod army at Hollabrünn, between Vienna and Znaïm, some few hours before the French had reached the spot.

To give Koutouzow the twenty-four hours' start which he needed to achieve his purpose, these 4000 men worn out with fatigue, were to keep the enemy busy and so save the army—it was obviously impossible. But capricious fortune made the impossible possible. The success of the trick by which the French had taken possession of the bridge at Vienna without drawing swords, suggested to Murat the idea of attempting a similar stroke with Koutouzow. When he met Bagration with his slender force he fancied that the whole Russian army was behind them, and being certain of crushing it as soon as his reinforcements should come up, he proposed an armistice for three days, during which both parties were to remain where they were. To make sure of its acceptance he asserted that preliminaries of peace were certainly under discussion, and that it was useless to shed blood. General Nostitz, an Austrian, who held the advanced posts, took his word for it, and by retiring, left Bagration exposed. Another emissary carried the same false assurance to the Russian camp. Bagration, however, replied that he could neither accept nor refuse any terms, that he must refer every-

[1] A verst is 3500 feet, about two-thirds of a mile.

174

thing to his commander-in-chief, to whom he would send an aide-de-camp.

This proposal was the salvation of the army; Koutouzow at once despatched his adjutant-general, Wintzengerode, to the enemy, charged, not merely to accept the armistice, but to discuss the terms of a capitulation. At the same time he sent off instructions to the rear to hurry on the army, as it was screened by Bagration's little force, which held its position unflinchingly in the face of eight times its own numbers. Koutouzow's anticipations were justified; his proposals bound him to nothing, but gained him precious time; Murat's blunder could not fail to become evident. When Bonaparte—who was still at Schoenbrünn, about sixteen miles from Hollabrünn—received Murat's despatch reporting the proposals for an armistice and a capitulation, he saw at once that the marshal had been duped, and he wrote to him as follows:

"To Prince Murat.
"*Schoenbrünn,* 25 Brumaire (16 Nov.), 1805.
[8 in the morning.]

"I cannot possibly find words to express my vexation. You command only the van and have no right to propose an armistice without my orders. You have made me lose the advantages of a whole campaign. Break the armistice at once and march on the enemy. Have it explained to him that the general who signed the capitulation had no right to do so, that no one has the right but the Emperor of Russia.

"If, after all, the Emperor of Russia should sign the agreement I would ratify it, but it is simply a trick. March in and destroy the Russian army. You are in a position to secure its baggage and artillery.

"The Russian aide-de-camp is a . . . Officers count for nothing when they have no powers, and this one had none. The Austrians were duped about the bridge at Vienna, but you have been duped by a Russian aide-de-camp.

"Napoleon."

The aide-de-camp who acted as courier with this fulminating letter rode like mad. Napoleon himself, fearing lest his easy prey should escape him, came up with all his Guards to give battle, while Bagration's 4000 men were contentedly lighting their fires, and warming and drying themselves for the first time in three days; cooking their porridge, and not one of them dreaming of the storm that was about to overwhelm them

CHAPTER XLIV

NAPOLEON'S aide-de-camp had not yet reached Murat when Prince Andrew, having extracted the permission he desired from Koutouzow, reached Grounth, where he found Bagration, at about four in the afternoon. No one there knew anything about the progress of affairs outside; they talked of peace without believing in it, and of a battle, but with no idea that it was imminent. Bagration welcomed Koutouzow's favourite aide-de-camp with every mark of distinction and kindness; he told him that they were certain to come to blows ere long, and offered him the choice of attaching himself to the commander's immediate following during the action, or of superintending the retreat of the rear, which was quite equally important.

"At the same time I do not expect an engagement to-day," he added, as if to set Prince Andrew's mind at ease, while he said to himself: "If he is only a young puppy sent to the front to win a medal he will do that just as well by keeping in the rear, but if he chooses to stick by me, so much the better; a brave officer is never one too many."

Prince Andrew gave no answer to either proposal, but begged Bagration's permission to go over the ground and see how the troops were placed that he might know where he was in case of need. The officer on duty with the detachment, a handsome and remarkably elegant man, with a large diamond on his forefinger, who spoke French readily but very badly, offered to guide him.

On all sides they saw officers, drenched to the skin, all searching for something, and soldiers dragging doors, palisades and benches.

"You see, prince, we cannot succeed in getting rid of fellows like those," said the officer, pointing to them and then to a vivandière's canteen. "The commanding officers are so weak; they allow them to collect here—I drove them all away this morning and the place is full again. One moment, excuse me, and I will clear them out."

"Let us go in," said Bolkonsky, "and I will get a bit of bread and cheese, I have had no time to eat."

"If you had told me I would have offered you some food."

They dismounted and went into the vivandière's tent, where a party of officers, looking weary but excited, were eating and drinking.

176

"For God's sake, gentlemen!" said Bolkonsky's companion, in a tone of emphatic reproof, which showed that it was not the first time he had spoken, "you know that the prince has forbidden you leaving your posts and assembling here. . . ." He turned to an artillery officer—a little man, very lean and slovenly, who had risen at their entrance with an awkward smile, having taken off his boots for the woman to get them dried. "You, too, Captain Touschine! Are you not ashamed of yourself? As an artillery officer you ought to set an example, and here you are with no boots; if the alarm should be sounded a pretty figure you would cut, barefoot. Come, gentlemen, you will have the goodness to return to your posts," he added, in a tone of command.

Prince Andrew could not help smiling as he looked at Touschine, who stood silent and smiling, and lifting first one foot and then the other, while his genial and intelligent eyes looked from one to another.

"The men say that it is more comfortable to go barefoot," replied Touschine humbly, trying to get out of his scrape by a laugh, but finding his sally ill-received, he looked uncomfortable.

"Back to your posts, gentlemen," repeated the staff-officer, doing all he could to keep his countenance.

Prince Andrew cast a parting glance at the artilleryman, whose comical individuality was of a peculiar type—anything rather than military, but curiously attractive.

Once outside the village, after passing and meeting soldiers and officers of every class, they saw on their left the entrenchments—earthworks of red clay—which the men were still busied in throwing up. Some battalions, in shirt sleeves in spite of a bitter north wind, were working like a swarm of ants. Having inspected these they galloped on and up the opposite slope. From the rising ground they could see the French.

"That is our battery over there, under our queer barefoot friend; we will go there, prince, it is our highest point, and we shall see better."

"A thousand thanks, but I can find my way alone," said Prince Andrew, to be rid of his escort. "Do not trouble yourself any further, I beg. . . ." And they parted.

At between six and seven miles from the French camp, on the road from Znaïm, which Bolkonsky had ridden over that morning, a scene of indescribable confusion was going on, and at Grounth the air seemed full of anxiety and unusual excitement· but here, much closer to the foe, he was glad to see the good order and confident feeling that prevailed. The soldiers, each in his grey capote, stood in well-formed ranks before the captain and sergeant-major, who were counting the men, laying a finger on each man's breast and making the last man of each little division hold up his hand. Some who had been told off to fetch wood and brushwood to build huts, were laughing and chatting; groups had gathered round the fires—some dressed, while some were half-stripped, drying their shirts, mending their boots or their coats, squatting round the kettles and the cooks. In one company the stew was ready, and the eager men watched the steam with greedy eyes, while a sergeant carried a basinfull to be tasted by the officer who sat on a log in front of his shanty.

The men of another and a luckier company—for they had not all a store of brandy—stood crowding round their sergeant, a broad-shouldered fellow marked with the smallpox, who poured for each a dram into the lid of his can, tilting his little barrel. The soldiers lifted it reverently to their lips, rolled it round in their mouths, wiped their lips on their sleeves and, after covering their cans again, went off in the best temper and spirits. They were all so cool that it was difficult to believe that the enemy were close by. They seemed to be resting in a quiet halting-place in their own country rather than on the eve of a struggle in which half of them perhaps would be left on the field. Prince Andrew rode past the regiment of Chasseurs and came to the serried ranks of the Kiew Grenadiers; these, though they had all their habitual martial neatness, were as peacefully employed as the rest; but he observed at a short distance from the taller hut of the officer in command, a knot of soldiers standing by a man who was stretched naked on the ground. Two held him down, two others whipped him on the back in regular time with thin, elastic canes. The victim cried out piteously, but a burly major, marching up and down in front of the detachment, took no heed of his howling and only said again and again: "It is a disgrace to a soldier to steal, a soldier must be honest and brave: if he robs his comrades it shows that he has no sense of honour, that he is a mean wretch—Go on! go on! . . ." And the switching and the howling continued.

A young officer who had just turned away his face, betraying some involuntary compassion, looked up in surprise at the aide-de-camp as he rode by.

Prince Andrew having reached the outposts inspected the position with care. The enemy's sharpshooters were parted from the Russians by a considerable space at each end of the line; but in the middle where the envoys had crossed in the morning, they were so near each other that the men could see each other's faces and exchange speech. Several inquisitive natives had mingled with the soldiers to examine this unknown and foreign foe, and though they were bidden again and again to quit the spot they remained as if nailed to it. The Russians were very soon tired of the amusement; they did not look at the French, but passed their time when on duty by cutting jokes on the new-comers.

Bolkonsky pulled up to study the enemy.

"Look, look!" cried one sentry to another, pointing to a third who had gone forward beyond the line and was carrying on a lively conversation with a French grenadier—"just see how he gabbles it out; the Frenchman cannot get a word in."

"What do you say to that, Siderow?"

"Stop—let me listen. The devil! how he goes at it!" said Siderow, who was supposed to speak French well.

The soldier they were admiring was Dologhow; he and his captain had come up from the left flank where their regiment was.

"Bravo, encore!" said the captain, leaning forward and trying not to lose a word, though it was all perfectly unintelligible to him. "Go on, not so fast! . . . What does he want?"

Dologhow, who had plunged into a hot discussion, made no reply. They were talking of the campaign: the Frenchman, mixing up the Russians with the Austrians, maintained that they had surrendered and abandoned Ulm, while Dologhow tried to prove to him that the Russians had beaten the French and had not given in: "And if we are told to clear you away from here we will do it," he added.

"You had better take care that when we go we do not take you with us, you and all your Cossacks," retorted the Frenchman, and his audience laughed.

"We will make you jump as Souvorow did," answered Dologhow.

"What nonsense is he talking?" asked a Frenchman.

"Ancient history!" sneered another, perceiving that the reference was to a past war.

"Our emperor will teach you Souvorow as he has taught others. . . ."

"What, Bonaparte?" said Dologhow, but the excited Frenchman interrupted him.

"There is no Bonaparte—there is the emperor, *sacré nom!*"

"Go to the devil with your emperor . . ." and Dologhow, swearing soldiers' oaths in Russian, hoisted his gun on to his shoulder and walked away saying to his captain:

"Come along, Ivan Loukitch."

"So much for his French!" said the soldiers, laughing. "Now, Siderow, it is your turn."

Siderow, with a sly wink, addressed the Frenchman, pouring forth a torrent of gibberish: "*cari, mata tafa, safi, murter, casca,*" trying to throw great expression into his voice. A Homeric roar rose up, such a jolly hearty laugh that the French caught the infection. A looker-on might have supposed that there was nothing more to do but to fire the guns in the air and go home; but the guns were not discharged, the loopholes in the houses and the outworks looked as sinister as ever, and the cannons placed in position and pointing at the enemy did not stir from their ominous guard.

CHAPTER XLV

AFTER riding along the front to the left flank Bolkonsky went up to the battery whence, as the staff-officer had told him, he could get a view of the whole ground. He got off his horse and stood at the end of the battery close to the fourth and last piece. The man on guard was going to present arms, but the aide-de-camp gave him a negative sign, and he resumed his regular walk. Behind the guns were the gun-carriages, and further off the horses were picketed and the bivouac fires were blazing. To the left, at a short distance, a little hut had been constructed of wattles, within which the eager voices of several officers could be heard.

He could, in fact, survey from this battery almost all the Russian troops and the larger part of the enemy's. On a hill in front of him the village of Schöngraben stood out against the sky; to the right and left, in three separate divisions, the French could be seen in the midst of their reeking fires, but the greater portion were collected in the village and behind the hill. To the left of the houses, through clouds of smoke, a dark mass was discernible, which might be a battery, but which was quite indistinct to the naked eye. The Russian right lay distributed over a moderately high ridge, commanding the enemy, and held by the infantry and dragoons, who could be clearly made out along the top. From the centre, occupied by Touschine's battery and where Prince Andrew was now standing, a road down an easy slope led straight to the stream which divided the Russian position from Schöngraben. On their left wing the Russians occupied the ground to the skirt of the forest, and the trees at the edge of it were lighted up in the distance by the fires made by the infantry. The enemy's front was the more extensive, and it was very evident that he could turn the Russians on both flanks, while a ravine, ending in a precipitous gully, made any retreat difficult for cavalry and artillery. Prince Andrew, leaning against a cannon, hastily sketched, on a scrap of paper torn from his note-book, the position of the troops, especially noting two points to which he intended to direct Bagration's attention: in the first place the concentration of all the artillery in the centre, and in the second the transfer of the cavalry to the other side of the ravine. Prince Andrew having been the constant companion of the commander-in-chief from the beginning of the campaign, had acquired practice in apprehending the moving of masses and the judicious distribution of the forces. He had carefully studied historical narratives of battles, and in the engagement now imminent he grasped only the main features, involuntarily reflecting on their bearing on the general conduct of the action. "If the enemy attacks the right wing," he said to himself, "the Kiew Grenadiers and the Podolie Chasseurs must defend their positions till they can be supported by the reserves in the centre, and then the dragoons can make a flank movement and cut them to pieces. If they attack the centre, which is covered by the principal battery, we can concentrate the left flank on this height and retire in good order to the ravine."—As he made these reflections he could still hear the voices in the officers' hut, though without paying the slightest attention to what they were saying. One, however, caught his ear by its honest ring, and he involuntarily listened: "No, my dear fellow," said the attractive voice which he fancied he knew, "what I say is that if we only knew what awaits us after death not one of us would be afraid of it; that is the fact, my dear fellow."

"Well, afraid or not," said a younger voice, "it is the same thing in the end; we cannot escape it."

"No; but meanwhile we are afraid."

"Oh, you know all about it of course!" came from a deeper throat. "You artillerymen are so cocksure, only because you always have your brandy and rations handy."

181

An infantryman's jest, no doubt.

"Yes; and yet we are afraid," the first voice began again; "afraid of the unknown, that is what it is! It is all very well to say that the soul goes up to Heaven. We know very well that there is no such thing as Heaven, nothing but space above us."

"Come, Touschine, give us a share of your absinthe," said the heavier voice.

"Then it is the little captain I saw without his boots in the vivandière's tent," thought Bolkonsky, pleased to recognise the voice of the philosopher.

"Absinthe, to be sure, why not?" said Touschine. "As to understanding the life to come. . . ." He did not finish the sentence, for at this moment a hissing whistle clove the air, and a ball, rushing down with giddy swiftness, plunged into the ground, flinging up the soil, two yards from the hut; the shock shook the earth. Touschine rushed out with his pipe in his mouth; his kindly, bright face was rather pale. After him came the infantry officer of the bass voice, buttoning his jacket as he ran off, full tilt, to join his company.

CHAPTER XLVI

PRINCE ANDREW remounted, and stood by the battery, seeking all round the wide horizon the piece which had fired the ball. He could detect a sort of undulation among the masses of French which till now had remained motionless, and made out the position of the battery he had suspected. Two men on horseback were galloping down the mountain side, and at the foot a small column of the enemy were advancing, evidently for the purpose of strengthening the outposts. The smoke of the first shot had not dispersed before a second cloud puffed up, and another roar was heard: the action had begun. Prince Andrew rushed off, full speed, towards Grounth to join Prince Bagration. The cannonade grew in violence behind him, and the Russians were answering. Below, where the envoys had met, a brisk fusillade was going on.

Lemarrois had just delivered Napoleon's irate letter to Murat. Murat, ashamed of having been duped, and only anxious to win forgiveness, at once marched his troops down on the Russian

182

centre, hoping to turn both flanks at once, and to demolish the small division that opposed him before nightfall, and before the arrival of Bonaparte.

"It has begun!" said Prince Andrew to himself. "But where am I to find my Toulon?"

As he rode through the companies which, only a quarter of an hour ago, had been quietly eating their soup, he found them everywhere astir; the soldiers seizing their muskets, and falling into their ranks, while the excitement he felt at the bottom of his heart was plainly legible on their faces. Like him, they, too, seemed to be saying with mixed emotions of dread and gladness: "It has begun!"

At a short distance from the unfinished earthworks he saw, through the dusk of a misty autumn evening, several officers on horseback riding towards him. The foremost, wrapped in a *bourka*,[1] was on a white horse; this was Bagration himself, who recognised Bolkonsky, and nodded to him. Bolkonsky drew up to wait for him, and report on what he had seen. As he listened Bagration gazed before him, and Prince Andrew could not help wondering with uneasy curiosity as he studied the details of his face—with its strongly-marked features, and half-shut, vague, dreamy eyes—what thoughts and feelings lay hidden behind that impenetrable mask?

"Very good," he said, bowing acquiescence, as though he had foreseen everything Prince Andrew could tell him. Prince Andrew, out of breath with the pace he had been making, talked volubly, while Prince Bagration accented all his words, dropping them slowly, in Eastern fashion, from his lips. He put spurs to his horse, but without the slightest appearance of precipitancy, and rode towards Touschine's battery, followed by his suite, which consisted of a staff-officer, of his personal aide-de-camp, of Prince Andrew, Gerkow, an orderly, the staff-officer on duty, and a civil official employed as auditor, who, out of sheer curiosity, had asked and obtained permission to look on at a battle. This burly, round-faced civilian, seated on a pack saddle, and jolted by his steed, in his thick camlet cloak, looked about with a placid, greenhorn smile, a queer figure in the midst of the hussars, Cossacks, and aides-de-camp.

"To think that he should want to see a battle!" said Gerkow to Bolkonsky, pointing out the civilian. "Why his stomach turns already."

[1] A *bourka* is a hooded coat of woollen stuff.

"Come now, you might spare me," said the stranger, who seemed very well content to be the butt of Gerkow's jokes, and tried to look more obtuse than he really was.

"Very amusing, *mon monsieur Prince*," said the officer on duty; he remembered that in speaking French the title must be preceded by another word, but could not hit it quite rightly. They were near Touschine's battery, when a ball fell at a short distance.

"What was that?" asked the civilian.

"A French pancake," replied Gerkow.

"That is what kills men then?" said the other. "Heavens! This is very alarming!" he added lightly.

He had hardly spoken when a terrific, an appalling whistle rang through the air. A Cossack slipped off his horse, and fell a little way to the right of the speaker. Gerkow and the officer on duty bent low, pulling their horses aside. The civilian stopped, looking with curious contemplation at the Cossack; he was dead; his horse was still struggling.

Bagration glanced over his shoulder, and guessing the cause of the commotion, coolly turned away, as much as to say, "It is not worth while to be worried about such trifles."

He drew up, however, and leaning over like a good horseman as he was, he disengaged his sword which had caught in his cloak. It was an old sword, unlike those commonly worn, a present from Souvorow in Italy.

When they reached the battery, Bagration asked the gunner in charge of the ammunition: "Whose company?" But he looked rather as if he were asking, "Are you not a little frightened?"

The man read it so.

"Captain Touschine's company, your excellency," he answered jovially—he was a red-haired fellow.

"Very good, very good," replied Bagration. He was riding along by the gun-carriages to reach the farthest field-piece when it rang out with a deafening roar, and in the midst of the smoke that hung around it he could see the men that served the gun toiling and struggling to get it back into its place. Then gunner No. 1, who held the ramrod, stood back by the wheel, while No. 2, with a trembling hand, put in the charge. Touschine, a short square figure, stood tottering on the carriage, and gazing into the distance, shading his eyes with his hands.

"Two lines higher will do it," he called out in his piping

voice, to which he tried to give a military severity that ill matched his appearance. "No. 2—Fire!"

Bagration called the little captain, who at once came up, saluting shyly and awkwardly, with his three fingers raised to his cap, more like a priest giving a blessing than a soldier's salute. Instead of sweeping the low ground, as had been intended, the guns were throwing shell into the village of Schöngraben, in front of which the enemy were swarming like ants.

No one had given Touschine any orders as to where or at what he was to fire; but having taken counsel of his sergeant-major Zakartchenko, for whose opinion he had a great respect, they had agreed that the best thing would be to try to set the village on fire.

"Very good," said Bagration, after listening to his account, and examining the field of action. From the foot of the slope where the Kiew Regiment was stationed, came up the mutter and rattle of musketry; further to the right, behind the dragoons, a column of the enemy could be seen turning the Russian flank; to the left the forest bounded the horizon.

Prince Bagration ordered two battalions from the centre to be sent up to support the right flank; the staff-officer took the liberty of representing that in that case the battery, would be exposed on that side. Bagration looked at the staff-officer with his dim eyes, and said nothing. Prince Andrew thought the observation was correct; there was nothing to be said. At this instant an aide-de-camp came up at full gallop from the officer in command of the regiment that was fighting down by the river. He reported that enormous masses of French were in motion across the low ground, and that his regiment was scattered, and that he was about to retire and join the Kiew Grenadiers. Bagration signed consent and approbation. Then he slowly went off to the right, sending an order to the dragoons to attack at once; about half an hour later his messenger came back to say that the dragoons had already retired to the other side of the ravine in order to avoid the terrific fire and useless loss of life; they were sending out sharpshooters among the brushwood.

"Very good," said Bagration once more, and he quitted the battery.

Firing could be heard in the forest; the left flank was too distant for the commander-in-chief to reach it in time, so he sent off Gerkow to desire the general in command — the very man whose regiment had been reviewed at Braunau by

185

Koutouzow—to retire as fast as possible beyond the ravine, as the right flank would not long be able to hold out against the enemy. Thus, Touschine was forgotten, and his battery left exposed and unprotected.

Prince Andrew listened carefully to the remarks that passed between the commander-in-chief and the different commanding officers, and to the orders that were given.

He was surprised to find that Bagration, in fact, never gave an order, but merely tried to give the impression that his own intentions had been implicitly carried out when, in reality, all that was done was the outcome of circumstances, of the resolution of his subordinates, or the caprices of chance. Nevertheless—and in spite of the unsatisfactory turn that events were taking, and that he had not expected—Prince Andrew was obliged to confess that his chief's perfect tact made his presence most valuable. The mere sight of him restored confidence to those who came up to him with grieved and anxious looks; officers and soldiers alike saluted him cheerfully, and spurred each other on to display all their courage in his presence.

CHAPTER XLVII

PRINCE BAGRATION mounted to the highest shoulder of the Russian ridge on the right, and rode down into the plain, where the firing never ceased, and where he and his suite were presently wrapped in the dense cloud of smoke, which hid the scene from their ken. At every step, though they could see nothing distinctly, they felt that they were getting nearer to the heart of the struggle. They met wounded men; one of them, who had lost his shako, and whose head was wounded, was being dragged along supported by two soldiers; he was vomiting blood, and his breath rattled; the bullet had, no doubt, gone into his mouth or throat. Another had dropped his gun and was striding bravely along, looking more scared than hurt, but wringing his smashed hand from the keen, unaccustomed smart, while the blood ran down over his coat. After crossing the high-road they went down a scarped incline where several men had fallen, and further on were met by some more soldiers, among whom were some wounded, but shouting and gesticulating in spite of the general's presence. At a few paces off, the lines of grey coats could be distinguished through the smoke, and an officer, seeing Bagration, ran to the men and desired them to return at once.

The commander-in-chief went down to the ranks; the incessant snap of shots rose above the hum of voices and the word of command. The men's eager faces were blackened with gunpowder; some were ramming the charge home, others were pouring powder into the pan, or taking cartridges out of their pouches; others, again, were firing at random, through the dense cloud of smoke that hung motionless in the air. Now and again, at short intervals, a sharp disagreeable whiz, unlike any other sound, jarred painfully on the ear.

"What is going on here?" thought Prince Andrew, approaching this mob. "It is not an attack, for they are standing still nor, on the other hand, is it a square. . . ."

The commanding officer, a lean and frail-looking old man, with heavy eyelids that almost hid his eyes, met Prince Bagration with a genial smile, as if he were receiving a welcome guest. He explained that his regiment had been attacked by the French cavalry, and had repulsed them, but with a loss of more than half its number. He used military language in calling the fray that had just taken place an attack, though, in point of fact, he had no clear idea of the position of his troops during the last half-hour, or whether the attack had been repulsed, or his regiment broken through. Nothing was certain but the hail of bullets and grenades which had incessantly decimated his men ever since they had begun fighting at the cry of: "Here comes the cavalry!" The cry was the signal for a general mêlée, and they had fired, not indeed on the cavalry, but on the French infantry, who had been seen in the valley.

Prince Bagration again nodded approbation of the report, as though it were all he could wish, and just what he had foreseen. Then turning to his aide-de-camp, he desired him to fetch down from the height the two battalions of the Sixth Chasseurs, whom he had seen as he rode past. At this moment Bolkonsky was struck by the change that had taken place in his chief's face: it expressed decision and self-reliance—the look of a man who takes a run and a leap to plunge into cool waters on a hot summer-day. The vague, sleepy gaze, the deceptive mask affecting to cover deep calculations, had vanished; his hawk's eyes, round and determined, looked up brightly without fixing on anything, with a sort of contemptuous enthusiasm, while his movements were as deliberate and methodical as ever. The general begged him to withdraw, as the spot was a perilous one: "In Heaven's name, your excellency! only look!" for the bullets were singing and rattling on every side.

He spoke with the persuasive tone of remonstrance that a carpenter might use, who saw his master trying to use a hatchet: "As for us, we are used to it—but you will get corns on your hands."

He himself seemed confident that the bullets would respect him, and the staff-officer vainly added his entreaties. Bagration, instead of answering them, ordered that the men should stop firing and form in ranks to make way for the battalions who were advancing. Even while he was speaking it seemed as though some invisible hand on the left were raising a corner of the curtain of smoke that shrouded the distance; every one looked at the hill, which was gradually unveiled before their eyes, and which the enemy were steadily descending. Already the fur hats of the grenadiers were recognisable, the officers could be distinguished from the rank and file, and the flag could be seen hanging in heavy folds round the staff.

"How well they march!" said a voice in Bagration's suite. The head of the column had now reached the bottom of the ravine, and on that side of the slope a collision was imminent.

The remains of the regiment that had stood the brunt of the attack hastily reformed and went off to the right, while the two battalions of Sixth Light Infantry came on with a heavy, regular, rhythmical tramp, driving the stragglers before them. On the left, nearest to Bagration, marched the captain in command; a man of splendid physique, with a broad face, and dull, self-satisfied expression—the man who had rushed out of the hut with Touschine. It was evident that he had but one idea: that of marching past his chief with an effective swagger. Balancing himself steadily on his feet, he walked bolt upright without the slightest effort, holding his short sword with its slender curved blade naked in his hand; he looked now at the prince, and now at his men, without ever losing step, and repeated as he strode on, turning his strong, supple form: "Left, left, left! The moving wall of men marched in time, and each face, all grave, all different, weighted as it were by the gun and knapsack, seemed, like him, to express but one idea, and to be repeating after him: "Left, left, left! . . ."

A breathless major lost step in getting round a bush in

The men's eager faces were blackened with gunpowder

the path; a straggler, frightened at his own heedlessness, was running to catch up his company.

A ball came singing over the heads of Bagration and his staff, and fell in the middle of the column, a grim accompaniment to the steady: "Left, left, left! . . ."

"Close up the ranks," shouted the captain with a swagger; the soldiers parted as they went past the spot where the ball had fallen, and an old sergeant with many stripes, who had been left behind in charge of the killed, fell into the ranks, and caught up his step with anxious haste; the word of command: "Left, left, left," again gave time to the regular tramp of the soldiers, a voice from the ominous silence.

"You have come through it like men, my children!" said Bagration. "Glad to have had the trouble!"[1] rose from each detachment in turn. One sullen man looked up at the general, as much as to say: "We know that as well as you do," and another, without looking round for fear of losing step, opened his mouth wide and shouted.

The word was given to halt and unstrap their knapsacks. Bagration rode down the ranks that had just marched past him, got off his horse, threw the bridle to his Cossack, gave him his bourka to hold, and stretched his legs. At this instant the front of the French column, with the officers leading, appeared from behind the hill.

"Forward! and God help you!" cried Bagration, in a firm clear voice; he glanced round at the men and went forward himself on the uneven ground, with the rolling gait of a cavalry officer on foot. Prince Andrew was carried away by an irresistible impulse; he felt perfectly happy.[2]

The French were not far off, he could see their faces, their belts and red epaulettes, and an old officer painfully climbing the height—his feet turned out and he wore gaiters. Bagration gave no new order but silent marched before the ranks. A shot—another—a third, and the hostile lines were shrouded in smoke, the battle had begun again. Some of the Russians fell, and among them the officer who had been at such pains to cut a figure in the eyes of his superiors. At the crack of the first shot Bagration shouted hurrah! And a prolonged cheer had

[1] This response is required of the soldiers in the Russian army when thanked or praised by their commander.
[2] Thiers gives the following account of this collision: "A rare thing in battle, the two masses of infantry marched resolutely to meet each other, neither giving way, till they were within range." And Napoleon on St. Helena said, "The Russians bore themselves valiantly."

answered him all along the line; the soldiers, outstripping their officers and each other, rushed triumphantly in pursuit of the French, whose ranks had given way.

CHAPTER XLVIII

THE attack of the 6th Chasseurs had covered the retreat of the right flank. In the centre, the conflagration caused at Schöngraben by Touschine and his neglected battery checked the progress of the French, who stopped to put out the fire which the wind fanned and spread, thus giving the Russians time to retire; the retreat of the centre across the ravine was effected with much noise and hurry, though in very good order. The left flank, however, consisting of the Azow and Podolie Regiments and the Pavlogradsky Hussars, which had been attacked at the same time and surrounded by superior numbers under Lannes, had completely given way.

Bagration sent Gerkow to instruct the general in command to retire at once. Gerkow, saluting with his finger-tips, set off at a smart gallop, but he had hardly started when his courage failed him; seized by an insane fit of fright, he could by no effort persuade himself to meet the danger; not venturing within range of the firing, he looked for the general and the other officers where they could not possibly be—of course the order was never delivered.

The officer in command of the left flank was by seniority and rank the chief of the regiment we saw arrive at Braunau, in which Dologhow was serving, while the extreme left was commanded by a colonel of the Pavlograd Regiment, to which Rostow belonged. These two officers were excessively angry with each other, and this occasioned a misunderstanding; they were still losing time in abusive recrimination when fighting had long since begun on the right flank, and the French were advancing. The cavalry and light infantry regiments were in no condition to take part in the engagement, and from the general to the private, no one expected to be called upon: the infantry were quietly making their fires, and the cavalry finding forage.

"Your chief is my senior in rank," said the German officer in command of the hussars to the aide-de-camp of the light infantry regiment; his face was purple with rage. "He may do as he pleases; I will not sacrifice my men. Buglers, sound a retreat!"

However, the battle waxed hot; cannon and musketry roared and rattled; in the centre and on the right Lannes' skirmishers were crossing the mill-dam and forming just beyond gun-shot range along the Russian flank. The infantry general clambered heavily into his saddle, and drawing himself up to his full height, rode off to speak to the colonel of cavalry. The extreme politeness of their manner concealed their animosity.

"Really, colonel, I cannot leave half my men in the wood. I beg of you . . ." and he emphasised the word—"I beg of you to occupy the ground and be prepared for an attack."

"And I beg of you to mind your own business; if you were a cavalry officer. . . ."

"I am not in the cavalry, colonel, but I am a Russian general; if you do not know it. . . ."

"I know it perfectly well, your excellency," said the other, digging his spurs into his horse and turning red.—"Would you like to come with me to inspect the outposts? Then you would see for yourself that the position is untenable; I have no fancy to see my men massacred to please you."

"You forget yourself, colonel; it is not to please me, and I cannot allow you to say so. . . ."

The general accepted this challenge to a test of courage: his breast swelling and his brows fiercely knit, he went forward with the colonel to the line of skirmishers, as if their disagreement could only be settled under fire. Having got so far they stopped in silence while a few bullets whistled over their heads. There was nothing fresh to be seen, for the impossibility of manoeuvring cavalry in the midst of rifts and brushwood was as obvious from the spot they had left as the movement of the French to surround the left wing. The two officers looked at each other like two gamecocks about to fight, each waiting in vain for the other to show a sign of yielding. They both stood the test with honour, and might have prolonged it for an indefinite period out of bravado, neither being willing to give in first, if, at this instant, a sharp volley and a confused outcry had not rung out close behind them.

The French had fallen on a fatigue party who were collecting firewood; the question as to whether the hussars should retire with the infantry was thus settled, for their retreat was cut off on the left by the enemy's outposts, and they had no choice but to attack and force a passage, in spite of the difficulties of the broken ground.

Rostow's squadron had barely time to mount; they were just in front of the enemy, and, as on the bridge at Enns, there was nothing between them and the foe but that space, that gulf of terror, and the unknown between the living and the dead, of which each was instinctively conscious as he wondered whether he would be one of those to cross it safe and sound!

The colonel rode to the front, answering the officer's questions with ill-temper; he flung out an order, evidently determined to go his own way. Nothing very clear was known, but something in the air gave warning of an attack, and suddenly the word came: "Fall in!" and the clash of unsheathing sabres. No one stirred: the indecision of the commanding officers was so apparent that it soon infected the troops, infantry and cavalry alike.

"Oh! if only it would come quicker, quicker," thought Rostow, feeling the moment of attack at hand—that supreme and triumphant joy of which he had so often heard his comrades speak.

"Forward, and God be with you, lads!" cried Denissow. The horses' haunches rose and fell; the "Crow" tossed his bridle and cantered off.

On Rostow's right were the foremost ranks of his hussars; in front of him a dark line, too far off to be distinctly visible, but which he knew to be the enemy. The crack of muskets in the distance.

"Charge!" And Rostow felt his blood fire in sympathy with his excited charger. A tree standing alone, which to his fancy had seemed to mark that mysterious line, was left behind them: "Well. we have passed it, and there is nothing terrible about it; on the contrary, it is livelier and more amusing every moment. Oh! how I will slash at them!" he muttered to himself, and he gripped the hilt of his sword.

A tremendous hurrah was shouted behind him. "Only let me get at them!" And giving his horse a lift he spurred him to top-speed; the enemy were in sight. Suddenly a tremendous crack of whips lashed the whole line—Rostow raised his hand to strike with his sword, but at the same moment he saw Nikitenka, the man who was riding in front of him, gallop off out of sight, and he felt himself rushing on at a giddy pace, as if in a dream, without moving from the spot. A hussar flew past and looked at him with a gloomy face.

"What is happening? I am not moving; have I had a fall? Am I dead?"

Questions and answers buzzed in his brain. He was alone in the midst of a field; no frenzied horses, no hussars, nothing to be seen anywhere but the still earth and the short stubble. Something warm—blood—was flowing round him.

"No, I am only hurt; my horse is killed."

The "Crow" tried to get on his feet, but fell back with all his weight on his rider; a stream of blood was flowing from his head, and he struggled in vain efforts to rise. Rostow attempting to get up also fell back; his sash had caught on the saddle.

"Where are our men? Where are the French?"

He could not imagine—not a soul was to be seen.

Having succeeded in freeing himself from the weight of his horse, he got on his feet; where now was the line that so clearly divided the armies?

"Something serious must have happened to me. Is this always the way I wonder? What ought I to do next?" He felt a strange heaviness about his left arm; it was quite numb, and his wrist did not seem to belong to him, still there was no sign of blood on his hand.

"Ah! here are some men at last, they will help me," he thought with much joy. The foremost of the men who were running towards him, a weather-beaten, sunburnt fellow with a hooked nose, wore a blue cloak and a shako of foreign shape; one of them spoke a few words in a language which was not Russian. Some others, dressed in the same fashion, were leading a hussar of his own regiment.

"A prisoner no doubt—but will they take me too?" said Rostow to himself, hardly believing his eyes. "Are they French?"

He looked sharply at the party as they drew nearer, and in spite of his recent valiant fit and wish to exterminate them all, their vicinity froze him with fear.

"Where are they going—are they coming after me? Will they kill me? — Oh! why — me — everyone loves me. . . ." And the affection that his mother, his family, everyone had shown him, rose up in his mind to make the idea seem monstrous.

He stood rooted to the spot, not fully understanding the predicament: the hook-nosed Frenchman, his queer face flushed with running, as Rostow could already make out, was coming straight at him with his bayonet fixed. Rostow clutched at his pistol, but instead of firing at his foe he flung it at his head with all his strength, took to his heels, and ran as fast as he could to hide among the brushwood.

The impulse of pugnacity and enthusiasm that he had felt on the bridge at Enns was utterly extinct; he ran like a hare with the dogs at her heels; the instinct of preserving his young and happy life possessed him wholly and lent him wings. Leaping ditches, skipping over furrows with all the nimbleness of his boyhood, he constantly turned his pale, good-natured face to look behind him while a shudder of fear spurred him to fly faster.

"It is better not to look back," he thought; but when he reached the first bushes he stopped. The Frenchmen were far behind, and the one who was pursuing him was going slower, and seemed to be calling his companions.

"It is impossible, they cannot want to kill me," said the lad to himself.

But his arm grew heavier every minute; he could have believed he had a hundredweight to carry—he could drag himself no farther. The Frenchman was aiming at him, he shut his eyes and ducked: a bullet, another, whistled past his ears. Then, collecting all his remaining strength, and carrying his left wrist in his right hand, he scrambled on through the bushes. There was safety—there were the Russian sharp-shooters.

CHAPTER XLIX

The infantry, taken by surprise in the wood, had rushed out in hot haste, and in complete confusion. A scared soldier had spoken the words of such terrible significance in war: "We are cut off."

A panic spread through the whole mass: "Surrounded, cut off, lost!" cried the fugitives.

At the first sound of firing, and the first outcry, the general understood that something terrible had happened. Struck with the thought that he—a punctilious officer, for so many years an exemplary soldier—might possibly be accused by his superiors of negligence and indifference, he grasped the bow of his saddle, and forgetful of the danger, and the unruly cavalry commander, spurred his horse to a gallop, and set off to join his regiment, under a storm of bullets, which fortunately did not even graze him. He had but one wish: to ascertain what had occurred, to repair the error if it should be attributed to him, and escape all blame—he who could show twenty-two years of untarnished service!

When he had thus happily crossed the enemy's line of fire, on the other side of the wood he fell into the midst of the fugitives, who were dispersing in every direction, and deaf to every word of command. It was the critical moment of moral vacillation which decides the issue of a battle. Would these frenzied troops obey the hitherto respected voice of their commander, or would they persist in flight? In spite of his despairing appeals, his face of fury, his threatening demonstrations, the men ran and still ran, firing in the air without looking back. Their fate was sealed; the balance at that doubtful crisis had been struck on the side of terror.

The general was nearly choking with shouting, the smoke blinded him; in his despair he did not even stir. All seemed lost, when suddenly the French in pursuit, without any apparent reason, turned round and fled back to the forest, where the Russian skirmishers were now to be seen. It was Timokhine's company; he alone had succeeded in keeping his men in good order, and had entrenched himself in the ditch at the edge of the wood, whence he had attacked the French in their rear; Timokhine, flourishing his short sword, had rushed upon the foe with such terrific impetus, and such rash courage, that the French, in their turn, took flight and fled, throwing away their guns. Dologhow, who ran too, and kept up with him, shot one point-blank, and was the first to seize an officer, who surrendered at once. The Russian fugitives paused, the battalions formed again, and the enemy, within an ace of cutting through the left wing, were driven back.

The commanding officer of the regiment was on the bridge with Major Ekonomow, watching the filing off of the companies as they retired, when a private came close up to his horse, pressing against him; the man held an officer's sword; he had on a dark blue French capote and a French cartridge-pouch and shoulder belt; his head was bandaged, and he had lost his shako and knapsack; there was a smile on his pale face, and his blue eyes looked proudly up at his chief, who could not forbear paying him some attention, though he was engaged in giving orders to Ekonomow.

"Your excellency, two trophies," said Dologhow, holding up the sword and the pouch. "I took an officer prisoner—I stopped the advance of a company. . . ." His short, panting breath betrayed his exhaustion; he spoke in jerks. "All my company will bear me witness; please to remember it, your excellency!"

"Very good, all right," replied the general, still listening to the major.

Dologhow, untying the handkerchief, pulled him by the sleeve, and pointing to the clots of blood in his hair: "A bayonet wound," he added. "I was in front—don't forget me, your excellency!"

As has been said, Touschine's battery had been completely forgotten; but, towards the end of the battle, Prince Bagration, hearing the cannon still thundering away at the centre, despatched first the staff-officer on duty, and then Prince Andrew, to order Touschine to retire as soon as possible. The two battalions which had been placed to defend the battery had been moved away, in obedience to an order of which Touschine knew not the source, to take part in the fighting; still the battery kept up its fire. The French, deceived by this vigorous display, and fancying that the main strength of the enemy was concentrated on that side, tried twice to take the battery, but were driven back each time by the grape-shot that poured from the mouths of these four solitary cannon left on these heights.

Not long after Bagration's visit of inspection, Touschine had succeeded in setting fire to the village of Schöngraben.

"Look, what a blaze! and what a smoke! See them run!" said the gunners, delighted at their success. All the pieces were directed on the village, and every hit was hailed with shouts of triumph. The flames, driven by the wind, spread rapidly; the French abandoned Schöngraben, and mounted ten guns to the right of it, which responded to Touschine's firing.

Their childlike delight at the sight of the conflagration, and the success of their labours, prevented the Russians from observing this hostile battery. They did not notice it till two balls, followed by others, plunged into their midst. A gunner had his leg shot off, and two horses were killed. This did not cool their ardour, but it changed its character; the horses were replaced by two from a reserve carriage, the wounded were carried under shelter, and the four guns were turned on the enemy's battery. The officer second-in-command to Touschine had been killed at the beginning of the action, and out of forty men to serve the guns seventeen met the same fate within an hour. But the survivors went on merrily at their work. The little captain, with his awkward ways, made his servant constantly refill his pipe, and sprang forward to see what the French were doing, shading his eyes with his hand.

"Fire, boys!" he would say, and point the cannon with his own hand. Backwards and forwards, through the smoke, deafened by the incessant roar and quivering at the shock of every shot, Touschine ran from one gun to another with his pipe between his teeth, adjusting the aim, counting the remaining charges, or changing the horses. In the midst of this infernal uproar his thin little voice gave unceasing orders, his face grew more eager every moment; it only clouded when a man fell dead or wounded, then he turned away to call out angrily to the survivors—always slow to remove the dead or disabled. The gunners—all fine men, and, as is often the case in the artillery, two heads taller, and of much broader build than their captain—looked at him inquiringly, like children in a difficulty, and the expression of his face was immediately reflected in their features.

Thanks to the incessant rating, to the din and the compulsory activity, Touschine felt not the smallest fear; he did not admit the possibility of his being wounded or killed. He felt as though it were quite a long time since he had fired the first shot at the foe, that he had been there since yesterday, that those few feet square of earth were familiar and long known to him. He forgot nothing, and made his arrangements with as perfect coolness as the most experienced officer could have done in his place, and nevertheless he was in a state bordering on intoxication or delirium. In the midst of the stunning clamour of the battery, of the smoke, of the enemy's balls—which were falling on the ground, on a gun, on a man or a horse—surrounded by his bustling men, while his face streamed with sweat, his brain was busy in a weird fantastic world full of feverish delights. In this waking dream the hostile cannon were gigantic tobacco pipes out of which an invisible smoker was blowing light clouds of vapour.

"Hallo! another puff!" said Touschine in an undertone, marking a white smoke-wreath borne away by the breeze, "Catch the ball and toss it back!"

"What are your highness's orders?" asked the man by his side, who half heard the words.

"Nothing. Go on, fire away. Give it them, Matvéevna!" he replied, addressing the large, old-fashioned field-piece at the further end of the row and which he called Matvéevna.

To him the French looked like ants swarming round their guns; a fine artilleryman, somewhat given to drink, who served the second cannon as No. 1, figured in Touschine's excited imagination as "the uncle," and he watched his slightest movements with particular interest; the volleys of musketry came up to him like the breathing of a living creature to whose sighing he listened eagerly.

"He is breathing hard," he muttered, and he seemed to himself a huge man, tall and strong, hurling ball at the enemy with both hands.

"Now then, Matvéevna, do your duty!" he had just said, quitting his favourite cannon, when he heard above his head an unknown voice: "Captain Touschine—Captain. . . ." He started and turned round. It was the staff-officer who addressed him.

"Are you mad? This is the second time you have been ordered to retire. You . . ."

"I—I am all right . . ." he stammered, raising his two fingers in a salute. "I . . ."

But the staff-officer did not finish. A ball, rending the air close to him, made him duck his head. He was going to speak again when another ball cut him short. He turned his horse and disappeared at a gallop, calling over his shoulder: "Retire!"

The artillerymen shouted with laughter. Almost immediately another aide-de-camp came, with the same message. This was Prince Andrew.

The first thing that struck his sight as he reached the spot was a horse that had his leg smashed and was whining with pain as he stood with his companions still in harness. Some of the killed were lying among the gun-carriages. Balls flew over his head in quick succession, and a nervous thrill ran down his spinal marrow; but the thought that this might be fear revived all his courage. He deliberately got off his horse in the middle of the battery and gave the order there, on the spot. He was quite determined to see it carried out under his own eyes, to convoy the guns himself, if necessary, under the murderous French fire, and he proceeded to help Touschine, striding over the bodies that lay stretched on all sides.

"Another messenger came just now, but he made himself scarce in no time—not like your highness!" said a gunner to Prince Andrew.

He and Touschine had not exchanged a word; indeed, they

"Retire !"

were both busy, and did not seem to see each other. Having succeeded in getting two of the four pieces safely limbered up, they set out down the slope, leaving two guns, one spiked.

"Now good-bye," said Prince Andrew, and he held out his hand.

"Good-bye, my friend—brave, good soul!" And Touschine's eyes filled with tears, though he could not have said why.

CHAPTER L

THE wind had fallen; the heavy clouds that seemed to mingle on the horizon with the reek of gunpowder hung low over the field of battle, and two blazing villages stood out against the black background more visible as night fell. The cannon were firing less steadily, but the fusillade behind and to the right was nearer and louder as they went on. Touschine had scarcely got his pieces beyond the range of the enemy's fire and down into the ravine when he met a party of staff-officers, among them he who had brought the order to retire, together with Gerkow, who, though twice despatched, had never reached him. All, with one consent interrupting and contradicting each other, gave him orders and counter-orders as to the road he should take, loading him with blame and criticism.

He, for his part, mounted on his worn-out horse, sat in gloomy silence, for he felt that if he spoke a word his nerves, in their utter reaction, must give way and he should betray some emotion. Though he had been instructed to leave the wounded, several had dragged themselves after him, imploring to be carried on the guns. The smart infantry-officer who, a few hours before, had come hurrying out of Touschine's hut, was stretched on "Matvéevna's" gun-carriage with a bullet in his stomach. A *junker* of hussars, pale and nursing a crushed hand, besought a little room.

"For God's sake, captain!" he said. "I am badly hurt—I can walk no farther!" It was evident from his tone of timid entreaty that he had repeated his request many times in vain. "For pity's sake do not refuse!"

"Find a place for him, tuck a cloak under him, little uncle," said Touschine to his favourite gunner. "Where is the wounded officer?"

"We took him down—he is dead," said a voice.

199

"Sit there, then, sit down: spread out the cloak, Antonow." The *junker*, Rostow himself, his teeth chattering with fever, was helped on to "Matvéevna" from which the dead man had just been removed. The blood on his cloak stained Rostow's trousers and hands.

"Are you wounded, friend?" said Touschine.

"No, only bruised."

"But there is blood on the cloak?"

"The officer's, your highness . . .!" said the gunner, wiping it away with his sleeve, as if apologising for the stain on one of his cannon.

With the help of the infantry to push, the guns were, with great difficulty, hauled up the hill as far as the village of Gunthersdorf; there they halted. It was now so dark that the different uniforms were indistinguishable at ten paces distance. The firing was gradually ceasing. Suddenly it began again and quite close, on the right; the flashes gleamed in the darkness. This was a last effort on the part of the French; the Russians replied from the houses in the village, and then rushed out. Touschine and his company, unable to advance, awaited their fate, looking at each other in silence. However, the firing was soon over, and a party of soldiers came out of a cross-street, talking loudly.

"We have given them a warming, lads; they will not try it again."

"Are you safe and sound, Pétrow?"

"It is impossible to see a thing," said a third. "It is as dark as pitch . . . I say, boys, can we get anything to drink?"

The French were finally driven off; Touschine went on with his guns into the remoter darkness, the noise and bustle of the infantry flowing on with him. It was like a black, invisible stream going steadily onwards, its deep murmur being represented by the dull sound of voices, the clatter of horses, and the rumble of wheels. Above this medley of noises rose, piercing and distinct, the groans and cries of the wounded, which seemed indeed to fill the darkness and become one with it—a single hideous impression. A little further on the moving mass was visibly excited: an officer on a white horse, followed by a numerous staff, had just ridden by, shedding a few words as he passed.

"What did he say? Where are we to go? Are we to stop here? Did he say anything by way of thanks?"

In the midst of this crossfire of questions the living stream was suddenly checked in front; the foremost ranks had halted: orders had been given that they were to stop for the night in the middle of this miry road.

Fires were lighted and tongues wagged again. Captain Touschine, after making his arrangements, sent a soldier to seek out an ambulance or a surgeon for the hapless *junker*, and sat down by the fire. Rostow dragged himself there, too; his whole frame shook with the feverish chill caused by pain, cold and damp; he was almost overpowered by sleep, but he could not give way to it for the acute suffering caused by his arm; he would shut his eyes for a minute or two, and then gaze at the fire, which he saw in a blood-red glare, or at Touschine's square little figure as he squatted like a Turk, and looked at Rostow with a kindly, shrewd twinkle, full of pity and sympathy. He would have helped him with all his heart if he could, but he knew he could not: on all sides they could hear steps and voices, the infantry settling down for the night, the horses' hoofs as they pawed the mud, and the splitting of wood at a distance.

It was no longer the roar of an invisible torrent; it was the swell and dash of the sea after a storm. Rostow saw and heard, but did not seem to understand what was going on round him. A trooper came up to the blaze, squatted on his heels and held out his hands to warm them, turning to Touschine with an apologetic look: "You will not object, highness? I have missed my company, I don't know where."

An infantry officer, with his face tied up, came to ask Touschine to have his guns moved; they blocked the way for a baggage-waggon; after him came two soldiers abusing each other and quarrelling for a boot.

"It is not true that you picked it up . . ."

A third, with his neck wrapped in bloodstained bandages, came to the artilleryman and asked for a drink in a hollow voice: "Must I be left to die like a dog?" Touschine bid them give him some water. Then a wag ran up wanting some fire for the infantrymen.

"Fire, fire!" he said. "Fire, all hot!—Good-luck to you, friend, and thanks for the fire; we will return it with interest," and he disappeared with his flaming brand.

After this, four soldiers went past, carrying something heavy wrapped in a cloak. One of them stumbled.

"D—— them! They have left the place strewn with wood!" he grumbled.

"He is dead—what is the use of carrying him?" said another.

"I tell you what . . ." And the four men with their burthen were lost in the gloom.

"You are in great pain?" said Touschine softly to Rostow.

"Yes, great pain."

"Highness, the general is asking for you," said an artillery-man to the captain.

"I am coming, friend," said Touschine rising and buttoning his uniform as he quitted the fire.

Prince Bagration was at dinner in a cottage a few steps away from the artillery camp-fires, talking with several commanding officers whom he had invited to share his meal. Among them was the old sleepy-eyed colonel—who was gnawing at a mutton-bone with an appetite; the general of twenty-two years' blame-less service, his face radiant with wine and a good dinner; the German with the diamond ring; Gerkow, who looked anxiously from one to another of the company; and Prince Andrew, very pale, his lips set, and his eyes glittering with a fevered light.

In one corner of the room there was a French flag; the civilian sat feeling the stuff it was made of and shaking his head: was it out of curiosity, or was it that the sight of the dinner-table, at which there was no place for him, was a trial to his famished stomach?

In the neighbouring cottage sat a French colonel, who had been taken prisoner by the Russian dragoons, and the officers were crowding round him inquisitively.

Bagration thanked the officers who had commanded the various divisions, and made inquiries as to the details of the battle and the losses sustained. The general whom we know as commanding the regiment at Braunau, explained to the prince how, quite at the beginning of the action, he had called together the men who were gathering wood, and had allowed the French to pass through, and had attacked them with two battalions with fixed bayonets and routed them.

"Then, your excellency, seeing that the first battalion was giving way I took up a position on the road and said to myself: we will let these get past and receive the others with a volley—and that was what I did."

The worthy man would so much have liked to do this, that he had ended by persuading himself that it had actually happened. But perhaps it really did happen? Who can tell anything in all that muddle?

"I should wish, too, to point out to your excellency," he went on, with a reminiscence of Dologhow's conversation with Koutouzow, "that Dologhow, the private, seized a French prisoner under my eyes, and distinguished himself conspicuously."

"At that very moment, excellency, I saw the attack made by the Pavlograd Horse," added Gerkow, with a rather doubtful manner, for he had not set eyes on a hussar during the whole day, and only knew by hearsay of what they had done. "They broke two of the enemy's squares, your excellency."

Some of the officers present smiled as Gerkow spoke; they were prepared for one of his usual pleasantries; but as this lie was not followed up by any jest, and as, after all, it was to the honour and glory of their troops, they looked grave again, although many of them knew that Gerkow was lying and what he said had no foundation in fact.

"I thank you all, gentlemen. Every corps—infantry, cavalry, artillery, all behaved heroically! But how is it that two guns were abandoned at the centre?" he asked looking round for someone.

Prince Bagration made no inquiries as to what had become of the cannon of the left flank, which had been abandoned quite at the beginning of the engagement.

"I fancy I gave you orders to bring them down," he added, turning to the staff-officer on duty.

"One was spiked," replied the officer. "With regard to the other, I cannot understand . . . I was there all the while . . . It was a hot corner to be sure," he added, modestly.

Someone observed that Captain Touschine had been sent for.

"But you were there?" said Bagration, addressing Prince Andrew.

"Of course . . . We just missed each other," said the staff-officer with an ingratiating smile.

"I had not the pleasure of seeing you," replied Bolkonsky, shortly and sharply.

There was a pause. Touschine had just come in, gliding shyly forward behind all these broad epaulettes; abashed, as usual, at the sight of them, he stumbled over the flag-pole, and his awkwardness gave rise to a smothered laugh.

"How is it that two guns were left on the height?" said Bagration, with a frown which was meant for Gerkow and the laughers rather than the little captain.

Now, for the first time, in the presence of this dread chief, did Touschine perceive with alarm the enormity of his delinquency in abandoning two guns while he himself had life.

In his bewilderment and the excitement he had gone through, he had entirely forgotten the incident. He succumbed, and only murmured: "I do not know, your excellency, there were not enough men . . ."

"You might have had men from the battalions which covered you."

Touschine might have replied that there were no such battalions: it was the plain truth. But he feared to compromise some superior officer, so he stood with his eyes fixed on Bagration like a schoolboy caught in mischief. The silence remained unbroken; his judge, evidently anxious to avoid useless severity, did not know what to say. Prince Andrew looked at Touschine from under his brows, and his fingers twitched nervously.

"Your excellency," he began, breaking the silence in a peremptory tone, "you sent me to Captain Touschine's battery and I there found two-thirds of the men and horses killed, two cannons burst, and no battalions to protect it." Bagration and Touschine never took their eyes off him. "And, if your excellency will allow me to express an opinion, it is to that battery and to Captain Touschine's heroic steadiness that the success of the action is in great measure due."

He rose from the table without waiting for a reply. Bagration looked at Touschine, and, not choosing to show his incredulity, he simply bowed and told him he might withdraw. Prince Andrew followed him.

"Thank you," said Touschine, wringing his hand. "You have got me out of a mess." Prince Andrew said nothing; he looked at him sadly and turned away. He felt a weight on his heart . . . everything was so strange, so different from what he had hoped.

"Who are they? What are they doing? When will it all end?" said Rostow to himself, as his eyes followed the shadowy figures that passed his unceasingly. His arm hurt him more and more; want of sleep weighed him down; red spots danced before his eyes, and all the various impressions of the voices and faces around him, and of his own loneliness, became one with the pain he was suffering: those wounded soldiers were crushing him, knocking up against him, those others were racking his muscles, roasting his broken arm.

To be rid of the sight he shut his eyes, and forgot himself for a moment; and in that brief instant a whole phantasmagoria danced before his brain: his mother, with her white hands,

Sonia with her thin shoulders, Natacha's smiling eyes; then Denissow, Télianine, Bogdanitch, and all his squabble with them—and the whole scene was epitomised in the figure of a soldier there, who hurt him so much and dragged his arm. He tried, but in vain, to free himself from the clutch that tortured his shoulder—that unlucky shoulder which would have been quite sound if only he had not bruised it so cruelly.

He opened his eyes: a narrow strip of the black veil of night was visible above the glare of the fires, and in the glare fluttered a silvery dust of fine, light snow. No surgeon—and Touschine did not return. With the exception of a poor little trooper, stripped to the skin, who was warming his starveling frame at the other side of the fire, he was quite alone.

"No one wants me," thought Rostow, "no one helps me or pities me—and at home I used to be strong and happy, and everyone loved me." He sighed, and his sigh was lost in a groan.

"What is the matter? Are you hurt?" asked the trooper, shaking his shirt over the blaze; and without waiting for a reply he went on: "What a lot of poor fellows have been cut and slashed this day. It is fearful!"

Rostow did not heed him, he sat watching the snow-flakes as they whirled in the air; he thought of his winters in Russia, of the warm, well-lighted house, of his soft furs, and swift sleigh— he saw himself happy, well, surrounded by his own people: "What on earth made me want to come here?" he asked himself.

The French did not renew the attack on the following day, and the remains of Bagration's division joined the army under Koutouzow.

BOOK THREE

CHAPTER LI

PRINCE BASIL never laid any plans beforehand; still less did he ever plot evil with a view to his own advantage. He was simply a man of the world who had been successful, and to whom success had become a matter of habit. He acted according to circumstances and to his position towards others, and he reconciled this mode of proceeding with the various schemes which were his chief interest in life, but which he never examined with conscientious narrowness. He had always a dozen in hand: some never got beyond the first stage, some worked out successfully, some again went overboard.

He never—for instance—said to himself: "So and so is in power; I must try to win his confidence and liking, and so gain this or that pecuniary advantage," or: "Peter is rich; I should do well to keep him about the house, so that he may marry my daughter and lend me those 40,000 roubles I want." But if the influential magnate came in his way, his instinct prompted him to make the best of his opportunities; he made advances, became intimate in the most easy and natural manner, flattered him, and made himself agreeable. In the same way, without any premeditation, he kept an eye on Peter at Moscow. Thanks to his good offices, the young man was appointed a gentleman-in-waiting—which in those days gave him the position of a councillor of state—and he invited him to return with him to St. Petersburg, and reside in his house. Prince Basil was certainly doing everything to bring about his daughter's marriage, but he did it with an air of supreme indifference and of perfect conviction that his conduct was obviously natural. If he had been in the habit of meditating his plots he could not have shown such absolute simplicity and frankness in his relations alike to his superiors and his inferiors.

Something always guided him towards those who were more powerful or richer than himself, and he had the rare gift of seizing the most favourable moment to profit by his chances.

No sooner was Peter rich and titled, forced out of his seclusion and indifference, than he found himself surrounded by society, and so overwhelmed with engagements of every kind that he had no leisure even to think, only in bed. He had to sign papers, to dance attendance in law-courts of which he had the very vaguest idea, to catechise his head steward, to look at his estates in the neighbourhood of Moscow, to receive crowds of visitors, who hitherto had ignored his existence, and who now would have taken offence if he refused to admit them. Men of law and men of business, distant relatives, and mere acquaintances—all were equally kind and civil to the young heir. All, too, seemed agreed as to his noble qualities; first one and then another would say to him: "thanks to your indefatigable kindness," or "thanks to your generous heart,"—or "you who are so high-minded,"—"if he were as wise as you. . . ." etc., etc. . . . He was beginning to believe in his own inexhaustible kindness and brilliant intelligence, all the more easily, indeed, because, at the bottom of his heart, he had always known himself to be kind and intelligent. Even those who had formerly been grudging and spiteful now became gentle and affectionate. The eldest princess—she of the long waist and the flat hair like a doll's—had come to him after the funeral, with downcast eyes and crimson cheeks, to say that she was sorry for their past mis-understandings, that she knew she had no claims, but that she begged him, after the blow that had come upon her, to allow her to remain a few weeks longer in the house she loved so much, and where she had so long lived a life of sacrifice; and seeing the poor woman, usually so rigid, melt into tears, Peter took her hand, and with much agitation begged her forgiveness, not knowing, indeed, what she was talking about. And that very day the princess began to knit for him a striped woollen comforter, and her manner towards him changed completely.

"Do this for her, my dear fellow, for, after all, she went through a great deal from her uncle's temper," said Prince Basil; and he made Peter sign a cheque for the princess, after duly reflecting, on his own part, that this bone to gnaw—this cheque for 30,000 roubles—would do to throw to the poor woman and stop her mouth as to the share he had had in the struggle for the famous note-book. Peter signed the cheque, and the princess was more affectionate than ever; her sisters followed her example, particularly the youngest—with the mole; indeed, Peter sometimes felt embarrassed by her smiles and her frank agitation when they happened to meet.

This universal good-will seemed to him so very natural that he could never have doubted its sincerity. But, in truth, he had no time to ask himself the question, his new experience was at once so soothing and so intoxicating. He was the centre towards which important interests gravitated; he must be constantly moving and doing; his inaction would be fraught with mischief to many people; and yet, though he fully appreciated the good he might do, he did no more than exactly what was required of him, leaving the completion of his task to some future time.

Prince Basil took entire possession of Peter and the control of his affairs; he was quite worn out, to be sure, still, he could not make up his mind to leave the owner of such a colossal fortune, the son of an old friend, to the vagaries of fate and the designs of scoundrels. During the first few days after the old count's death he advised him on every point, telling him what he ought to do in a weary voice which seemed to imply:

"You know I am overwhelmed with business, and that I take all this trouble out of pure charity—but of course you see that what I say is right; you have no choice. . . ."

"Well, my dear boy, we are off to-morrow," he said one day in a tone of decision, closing his eyes and drumming with his fingers on Peter's arm, as though their departure had long since been discussed and fixed. "We are off to-morrow; I shall have much pleasure in offering you a seat in my carriage. Everything pressing is settled here, and I must positively get back to St. Petersburg. This is what I have got from the chancellor, to whom I applied on your behalf: you are appointed gentleman-in-waiting and attaché to the diplomatic corps. Now the diplomatic road is open to you."

Notwithstanding his authoritative tone, Peter, who had thought a great deal about the life he meant to follow, tried to protest; but in vain, he was stopped at once by Prince Basil. In such a crisis the prince had a way of talking on, in a low, hollow voice, which made it impossible to interrupt him.

"My dear fellow, I did it for my own sake—to satisfy my own conscience—you have nothing to thank me for. No one ever yet complained of being too much beloved. And you are quite free, you can go out of residence whenever you please. You will see for yourself at St. Petersburg. It is high time to turn our backs on all these painful memories. . . ." And he sighed.

"My man can follow us in your carriage. By the way, I forgot to tell you, my dear boy, we had some accounts to settle with the late lamented.—I have therefore kept the sum paid in from the Riazan property, you are not in need of it, and we will make it all square by and by."

Prince Basil had, in fact, received and kept several thousands of roubles from the estates in question.

The atmosphere of affection and kindliness that had enveloped Peter at Moscow he again found at St. Petersburg. He could not possibly decline the office—or rather the dignity, for he had nothing to do—which Prince Basil had procured for him. His crowd of acquaintances, and the invitations that were showered upon him, kept him here, even more than at Moscow, in a waking dream—in a whirl of excitement which deluded him with the sense of expectation of attaining some great good which was never quite attained. The companions of his former follies were for the most part dispersed. The Imperial Guard were on the march, Dologhow was serving as a private, Anatole had joined his regiment in the interior, and Prince Andrew had gone to the front; hence Peter could not spend his nights in the amusements to which he had formerly been addicted, and had no opportunities of intimate visits and discussions such as he had before enjoyed. All his time he was taken up with dinners and balls in the society of Prince Basil, of his stout and imposing wife, and of the fair Helen.

Anna Paulovna Schérer was far from being the last to make Peter aware of the changed estimation in which he was now held. Of old, whenever he had found himself in this lady's presence, he had always been conscious of his want of tact and aptness in all that he said; his most intelligent judgments seemed to lose all their sense as he put them into words, while Prince Hippolyte's most idiotic remarks were received as flashes of wit. Now, on the contrary, everything he said was pronounced "*charmant*," and when Anna Paulovna did not directly express her approbation, he could see that it was out of consideration for his diffidence.

One day early in the winter season of 1805–6 Peter received from her the usual little pink note of invitation. There was a postscript:

"You will meet *la belle Hélène*—one can never tire of seeing her."

As he read this it struck him for the first time that between himself and Helen there was a certain tie, which was quite evident to a great many persons; and the idea alarmed him, for it brought in its train various new responsibilities, which he had no wish to undertake, while, at the same time, it amused him as a strange and not unpleasing suggestion.

Anna Paulovna's evening party was in every respect like that of the previous July, with the difference only that the lion of the occasion was not Mortemart, but a secretary all hot from Berlin, and brimful of details concerning the czar's visit to Potsdam, where the august friends had sworn an eternal alliance for the defence of the good cause against the arch-enemy of the human race. Anna Paulovna received Peter with the shade of melancholy that she deemed due to his recent loss—for all the world seemed to have agreed that it had been a great grief to him to lose the father whom he hardly knew—the same pathetic tone which she affected in speaking of the Empress Maria Féodorovna. Then she drew her company into groups with her usual tact: the seniors—some generals and Prince Basil enjoyed the *diplomat's* society; the second group gathered round the tea-table. Their hostess was as much agitated as a commander-in-chief on a field of battle, whose head is full of brilliant combinations if only he could have time to carry them out. Seeing Peter go forward to join the elders, she lightly touched his arm:

"Stop," she said, "I have something for you to do this evening." She looked at Helen and smiled. "My dear Helen, you must take pity on my poor aunt, who adores you; go and talk to her for ten minutes, and the count will not mind sacrificing himself in your company."

She detained Peter an instant and said, with a confidential air: "Is not she quite charming?" while Helen majestically went towards *"la tante."* "What dignity for such a young creature! What tact! And what a heart! Happy the man who wins her! The man who marries her, however humble his pretensions, is sure to rise to the highest rank. . . . Don't you think so?"

Peter responded warmly to Anna Paulovna's praises, for whenever he thought of Helen it was always her beauty and her grand, serene manner that first rose before his fancy.

The old lady, ensconced in her chair, received them both kindly but without showing any enthusiastic pleasure at seeing Helen; on the contrary, she threw a scared glance at her niece as if to ask her what she was to do in the matter. Without noticing this, Anna Paulovna again lightly touched Peter's sleeve and said: "I hope you will no longer think it a bore to come to my parties!"

Helen smiled, much surprised that such an idea should suggest itself to anyone who had the distinguished happiness of admiring and talking to her. The aunt, after clearing her throat by two or three little coughs, expressed in French to Helen her pleasure at seeing her there, and then, turning to Peter, she went through the same formality with him. While this soporific conversation dragged lamely on, Helen shed on Peter one of those lovely and radiant smiles of which she was so lavish to everyone—he was so much accustomed to them that he did not even notice it! The old lady proceeded to question him as to a fine collection of snuff-boxes, that had belonged to old Count Bésoukhow, and showed him her own, with a portrait of her husband on the lid.

"Painted by Vines, no doubt," said Peter, alluding to a famous miniature painter.

He leaned across the table to take the snuff-box—he was listening all the time to the conversation of the others. He was about to rise when the old lady lifted up the box and held it out, above Helen's head. Helen bent forward, smiling. Her dress, as was then the fashion, was cut very low, and her shoulders, which to Peter looked as white as marble, were so close to him that, in spite of his short sight, he could see the outline of her throat and bosom so close to his lips that by stooping half an inch lower he might have touched them. He was aware of the warmth of her body, the fragrance of some perfume, and a vague creaking of stuffs at her slightest movement. It was not, however, the perfect union of beauties in the marble form that struck him at this instant: it was the charm of the lovely woman under the gauzy dress that flashed upon his senses. The shock thrilled through every fibre of his being and completely effaced every former impression; thenceforth he could no more have recalled them than we can reinstate a lost illusion.

"Did you never know before how beautiful I must be?" This was what she seemed to say to him. "Did it never occur to you that I am a woman—a woman to be won—and to be won by you?" This was what he read in her eyes.

He knew, all at once, not merely that Helen might be his wife, but that she would be his wife; he was as sure of it as if they had then and there been standing in front of the priest. How—when? He knew not. Would it be happiness? He could not tell. If anything he had a presentiment of misfortune, but he was sure it would happen. He looked down and then he looked up, trying to see in her the cold beauty by which, till this moment, he had been quite unmoved; he could not, as a man seeing a small plant in a fog and taking it for a tree cannot again see a tree on seeing a small plant; he had succumbed to her influence; nothing stood between them but his own free will.

"That is well; I can leave you to yourselves; I see you are getting on very well," said Anna Paulovna, as she went past. Peter wondered with some terror whether he had not committed some monstrous impropriety and betrayed his agitation.

He joined the principal group.

"I hear that you are improving your St. Petersburg house?" said Anna Paulovna. It was true: his architect had told him that certain alterations were indispensable and he had given way. "That is very wise; but do not give up your quarters at Prince Basil's; it is a good thing to have such a friend as the prince—I know something about that," said Anna Paulovna, smiling at Prince Basil. "You are so young, you need advice —you must forgive me for exercising my privileges as an old woman. . . ." And she paused, expecting a compliment, as women do who talk of their age. "If you marry, of course it will be another thing." And she cast an all-meaning glance at Peter and Helen. They did not look at each other, but Peter felt that she was dangerously near him, and he murmured some commonplace reply and grew scarlet.

When he went home he could not sleep; he could not help thinking of the shock he had gone through. He had suddenly discovered that this woman, whom he had known as a child, of whom he had been able to say indifferently: "Yes, she is very handsome," might be his.

"But she is brainless, I have always said so," he thought to himself. "There's something evil in this feeling that she inspires me with, something forbidden. And did I not hear that she was in love with her brother Anatole who was in love with her and had to be sent away from St. Petersburg in consequence. There must be something wrong in the feelings she has stirred in me—Hippolyte is her brother; Prince Basil is her father; there is something wrong about it."

And yet, through all his wandering reflections as to Helen's moral worth, he found himself smiling as he dreamed of her— dreamed of her as his wife, hoping that she might love him, that any ill that could be spoken of her was false—and suddenly she rose before him, not herself, but that fair form veiled in white drapery.

"How is it that I never saw her in this light before? . . ." And then, thinking there was something dishonourable in the notion of such a marriage, he blamed himself for his weakness. He thought over her words, her looks—and the words and looks of others who had seen them together. Anna Paulovna's transparent hints, and Prince Basil's, too; and he wondered with horror whether he were not already pledged to do a thing that he felt must be wrong and against his conscience . . . but, even as he pronounced judgment, in his innermost soul he was gazing at the brilliant image of Helen in all the glory of her womanly beauty.

CHAPTER LII

SOME weeks after this Prince Basil was sent on a tour of inspection of four governments; he had begged for the appointment with a view to visiting his own ruined properties, taking up his son Anatole by the way, and going with him to see Prince Bolkonsky, in the hope of marrying him to this wealthy old man's daughter. But, before setting out on their fresh enterprise, it was necessary to bring Peter's indecision to a point; the young man spent all his days with him, and looked sheepish and awkward—as all lovers are—in Helen's company, but never took the decisive step.

"This is all very well, but it must come to an end," said Prince Basil to himself one morning, with a weary sigh, for he was beginning to think that Peter, who owed so much to him, was not behaving quite rightly in the matter. "Is it the giddiness of youth? God bless the lad!"—and Prince Basil reflected with satisfaction on his own indulgent kindness— "but it must end somehow. The day after to-morrow is her birthday: I will ask a few friends, and if he does not find out what he ought to do next, I must see to it; it is my duty as a father."

Six weeks had passed since Anna Paulovna's party and the sleepless night, during which Peter had made up his mind that a marriage with Helen would be his ruin, and that he had no choice but to go away and avoid her. Still he had not quitted her father's house; he felt with horror that every day entangled him more deeply, that he would no longer meet Helen with his former indifference; he had not strength of mind enough to break away from her; he seemed to be dragged into marrying her though he knew that nothing but misery could come of it. Perhaps he might have escaped in time even now, if Prince Basil, who had never been known to have anyone in his house, had not taken it into his head to have company every evening, and Peter's absence, as he was assured, would have removed a pleasurable element from these gatherings and have disappointed everyone. During the short time which Prince Basil spent in the house, he constantly, as he offered him his clean-shaven cheek, took the opportunity of saying: "Till to-morrow," or "till we meet at dinner," or "I am staying at home on your account," though, if in fact he stayed at home on Peter's account, as he said, he paid him no special attention.

Peter lacked the courage to disappoint his hopes. Every day he said to himself: "I must learn to know her better; was I mistaken then, or am I deceiving myself now? She is not stupid, she is delightful! she does not talk much, to be sure, but then she never talks nonsense, and never gets into difficulties, she is never disconcerted and, therefore, cannot be a bad woman."

He would sometimes try to draw her into some discussion; she would reply, in a soft voice, but with some remark which showed how little interest she felt in the matter, or else by a smile and a look, which, in his eyes, were an infallible sign of her superiority. She was right no doubt, to treat these discussions as worthless in comparison with her smile: she had a particular smile for him, of radiant confidence, quite unlike the stereotyped smile that generally lighted up her lovely face. Peter knew well enough that something was expected of him—a word, a step beyond the line; and he knew that sooner or later he would cross the line, in spite of the unaccountable horror he felt at the mere idea. How many times during these last weeks had he felt himself carried away, hurried on towards the abyss, and had asked himself: "Where is my firmness? Have I lost it all?"

During these struggles his strength of will did in fact seem to have disappeared entirely. Peter was one of those men who have no power of will, excepting when the conscience is absolutely clear; and from the moment when, over the old lady's snuff-box, a sensual impulse had taken possession of him, a sense of guiltiness had paralysed his will and tenacity.

A small party of intimates, relations and friends, as the princess called them, supped at the Kouraguines' on the evening of Helen's birthday, and they had been given to understand that the fate of the heroine was to be decided on this occasion. Her mother, who had formerly been a majestic beauty, but who had grown very stout, sat at the head of the table; near her were the most distinguished guests, an old general officer, his wife, and Anna Paulovna. At the other end were placed the elders of the party and the residents in the house; Helen and Peter were side by side. Prince Basil would not sit down: he walked round the table from one to another of his guests, in the best possible humour, saying a kind word to one and another, excepting Peter and Helen, whom he totally ignored. Wax-candles lighted up the scene, silver, glass, the ladies' dresses and gold and silver lace sparkled in their rays; round the table blazed the scarlet liveries of the menservants. On all sides there was a rattle of knives, a clatter of plates and glasses, and the lively confusion of voices in conversation. An aged chamberlain was making ardent professions of love to an equally aged baroness, who answered with fits of laughter; another was telling some misadventure that had happened to a certain Maria Victorovna, while Prince Basil, standing half-way down the room, attracted general attention by describing, with much zest, the latest meeting of the Imperial Council, in the course of which the newly-appointed Governor of St. Petersburg (Sergueï Kousmitch Viasmitinow) had received and attempted to read a despatch addressed to him from head-quarters by the Emperor Alexander. In this epistle the czar had acknowledged the endless proofs of fidelity shown him every day by his people, and added that those of the citizens of St. Petersburg were especially precious in his eyes, that he was proud to be the monarch of such a nation, and hoped to prove himself worthy of the honour.

"The letter began: 'Sergueï Kousmitch, from all sides I learn . . .'"

"And he got no further?" asked a lady.

"Not another word: 'Sergueï Kousmitch, from all sides . . . from all sides, Sergueï Kousmitch'—and poor Viasmitinow could get no further," said Prince Basil laughing. "He tried again and again, but as soon as he had read his name, 'Sergueï,' his voice broke, at 'Kousmitch' the tears came, and when he had read, 'from all sides,' he was so choked with sobs that he could not go on. Then he pulled out his handkerchief and began again: 'Serguei Kousmitch, from all sides . . .' and tears stopped him again, and someone offered to read the despatch."

"Kousmitch . . . from all sides . . . tears," repeated someone laughing.

"Do not be naughty!" said Anna Paulovna, shaking her finger. "Viasmitinow is such a thorough good soul!"

Everyone was laughing and gay, excepting Peter and Helen, who sat silent, and at the greatest pains to hide the beatific and bashful smile which their own feelings brought involuntarily to their lips.

It was all very well to chatter and laugh and jest, to eat fricass es and ices and sip Rhine wine, to avoid noticing them, and to seem to ignore their existence—everyone knew instinctively that this was but a pretence, and betrayed it by their furtive glances at the couple, and shouts of laughter over the story of "Serguei Kousmitch." By degrees, indeed, the attention of the whole party was concentrated on them. Even while he was imitating Kousmitch's sobbing, Prince Basil cast a searching eye on his daughter: "It is all right," he said to himself, "it will be settled this evening." And Anna Paulovna's warning finger seemed to be wagging congratulations on the approaching marriage.

The elder princess, fixing a wrathful gaze on her daughter while with a melancholy sign she offered wine to the lady near her, seemed to imply: "Alas! there is nothing left for us but to drink sweet wine; it is their turn, in their youth and insolent happiness."

"Yes, that is true happiness," thought the old courtier, as he looked at the lovers. "What rubbish all the nonsense I can talk is in comparison with that."

In the midst of all the mean and artificial interests which stirred this circle of souls, a genuine and natural emotion had pierced the crust, the reciprocal feeling of two fine, warm-blooded young creatures; it rose superior to this skeleton structure of affectations and conventionalities and crushed it utterly Not the company only, but the very servants seemed conscious of it, and lingered to gaze at Helen's dazzling beauty and Peter's blushing and eager face. It seemed as if even the light of the candles was concentrated on those two happy faces. Peter was happy, and at the same time embarrassed at feeling himself the centre of attention. He sat in the bewildered state of a man so absorbed that he has only a vague idea of what is going on around him, and only catches flashing glimpses of the realities of life.

"It is all over—how has it come about so quickly—for I cannot go back now, it is inevitable—for her sake, for mine, for everyone's. . . . They are so confident that I cannot disappoint them."

This was what Peter thought as he looked at the white shoulders that gleamed so close to him. Now and again a feeling of shame came over him; it annoyed him to be an object of general attention, to know that he looked so frankly happy, to be playing the part of Paris to his brilliant Helen—he, with his plain face. But it was all as it should be, no doubt, so he comforted himself. He had done nothing to bring matters to this pass: he had come from Moscow with Prince Basil, and had stayed in his house . . . well, and why not? Then he had played cards with her, had picked up her workbag, and walked out with her. . . . When did it all begin? . . . And now they were as good as betrothed. . . . She is by his side, close to him; he can see her, feel her breathe the same air—he admires her beauty. . . . And then again it would seem as if it were not she but he who is so extraordinarily good-looking, and that is why everybody is gazing at him, and he, happy in this general astonishment, draws himself up, raises his head and beams at his own happiness." And a well-known voice asking him the same question a second time roused him from his day-dream:

"Tell me, when was it that you received Bolkonsky's letter? You are so absent this evening! . . ." said Prince Basil. Then Peter saw that everyone was smiling at him and at Helen.

"After all, if they all know it," he thought, "it is well that it should be true. . . ." And a bright smile lighted up his face again.

"When did the letter come? From Olmütz, was it not?"

"How can he think of such trifles!" thought Peter. "Yes, from Olmütz," and he sighed.

When supper was ended he offered her his arm, and led her back into the drawing-room, behind the other guests. The party broke up, and some went away without saying good night to Helen, as if to mark that they did not wish to occupy her attention; those who went to bid her good-bye only detained her an instant, and begged her not to think it necessary to see them to the door. The old chamberlain went away depressed and saddened. What was his futile career as compared with

217

the happiness of these young things? The old general, when his wife inquired after his leg, growled out a reply and added in a mutter to himself: "Silly old fool! . . . Look at Helen Vassilievna, she will be handsome when she is fifty."

"I might almost venture to congratulate you," murmured Anna Paulovna, tenderly embracing the elder princess. "If it were not for a bad headache, I would stay a little longer."

Princess Kouraguine made no reply; she was envious of her daughter's happiness. While all the world was saying good night, Peter had been left alone with Helen in a little drawing-room; he had often been alone with her before and had never made love to her. He knew now that the hour had come, but he could not make up his mind to take the final plunge. He was ashamed: he felt as if had usurped a place that had never been meant for him: "You have no right to this happiness," said a voice within him. "It is for one who has not what you have already."

But this silence must be broken: he asked her if she had enjoyed the evening. She answered with her usual directness that she had never had a pleasanter birthday.

Her more immediate relations were still chatting in the big drawing-room. Prince Basil dropped in upon them, coming towards Peter, who could think of nothing better than to rise hastily and observe that it was growing late. A gaze of stern inquiry met his eye, as much as to ask what he meant by this strange remark; but Prince Basil at once recovered his insinuating expression, and made him sit down again.

"Well, Helen?" he said, in the tender tone of affection that comes natural to parents who are fond of their children, and which the prince could put on without feeling it. . . . "Sergueï Kousmitch, from all sides . . ." he began, and he fidgeted with his waistcoat button.

Peter quite understood that this anecdote was not what interested Prince Basil at this juncture, and Prince Basil saw that he understood. He hastily left the room, and the agitation which the young man fancied he could detect in the old one touched him deeply; he turned to Helen: she was confused and awkward; he fancied she implied: "It is all your fault."

"It is inevitable—I must do it—I cannot!" and he began talking on all sorts of subjects, asking her where the point lay of this story about Sergueï Kousmitch. Helen said she had not even heard it.

In the next room her mother was discussing Peter with an

old lady: "Of course it is a very splendid match, but for happiness, my dear friend . . ."

"Marriages are made in Heaven!" said the old lady.

Prince Basil returned at this moment; he went into a remote corner, sat down, shut his eyes and fell asleep. His head dropped forward and he woke with a start.

"Aline," he said to his wife, "go and see what they are about."

The princess walked past the door of the inner room, just glancing in as she went by.

"They have not stirred," she said to her husband.

Prince Basil frowned and screwed his mouth on one side with a vulgar expression of disgust and ill-humour, the muscles of his cheeks twitched; then he gave himself a shake, and tossing back his head, he walked resolutely into the little drawing-room. He looked so solemnly triumphant that Peter started to his feet, quite scared.

"Thank God!" he said. "My wife has told me all." And he clasped Peter and his daughter in his arms. "Helen, my darling, what happiness! I am so glad! . . ." His voice quavered.

"And I was so much attached to your father. . . . She will be a devoted wife! God bless you!"

Real tears rolled down his cheeks.

"Princess," he called out to his wife, "come here, come quickly!" The princess came in, bathed in tears; the old cousin, too, was wiping her eyes; they embraced Peter; Peter kissed Helen's hand. A few minutes later they were alone again.

"It had to be," said Peter to himself, "so it is of no use to ask whether it is for good or for evil; for good so far, at any rate, as that I am out of suspense." He was holding Helen's hand, while her fair bosom rose and fell.

"Helen," he said, simply and distinctly; then he paused.

"It is customary, of course," he thought, "to say something under these extraordinary circumstances—but what?"

He could not remember; he looked at her, and she came closer to him, colouring deeply.

"Take them off—oh, take them off!" she exclaimed, pointing to his spectacles. Peter took them off, and his startled, inquiring eyes had the odd look which eyes accustomed to see through glasses always assume. He bent over her hand, but she, with a hasty and violent movement, intercepted the action,

and passionately pressed her lips to his. The sudden break-
down of her usual reserve and her utter self-abandonment
struck Peter painfully.

"Too late—too late," thought he. "It is done now—and
after all I love her!"

"I love you!" he said aloud, being obliged to say something.
But the confession sounded so thin that he was ashamed of it.

Six weeks later he was married and settled as the saying is;
the happy owner of a beautiful wife and of several millions, in
the splendid mansion of the Bésoukhows, which was entirely
refitted for the occasion.

CHAPTER LIII

In the month of November 1805, old Prince Bolkonsky had
a letter from Prince Basil announcing his intention of paying
him a visit, with his son, at an early date.

"I have been sent on a tour of inspection," he wrote, "and
a hundred versts of cross-country shall not prevent my paying
you my respects, my worthy benefactor. Anatole is with me,
on his way to join the army, and I hope you will grant him the
opportunity of expressing in person the regard for you that he
has inherited from his father."

"So much the better; we shall not have to take Maria into
society since suitors seek us out here." This was the indiscreet
comment that escaped the little princess when she was informed
of the news. The prince frowned and said nothing.

A fortnight after the receipt of this letter Prince Basil's
servants one day made their appearance; they had preceded
their master, who was to arrive next day.

Prince Bolkonsky had always had a very low opinion of
Kouraguine, and his splendid success during the last few years,
with the high position he had contrived to win under the last
two emperors, had strengthened his distrust. He guessed what
the under-purpose of his visit was, from the transparent hints
in his letter and the little princess's insinuations, and his dislike
took the form of deep contempt. He sniffed contemptuously
whenever he mentioned him, and on the day of his arrival was
more morose than ever. Was it Prince Basil's advent that had
put him out, or did it merely aggravate his usual ill-temper?
Be that as it may, he was as surly as a bear.

Tikhon even advised the architect not to go into the prince's room: "Listen to his tramp," he said, directing the architect's attention to the sound of their master's steps. "He is walking on his heels, we know what that means."

Nevertheless, at nine o'clock, Prince Bolkonsky, wrapped in a velvet pelisse with a sable collar and a cap of the same fur, went out for his daily walk. It had snowed the day before; the alley which led to the greenhouse had been swept; traces of the gardener's presence were still visible, and a spade was stuck upright in the ridge of soft snow that was piled up at the side of the path. The prince went the round of the greenhouses and outbuildings with a gloomy look and in total silence.

"Can sleighs come up?" he asked the steward who followed him, and who looked like the exact double of his master.

"The snow is very deep, highness; I have ordered them to clear the high road."

The prince nodded approval and went up the steps.

"Thank Heaven!" thought the man, "the storm has not burst," and he added aloud: "It would have been difficult to drive up, highness, and hearing that a minister was coming to see your excellency. . . ."

The prince turned upon him at once and fixed him with a furious glare:

"A minister! what minister? Who gave you any orders?" he said, in his loud, harsh voice. "The road is not cleared for the princess, my daughter, but for a minister! There is no minister coming!"

"Your excellency, I thought. . . ."

"You thought! Villain, rascal, beggar—I will teach you to think!"

He raised his cane, which would certainly have fallen on Alpatitch if he had not instinctively drawn back. Frightened at his own daring, though the impulse was a natural one, Alpatitch bowed his bald head before his master, who, in spite of the submissive gesture—or by reason of it perhaps—did not lift his stick again, though he continued to scold:

"Rascal!—Have the snow thrown back on the roadway." He went into the room and slammed the door.

Princess Maria and Mademoiselle Bourrienne stood waiting for the prince to come to dinner; they knew that he was in a very bad temper, but Mademoiselle Bourrienne's lively face seemed to imply: "Much I care! I am always the same."

As to Princess Maria, she was very conscious that she would have done well to imitate this placid indifference, but she simply could not. She was pale and frightened, and stood with downcast eyes.

"If I pretend not to notice his ill-humour he will think I have no sympathy with him," she said to herself, "and then he will accuse me of being tiresome and sulky."

The prince glanced at his daughter's scared face.

"A double-distilled simpleton!" he muttered between his teeth, "and the other one—not here? Have they told her? Where is the princess? In hiding?" he asked.

"She is not very well," said Mademoiselle Bourrienne, "she will not come down—it is only natural—under the circumstances."

The prince cleared his throat, and sat down. His plate not being wiped to his satisfaction he flung it behind him; Tikhon caught it and handed it to the butler.

The little princess was not ill, but hearing of her father-in-law's angry mood she had made up her mind to stay in her own rooms.

"I am afraid—for my baby; God knows what might happen if I were frightened," she said to Mademoiselle Bourrienne, to whom she had taken a great fancy, and who spent her days with her, and indeed slept with her sometimes. The princess had no reticence with her, but freely judged and criticised her father-in-law, of whom she felt the utmost terror and dislike. As to the antipathy it was reciprocal, but on the prince's part it took the form of contempt.

"We have company coming, I hear, prince," said the Frenchwoman, as she unfolded her napkin with her dainty pink fingers. "His Excellency Prince Kouraguine and his son, I am informed."

"Hm! His excellency is a whipper-snapper—and I helped him into the ministry," growled the prince, much offended. "As to his son, I am sure I do not know why he is coming; Princess Elizabeth Carlovna and Princess Maria know perhaps: for my part, I don't know, and I don't want to know." He looked at his daughter, who coloured.

"You—are you ill?" he asked. "Are you afraid of the minister—as that idiot Alpatitch called him this morning."

"No, father."

Mademoiselle Bourrienne was unlucky in her choice of a subject; but this did not stop her chatter—she talked about the orangeries, and about the beauty of some plant that had just blossomed, till, after the soup, Prince Bolkonsky had somewhat softened.

When dinner was over he went to see his daughter-in-law, who was seated at a little table and gossiping with her maid, Macha. She turned pale at the sight of the old prince, and she did not look pretty—on the contrary, rather ugly. Her cheeks had sunk, her eyes were set in dark circles, and her short upper lip showed her teeth.

"Nothing, it is nothing," she said, in reply to her father-in-law's inquiries. "I was not very comfortable."

"Want nothing?"

"Nothing, thank you."

"All right, all right." And he went away.

Alpatitch met him in the ante-room.

"You have thrown the snow back on the road?"

"Yes, highness—forgive me! It was my stupidity. . . ."

His master interrupted him with a forced smile: "All right —very good," he held out his hand, which the man kissed, and then he retired to his study.

Prince Basil arrived in the evening; in the road he found the drivers and stablemen of the estate who, with much shouting and swearing, dragged his *vasok* [1] over the snow that had been thrown back on the road.

Separate rooms had been prepared for the visitors. Anatole, in his shirt sleeves, his hands on his hips, sat staring with his large, fine eyes, smiling absently at the little table before him. To him life was one uninterrupted series of amusements, which somebody, for some unknown reason had undertaken to supply him with, even when it included a visit to a morose old man and an ugly heiress; take it for all it might have its comic side— why not marry her since she was rich? Money is no marplot. He shaved and scented himself with the elegant care which he always devoted to every detail of his toilet, and holding up his head with the all-conquering air that was natural to him, he went to find his father, on whom two valets were busily attending. Prince Basil nodded to him gaily, as much as to say: "You look very well."

"Come, father, without any nonsense, is she positively monstrous?" asked Anatole, returning to a question he had discussed several times in the course of their journey.

"No nonsense, I entreat you; do all you can to make yourself

[1] A carriage mounted on runners.

acceptable and respectful to the old man. That is the chief point."

"But if he fires any very unpleasant shots at me, I shall go away, I warn you. I hate your old men."

"Do not forget that it depends entirely on yourself."

Meanwhile the ladies in the female-servants' hall had been informed, not merely of the arrival of the minister and his son, but of every detail concerning them. Princess Maria had gone to her own room, and was vainly endeavouring to control her agitation.

"Why did they write? Why did Lisa say anything about it? It is impossible—I know it is . . ." and she added, as she looked at herself in the glass: "How can I go into the drawing-room? I can never be quite myself, even if I like him!"

The mere thought of her father filled her with terror. Macha had told the little princess and Mademoiselle Bourrienne how this handsome young gentleman, with his bright colour and black eyebrows, had flown upstairs "like an eagle," three steps at a time, while his old father had hobbled slowly behind, dragging one leg after the other.

"They are come, Maria, did you know?" said her sister-in-law, as she and Mademoiselle Bourrienne entered Maria's room. Lisa dropped into an arm-chair; she had changed her morning dressing-gown and put on one of her prettiest dresses; her hair, too, was carefully dressed, but even her brightened expression could not disguise the alteration in her features; on the contrary, her elegant toilet showed it more plainly. Mademoiselle Bourrienne, too, had taken much pains to make the best of her engaging person.

"Are you not going to dress, dear princess?" she said. "They have just brought word that the gentlemen are now in the drawing-room. . . . Will you make an alteration in your dress?"

Princess Lisa rang for a maid and merrily reviewed all her sister-in-law's wardrobe. Princess Maria hated herself for her own excitement, which she felt to be undignified, and almost hated her two companions who took it as a matter of course. It would have been self-betrayal to reproach them, and a refusal to dress would have entailed an endless fire of raillery and advice. She blushed, her fine eyes grew dim, her colour faded in patches, and she resigned herself like a victim to the tyranny of Lisa and Mademoiselle Bourrienne, who set to work to vie with each other in trying, *in perfect sincerity*, to beautify her. She, poor girl, was so plain, that any rivalry with them was quite out of the question, and they did their best to dress her becomingly, with all the simple faith in adornment that is inherent in woman.

"Really, my dear, that gown is not pretty," said Lisa, drawing back to judge of the effect. "Try the other one; your whole life may be in the balance. . . . No! It is too light, it does not suit you."

It was not the gown that was in fault but the wearer. The little princess and the Frenchwoman could not see this; they were convinced that a blue bow here, a curl pinned up there, a scarf across the brown dress would set everything right. They failed to see that nothing could alter the expression of that careworn face; they might change the setting as much as they liked, it would still be insignificant and unattractive. After three or four experiments Princess Maria, still submissive, saw herself dressed in the light gown with a blue sash, her hair turned up from her face, which made her look worse than ever; the little princess having walked round her twice to examine her from every side and arrange the folds, exclaimed in despair: "It will never do! No, Maria, it certainly does not suit you. I like you better in your everyday grey frock. To please me, Katia," she added to the maid, "bring the princess her common grey gown. You will see," she went on to Mademoiselle Bourrienne, smiling at her artistic schemes, "you will see what I will do!"

Katia fetched the dress; Maria stood motionless in front of the glass. Mademoiselle Bourrienne saw that her eyes were tearful, that her lip quivered and she was ready to cry.

"Come, dear princess, try once more." And Lisa, taking the grey gown from the maid, came towards her.

"Now, Maria, we will try something quite plain, quite simple." And all three chirped and fluttered like so many birds.

"No—that will do; let me be." There was something so serious and melancholy in her voice that the three birds ceased chirping at once. They saw in the beseeching expression of her dark eyes that it was of no use to persist.

"At any rate do your hair differently! I told you so," said Lisa to Mademoiselle Bourrienne, "Maria has one of those faces which that style of hair-dressing never suits—never in the least. Alter that at any rate."

"No, no; let it be, I do not care a single pin."

Her companions in fact could not help seeing that. Dressed

out like this she was plainer than ever, but they knew the meaning that lay behind that melancholy gaze, the expression in her of a firm determination.

"You will alter it, won't you?" repeated Lisa; but Maria said no more.

The little princess quitted the room, and Maria, left to herself, did not look in the glass again. She stood motionless. She was dreaming of the husband—of the strong, commanding man, gifted with a mysterious charm, who would carry her off into his own world, so unlike this in which she lived, and bright with happiness. Then she thought of a child—her child—a little baby like her nurse's grandchild which she had seen only the day before. She felt it in her arms, clasped it to her bosom —her husband looking on, gazing fondly at her and their child. . . . "But it is impossible, I am too ugly!" she thought.

"Tea is served and the prince is coming out of his room," the maid called to her through the door, and she started and trembled, frightened at her own imaginings.

Before going down she went into the oratory, and fixing her gaze on the blackened image of the Redeemer in the softened light of the lamp, she clasped her hands and spent a few minutes in silent prayer. Her soul was tossed by doubts: would the joys of love—of earthly love—ever be vouchsafed to her? In her visions of marriage she always pictured domestic happiness as completed by a family of children; but her secret dream, unconfessed even to herself, was to know that earthly passion, and the craving was all the stronger because she buried it out of sight of others and of herself: "O God! how can I purge my heart of these promptings of the devil? How can I escape these horrible ideas and teach myself to bow calmly to Thy will?" And she hardly put the prayer into words when she found the answer in her own heart: "Ask nothing for yourself, seek nothing, do not worry yourself, and envy no one; the future must remain hidden, but when it comes it must find you ready for whatever it may bring. If it should be God's will to try you by the duties of married life, His will be done!"

These reflections composed her spirit; still, at the bottom of her heart she cherished the wish to see her dream realised; she sighed and crossed herself. Then she went downstairs without another thought for her dress, or her hair, or her appearance in the room, or what she should say. What did these miserable trifles signify in the plans of the Almighty, without whose will not a hair can fall from a man's head.

BEFORE TILSIT

CHAPTER LIV

SHE found Prince Basil and his son in the drawing-room, talking to the little princess and Mademoiselle Bourrienne. She went forward awkwardly, treading heavily on her heels. The two men and Mademoiselle Bourrienne rose, and the little princess exclaimed: "Here is Maria!"

Her eye took in the whole party at a glance. She saw the grave face that Prince Basil had put on at seeing her give way to an affable smile; she saw her sister-in-law's eyes inquisitively watching their visitors' expression to see the effect she was producing; she saw Mademoiselle Bourrienne, with her ribbons and her pretty face, more eager than she had ever seen it, turned towards *him*—but *him* she did not see—she was only aware that something tall, radiant and beautiful, came towards her as she entered. Prince Basil was the first to kiss her hand, her lips lightly rested on the bald forehead that bowed over her,[1] and in reply to his compliments she assured him that she had not forgotten him. Anatole followed his father's example, but she could not see him: she felt her hand firmly held in a soft grasp, and her lips scarcely touched a white brow shaded by thick, chestnut hair. Then looking up, she was struck at seeing him so handsome. He stood before her with one finger hooked into a button-hole of his uniform, slight and well made, his weight thrown on one leg, looking at her without speaking —and without thinking of her. Anatole had not a swift apprehension nor was he eloquent, but on the other hand he was possessed of that presence of mind which is invaluable in society, and which nothing could disturb. A shy man who had betrayed any embarrassment at the rudeness of being speechless on a first introduction, and who had floundered in his attempts to get out of it, would have made matters worse; while Anatole who did not allow it to disturb him, calmly gazed at Princess Maria's coiffure, and was in no hurry to break the silence.

"You can talk if you like," he seemed to convey, "I do not care to talk."

His sense of superiority infused a shade of contempt into his manner towards women and excited their curiosity and fear, nay, even their love. He always seemed to be saying: "I

[1] It is always customary in Russia for a lady to kiss the man who kissed her hand.

227

know you thoroughly, take my word for it. What is the use of attempting any concealment?—And you are quite satisfied!"

He may not have thought this; indeed, he probably did not, for he rarely took the trouble to think; but he conveyed this impression, and Princess Maria felt it so strongly that she at once addressed herself to Prince Basil in order to show his son that she considered herself unworthy to engage his attention. The conversation was lively and brisk, thanks chiefly to the gay chatter of the little princess, who was very ready to open her lips and show her pretty white teeth. She and Prince Basil had rushed into a flow of gossip which might have led the hearer to believe that between her and her interlocutor there was an exchange of reminiscences and anecdotes known only to themselves, while in fact it was no more than a give and take of sharp speeches based on no real previous intimacy. Prince Basil paid her in her own coin, and so did Anatole, who scarcely knew her. Mademoiselle Bourrienne thought it her duty to take a part in this gossip, and Princess Maria found herself drawn into the gay discussion.

"We can enjoy your society all to ourselves, my dear prince: it is not as it used to be at Anna's parties: you always fled . . . poor dear Anna."

"But, at any rate, you will not talk politics, as Anna does?"

"And our tea-table then?"

"To be sure!"

"Why did you never come to Anna's parties?" she said to Anatole. "Oh! I know. I remember—your brother Hippolyte told me of all your exploits. I know, I know," she went on, shaking her pretty finger at him, "I have heard of your doings in Paris."

"And did Hipployte tell you," said Prince Basil to his son, while he took Lisa's hand as if to secure her, "how he pined in vain for this sweet little lady who would have nothing to say to him? A pearl among women!" he added, turning to Princess Maria.

Mademoiselle Bourrienne at the word "Paris" took advantage of the cue to throw in a few personal reminiscences. She questioned Anatole as to his stay there: "Did he like Paris?"

Anatole was delighted to answer, smiling in her face; he had quite made up his secret mind that he was not likely to be too much bored at Lissy-Gory.

"She is not bad, not at all bad, this lady-companion," he said to himself. "I only hope that when the other marries

228

me she will bring her with her. She is a very nice little person, upon my soul."

The old prince meanwhile was not hurrying over his toilet; he was gloomy and cross, and meditating what was to be done. This visit put him out excessively.

"What can Prince Basil and his son want of me? The father is an empty-headed chatterbox—the son must be a nice specimen."

Their coming annoyed him chiefly because it brought up a subject which he constantly endeavoured to set aside, trying to cheat his own judgment. He had often asked himself whether he must not one day make up his mind to part from his daughter; but he never put the question point blank, for he knew that if he were to answer it fairly and plainly, it would be in direct antagonism not only to his feelings, but to his most cherished habits. To live without her, little as he appeared to care for her, seemed to him a total impossibility.

"What can she want to marry for, and be miserable? Look at Lisa, who certainly could not have had a better husband. Is she satisfied with her lot? And plain and awkward as Maria is, who would marry her for her own sake? It would be for her money and her connections! Would she not be much happier unmarried?"

So thought Prince Bolkonsky as he dressed himself, and he owned to himself that the terrible dilemma was on the eve of a solution, for it was Prince Basil's evident intention to make the offer, if not this evening, quite certainly to-morrow. His name, to be sure, his position in society—all was very suitable; but was he worthy of her? "That remains to be seen," he said aloud to himself.

He went to the drawing-room with a decided step and manner. As he went in, his eye seized every detail; his daughter-in-law's evening dress, Mademoiselle Bourrienne's bows, his daughter's preposterous head-dress, her evident isolation and the graces of the Frenchwoman and Anatole.

"She is bedizened like a simpleton," thought he, "and he does not seem to care a straw for her!"

"How do you do?" he said to Kouraguine; "I am happy to see you here."

"Friendship ignores distance," said Prince Basil, in his usual tone of confident familiarity. "This is my younger son—give him your regard; I recommend him to your good graces."

"A handsome lad! Very fine boy!" said the host, examining

Anatole. "Kiss me—come here." He offered him his cheek, which Anatole duly kissed, looking closely at the prince, but with perfect composure, and expecting one of the rough quaint speeches of which his father had warned him. The old man seated himself in the usual corner of the sofa, and after offering an easy chair to Prince Basil began talking of the news and politics of the day; while he listened attentively to his guest, he kept his eye on his daughter.

"Yes, that is the latest from Potsdam!" And as he repeated his guest's last words, he rose and went up to Maria:

"Is it to do honour to your company that you have made such a figure of yourself? Beautiful! Upon my soul, quite beautiful. For the guests you have done your hair differently, well, understand clearly, in their presence I forbid you ever again to fig yourself out without my leave."

"It is I who am to blame, father," interposed the little princess, growing red.

"You, madame, have every right to dress yourself out as you please," he replied bowing low, "but she need do nothing to disfigure herself; she is ugly enough without that." And he went back to his seat, and took no further notice of his daughter, who was ready to cry.

"It seems to me that the way the princess has dressed her hair is very becoming," said Prince Basil.

"Well, young man—what is your name? Come here and talk to me; we must make acquaintance."

"Now the fun is going to begin," said Anatole to himself as he sat down by his host.

"So you have been brought up abroad, as I understand.— Very different from your father and me, who were taught to read and write by the parish deacon! And now, my young friend, you are one of the Horse Guards?" and he looked very closely into the young man's face.

"No—I have joined a marching regiment," said Anatole who had much difficulty in restraining his inclination to laugh.

"Very good, very good. You are anxious to serve your czar and country. We are at war, and a fine fellow like you ought to see service—active service!"

"No, prince, the regiment is gone to the front, and I am attached. . . . What am I attached to, papa?" he asked with a laugh.

"Service! he is on service! ha, ha! and he asks his father what he is attached to?"

Bolkonsky went into a fit of laughing in which Anatole joined, till the prince stopped short, and said with a scowl:

"Go—get along with you."

Anatole obeyed, and rejoined the ladies.

"You had him educated abroad, I think, Prince Basil?"

"I did the best I could for him," replied Prince Basil, "for the education there is far better than here."

"Yes, everything is changed nowadays—everything is new, a very handsome boy—very. Will you come into my study?"

No sooner were they alone than Prince Basil hastened to pour out his hopes and wishes.

"Do you suppose I keep her chained up, or cannot part with her? What have they got into their heads?" exclaimed Bolkonsky indignantly. "To-morrow, if she likes, for aught I care! . . . But I must know more of my son-in-law. You know what my principles are: act frankly. I will ask her to-morrow, in your presence, if she wishes it; if so he may stay. He can stay here " He finished his speech with his usual snort, speaking in the same sharp pitch as when he had taken leave of his son Andrew.

"I will be quite frank with you," said Prince Basil in the tone of a man who is convinced that it is of no use to try cunning with a too acute opponent. "You see through people. Anatole is not a genius, but he is a very good fellow, and an excellent son."

"Well, well; we shall see."

When Anatole appeared on the scene, the three ladies who had lived so long in solitude and bereft of masculine society each and all felt that, till this moment, life had lacked an important element. The faculties of thought, feeling, and observation were suddenly multiplied tenfold, and the darkness that enfolded them was lighted up by an unexpected and vivifying flash. Princess Maria did not give another thought to her luckless coiffure; she gave herself up to contemplation of this handsome, radiant being, who might be her destined husband. He seemed to her good, brave, spirited, generous; she was convinced he must be; her fancy was full of pictures of domestic happiness which she tried to get rid of and bury in the depths of her heart.

"Am I very cold, I wonder?" she said to herself. "But if I am too reserved, it is only because I am too strongly attracted by him. Still, he cannot guess what I feel, and might think I do not like him." So she did her utmost to make herself attractive, but without success.

231

"Poor girl! She is diabolically ugly!" thought Anatole.

Mademoiselle Bourrienne's imagination, too, was excited by the young man's presence. She was a pretty girl, with no sort of position; an orphan, friendless, homeless; and had never had any serious prospect in life beyond that of being the princess' companion and reader for the rest of her days. She had long been waiting for the young Russian prince who, at the first glance, would discern her great superiority to all his plain and ill-dressed country-women, who would fall in love with her and carry her off; and here was the young prince. Mademoiselle Bourrienne knew a little story which her aunt had told her, and to which her fancy supplied a sequel—a pitiful romance of a young girl led astray, abused and cast out by her mother; she had often melted into tears over a dream of telling this tale to some imaginary seducer. . . . The Russian prince who was to conquer her was here—he would declare his passion—she would tell the little tale: "My poor mother," she would say, and he would marry her at once. This was the romance Mademoiselle Bourrienne composed, piece by piece, while she talked of the delights of Paris. She had no preconceived scheme, but everything had its logical sequence in her mind, and the fragmentary episodes grouped themselves round Prince Anatole, whom she was determined to fascinate at any cost.

As to Princess Lisa, she was like an old war-horse who pricks his ears at the sound of the trumpet; she made ready to charge full tilt, forgetting her condition, to set up a flirtation without meaning the slightest harm, out of pure and giddy light-heartedness. It was Anatole's way in the company of women to pose as a man weary and sick of their allurements; still, seeing the impression he had produced here, he could not repress a genuine impulse of gratified vanity, all the more because he felt surging up within him for the bewitching little Frenchwoman one of those reckless passions which carried him away to commit the most brutal and daring outrages.

After tea they adjourned to the music-room, and Princess Maria was requested to play. Anatole stood with his elbows on the instrument, next to Mademoiselle Bourrienne, his sparkling, laughing eyes set on Maria, who felt his fixed gaze with a strange mingling of pain and pleasure. Her favourite sonata bore her spirit into a realm of delicious and secret harmony, and its poetry grew fuller and more thrilling under the inspiration of those eyes. Yes, they were fixed on her—but their look was for Mademoiselle Bourrienne, whose little foot his tenderly pressed. She, too, looked at Maria, and her pretty eyes shone with uneasy happiness and hope.

"How fond she is of me," thought Princess Maria. "How happy I am to have such a friend, and such a husband! Ah! will he ever be my husband?"

After supper, when they parted for the night, Anatole kissed Maria's hand, and she summoned up courage to look him in the face; he also kissed the Frenchwoman's hand, a great breach of etiquette; but he did it with his usual confidence. She coloured and looked at the princess in some alarm: "What nice feeling!" thought Maria. "Amélie is afraid I shall be jealous perhaps. Does she suppose that I can fail to appreciate her pure affection and devotion?"

She went up to Mademoiselle Bourrienne and kissed her affectionately. Anatole turned to Lisa and was gallantly about to kiss her hand, too. "No, no. When your father writes me word that you are quite a good boy you shall have my hand to kiss—not before." And she left the room smiling and shaking her finger at him.

CHAPTER LV

THEY all went to their rooms, but, with the exception of Anatole who went to sleep at once, it was long before any one could close an eye.

"Will he really be my husband? That man! so good and so handsome—so good!" thought Maria. She shuddered with tremors which were not natural to her; she was afraid to turn round, to move; she felt as if there was someone lurking in that dark corner behind the screen, and that that someone was the Devil—that someone was the tall man with a white forehead, black eyelashes, and scarlet lips! She called her maid, and desired her to sleep in the room with her.

Mademoiselle Bourrienne spent a long time in walking up and down the conservatory; she was vainly expecting someone, smiling at someone, shedding a few tears now and again as she thought of her poor mother reproaching her for her sin.

The little princess was scolding her maid: her bed was badly made; she could not lie comfortably; the clothes were heavy and dragged her—she herself was uneasy and uncomfortable.

This evening she was doubly aware of her discomfort, for Anatole's company had carried her thoughts back to a time when she had been light and gay, without a care; now, she was sitting in her dressing-gown and night-cap, deep in a large arm-chair, while the maid turned the mattress and smoothed the sheets for the third time.

"I told you it was all lumps and hollows; I did not wish to lie awake you may suppose. It is not my fault," she said in the peevish tone of a child on the point of crying.

The old prince could not sleep either. Tikhon, through his slumbers, heard him walking about and snorting; his dignity was insulted, and he felt the insult all the more keenly because it was addressed not to himself, but to his daughter—the daughter he loved better than himself. In vain he said to himself that he should be in no hurry to make up his mind what line he should take in this matter—a line of action strictly just and equitable; his cogitations only fomented his indignation.

"She, she could forget everything for the first-comer; everything, even her father. . . . She flies upstairs, and dresses herself out, and gives herself airs and graces till she is not in the least like herself! She is delighted to get away from her father—and yet she knew I should notice it! Brr . . . brr. And cannot I see that that jackanapes stares at Bourrienne all the time! I must get rid of her! And not a pinch of pride to make her see clearly; if she has none for herself she might have some for me! I must make her see that the coxcomb thinks only of Bourrienne. She has no pride! I must tell her."

If he were to tell his daughter that she was under a delusion, and that Anatole's whole attention was for the Frenchwoman, that, he knew, would be the surest way to wound her self-respect; his case would be won, or, in other words, his wish to keep his daughter would be fulfilled. This idea soothed him, and he called Tikhon to help him to undress.

"The devil himself sent him here," he growled as Tikhon slipped his night-dress over his parchment-coloured shoulders and covered his chest that was furred with grey hairs. "I did not ask them here; and they come and turn my life topsy-turvy —and I have not so long to live. Devil take them!"

Tikhon was accustomed to hear his master think aloud and his face never changed before the furious glare in the prince's eyes as his head came up through the night-gown.

"Are they in bed?" Tikhon was too well trained not to

know his master's wishes: "In bed, and their lights out, excellency."

"High time, too, high time, too!" growled the old man. He shuffled his feet into his slippers, wrapped himself in his dressing-gown, and lay down on a couch which served as his bed.

Though Anatole and Mademoiselle Bourrienne had not exchanged many words, they had perfectly understood each other, as regarded that part of the romance which must precede the introduction of "my poor mother." They both felt that they had much to say to each other; they met—by the merest accident —in the conservatory next morning, just as Maria, more dead than alive, was making her way as usual to her father's room. She felt that not only did everyone know that her fate was to be settled to-day, but that she herself was prepared to meet it. She read it in Tikhon's face, and in that of Prince Basil's valet, whom she met in the passage carrying up his master's hot water, and who made her a low bow.

Her father was unusually kind and gentle to her that morning; she knew his mood of old: it would not prevent his hands clenching with rage over a problem in arithmetic that she could not work out fast enough, and that would make him start up and walk away from her and say the same thing over and over again in a hollow, sternly-controlled voice.

He began at once on the matter in hand.

"A proposal has been laid before me which concerns you," he said with a forced smile. "You have guessed, no doubt, that Prince Basil did not bring his pupil"—so he chose to call Anatole without exactly knowing why—"to Lissy-Gory for the sake of showing him to me. You know what my principles are —for that reason I appeal to you."

"What am I to understand by that, father?" asked the princess, turning red and white by turns.

"Understand!" exclaimed the old man hotly. "Prince Basil thinks you will suit him for a daughter-in-law, and he has proposed for you in his pupil's name. It is plain enough. What are you to understand? And I leave the answer to you."

"I do not know . . . whatever you . . . father . . ." stammered the young girl.

"I! I have nothing to do with it; he does not want to marry me; put that quite aside. What do you wish? That is what I should be glad to learn."

Princess Maria could gather that her father viewed the marriage with no particular favour, but she warned herself that

235

now or never was the decisive moment. She looked down to avoid meeting that gaze which deprived her of all power of thought, and to which she was accustomed always to yield.

"I desire only one thing—to act as you think rightly: but if I may be allowed to express a wish. . . ."

"Exactly so!" cried the prince, interrupting her. "He will take you with your fortune, and hook on Mademoiselle Bourrienne; she will be his wife, and you . . ." But he stopped, seeing what a painful impression his words produced on his daughter. She hung her head, and was on the point of melting into tears.

"Come, come; I was only in jest. Remember one thing, my principles have always led me to consider that a young girl has a right to choose for herself. You are free; but do not forget that the happiness of your whole life depends on your decision. . . . I am not speaking of my own."

"But, father, I do not know."

"I cannot talk about it. He will marry as he is bid; but you, I tell you, are free. Go to your own room and think it over, and let me have your answer in an hour hence. You will have to give your reply in his presence. I know you will pray over it—well, well, I do not want to prevent you; pray, if you will, but you would do better to exercise your judgment. Go—yes or no, yes or no, yes or no," he repeated, as his daughter quitted the room with an unsteady step, for her fate was already decided—decided for happiness.

Still, her father's hint about Mademoiselle Bourrienne had shocked her; believing it to be false even, she could not think of it calmly. As she went through the conservatory on her way back to her own rooms a well-known voice startled her from her painful reflections. She looked up and saw, at two yards in front of her, Anatole kissing the Frenchwoman and whispering in her ear. Anatole's face plainly revealed his violent excitement as he turned towards the princess, quite forgetting that his arm was still round the girl's waist.

"Who is there—who wants me?" he seemed ready to ask.

Maria stopped, petrified, looking at them in blank bewilderment. Mademoiselle Bourrienne gave a cry and fled. Anatole bowed to Maria with a smile of audacious triumph, and, shrugging his shoulders, vanished through the door leading to his rooms.

An hour later Tikhon, who had been desired to call the Princess Maria, informed her that her father was waiting for her, and that Prince Basil was with him. He found her seated on the sofa in her room, softly stroking Amélie's hair, while the Frenchwoman was crying bitterly. Maria's soft eyes, with their loving and gentle expression, were calm and bright and beautiful once more.

"Oh, princess, I must have fallen for ever in your opinion."

"Why? I love you more than ever, and will do my best . . ." said Princess Maria, with a melancholy smile.

"But you despise me, you, so pure, will never understand how one can forget oneself through passion. Oh, if only my poor mother . . ."

"I understand everything," answered Maria, sadly. "Now compose yourself, my dear. I must go to my father."

Prince Basil, sitting with his legs crossed and his snuff-box in his hand, affected deep emotion, which he pretended to conceal under an anxious smile. As the princess entered the room he hastily disposed of a small pinch of snuff, and took both her hands.

"Ah, my dear, my dear: my son's fate is in your hands. Decide, my dear, sweet Maria, whom I have always loved as a daughter." And he turned away, for he had really brought tears into his eyes.

"Brrr . . . !" snorted old Nicholas Andreitch. "The prince, in his own name and that of his son, asks whether you will become the wife of Prince Anatole Kouraguine—yes or no. Yes or no, I say—and I reserve my right to express an opinion afterwards. Yes, my opinion, merely my opinion," he went on, in answer to a beseeching glance from Prince Basil. "Well, yes or no?"

"It is my wish, father, never to leave you, never to part while we both shall live. I do not intend to marry," said Princess Maria, looking frankly and steadily at Prince Basil and at her father.

"Folly, stuff, and nonsense!" cried the old prince, drawing his daughter towards him, and wringing her hand so hard that she cried out with pain. Prince Basil rose.

"My dear Maria, this is a moment I can never forget. But tell me, can you not give us some little hope? Can he never touch your kind and generous heart? I only ask you to say: perhaps!"

"I have said what my heart prompts. I thank you for the honour you have done me, but I can never be your son's wife."

"That is an end of it, my dear fellow. Very glad to have

seen you, very glad. You may leave us, princess. . . . Very glad, very glad, indeed," repeated Bolkonsky.

"My happiness lies in a different vocation," said Princess Maria to herself. "I shall find it in devoting myself to making others happy; and cost what it may, I will always stand by poor Amélie. She loves him so passionately, and is so bitterly penitent. I will do all I can to promote their marriage. If he is not rich enough I will give her something, and I will entreat my father and Andrew to allow it—I should be so happy in seeing her his wife, she is so lonely, so sad, so forsaken. . . . How she must love him to have forgotten herself so far! Who knows? I might have done the same."

CHAPTER LVI

THE Rostows had received no news of Nicholas for a long time when, one day in the winter, the count got a letter, and recognised his son's writing. He stole off at once to his own room, walking on tiptoe that no one might hear him, and shut himself in to read it. Anna Mikhaïlovna, who had known somehow of the arrival of the letter—nothing that occurred in the house ever escaped her—softly followed the count to his study, where she found him crying and laughing both at the same time.

"My dear friend?" said the lady, in a tone of melancholy interrogation, fully prepared to be sympathetic whatever might happen. In spite of the improvement in her affairs she still stayed on with the Rostows.

"It is from Nicolouchka . . . a letter . . . he has been wounded, my dear; wounded, poor, dear child . . . and the little countess . . . made an officer, my dear—thank God! How can I tell her?" He sobbed out.

Anna Mikhaïlovna sat down by him, wiped away his tears, which were dropping on to the letter, read it herself, and then, after wiping her own eyes, soothed the count's agitation by promising him to prepare the countess during dinner, so that in the evening, after tea, the news might be broken to her.

She kept her word. During dinner she returned again and again to the subject of the war, asked when Nicholas had last written, though she knew very well, and observed that now they might expect to hear from him any day—this very day, perhaps, who could tell? Every time she returned to her hints the countess glanced anxiously at her and at her husband, and then Anna Mikhaïlovna adroitly changed the subject. Natacha, who was the one of all the family most keenly alive to the slightest inflection of voice, the faintest shade of expression in face or manner, at once pricked up her ears, guessing that under all this there must be some mystery between her father and Anna Mikhaïlovna, and that the lady was manœuvring to prepare her mother. But in spite of her native audacity, she knew her mother's sensitiveness about her absent son too well to dare to ask questions: her uneasiness prevented her eating; she could do nothing but twist and wriggle on her chair, to the governess's great vexation. As soon as dinner was over she flew after Anna Mikhaïlovna, whom she found in the drawing-room. She sprang up and flung her arms round her neck.

"Aunt, dear little auntie, what has happened?"

"Nothing, my child."

"Dear soul of an aunt, I am sure you know something, and I will not leave go till you tell me."

Anna Mikhaïlovna shook her head.

"You are too clever by half, child."

"A letter from Nicholas, is it not?" cried Natacha, reading the answer in her aunt's face.

"But hush, be discreet. You know how excitable your mother is."

"I will be, I promise: only tell me what he says. You will not? Then I shall go straight to her and tell her."

Anna Mikhaïlovna told her the facts in a few words, and repeated her charge of secrecy.

"On my word of honour," said Natacha, crossing herself. "I will tell no one . . ." But she flew to Sonia and told her with exuberant delight: "Nicholas is wounded—he has written!"

"Nicholas!" cried Sonia, turning pale.

At the sight of the impression produced by her news, Natacha suddenly understood all the sad feeling that was mixed up with this happy news. She threw her arms round Sonia and burst into tears: "He is only slightly wounded, and he has been promoted, and he must be quite well since he writes himself."

"What cry-babies you women are," said Pétia, striding up and down the room with a truculent air. "I am glad, very glad that my brother should have distinguished himself! You are only cry-babies, and you don't understand at all."

Natacha laughed through her tears.

"Have you seen the letter?" asked Sonia.

"No, I have not read it; but Anna Mikhaïlovna told me that the worst was over, and that he is an officer."

"Heaven be praised!" said Sonia, crossing herself. "But perhaps she is not telling you the truth. Come to mamma."

Pétia was still marching up and down the room.

"If I had been in Nicolouchka's place I would have killed a great many more Frenchmen; they are miserable scoundrels; I would have killed a lot and made a mountain of them! There!"

"Hold your tongue, Pétia: you are a little goose!"

"It is not I that am a goose, it is you who are simpletons. Fancy crying for such a trifle!"

"Do you remember him?" asked Natacha, after a pause.

"Do I remember Nicholas?" asked Sonia, smiling.

"No, no: what I mean is—do you remember him clearly—quite distinctly? Do you remember all about him?" And she gesticulated emphatically to add force to her words. "Now I—I remember Nicholas—very well. But as for Boris, I cannot remember him at all—really not in the least."

"What! you do not remember Boris?" said Sonia, puzzled.

"I do not mean that I have forgotten him; I know what he is like. If I shut my eyes I can see Nicholas, but Boris. . . ." She shut her eyes: "Nothing—no one—nothing at all!"

"Oh, Natacha!" said Sonia, in rapturous earnest; she thought her unworthy no doubt to hear her confession, but that did not prevent her emphasising her words with emotional conviction: "I love your brother, and whatever may happen to him or to me I can never cease to love him."

Natacha gazed at her with wondering eyes; she felt that Sonia had spoken the truth; that this was love, and that she had never felt anything like it; she saw what it might be, but she did not understand it.

"Will you write to him?"

Sonia did not reply immediately, for this was a question which she had long been debating. How should she write to him? Nay, in the first place, ought she to write? Now that he was promoted and a wounded hero, would she be right to remind him of herself and the promises he had made.

"I do not know," she said, blushing. "If he writes to me, I will write to him."

"And you would not feel shy about it?"

"No."

"Well, I should be ashamed to write to Boris, and I shall not write."

"Ashamed! why?"

"I don't know—but I should be."

"I know why," said Pétia, indignant at his sister's declaration. "It is because she fell in love with that big fellow in spectacles"—this was Pétia's description of his namesake, Peter Bésoukhow—"and now it is the singer's turn"—the singer was Natacha's Italian singing-master—"that is why she would be ashamed."

"Pétia, you are too silly."

"Not sillier than you, my lady!" retorted the brat of nine, with all the coolness of a brigadier.

The countess had meanwhile grown suspicious over Anna Mikhaïlovna's mysterious reticence, and was sitting in her own room, with her eyes riveted on her son's miniature on the lid of a snuff-box, ready to cry at any moment. Anna Mikhaïlovna with the letter in her hand, stopped at the door of the room.

"Do not come in," she said to the count, who was behind her. "Presently. . . ." And she closed the door upon him.

The count put his ear to the keyhole, but at first could hear nothing but a series of commonplace remarks; then Anna Mikhaïlovna made a long speech; then there was a cry and a silence—and presently the two voices in an eager and joyful duet. Anna Mikhaïlovna showed in the count: her face beamed with the proud satisfaction of an operator who has performed a tedious and dangerous amputation with complete success, and who wishes the public to appreciate his skill.

"It is all over!" she said to the count; while the countess, holding the miniature in one hand and the letter in the other, kissed them in turn. She held out her hands to her husband, kissed his bald head, gazing over it at the letter and the portrait; then she pushed him gently away and again pressed them to her lips. At this moment Vera, Natacha, Sonia, and Pétia came in; Nicholas's letter was read to them. In it he described in a few lines the course of the campaign, the two fights in which he had taken part, and his promotion, ending with these words: "I kiss your hands—papa's and mamma's, and ask your blessing. Much love to Vera, Natacha, and Pétia."

He also sent his respects to Mr. Schelling and to Miss Schoss, his old nurse, and begged his mother kiss his dear Sonia for him, and tell her that he constantly thought of her and loved her truly. Sonia turned crimson at this message, and her eyes filled with tears. Then, unable to bear the gaze of so many bystanders she ran away into the drawing-room, danced round it, made a pirouette on her heel, spinning round like a top, till her dress flew out, and ended by making a balloon on the floor.

The countess shed floods of tears.

"But there is nothing to cry for, mamma," said Vera. "You ought to be glad." It was quite true, and yet her father and mother and Natacha all looked at her reproachfully.

"I do not know whom she takes after," thought the countess.

The beloved son's letter was read and re-read a hundred times, and all those who were considered worthy of hearing it had to go to the countess's room, for she would not let it go out of her hands. As she read it to the tutor, to the governess, to Mitenka, to her acquaintances, it was each time a fresh delight to her, and each time she discovered some new merit in her darling Nicholas. It was so strange for her to think that the child she had brought into the world twenty years ago—how often she had scolded her husband for spoiling him—the child she could still fancy she heard trying to say mamma—was so far away, in a foreign country, fighting as a brave man should, and doing his duty as an honest gentleman without any one to guide him! The daily experience which shows us the road trodden by a boy from the cradle to manhood had never been real to her. Every step her son took in that direction was as wonderful in her eyes as though he had been the first example of such a process of development.

"What a nice style! what pretty description! And what a noble heart! Not a word about himself, not a detail! He speaks of a man named Denissow, and he himself, I am sure, showed more courage than all the rest. What a good heart! But I always said it of him, even when he was quite little—always."

For the next week every one was busy with rough copies, written and re-written, of letters to be sent to Nicolouchka: the count and countess superintended the preparation of a parcel of necessaries, to be forwarded, with a supply of money, for the equipment of the newly-appointed officer. Anna Mikhaïlovna, with her practical wit, had secured for her son a personal protector in the army, and greater facilities for correspondence, by forwarding her letters through the Grand Duke Constantine, in command of Guards. The Rostows, on the contrary, took it for granted that the address on their letters to "The Russian Guards, on service, abroad," was perfectly clear and explicit, and that if the letters reached the commanding officer there was no reason to suppose that they would fail to reach the Pavlograd Regiment, which was, no doubt, in his immediate vicinity. However, it was settled that this packet should be sent to Boris by the grand duke's courier, and forwarded by him to Nicholas. Father, mother, Sonia, and all the children wrote letters, and the count added 6000 roubles for his son's outfit.

CHAPTER LVII

On the 12th of November Koutouzow's army, encamped in the neighbourhood of Olmütz, made ready for inspection by the czar and the Emperor of Austria. The Guards had just come up, and had encamped about fifteen versts away; they were to march forward to the parade-ground next morning by ten o'clock. That very morning Nicholas Rostow had received a note from Boris, informing him that the Ismaïlovsky Regiment would halt at fifteen versts' distance, and that he wanted to see him to give him some letters and money. Nicholas was fully alive to the desirability of this last item, for after the campaign and during his stay at Olmütz he had been exposed to various temptations from the well-furnished canteens of the vivandières, not to mention the Austrian Jews who swarmed in the camps. In the Pavlograd Hussars there was no end to the entertainments in honour of promotions; or of excursions into the town, where a restaurant had been opened by a certain "Caroline la Hongroise," in which all the waiters were girls. Rostow had given a supper to celebrate his promotion, had bought Denissow's horse "Bedouin," and was up to his ears in debt to his comrades and to the mess-steward. So, after dining with some friends, he set out in search of his old companion in the Guards' camp.

He had not yet had time to procure his new uniform, and wore his shabby *junker's* jacket, with a private's cross, his leather-backed cavalry trousers and belt, with an officer's sword: his mount was a Cossack pony that he had bought cheap, and his bruised shako was stuck rakishly on one side. As he rode towards the Ismaïlovsky camp he could think of nothing but his glee at astonishing Boris and his comrades by

243

his war-stained appearance, with no trace of the inexperienced soldier who has never smelt powder.

The Guards had made a pleasure trip rather than a march, with a great display of smartness and elegance. The knapsacks were brought on in baggage-waggons, and after each short stage the officers had found a capital dinner provided by the Austrian authorities. The regiments had marched in and out of the towns with bands playing, and throughout the march the men, in obedience to the grand duke's orders, had marched in step, and the officers dismounted and each in his place; of this the Guards were exceedingly proud. From the first Boris had marched alongside, and shared quarters with Berg, who was now captain of a company, and who, by his punctuality, had gained the goodwill of his superiors and arranged matters very much to his own advantage. Boris had also taken care to make several acquaintances, among them Prince Andrew Bolkonsky, to whom he had a letter of introduction from Peter, and by whose intervention he hoped to get an appointment on the staff of the commander-in-chief. Berg and Boris, both as smart as a new pin, and quite recovered from the fatigues of their last stage, were playing chess at a round table in the clean, snug quarters that had been assigned to them. The stem of Berg's long pipe rested between his knees, while Boris was placing the pieces with his white fingers, and never taking his eyes off his antagonist, who, as usual, was wholly absorbed in the idea of the moment.

"Well, how will you get out of that scrape?"

"We shall see."

At this instant the door opened.

"At last!" cried Rostow. "Ah, and Berg too!" "Bye-bye, babies," he went on, humming a tune his old nurse used to sing, and which never failed to send Boris and himself into fits of laughter.

"Merciful Heaven! How you have altered."

Boris rose to receive them, taking care, however, not to upset the chessmen, and he was going to embrace him when Rostow dodged on one side. The youthful impulse to escape from beaten paths was strong in Nicholas, and he constantly longed to express his feelings in some new and original way, to avoid conformity to ordinary formalities. His one idea was to do something odd—to pinch his friend—at any rate, to escape the customary greeting. Boris, on the contrary, pressed the three regulation kisses on his cheek quite calmly and affectionately

They had been separated scarcely six months, and meeting again at the very time when they were just making their first real start in life, each was struck by the great change in the other, the inevitable result of the surroundings among which they had been developing.

"You—you rascally carpet-knights, who just go out for a ride and come in spruce and shining—look at us miserable sinners in the working regiments . . ." exclaimed Rostow, who endeavoured, with his fresh, young bass and affected roughness, to give himself something of the rollicking air of a fighting man, in contrast to the dandyism of the Guards, exhibiting his mud-splashed trousers. At this moment their German hostess put her head in at the door: "By Jupiter! Is she pretty?" cried Rostow with a wink.

"Don't shout so loud—you will frighten them all!" said Boris. "Do you know, I did not expect you so soon, for I gave my note to Bolkonsky only last evening—he is an aide-de-camp I know here. I had no hope of its reaching you so quickly. Well, and how are you? You have smelt powder, I see."

Rostow did not answer, but he fidgeted with his private's Cross of St. George that hung at his buttonhole, and pointed to his hand in a sling:

"You see. . . ."

"Well, well," said Boris, smiling, "we also have had a delightful campaign. His imperial highness marched with the regiment, and we have taken it easy. In Poland, entertainments, dinners, balls without end. . . . The czarevitch is most kind to all his officers."

Then they related the various phases of their military experience: Nicholas his camp-life, Boris the advantages of his position in the Guards under distinguished favour.

"Oh, yes! The Guards! . . ." said Rostow. "Give me a glass of wine."

Boris made a face, "Well, if you really want it," said he. He took out his purse from under his white pillows and sent for some wine.

"By the way, here are your letters and your money."

Rostow tossed the bag of money on to the sofa and tore open the letter, setting his elbows on the table to read it more comfortably. Berg's presence disturbed him; feeling his eyes fixed on him, he held up the letter so as to screen his face.

"They have been free with the money!" observed Berg as he looked at the full bag sunk in the sofa cushion. "We are almost at the end of our tether here, with nothing but our pay. Now to tell you about myself."

"Look here, old fellow, if ever I find you with a letter from home and a friend you want to talk to about a hundred things at once, I promise you I will take myself off and leave you in peace; so now vanish, bolt, go to the devil. . . ." And he gave Berg a spin and a friendly glance to mitigate the ultra-frank vehemence of his words. "You will not be angry with me—I venture to treat you as an old friend!"

"Not at all, count—I understand perfectly," said Berg in his husky voice.

"Go and pay the people of the house a visit; they asked you," added Boris.

Berg put on a spotless overcoat, pushed his hair off his forehead after the fashion of the Emperor Alexander, and, satisfied that his appearance must be irresistible, he left the room with a blissful smile.

"Oh, what a brute I am!" cried Rostow, as he went on with his letter.

"What for?"

"A perfect brute not to have written to them again; they were frightened out of their wits. Well, have you sent Gavrilo for the wine? That is well; we will treat ourselves handsomely."

Among the letters in the packet there was one of introduction to Prince Bagration. The countess, following Anna Mikhaïlovna's advice, had begged it of an acquaintance, and she desired her son to present it as soon as possible, and take every advantage of it.

"What nonsense! What do I want with that?" said Rostow, tossing the letter on the table.

"Why have you thrown it aside?"

"It is a letter of recommendation—why, I laugh at it!"

"Laugh at it? But it is very necessary."

"No, I do not want anything; I am not going begging to be made aide-de-camp."

"Why not?"

"It is a footman's place!"

"Ah! you are just the same as ever, I can see," said Boris.

"And you, too—as diplomatic as ever. However, that is of no moment. . . . What are you going to do?"

"Till now, as you see, I have been getting on very well; but I must confess that my ambition is to be made aide-de-camp, and not have always to stick to my regiment."

"But why?"

"Because if once you go in for a military career, the more brilliant it is the better."

"Ha! you think so!" Rostow gazed in his friend's face, thinking of something else, and he looked fixedly at his friend evidently vainly searching for an answer to some thought. Old Gavrilo brought in the wine that had been ordered.

"You had better send for Alphonse Carlovitch," said Boris; "he will drink with you instead of me."

"Just as you please. What is the Teuton like?"

"He is really a very good fellow, very straightforward and pleasant." Again Rostow looked narrowly at Boris, and sighed. Berg being sent for returned, and the conversation became livelier over the bottle of wine. The two guardsmen gave Rostow a full account of all the entertainments they had been asked to on their march through Russia, Poland, and Austria. They told stories and quoted jokes to illustrate the kindness and the violent temper of the grand duke their colonel. Berg, who, as usual, said nothing when the subject was not of personal interest to himself, related with much complacency how, in Galicia, he had had the honour of a few words with his imperial highness, how the grand duke had complained to him of the bad order in which the men marched, how he had called them "Arnauts," and sent for the captain. This was the czarevitch's favourite term of abuse when he was in a passion.

"You will hardly believe it, count, but I was so sure of my own blamelessness, that I stood before him without a qualm. Without boasting, I may say that I know all the order of the day and regimental regulations as well as I know the Lord's Prayer. My company never have to be pulled up for breach of discipline; and I could stand in his presence with an easy conscience." As he spoke he rose to show how he had gone forward to meet his chief with a military salute. It would have been hard to imagine a face more expressive at once of respect and of self-satisfaction. "He foamed over," Berg went on, "sent me to the devil, and heaped me with 'Arnauts!' and hints of Siberia. I took care not to say a word. 'Are you dumb?' he roared. Still I did not speak. And would you believe, next morning in the general orders not a word about it all! That is what comes of not losing one's head. Yes, count, that is the great secret," he said, lighting his pipe, and puffing rings of smoke into the air.

"I congratulate you," said Rostow. Boris, seeing that his

friend was inclined to laugh at Berg, adroitly turned the conversation by asking Nicholas how and where he had been hurt. Nothing could have pleased him better, and he began a full account of the fight at Schöngraben—growing more eager as he went on, and relating it, not so much as it had actually happened, but as he would have liked it to happen—embellished, that is to say, by his vivid imagination. Rostow respected truth, and by preference adhered to it; however, imperceptibly and quite unconsciously, he deviated from it considerably. An exact and prosaic narrative would not have met with any acceptance; for his companions, like himself, had often heard a battle described, and had formed a clear idea of the scene; if he had stuck to the facts, they would not have believed him, and might very likely have accused him of not actually seeing the whole of what had taken place under his very eyes.

How could he tell them in so many words that he had simply set off at a trot; that he had fallen off his horse, sprained his wrist, and then run away from a Frenchman as fast as his legs would carry him? It would have been a great effort on his part to confine himself to these simple facts. He gave the reins to his imagination, and described how, in the hottest of the fire, he had been overmastered by mad frenzy, had forgotten everything, had rushed down on the enemy's square like a tornado, slashing right and left, had dropped at length from sheer exhaustion, and so on, and so on. . . .

"You cannot imagine," he added, "what wild fury possesses you in the thick of the fray!"

As he uttered this grandiloquent peroration, Prince Bolkonsky came into the room. Prince Andrew was flattered by the respect of his juniors, and liked to help and encourage them. He had taken a fancy to Boris, and would have been sincerely glad to serve him. Koutouzow had despatched him to carry some papers to the czarevitch, and on his way he had looked in. Seeing the young hussar on service evidently all hot from narrating his own exploits—he hated that stamp of man—he scowled, though he nodded kindly to Boris as he took his seat on the sofa. There was nothing he disliked so much as dropping in on company that was distasteful to him. Rostow, sympathetically conscious, coloured scarlet; in spite of his general dislike and contempt for the fine gentleman of the staff, there was something in Prince Andrew's dry, satirical tone that upset him considerably, and perceiving that Boris seemed to be ashamed of him, he lapsed into silence. Boris asked whether there was any news, and if he might, without indiscretion, ask what was being planned at headquarters.

"We shall probably move forward," said Prince Andrew, anxious not to compromise himself in the society of strangers. Berg took the opportunity of inquiring, with his unfailing politeness, if the captains of companies were not to be allowed double rations of forage. Prince Andrew smiled, and said that he was unable to reply on so serious a state secret.

"I have a few words to say to you about your own business," he added to Boris; "but we will talk of that another time. Come to me after the review: we will do all in our power. . . ."

Then, turning to Nicholas, and feigning not to observe his gloomy and irritable manner, he said, "You were talking of the fight at Schöngraben? You were there?"

"I was there," said Rostow, rather offensively. The opportunity of amusing himself over the lad's angry mood being obviously eligible, Bolkonsky went on:

"There have been a good many stories invented about that affair."

"Oh! yes, many stories are invented!" replied Rostow, casting furious glances at Boris and Bolkonsky alternately. "Oh! yes, plenty of stories; but our reports—the reports of those who faced the enemy's fire—are not without weight. They are of a very different order of merit from those of the staff-puppies, who have medals given them which they have never won. . . ."

"And in your opinion I am one of them?" said the prince coolly, with a sweet smile. Rostow was torn between his irritation and the respect he could not help feeling for Bolkonsky's calm dignity.

"I do not allude to you, for I do not know you—and, what is more, I do not want to know you any better. But I speak of staff-officers in general."

"I see," said Prince Andrew, interrupting him in a quiet measured voice, "that you are bent on insulting me, and you will find it only too easy if you forego your self-respect. At the same time you cannot fail to see that the time and place are ill chosen. We are all on the eve of a great and terrible duel, and it is no fault of Droubetskoï's—your friend from childhood—if my face is so unlucky as to displease you. At any rate, you know my name, and where to find me. Remember, I am not in the slightest degree offended; and as I am older than you, I venture to advise you to let your ill-temper carry you no further. Then on Friday, Boris, after the review, I shall expect you. . . ."

He bowed and went away. Rostow was too much bewildered to recover himself. He hated himself for having had no answer ready; he had his horse brought round, and took his leave rather drily.

"Now, ought I to have insulted that airified aide-de-camp," he asked himself, "or shall I let the matter drop?"

The question worried him all the way home. He alternately pictured his satisfaction at seeing the haughty little man's alarm, and found himself, to his great astonishment, wishing with more eagerness than he had ever felt before, to win the regard of this aide-de-camp he detested so much.

CHAPTER LVIII

On the following day all the troops, Russian and Austrian, to the number of 80,000, including those just arrived from Russia, and those that had gone through the campaign, were reviewed by the czar, accompanied by the czarevitch, and the Emperor Francis attended by one of the archdukes.

At break of day the troops, in light marching order, were drawn up on the plain beneath the fortifications. The moving mass, with standards flying, halted at the word of command, parted, formed into detachments, and stood still to let another body pass by in compact bands of variously-coloured uniforms. Further away the cavalry manœuvred, in blue, green, and red, with their gorgeous trumpeters in embroidered jackets mounted on black, grey, or bay horses that ambled along to the rhythm of the music; and after them came the artillery in a long line, making its way between the infantry and cavalry to the position it was to occupy, the shining guns jumping on their carriages with a brazen clatter, and leaving a smell of burning matches behind them. Generals in dress-uniforms—blazing with decorations, buttoned up to the chin, and tightened in at the waist —officers in their smartest trim, soldiers freshly shaved, with their accoutrements brightly polished, horses groomed and brushed till their coats glistened like satin, and their manes hung like fringe—each and all were conscious that serious work was on hand. From the general to the private, every man felt that he was no more than a grain of sand in this great, living sea, but he had, at the same time, a sense of power as a unit in this grand total.

By dint of hard work, by ten o'clock all was ready. The army was drawn up in three main divisions: the cavalry in front, behind them the artillery, and the infantry in the rear. Between each corps there was a wide space left, and each stood out in conspicuous contrast to the other two. Three divisions of the army were in sharp contrast to each other. Koutouzow's forces, with the Pavlograd Regiment on the right, then the regiments of the line and the Guards just arrived from Russia, and next to them the Austrian army—all stood on the same line, and all under the same command, and in the same order.

Suddenly a murmur like the whisper of the wind in the trees ran along the ranks:

"They are coming! Here they are!" said one and another, and the crisis of expectation flew down the line.

A party of horsemen was visible in the distance. At the same moment a breath as it were stirred the air and fluttered the clinging folds of the flags; the gleaming lances quivered; a shiver seemed to express the gladness of the army at the approach of the sovereigns.

"Attention!" shouted a voice. Then, like the answering crow of cocks at daybreak, the shout was repeated at various points, and silence fell. Not a sound was to be heard in the stillness but the tramp of the approaching horses: then the trumpets of the 1st Regiment gave out a triumphant flourish, and the jubilant strain seemed to come from all those thousand breasts beating high with excitement at the advent of the two emperors. The trumpets had hardly ceased when the Russian emperor said very distinctly, in his fresh, soft voice: "Good day, my children!"

The men of the 1st broke into a shout, leading a cheer so overwhelming and so prolonged that each man thrilled as he thought of the number and strength of the mass of which he was but a fraction.

Rostow, whose place was in the front rank of Koutouzow's division which was the first that the emperors rode past, felt, like every man on the ground, a sudden self-oblivion, a proud consciousness of strength and passionate devotion to the hero of the splendid ceremonial. At one word from that man, he thought, this whole mass, including himself, an insignificant atom, would plunge through fire and flood, ready to commit any crime or act of heroism; and he fairly trembled and turned faint as he looked at the man who was the embodiment of that word. Shouts of hurrah, hurrah! rang out on every side; each regiment in turn, roused from their death-like and stony silence, woke to life as the czar rode by, hailing him with trumpet-blasts and cheers that mingled with those of the last ranks in deafening acclamation. Until the emperor rode up to it, each regiment in its silence and immobility seemed like a lifeless body, but as soon as he reached it, it came to life and joined its thunder to the line that had already been passed.

In the midst of these black lines, so motionless that they might have been petrified, some hundred horsemen were prancing in elegant array; these were the suite of the two emperors on whom the suppressed excitement of 80,000 men was centred. The handsome young czar especially, in his Horse Guards' uniform and his cocked hat on one side, with his pleasant face and full, sweet voice, attracted general attention. Rostow, whose post was close to the trumpets, kept his keen eyes fixed on his sovereign; and when, at a distance of about twenty yards, he could clearly distinguish his features, beaming with good looks, youth, and happiness, he felt a warm gush of love and enthusiasm; the emperor's appearance completely bewitched him.

The young czar paused in front of the Pavlograd Regiment, and turning to the Emperor of Austria, he smiled and said a few words in French. Rostow smiled in sympathy, and felt his loyal passion swell within him; he longed to give some proof of it, and the impossibility of doing so made him quite miserable. The emperor called the general in command.

"Good God! how should I feel if he spoke to me! I should die of joy!"

"Gentlemen," said the czar, addressing all the officers—and Rostow felt as if he were listening to a voice from heaven—"I thank you with all my heart. You have well earned the standard of St. George, and you will prove yourselves worthy of it!"

"Only to die—to die for him!" thought Rostow.

At this moment there was a tremendous cheer, in which Rostow joined with all the strength of his lungs, to vent the ardour of his enthusiasm even at the risk of bursting his throat. For a minute the czar seemed to hesitate.

"How can he hesitate or doubt?" said Rostow to himself; still, this indecision seemed to him no less majestic and full of

The approach of the sovereigns

charm than all else the emperor did; and at this moment Alexander, touching his handsome dark bay with the heel of his boot—a pointed narrow boot, as was then fashionable—gathered up his bridle in his doeskin-gloved hand and rode off, followed by his crowd of aides-de-camp. He stopped in front of each regiment in turn, farther and farther away, till at last all that could be seen of him was the white plume of his cocked hat waving above the heads of his suite.

Rostow had noticed Bolkonsky among the officers of the imperial suite, and was debating whether he should challenge him or no . . . "No, certainly not," he said to himself; "how can I think of such a thing now? What can our petty quarrels and offences matter when our hearts are overflowing with love, and devotion, and enthusiasm? I love and forgive everybody."

When the emperor had ridden past all the regiments, the march past began. Rostow, mounted on Bedouin, which he had just bought of Denissow, came the last of his division, alone and sufficiently conspicuous. He was a capital horseman, and spurring his horse he rode forward at a trot. Bedouin himself, with his foaming jaw held back against his breast, and his tail in the air, tossing up his heels and graceful, slender legs, seemed no less conscious that the eyes of the czar were upon him. His rider, on his part, with his legs pressed back, and his anxious, beaming face, sat bolt upright as if he and his horse were one; they flew past the emperor in all their beauty. "Well done, Pavlograd Hussars!" cried the emperor.

"Good heavens! how happy I should be if only he would bid me ride straight into the fire!" thought Rostow.

When the review was over, the officers fresh from Russia gathered into groups with those of Koutouzow's army, discussing the distinctions that had been conferred, the Austrians and their uniforms, Bonaparte and the critical position he would be in—especially when Essen's division should have joined them, and when Prussia and Russia were openly allied. But the Czar Alexander was the principal theme of conversation: every word he had said was repeated, every gesture discussed, and their enthusiasm grew as they talked. All they asked was to march against the foe under his command; for with him they were confident of victory, and the review had produced a stronger assurance of triumph than two battles gained.

CHAPTER LIX

THE day after the review Boris in his handsomest uniform, set out for Olmütz, with the best wishes of Berg to encourage him, to take advantage of Bolkonsky's disposition to serve him. Some snug little post, that of aide-de-camp to some important person, was all he asked.

"It is all very well for Rostow," said he to himself, "whose father sends him 10,000 roubles every now and then, to give himself airs and call it footman's work; but I have nothing but my wits, I must make my own way and take advantage of every opportunity that offers."

He did not find Prince Andrew at Olmütz that day. But the sight of the town, gay and busy with the bustle of headquarters, and with the presence of the corps diplomatique and of the two emperors, with their suite, their court and their hangers-on only added fuel to his ambition to move in these exalted circles.

Though in the Guards himself, he knew no one here. All these splendid beings with orders, and ribands, and plumes of every hue, rushing about the streets in handsome carriages— civilians and military alike—seemed to him so infinitely above himself, a humble subaltern, that they neither could nor would dream of his existence. At the house whither he was directed in search of Prince Andrew, the headquarters of Koutouzow, the reception he met with from the aides-de-camp and the servants conveyed very plainly that they had more than enough of idlers like him. Nevertheless, on the following day, it was the 15th, he repeated his visit. Prince Andrew was at home, and Boris was shown into a large room; it had formerly been a ball-room, and was now occupied by five beds and other furniture of every kind—tables, chairs, and a piano. An aide-de-camp, in a Persian dressing-gown, was writing close to the door; another—the red faced, powerful Nesvitsky—was stretched at full length on his bed, his head propped on his arm, laughing and talking with a brother officer who sat at his feet. A third was playing a Viennese waltz, and another, lolling half across the instrument, hummed the tune. Bolkonsky was not there. No one stirred as Boris went in, excepting the gentleman in the dressing-gown, who crossly told him that Bolkonsky was on duty, and that he would find him in the audience-chamber

—the door to the left of the corridor. Boris thanked him, went as he was desired, and found a party of about a dozen officers and generals.

At the instant when he entered Prince Andrew was listening to a Russian general with the languid politeness which duty demands as a cover to weariness. The Russian, a red-faced man past middle age, and wearing many medals, stood leaning forward and explained his case with the timid anxiety that is common in soldiers.

"Very good—be so kind as to wait," replied Bolkonsky in Russian, but with the French accent he affected when he wished to be superior. Then, catching sight of Boris, without troubling himself any further about the petitioner, who ran after him repeating his request, and assuring him that he had not done, he came forward and greeted Boris kindly. This marked change of manner made Boris fully aware of what he had in fact already suspected, namely: that outside and apart from discipline and routine as they were laid down in the military code, there was another law of conduct, far more important, which compelled this rubicund general to await Captain Andrew's good pleasure with such patience as he might, if Prince Andrew preferred to give his attention to Lieutenant Droubetzkoi. And he promised himself that henceforth he would serve where this code was in force and not the other. Thanks to the introductions he had brought, he felt himself a hundred times a greater man than this general, who, if he met him in the ranks, could utterly crush the sub-lieutenant in the Guards.

"I am sorry to have missed you yesterday," said Prince Andrew, shaking hands with him; "I was running about all day with the Germans. I went with Weirother to inspect and arrange for distributing the troops; and, as you know, when a German takes it into his head to be precise, there is no end of it."

Boris smiled with a pretence of knowing what everyone was supposed to know, though it was the first time he had ever heard the name of Weirother, or of distributing troops. "And so, my dear fellow, you want to be appointed aide-de-camp?"

"Yes," said Boris, blushing in spite of himself, "I should like to make the request of the commander-in-chief: Prince Kouraguine has no doubt written to him about it. I particularly wish it, because I very much doubt whether the Guards will see any fighting," he added, delighted to have hit on so plausible an excuse for his request

"Well, well, we will talk it over," said Prince Andrew. "As soon as I have reported this gentleman's business, I am at your service."

While he was gone the general, who took a different view of the privileges involved in social and military discipline, cast an indignant eye on this audacious sub-lieutenant, who had intervened to prevent his unfolding all the details of his case; Boris was somewhat abashed, and impatiently longed for Prince Andrew's return. Bolkonsky led him away to the room with the five beds.

"Now, my dear fellow, this is the conclusion I have come to: It is not of the slightest use for you to call on the commander-in-chief; he will be extremely civil, and ask you to dinner—" (not so bad that, as regards that other code of discipline! thought Boris), "and that will be the end of it, for there will soon be enough aides-de-camp and staff-officers to form a battalion. So I have another plan to propose which is all the more advantageous, because Koutouzow and his staff are not just now in the ascendant. For the present the emperor himself is the grand focus; so we will go to see General Prince Dolgoroukow, the emperor's aide-de-camp. He is my very good friend, and I have mentioned you to him. Perhaps he may be able to place you in his own suite, or even higher and nearer the sun."

Prince Andrew was always ready to help a young man and smooth his way for him, and he carried out the task with particular pleasure; under cover of the patronage he procured for others, and would never have accepted himself, he gravitated towards the star which attracted him in spite of himself, and whence all advancement radiated.

It was already late when they made their way into the palace occupied by the two emperors and their immediate suite.

Their majesties had that day been present at a council of war, at which all the members of the "Hofkriegsrath" had assisted. It had been decided, against the advice of the older officers—Koutouzow, Prince Schwarzenberg, and others—that they must act on the offensive, and force Bonaparte to a pitched battle. When Prince Andrew arrived in search of Dolgoroukow, the impression produced by this victory of the younger party was legible on every face. The voice of the temporisers who counselled delay had been so effectually drowned by their opponents, and their arguments converted by such positive proofs of the advantage of definite action, that the impending battle and the victory which must inevitably ensue, seemed to be things of the past rather than hopes of the future. The allied forces, far outnumbering those of Napoleon no doubt—were concentrated on a single point. The allied armies, under the incitement of the presence of the two sovereigns, were only too eager to fight; the field on which the engagement must be fought was well known in every detail to General Weirother, who would advise as to the distribution of the Russian and German forces. By a fortunate coincidence, the Austrian troops had manœuvred on that very ground only the year before; it was laid down on the maps with mathematical exactness; and Napoleon's present inaction argued a state of weakness.

Prince Dolgoroukow, who had been one of the warmest advocates of decisive action, had just come away from the council, tired and agitated but jubilant, when Prince Andrew introduced his protégé. Quite incapable, however, of keeping his excitement and his ideas to himself, he took no notice of Boris.

"Well, my dear fellow!" he began, addressing Prince Andrew in French: "We have gained the day! God grant that the victory to follow may be equally brilliant! I confess all my former injustice to these Austrians, above all to Weirother. What minute knowledge! What an exact acquaintance with every spot of ground! What foresight with regard to every contingency, every chance, every detail! Any position more advantageous than ours at this moment is simply inconceivable. A combination of Austrian precision and Russian valour. What more could you have?"

"Then an action is certain?"

"Yes—and Bonaparte seems to me to have lost his head. The czar had a note from him only to-day. . . ." And Dolgoroukow broke off with a meaning smile.

"The devil he had! And what does he write about?"

"What can he write about? This, that, and the other . . . it is simply to gain time. He will fall into our hands, take my word for it! But the best of the joke," and he smiled with good-humoured relish, "was that no one knew how to address him in reply. He could not be addressed as consul, and obviously he could not be addressed as emperor—there was nothing for it but to call him General Bonaparte, at least that was my opinion."

"But," said Bolkonsky, "it seems to me that there is a wide

difference between refusing to acknowledge him as emperor and calling him general."

"Of course, that was the difficulty," said Dolgoroukow. "Now Bilibine, who is a man of resource, proposed to address the note to 'the Usurper, and foe of humanity.'"

"Only that!"

"Well, it was Bilibine after all who evaded the difficulty with his usual wit. . . ."

"How?"

"To the head of the French Government. Very good, don't you think."

"Very good, but it will make him very angry," said Bolkonsky.

"Oh, no doubt it will. My brother, who knows him and has dined more than once with this emperor at Paris, tells me he never met a subtler or môre finished diplomatist. French readiness grafted on to Italian play-acting. Of course you know all the stories that are told of Count Markow, the only man who proved a match for him. Do you know the story of the handkerchief? It is delightful. . . ." And Dolgoroukow, chattering on, turning first to the prince and then to Boris, told them how Napoleon, wanting to test the Russian ambassador, had dropped his pocket-handkerchief at Markow's feet, and stood still to see if he would pick it up; but Markow, dropping his own close to Napoleon's, picked it up again without touching the other.

"Delicious!" said Bolkonsky. "But just two words, prince: I came on behalf of my young friend here. . . ."

An aide-de-camp, sent to fetch Dolgoroukow to speak with the czar, gave Prince Andrew no time to finish his sentence.

"Ah! what a bore," said Dolgoroukow, starting up and shaking hands with his two visitors. "I will do everything in my power, everything that depends only on myself, for you and your charming young friend. But it must be another time— you see . . ." and he again shook hands with Boris with easy, good-natured familiarity.

Boris was quite agitated by his contact with this powerful personage and with one of the springs that gave motion to those masses of men in which he himself, as a unit in his regiment, felt that he was but a minute and subordinate speck. They followed Dolgoroukow down the corridor, and just as Dolgoroukow went into the emperor's private rooms a tall man came out of them in civil uniform; his face was shrewd, with a heavy jaw which, far from disfiguring it, lent energy and mobility to his expression. He nodded to Dolgoroukow as to an intimate acquaintance, and fixed Prince Andrew with a cold stare as he walked straight on, quite confident that Bolkonsky would bow and make way for him; but Prince Andrew did neither, and the stranger, with a look of annoyance, turned away and went down the other side of the corridor.

"Who is that?" asked Boris.

"One of our most remarkable and, to my mind, most odious men. Prince Adam Czartorisky, Minister for Foreign Affairs. . . . And those are the men," added Bolkonsky with an irrepressible sigh, "who decide the fate of nations."

The army was set in motion next day, and Boris saw no more of either Prince Andrew or Dolgoroukow during the days that elapsed till the battle of Austerlitz; so he remained with his regiment.

CHAPTER LX

At break of day on the 16th, Denissow's squadron, forming part of Prince Bagration's division, set out from its last halting-place to take up its position on the field of battle with the other regiments; but at about a verst off they were ordered to stop. Rostow saw the division march past him: the Cossacks, the 1st and 2nd squadrons of hussars, some battalions of infantry and artillery with the generals in command: Bagration, Dolgoroukow and their aides-de-camp. The struggle he had had with himself to overcome the terror which seized him at the moment of going into battle, and all his bright dreams of distinguishing himself in the immediate future, vanished in smoke, for his squadron was left in reserve, and the hours went by in dreary inaction. At nine o'clock in the morning, however, he heard musketry in the distance, shouts, cheers—he saw a few wounded brought to the rear, and presently, surrounded by Cossacks, a whole detachment of French cavalry came past— the engagement had evidently been a short one, but at any rate it had been successful; the officers and soldiers all talked of a brilliant victory, of Vischau having been taken, and a French squadron cut off and captured.

The weather was clear, the sun thawed the air after a hard frost during the night, and the fresh splendour of a fine autumn day was in harmony with the jubilant sense of victory, and reflected in the faces of the privates, the officers, and the aides-de-camp who were hurrying about in all directions. After going through all the agonies of anticipation which must precede a battle, Rostow was out of all patience at having to spend this day of triumph in idleness.

"Here, Rostow—come here; we will drown our disappointment!" cried Denissow, who was sitting by the roadside with some provisions and a bottle of brandy by his side, while a party of brother-officers were sharing his meal.

"Here comes another prisoner!" said one, pointing to a French dragoon between two Cossacks, one of whom was leading the Frenchman's horse, a fine powerful charger.

"Sell us the horse?" said Denissow to the Cossack.

"With pleasure, highness."

The officers rose and gathered round the Cossacks and their prisoner, a young Alsatian who spoke French with a strong German accent. He was crimson with confusion; having heard them speaking his own language he appealed first to one and then to another, explaining that it was not his fault that he had been taken prisoner, that it was the corporal's doing, that he had been sent to fetch some horse-cloths, though he had told him that the Russians were on the spot; and he finished every sentence with: "But don't hurt my little horse," and he patted its coat.

He hardly seemed to know what he was saying: he apologised for having been taken prisoner, then he boasted of his strict attention to his duties as a soldier, as if he were on his trial before his own officers. He was a typical specimen of the French soldier, of which the Russians as yet knew very little. The Cossacks sold the horse for two gold pieces, and Rostow, who was most in funds of the party, became its owner.

"But don't hurt my little horse," the Alsatian said to him once more. Rostow reassured him and gave him some money.

"Now, come on," said the Cossack, taking the Frenchman by the hand to get him along.

"The Emperor! the Emperor!" they suddenly heard shouted close to them. All was stir and excitement, each man ran to his post; Rostow, seeing some horsemen with white plumes riding towards them, nimbly remounted his horse. All his annoyance, weariness, personal feeling even vanished in an instant before the exquisite pleasure that surged through his being at the approach of his soveriegn. To him it was ample

At break of day the squadron set out to take up its position on the field of battle

indemnification for the morning's disappointment; he was as excited as a lover who has gained a longed-for rendezvous—he dared not look round even, but divined *his* presence, not by the tramp of the horses, but by the rapturous emotion that fired his senses and glorified everything within his ken. That Sun was coming nearer, nearer—Rostow felt himself wrapped in its soft, majestic light—he heard that kind, calm voice, at once impressive and simple, audible in the deathlike silence: "The Pavlograd Hussars?"

"The reserve force, sire," said a human voice after the divine voice that had just spoken.

The czar paused in front of Rostow. His handsome face— handsomer now than even on the day of the review, was radiant with youth and eagerness, and his look of boyish innocence, bright with vehemence of early manhood, in no way detracted from the dignity of his features. As his eyes glanced down the ranks for an instant they met Rostow's eager gaze. Had he read the feelings that were seething within him? Rostow was sure that he had; for he thrilled under the soft influence of those fine blue eyes. The czar's brow lifted, he hastily set spurs to his horse and galloped off towards the front.

The young monarch had not been able to resist the temptation of being present at the fight in spite of the advice of his counsellors; at about noon he left the third column with which he had been riding, and was about to join the corps in front when, just as he passed the Hussars, several aides-de-camp came up bringing the news of a happy conclusion to the engagement.

This battle, which had in fact consisted merely in the capture of a French troop of horse, was described to him as a great victory: so much so that the czar, and even the army, were convinced—till the smoke cleared off—that the French were defeated and retreating. A few minutes after he had ridden forward the Pavlograd Hussars were ordered to advance, and Rostow again had the happiness of seeing the czar in the little town of Vischau. Some killed and wounded, whom there had not yet been time to remove, were still lying on the ground where the fire had been hottest. Alexander, followed by his civil and military suite, and riding a bay horse, was leaning over in a graceful attitude, and with a gold eye-glass was gazing at a soldier who lay stretched below him, bareheaded and blood-stained. The sight of this wounded wretch, horrible to look at, so close to the emperor, sickened Rostow; he could see the pained look in the czar's face and the shudder that ran through his frame; he saw his foot nervously thrust against the ribs of his horse, which was too well trained to stir an inch. An aide-de-camp dismounted to raise the sufferer, who groaned as he laid him on a litter.

"Gently, gently—can it not be done more gently?" said the czar in a compassionate tone, which betrayed keener pain than that of the dying man.

He moved away, and Rostow, who had seen that his eyes were full of tears, heard him say in French to Czartorisky: "What a fearful thing is war!"

The advance guard, posted in front of Vischau, within sight of the foe which had given way without making any stand, had been thanked by the emperor with promises of medals and double rations of brandy to the men. The great bivouac fires blazed even more merrily than on the previous evening, and the air rang with soldiers' songs. Denissow must celebrate his promotion to the rank of major, and Rostow, who by the end of supper was somewhat excited, proposed the health of his majesty the czar, not as the emperor but as a man of feeling— a charming man.—"Let us drink to his health," he exclaimed, "and to our next victory. If we fought well and never yielded an inch to the French at Schöngraben, what can we not do now with him—himself to lead us? We would die gladly for him, gentlemen, would we not? I do not express myself well, but I feel it, and you too. To the health of the Czar Alexander the First! Hurrah!" And the hurrah was answered in chorus, old Kirstein shouting with as much enthusiasm as the twenty-year old Rostow. When their glasses were emptied and broken, Kirstein filled fresh ones, and going, in shirt-sleeves, up to the soldiers who were squatting round the fire, he raised his glass above his head, while the flames threw a ruddy glare on his triumphant figure, his great grey moustache and his white breast visible under his unbuttoned shirt-front.

"Lads! To our Emperor's health and a victory over the enemy!" he said, in his deep ringing voice. His men crowded round him cheering lustily.

When they parted for the night, Denissow slapped his favourite Rostow on the shoulder: "No room for love affairs, eh? when one is in love with the czar!"

"Denissow, no jests on that subject. It is too lofty, too sublime a feeling!"

"Yes, yes, boy, I know. I agree with you. I share it and approve."

"No—you cannot understand it."

And Rostow took himself off to wander about among the camp-fires which were dying out by degrees, and to dream of the joy of dying without a care for life, of simply dying before the emperor's eyes. He was quite beside himself with enthusiasm for his person, for the glory of the Russian arms and the impending victory. Though, indeed, he was not the only man in this frame of mind; nine-tenths of the soldiers felt the same intoxicating impulse, though in a minor degree, during the memorable days which preceded the battle of Austerlitz.

CHAPTER LXI

THE emperor spent the next day at Vischau. His chief physician, Wiley (an Englishman), having been sent for to see him several times, a rumour that he was ill got about at headquarters, and the nearer-lying portions of the army said he could neither sleep nor eat. This state of things was due to the painful impression produced on his tender soul by the sight of the dead and wounded.

Early in the morning of the 17th a French officer, under shelter of a flag of truce, requested an audience of the czar, and was guided past the outposts. This was Savary. The emperor had just fallen asleep, and Savary had to wait. At noon he was admitted, and an hour after he returned, accompanied by Prince Dolgoroukow. His errand, it was said, was to propose a meeting between the Czar Alexander and Napoleon. To the great satisfaction of all the army the interview was refused, and Prince Dolgoroukow, the captor of Vischau, was sent with Savary to enter into negotiations with Napoleon in case his proposals, contrary to every expectation, should be in favour of peace. Dolgoroukow, on his return the same evening, was closeted for a long time with the czar.

On the 18th and 19th the troops again moved forward two stages, while the French only withdrew steadily after the exchange of a few shots. During the afternoon of the 19th there was an unusual stir among the superior officers in command of the army, and this went on till the next morning, the 20th of November—the date of the great battle of Austerlitz.

Until the afternoon of the 19th the unwonted excitement, eager conversations, and rushing about of aides-de-camp had

263

not gone beyond the boundaries of the headquarters of the imperial staff; but in the afternoon they spread to Koutouzow's quarters, and soon after to those of the generals of divisions. By the evening the orders communicated by the aides-de-camp had set every corps of the army in motion, and in the night of the 19th–20th the nine–verst long, enormous mass of 80,000 souls rose as one man.

The motion which in the morning had centred in the imperial headquarters had spread from one to another, had reached and started the remotest springs of the vast military machine, which might be compared to the complicated mechanism of a great clock. The impetus once given, nothing can stop it; the great central wheel, rotating with increasing rapidity, involves all the others; once started at their full speed, without any consciousness of the end to be gained, the cog-wheels catch, the springs creak, the weights groan, the puppets move, and the hands point to the hour—the sum total of the result of the impulsion given to this elaborate structure which looked as if it were never meant to move at all. Thus, the wishes, humiliations, and sufferings, the flashes of pride, terror, and enthusiasm —the whole mass of feelings experienced by 160,000 men, Russians and French, resulted in an event marked on the dial of the history of the human race as the great battle of Austerlitz, the Battle of the Three Emperors.

Prince Andrew was on duty that day, and never once quitted General Prince Koutouzow, who, after arriving at six in the evening at the imperial headquarters, had a short audience of the czar, and then went to see Count Tolstoï, the grand marshal of the household. Bolkonsky, noticing that Koutouzow seemed annoyed and dissatisfied, took advantage of his visit to Tolstoï to go to see Dolgoroukow, and get some information from him as to what was going on. He fancied he had perceived that there was some grudge felt towards his chief at headquarters, and that he was treated with the tone adopted by those who are better informed.

"How are you?" said Dolgoroukow, who was drinking tea with Bilibine. "So the fun is fixed for to-morrow. What is wrong with your old man? He seems very much out of temper."

"I should not say out of temper; but I think he would have liked to be heard."

"But he was heard at the council of war, and he always will be listened to when he talks sense; but to prolong delay and wait for ever when Napoleon is evidently afraid to fight—it is impossible."

"But you have seen Bonaparte. How did he strike you?"

"Yes, I saw him, and am quite convinced that he is dreadfully afraid of this battle," repeated Dolgoroukow, delighted with the conclusion he had drawn from his interview with Napoleon. "If he were not afraid why should he have asked for this interview or have proposed negotiations? Why should he have retired, when a retreat is against all his principles of tactics? Take my word for it, he is frightened—his hour is come, rely upon it."

"But what is he like?" asked Bolkonsky.

"A man in a grey overcoat, extremely anxious that I should address him as 'your majesty,' but I gave him no title at all, to his great disgust. That is the man he is, neither more nor less! And in spite of the deep respect I entertain for old Koutouzow, we should be in a pretty position if we remained waiting for the unknown, and so gave him the chance of withdrawing or of tricking us, while, as it is, we are sure to beat him. We must not forget Souvorow's maxim: 'that it is better to attack than to be attacked.' The eagerness of the young is in war a safer guide than all the experience of your old tacticians, take my word for it."

"But what is his position? I went down to the outposts to-day, and it is impossible to discover where he has posted the main body of his troops," said Prince Andrew, who was dying to explain to Dolgoroukow what his own plan of attack had been.

"That does not matter in the least. Every contingency has been considered; if it is at Brünn . . ." said Dolgoroukow, rising to spread a map on the table and to explain in his own words Weirother's plan of attack by a flank movement. Bolkonsky raised certain objections, to prove that his plan was as good as Weirother's, which, in his opinion, had only had the good luck to be approved. While Prince Andrew was pointing out its weak places and the advantages of his own scheme, Dolgoroukow ceased listening, and glanced absently from the map to the speaker.

"There will be a council of war held this evening at Koutouzow's," he said, "and you can put forward your objections."

"I shall undoubtedly do so," replied Prince Andrew.

"What is disturbing your minds, gentlemen?" said Bilibine, who, after listening to them in silence, was prepared to make some fun of them. "Whether we have a victory or defeat to-morrow the honour of the Russian army is safe, for, with the exception of Koutouzow, there is not a single Russian among the generals of division: General Wimpfen, Comte de Langeron, Prince of Lichtenstein, Prince of Hohenlohe, and finally Prsch —Prsch with all the letters of the alphabet to follow—like all Polish names."

"Silence, gabbler!" said Dolgoroukow, "you are mistaken; there are two Russians: Miloradovitch and Dokhtourow; indeed, there is a third: Araktchéiew, but he has not strong nerves."

"I am going back to my chief," said Bolkonsky. "Good-luck to you, gentlemen," and he shook hands with both and left them.

As they rode forward Prince Andrew could not refrain from asking Koutouzow, who sat in silence by his side, what he thought of the chances of the morrow. The general looked very grave, and after a short pause, replied: "I believe we shall be defeated, and I begged Count Tolstoï to communicate my opinion to the emperor. Well, and what do you think he answered? 'Oh, my dear general, it is my business to see to rice and cutlets; it is your business to manage the war.' Aye, that's the reply I got."

CHAPTER LXII

At ten o'clock that evening Weirother carried his scheme to Koutouzow's lodgings, where the council of war was to be held. All the chiefs of divisions had been summoned, and all, with the exception of Bagration, who excused himself, had assembled at the appointed hour.

Weirother, the moving spirit of the impending engagement, was a man of vehement and feverish impetuosity, a marked contrast to Koutouzow, with his sleepy, dissatisfied look, who, in spite of himself, had to preside at the council. Weirother, as the leader of an advance which nothing now could arrest, was in the position of a horse harnessed to a coach and started full-tilt down hill—at a certain point he ceases to know whether he is dragging the coach, or the coach is forcing him on. He was carried away by the irresistible momentum, and could not stop now to consider the consequences of the plunge. Twice during the evening he had reconnoitred the enemy's lines, twice he had waited on the emperors to make a report and explain matters; and between whiles he had gone to his private room to dictate, in German, his scheme for the distribution of the troops. By the time he came to the council he was quite worn out. His absence of mind was so complete that he even failed in deference to the commander-in-chief; interrupting him constantly, and not even addressing him; nay, not replying to his questions. His dress was bespattered with mud, and he looked haggard, weary, and distracted, though pride and swagger pierced through it all.

Koutouzow's quarters were in an old mansion. Here, in the great drawing-room, were met Koutouzow, Weirother, all the members of the council of war. They drank tea. They were only waiting for Prince Bagration to begin the council. At eight o'clock an orderly arrived from Bagration with the information that the prince could not be present. Prince Andrew came in to report this to the commander-in-chief, and taking advantage of Koutouzow's previously given permission to be present during the proceedings, remained in the room.

"As Prince Bagration is not coming we may open the meeting," said Weirother, eagerly rising and going to the table, on which lay a large and detailed map of the environs of Brünn. Koutouzow, with his uniform unbuttoned to air his great bull-neck, was sunk in a deep easy chair with his little, fat, old-man's hands laid squarely on the arms of it; he seemed to be asleep, but at the sound of Weirother's voice he opened his remaining eye:

"Yes, pray do," he said, "or it will be too late." His head sank again on his breast, and he closed his eye.

When Weirother began to read, his colleagues might perhaps have fancied that he was pretending to be asleep, but his loud breathing soon showed that he had yielded to the invincible need of sleep to which human nature is liable, in spite of his earnest wish to parade his contempt for the plans that had been decided on. In point of fact he was sleeping soundly. Weirother, too much excited to waste a moment, took up a paper and began reading in a monotonous voice the complicated details of the distribution of the forces which his hearers found great difficulty in following.

"Distribution of the forces to attack the enemy's positions behind Kobelnitz and Sokolenitz, November 20th, 1805.

"Seeing that the enemy's left flank is protected by wooded

heights, while his right wing skirts the pools behind Kobelnitz and Sokolenitz, and that our left wing is greater than his right wing, it will be to our advantage to attack the enemy's right wing; above all, if we succeed in taking possession of the villages of Kobelnitz and Sokolenitz, we shall then be able to fall on the enemy's flank and pursue him across the plain that lies between Schlapanitz and the wood of Turass, avoiding the defiles of Schlapanitz and Bellovitz which protect his front. To this end it is indispensable—the first column marches . . . the second column moves . . . the third column advances . . . etc., etc.''

Weirother read on, all the generals trying to follow, but with manifest displeasure. General Bouxhoevden, a tall, fair man, standing with his back against the wall and his eyes fixed on the flame of one of the tapers, affected not to listen. Miloradovitch, with a highly-coloured face and his moustache tightly twisted, sat facing Weirother in a very bellicose pose, his elbows stuck out and his hands on his knees. He did not speak a word, but fixed the reader with his large shining eyes, only glancing round at his colleagues whenever there was a pause, with some meaning which they failed to interpret. Was he for or against, content or adverse, to the proposed scheme? Close to Weirother sat the Comte de Langeron; his face was that of a southern Frenchman; all through the reading it was lighted up by a subtle smile, while his eyes were fixed on his slender fingers, and he fidgeted with a gold snuff-box set with a miniature. In the middle of one of the longest sentences he suddenly raised his head, and was on the point of interrupting Weirother with an elaborate politeness that was almost offensive; but the Austrian had not paused; he frowned, and impatiently waved his hand, as much as to say: "Presently, presently, you can make your comments; just now look at the map and attend." Langeron cast up his eyes in astonishment, and then looked round at Miloradovitch for an explanation, but meeting his gaze his head drooped again, and he returned to the study of the snuff-box.

"A geography lesson!" he murmured, loud enough to be heard.

Przebichewsky, holding his hand to his ear as an ear-trumpet, with respectful but dignified politeness, sat like a man whose whole attention is given to the matter in hand. Dokhtourow, a little man of modest exterior, leaned over the map, conscientiously studying the ground, which was new to him.

He several times begged Weirother to repeat some word he had not caught distinctly, and the names of villages, which he then wrote down in his note-book.

When the reading—which took more than an hour—was over, Langeron, ceasing to twirl his snuff-box, expressed his opinion without addressing any one in particular: it would be difficult, he thought, to carry out the plan, which entirely depended on a hypothetical position of the enemy, whereas his real position could not be precisely ascertained, as it was constantly being shifted. His objections were well founded, but their evident aim was to make the Austrian general feel that he had unfolded his scheme with the assurance of a lecturer laying down the law to schoolboys; and that the men he had to deal with were not simpletons, but perfectly capable of giving him a lesson in the art of war.

When Weirother's monotonous voice ceased, Koutouzow opened his eye—as a miller wakes when the soporific rumble of his mill-wheels stops; he listened to what Langeron had to say, and then nodded to sleep once more, with his head sunk deeper on his breast, to show how little interest he took in the discussion.

Langeron, doing his best to irritate Weirother and gall his vanity as an author, went on to point out that Bonaparte was quite as like to take the initiative and attack, instead of letting himself be attacked, and that in that case he would at one stroke upset all these combinations. His opponent's only reply was a smile of profound contempt which supplied the place of words: "If he could have attacked us he would have done so."

"Then you do not think he is strong?" said Langeron.

"If he has 40,000 men that is the most," replied Weirother, with the scorn of a physician to whom an old woman suggests a remedy.

"In that case he is courting ruin by waiting for us to attack him," added Langeron ironically.

He looked to Miloradovitch for support, but he was miles from the point of the discussion.

"*Ma foi!*" said he, "we shall see to-morrow on the field of battle."

It was easy to see in Weirother's face that he was amazed at meeting with objections from the Russian generals, when not only himself, but the two emperors, had been satisfied of the merits of his scheme.

"The fires are out in the enemy's camp, and there is a constant stir," he said. "What can that mean? either they are retreating, which is the only thing we have to fear, or they are changing their position. But even supposing they occupy Turass, they will only be saving us trouble, and our plans will remain unaltered down to the minutest details."

"In what way?" asked Prince Andrew, who had been watching for an opportunity for expressing his doubts.

Koutouzow woke up with a loud fit of coughing.

"Gentlemen," he said, "our plans for to-morrow—I might say for to-day, since it is one in the morning—cannot be altered now. You all know them; we will all do our duty. And nothing is so important on the eve of a battle as—" he paused, "as a good night's rest." He prepared to rise; the generals all bowed, and the meeting broke up.

This council of war, at which Prince Andrew had had no chance of expressing his own views, had left him doubtful and uneasy, and he asked himself anxiously who, after all, was right: Dolgoroukow and Weirother, or, on the other hand, Koutouzow and Langeron? Why could not Koutouzow frankly explain his opinion to the czar? Were matters always managed thus? "Must thousands of lives—and mine, too—" he thought, "be risked for the sake of private Court interests? Yes, I may be killed to-morrow . . ." And the idea of death awoke a whole train of remote but familiar memories: his parting from his father, his wife, the early days of their marriage, and his love for her. He thought of the child she was to bear him, and grew quite pathetic over her and himself; then starting up he went out of the hut which he shared with Nesvitsky, and walked up and down. The night was hazy, and a mysterious moon struggled to pierce the mist.

"To-morrow, yes to-morrow!" he said to himself, "all will be over with me perhaps, and these reminiscences will be as nothing. To-morrow I feel sure I shall have a chance of showing what I am good for . . ." And his fancy painted the fight, the slaughter, the concentration of the struggle on a single point, the bewilderment of the leaders: "This is the longed-for opportunity—the Toulon I have waited for!"

Then he pictured himself laying his opinion clearly and positively before Weirother, Koutouzow, and the sovereigns. All were struck by the accuracy of his forethought, but no one dared take the responsibility of executing his plan. . . . He selected a regiment, a division; made it a condition that no one should interfere with his actions; led his men to the critical spot, and gained the day. . . . "And suffering, death?" . . . whispered another voice.

But still he pursued his visions of success. He would be entrusted with the tactics of the next engagement. He was, to be sure, no more than an officer on duty in Koutouzow's staff, but he was omnipotent—and the next battle, too, was won! . . . Then he filled Koutouzow's place! . . . "Very good, and what then?" said another voice. "If, meanwhile, you are not wounded, killed, or thrown over, what next? . . ."

"After that," replied Prince Andrew, "I know not—I do not care to know. It is no fault of mine if I crave for glory, if I long to make myself famous, to win the affections of other men—if that is my one aim in life. I should not tell anyone, but how can I help it if I care for nothing in the world, but glory and devotion of my fellow men? Death, wounds, the loss to my family—nothing can terrify me. And however dear those I love may be—my father, sister, wife—strange as it may seem, I would give everything for one minute of glory, of triumph, of the enthusiastic love of men whom I do not know, and never shall know!" thought he, listening to the talk in Koutouzow's yard.

Half-listening to the confusion of sounds that proceeded from Koutouzow's quarters, he could distinguish the voices of the servants busied in packing, especially that of a coachman, who was laughing at Koutouzow's old cook for his name, which was Titus.

"Go to the devil!" growled the old man, in the midst of shouts of laughter.

"And yet," thought Bolkonsky, pursuing his reverie, "I ask nothing but to rise above them all, I care for nothing but that mysterious glory which I seem to feel in the haze that hangs above my head."

CHAPTER LXIII

ROSTOW spent the night with his company at the outposts of Bagration's detachment. His hussars were posted to watch in couples, and he kept moving along the line, walking his horse to conquer his invincible inclination to sleep. Behind him scattered over a vast extent of ground, the Russian fires glared dimly through the mist, while in the immediate vicinity the night was black in front and around him. In spite of every effort to look through the haze, he could see nothing. Now and again he fancied he perceived a doubtful gleam, the glimmer of a camp-fire; then it vanished again, and he told himself it had been an illusion—his eyes closed and his fancy pictured the czar, or Denissow, or his own people, and he awoke to see nothing but his horse's ears and head, and the darker silhouettes of the hussars on guard in the general darkness.

"Why should not such a chance favour me as has befallen so many others?" he said to himself. "Why should I not happen to come in the emperor's way, to receive some command as any other officer might, and when I have fulfilled it to be employed about his person? Ah! if that could be! How I would watch over him, how I would tell him the truth, how I would unmask all falsehood!" And Rostow, to give colour to the picture of his love and devotion to the czar, fancied himself struggling with a German traitor whom he thrashed and killed under his sovereign's eyes. A distant cry startled him.

"Where am I? To be sure, at the outposts! The password is 'Timon and Olmütz!' What ill-luck to be left behind in the reserve to-morrow! If only I might take part in this engagement. It will perhaps be my only chance of seeing the emperor. I shall be relieved presently, and I will go and ask the general."

He settled himself in his saddle to inspect his men once more. The night seemed a little less dark; he could just make out a slight declivity to the left, and opposite to him rose a black knoll on the top of which there was a white patch which he could not clearly distinguish. Was it a clearing on which the moon was shining—a group of white houses—or a sheet of snow? Then he thought he saw some motion in it. "A white patch?" he said to himself. "It is snow, no doubt—a patch!" he murmured, half asleep again, and he drifted off into dreams

"Natacha! She will never believe that I have seen the czar."

"Keep to the right, highness, there are bushes there," said the man he was just then passing.

He looked up and stopped. He was quite overcome by the sleepiness of youth.

"What was I thinking of? How I can speak to the emperor? No, it was not that. . . ." And again his head drooped; then in his dream he fancied someone was firing on him, and he woke with a start, exclaiming: "Who goes there?"

At this instant, from the side where he supposed the enemy to be, he heard a thousand voices calling and shouting; his horse and the man's both pricked up their ears. On the spot whence the sound came, a fire-flash sparkled and died out, then another started into life, and all the line of the enemy's troops, posted on the hill-side, was suddenly lighted by a thread of fire, while the clamour grew louder. Rostow could distinguish by the intonation that it was in French, though the noise was too confused for words to be distinguishable.

"What is it? What do you think?" he asked the man. "It is in the enemy's camp, at any rate?—Do not you hear?" he added, as the soldier did not reply.

"Who can tell, highness."

"Judging from the direction it must be the enemy."

"Perhaps it is, perhaps not. Queer things happen at night! Now then, steady! No nonsense!" he added, to his horse.

Rostow's horse, too, was growing fidgety and pawing the frozen ground. The shouts grew louder and louder, and rose to a great uproar, such as only could proceed from an army of thousands of men. Fires blazed out in every direction. Rostow's sleepiness had been quite dispelled by the sound of cheers and acclamations: "*Vive l'Empereur! Vive l'Empereur!*" he could hear the words clearly now.

"They are not far off; they must be beyond the brook," he said to his hussar. The man made no answer, but sighed and coughed a little grimly.

Then he heard a horse coming towards him and saw, looming suddenly out of the fog, a figure that looked gigantic: it was a sergeant who came to announce that the generals were at hand, and Rostow rode to meet them, looking back at the enemy's fires. Prince Bagration and Prince Dolgoroukow had come in person to see this phantasmagoria of lights and investigate the noise the foe were making. Rostow went up to Bagration, and, after making his report, fell in among the suite, listening to what was being said by the two commanders.

"Take my word," said Dolgoroukow, "it is only a stratagem; they have retired, and the rear have been ordered to light the fires and make as much noise as possible to take us in."

"I can hardly think it," said Bagration. "They occupied this mamelon last evening; and if they were retiring they would certainly have abandoned it. You, sir," he said, turning to Rostow, "are their scouts about there still?"

"They were last evening, your excellency, but I do not know now. Shall I take my men down and find out?"

Bagration tried in vain to make out Rostow's face. "Well, yes, do so," he said, after a moment's hesitation.

Rostow darted forward, calling a sergeant and a couple of men to follow him, and then rode down the slope in the direction of the noise at a brisk trot. He felt a strange mixture of trepidation and excitement at losing himself thus, with his three hussars in the gloom, full of mysteries and perils. Bagration called after him, from the height where he stood, not to cross the brook, but Rostow pretended not to hear. On he went, on and on, mistaking bushes for trees, and rifts for men. At the foot of the hill he saw no one, neither friend nor foe; the noises, on the other hand, were more distinct. At a few paces in front of him he saw a river, as he thought, but on going nearer he found it was the high road, and he doubted which way to turn: had he better follow it, or cross it and ride over the fields towards the opposite hill? It was more prudent to follow the road, which was visible through the haze, because one could see a few yards before one.

"Follow me," he cried, and he dashed across and up the opposite slope, which had been held since the day before by a French outpost.

"Here he is, highness!" said one of the men.

Rostow had scarcely time to note a black spot in the fog when there was a flash and a report, and a bullet whistled past, regretfully as it seemed, high up in the air, and was lost in the distance. A second lightning spark—but it was a flash in the pan. Rostow turned about and galloped off. Four shots at once followed, and the bullets sang past, each in a different pitch. In a moment Rostow held in his charger, no less excited than himself, and brought him to a walk.

"More! go on, more!" he said lightly. But the shots had ceased.

From the side where he supposed the enemy to be, he heard a thousand voices calling and shouting

He galloped up to Bagration and saluted. Dolgoroukow was still maintaining his opinion:

"The French have retired and lighted their fires to deceive us. They could quite well retire and leave their picquets."

"Well, they are certainly not all gone, prince," said Bagration. "We shall know to-morrow."

"The picquets are on the hill, your excellency, and in the same position," said Rostow, unable to conceal a smile of exultation after his ride and the whistling of the shot.

"Very good, very good. Thank you, sir. . . ." said Bagration.

"Excellency," said Rostow, "allow me. . . ."

"Well, what is it?"

"Our squadron is to be left in reserve. If you would do me the favour of ordering me to join the 1st squadron."

"What is your name?"

"Count Rostow."

"Ah! Very good, very good! I will keep you with me as orderly."

"You are the son of Elias Andréiévitch?" said Dolgoroukow.

Rostow, without heeding him, asked Prince Bagration:

"Then I may hope, your excellency . . ."

"I will give the necessary orders."

"To-morrow, then," he thought, "to-morrow perhaps I may be sent on a message to the czar. Thank God!"

The shouts and bonfires had been in honour of the Emperor Napoleon's address to the army, which had been read publicly while he himself rode round and about the camp. The soldiers, having seen him, had lighted wisps of straw, and ran after him crying, "*Vive l'Empereur!*" The order of the day with Napoleon's proclamation, which had just been given out, was as follows:

"Soldiers! The Russian army confronts you in order to avenge the Austrian army at Ulm. They are the same men whom you have already beaten at Hollabrün, and that you have followed up to this spot.

"We occupy a formidable position, and while they advance to turn my right wing their flank will lie open to us. Soldiers, I myself will direct your movements. I shall keep out of the way of fire if you, with your usual valour, carry disorder and confusion into the enemy's ranks; but if victory should for a moment seem doubtful, you will see your emperor expose himself to the foremost fire; for victory must not tremble in the balance on a day when the honour of the French infantry is at stake, that honour is essential to the honour of the whole nation.

"Do not allow the ranks to be broken under pretence of rescuing the wounded; let every man be possessed with the idea that we must beat these mercenaries subsidised by England and fired by such deep hatred of our country.

"This victory will close the campaign; we can withdraw to winter quarters, where we shall be reinforced by fresh armies now forming in France, and then the peace I shall conclude will be worthy of my people, of you, and of myself. NAPOLEON."

CHAPTER LXIV

IT was five in the morning, and day had not yet dawned. The forces in the centre, the reserve, and Bagration's right wing remained motionless; but on the left the various columns of infantry, cavalry, and artillery, who were under orders to go down into the valleys and attack the French right so as to force them back into the Bohemian highlands, were rousing themselves and beginning their preparations. The smoke of the bonfires, into which everything that was not wanted was thrown, made the eyes smart. It was cold and gloomy. The officers were hastily breakfasting and swallowing their tea; the privates munched their biscuits, stamped about to warm themselves, and gathered round the fires, throwing in fragments of chairs, tables, wheels, barrels, hurdles—in short, everything they could not carry away. The advent of the Austrian guides was the signal for the start: as soon as an Austrian officer appeared near the regimental commander, the regiment began to stir, the soldiers left the fires, stuck their pipes into the tops of their boots, and, putting their knapsacks into the waggons, shouldered their guns and formed into good order. The officers buttoned up their uniforms, tightened their belts, strapped their knapsacks, and carefully inspected the ranks. The men on duty with the baggage-waggons and the officers' servants put to the horses and stowed away the luggage. The aides-de-camp, the colonels of regiments, and other officers in command, mounted their chargers, crossed themselves, gave their last instructions and commissions to the suttlers and servants, and the columns moved on to the rhythmic tramp of thousands of feet, not knowing whither they were going, not even seeing through the smoke and dense fog the spot they were leaving, or the ground on which they were to fight.

A soldier on the march is quite as much fettered in his actions and as dependent on his regiment as a sailor is on board ship. To one the deck, the mast, the hawser, is always the same; the other, in spite of the vast distances he traverses and the dangers he has to face, has always the same comrades, the same sergeant, the same company's dog, and the same captain. A sailor rarely cares to take account of the enormous extent of sea his ship has sailed over; but on a day of battle, why or how no one knows, a single solemn note finds a response in the moral consciousness of every soldier; a chord is set vibrating by the nearness of the inevitable and fateful unknown, and rouses him to unwonted anxiety. He is excited and eager, looks, listens, asks questions, and tries to find out what has been happening outside the circle of his daily interests.

The fog was so dense that the first gleam of day was too feeble to pierce it, and nothing was distinguishable at ten yards off, the shrubs looked like large trees, plains and slopes were transformed into ravines, and the Russians were in imminent danger of finding themselves unexpectedly face to face with the enemy. The column marched for a long time through this cloud, up and down, along by walls and gardens in an unknown land without coming on the foe Before, behind, and on every side, they could hear the Russian army marching in the same direction, and they were elated to think how largē a number of their fellow-men were converging on that unknown goal.

"Did you hear? The Koursk men have just gone by," said a voice in the ranks.

"The number of our troops is something tremendous," said another. "When the fires were lighted last evening I looked round—it was like Moscow itself. . . ."

The men marched on in good spirits as they always do to an attack, thought their leaders had not yet come near them nor said a word to them—indeed, all those who had met at the council of war were sore and angry and disapproved of the plan decided on; they restricted themselves to executing the orders they had received, and did not trouble themselves to inspirit the men.

This went on for about an hour; then the main body halted, and immediately there was a general and instinctive sense of great confusion and disorder. It would be difficult to explain

277

how this feeling, at first vague and doubtful, quickly became a dead certainty; but it ran on from one to another with an overwhelming rapidity, as water rushes down a ravine. If the Russian army had stood alone, without allies, it would have taken longer to grow from an apprehension to a conviction; but, as it was, there was a keen and natural satisfaction in ascribing it to the Germans, and every man was at once sure that this fatal muddle was due to the "sausage-eaters."

"Here we are at a standstill. What stops the way? The French? No, or they would have fired on us by this time; That's it; hurried us to advance, and now that we have advanced, we have to stand about senselessly in the middle of a field. Those d——d Germans make a mess of everything—wretched devils, with their brains topsy-turvy. They ought to have been sent on in front, instead of which they are pushing on from behind. And here we are stuck with nothing to eat! How long are we to wait? . . ."

"And there is the cavalry now right across the road!" exclaimed their officer. "Devil take these Germans, who don't know their own countryside," said another.

"What division is this?" asked an aide-de-camp coming up.

"The eighteenth."

"Then what are they doing here? You ought to have been in front long ago. Now you cannot get forward till the evening."

"What monstrous arrangements! They do not know what they are about themselves!" said the officer as he rode off.

Then came a general sputtering with rage in German.

"And they wonder we do not understand them!" said a soldier. "I would have shot them all down, the blackguards!"

"We ought to be in position by nine o'clock and we have not got half-way. What a muddle!"

This was the cry on all sides, and the first ardour of the troops was gradually waning into violent irritation caused by the blundering instructions given by the Germans.

The first cause of the obstruction was a movement towards the left flank effected by the Austrian cavalry. The commander-in-chief, thinking the Russian centre too far away from the right wing, had made all the cavalry return and move towards the left; and in consequence, several thousand horse had to cross the infantry which was of course brought to a standstill.

A dispute had then arisen between the Austrian guide and the Russian general. The Russian talked himself out of breath, insisting that the cavalry must be stopped; the Austrian persisted that the fault was not his but his chief's; and all this time the troops, standing motionless and silent, were gradually losing their first spirit. After waiting for about an hour they started once more and were going down into the valley—where the mist was thicker than ever, while it was clearing off the heights—when, just in front of them, a gun was fired into the dense fog; then another, and several more at irregular intervals, followed up by a brisk and steady fire over the brook called the Goldbach. The Russians not expecting to find the enemy, and coming upon them unawares, receiving no encouragement from their officers, depressed by a sense of unnecessary delay, and completely shrouded by the thick fog—fired dully and without briskness; they advanced, they halted, the word of command never reaching them soon enough from their officers, nor from the aides-de-camp who were wandering about the dells in search of their own divisions. This was what happened to the first, the second, and the third columns, who had all made their way down the slope. Was the main body of the enemy at a distance of ten versts, as every one supposed, or close at hand but invisible?

Till nine in the morning no one knew. The fourth column, commanded by Koutouzow, was placed on the plateau of Pratzen.

While this was going on Napoleon and his marshals occupied the height of Schlapanitz. A blue sky spread above his head and the low sun floated like a blazing fire-ship on a milky sea of mist. Neither he and his staff, nor the French army, was located on the further side of the stream and beyond the hollow ground near the villages of Sokolenitz and Schlapanitz which the Russians had counted on occupying as the base of their attack. On the contrary, they were on the hither side, and so close to the Russians that Napoleon could distinguish a horseman from a foot-soldier without a glass. Dressed in his blue capote—the same he had worn throughout the Italian campaign —and mounted on a small grey arab, he was a little in front of his suite, silently studying the outline of the hills which emerged one after another from the mist, and on which the Russian troops were manœuvring, and listening to the cross-fire in the valley below. Not a muscle of his face moved—it had not yet grown fat—and his bright eyes were steadily fixed on a particular point. His prevision was justified; a large body of Russians had gone down into the ravine and were marching towards the pools of water. The remainder were now abandoning the height of Pratzen which Napoleon, who regarded it as the key to the position, had intended to attack. He could watch the thousands of Russian bayonets glittering as they filed off through the fog, down the slope from Pratzen into a deep ravine between two mountains; all going in the same direction along the valley, till they were lost in the sea of haze. From the information brought to him on the previous evening, and the unmistakable noise of wheels and footsteps that the outposts had overheard during the night, and from the confused movements of the Russian forces, he plainly perceived that the allies supposed him to be at a considerable distance; also that the columns that had occupied Pratzen constituted the Russian centre, and that this centre was now weak enough to be attacked with success—still, he did not give the word.

This was a solemn day with him; the anniversary of his coronation. He had fallen into a light sleep towards morning, and had risen fresh, and in the happy frame of mind in which everything seems possible and sure to succeed; then he got on his horse and went out to reconnoitre the ground. His calm, set features betrayed in their rigidity a consciousness of well-earned happiness, such as may be sometimes seen in the face of a young and happy lover. His marshals stood a little behind him. He looked sometimes at the Pratzen heights, and sometimes at the sun now appearing through the fog.

When the sun was fairly above the fog, and its shafts of dazzling glory lighted up the plain, Napoleon ungloved his white and faultless hand, and by a sign gave the order to attack. The marshals, followed by their aides-de-camp, galloped off in various directions, and a few minutes later the main body of the French army was marching rapidly on Pratzen, which the Russians were fast abandoning, making their way to the valley on the left.

CHAPTER LXV

AT eight that morning Koutouzow had ridden up to Pratzen at the head of the fourth division—that of Miloradovitch—which was to take the place of those of Przebichewsky and Langeron, who had moved down into the hollow. He greeted the men of the 1st Regiment, and himself gave the word to march, thereby signifying his intention of commanding in person. At the village of Pratzen he halted. Prince Andrew, excited and elated, though apparently calm and cool, as a man commonly is who feels he has reached the goal he had longed to gain, was one of the commander-in-chief's numerous suite. The day that was beginning was assuredly fated to be his Toulon or his Arcole. How this would happen he did not know, but he was firmly convinced that it was to be. The land and the position of the troops were as well known to him as they could be to any superior officer in the Russian army—as to his own scheme of action, he had entirely forgotten it. As he thought over Weirother's, he only wondered what stroke of fate or unforeseen incident would give him a chance of showing his steadiness and the promptness of his apprehension.

To the left, at the foot of the hill, through the fog, invisible lines of men were exchanging volleys. "There," said he to himself, "the fighting will be hottest; that is where difficulties will arise; it is there that I shall be sent with a brigade or a division, and lead the way with the standard in my hand, sweeping everything before me!" Nay, as he saw the battalions file past, he could not help saying to himself: "Perhaps that is the very flag I shall carry to the front."

A light hoar-frost lay on the ground, which soon melted into dew, while the ravine was still shrouded in dense mist. Literally nothing could be seen in it, especially on the left, where the Russian forces had been swallowed up, and where the musketry might be heard. The sun blazed in all its glory above their heads in a deep blue sky. A long way in front, on the farther shore of this white flood, wooded hill-tops rose—that was where the foe must be lying. To the right the Imperial Guard was engulfed, leaving no trace but the echo of its steps; from behind the village on the left came squares of cavalry, to vanish in their turn. Before and behind them the infantry filed past. The commander-in-chief was keeping an eye on the troops as they came out of the village; he looked exhausted and annoyed. Then the infantry halted suddenly without any orders, evidently in consequence of an obstacle in the way of their advance.

"But do command them to break up into battalions and get out of the village," said Koutouzow drily to the general who came up with him. "Don't you understand that it is quite impossible to form in open order in the streets of a village when marching against an enemy?"

"Your excellency, I propose to form outside the village."

Koutouzow smiled sourly: "A happy thought certainly to form in the face of the enemy!"

"The enemy is a long way off yet, excellency. In accordance with the plan. . . ."

"What plan?" he exclaimed in a rage. "Who told you that? Have the goodness to obey my orders."

"I obey," said the other.

"My dear fellow," Nesvitsky whispered to Prince Andrew, "the old man is in a dreadfully bad temper."

An Austrian officer, in a white uniform with a green plume, at this moment came up to Koutouzow and asked him, from the emperor, whether the fourth division were taking part in the engagement. Koutouzow turned away without replying; his eye happened to light on Bolkonsky, and he softened, as if to exclude him from the effects of his ill-temper.

"Will you, my dear fellow, go and see if the third has got past the village yet. Tell them they are to stop and wait for orders from me. And ask," he added, detaining him, "if the skirmishers are placed, and what they are doing—what they are doing," he repeated, without stopping to answer the Austrian messenger.

Prince Andrew rode past the foremost battalions, paused at the third division, and noted that the sharpshooters were not in fact in their places in front of the columns. The colonel of the regiment was amazed at receiving the commander-in-chief's instruction to send them forward; he was persuaded that other Russian troops were forming between him and the enemy, whom he supposed to be at least ten versts away. Indeed, he could see nothing before him but a waste of ground that sloped away under the dense mist; Prince Andrew returned at once to make his report to the commander-in-chief, whom he found in the spot where he had left him on horseback, and sitting hunched in his saddle with the whole dead weight of his body, yawning, and with his eyes shut. The troops had halted and were standing with the butt-ends of their guns on the ground.

"Very well," was all he said; and turning to the Austrian, who stood by him with his watch in his hand, assuring him that it was high time to go forward, as the left wing had made their movement down hill: "There is no hurry, your excellency," he said, with a yawn. "We have plenty of time."

At this moment they heard cheers from the troops behind them in response to greetings from various voices which approached rapidly along the marching columns. When the men of the regiment he was leading took up the cry, Koutouzow frowned and drew back a few paces. Along the Pratzen road

282

came a many-coloured squadron of horsemen riding fast, two conspicuously in front of the rest: one in a black uniform with a white plume rode a chestnut horse; the other, in white, rode a black horse. These were the two emperors, followed by their suite. Koutouzow, with the affected precision of an officer at his post, commanded silence, and with a formal salute went forward to meet the czar. His manner and person were suddenly metamorphosed, and had assumed the aspect of blind submission as an inferior who has no opinion of his own. His affected deference seemed to impress the Emperor Alexander unpleasantly, but the feeling was transient and vanished at once, leaving no trace on his youthful and beaming features. His little indisposition had made him thinner than at the Olmütz parade when Bolkonsky had seen him for the first time abroad, but had not deprived him of the really fascinating union of dignity and gentleness which characterised his delicate lips and fine blue eyes. If he had been imperial at the review at Olmütz, to-day he was more eager and bright. His face was flushed with his swift ride; he pulled up his horse and breathed deeply, turning to his staff—as fresh and youthful as himself—Czartorisky, Novosiltsow, Volkonsky, Strogonow, and others were among the number; they were laughing and chatting together. Gorgeous in their uniforms, and mounted on fine, well-trained horses, they remained a few paces behind the sovereigns. Grooms, too, were in attendance with led horses for the emperors to change, saddled with embroidered horse-cloths. The Emperor Francis, himself still young, thin, tall, and stiffly upright on his handsome stallion, glanced about him anxiously, and signed to one of his aides-de-camp to come to him.

"He is going to ask him at what hour they set out," thought Prince Andrew to himself, as he watched his former acquaintance, remembering the questions the Austrian Emperor had asked him at Brünn.

The sight of all this splendid youth, so full of vigour, and so sure of triumph, dissipated the sullen mood that had fallen on Koutouzow's staff, as a fresh, moorland breeze, blowing in at a window, clears away the vapours of an overheated room.

"Why do you not begin, Michael Larionovitch?"

"I was waiting, your majesty," said Koutouzow, bowing low.

The czar leaned towards him as if he had not heard.

"I was waiting, your majesty," Koutouzow repeated—and Prince Andrew noted the curl of his lip as he said: "I was waiting. The columns are not all assembled, sire."

The answer annoyed the czar; he shrugged his shoulders and looked at Novosiltsow as though to reflect on Koutouzow.

"But we are not on the parade-ground, Michael Larionovitch, that we should wait till all the regiments are assembled before the review begins," said Alexander, and he now cast a glance at the Emperor Francis, as if to invite his attention at any rate, if he would not join in the conversation; but the emperor paid no heed.

"That, sire, is the very reason why I do not begin," said Koutouzow, loudly and distinctly. "We are not at a review, it is not a parade-ground."

At these words the officers in attendance looked at each other. "Old as he is he ought not to speak like that," their disapproving expression plainly said.

The czar looked steadily and inquiringly at Koutouzow, waiting for what further he was going to say. Koutouzow, with a respectful bow, sat silent.

The silence lasted a few seconds, and then, again putting on the attitude and tone of an inferior waiting for orders, he added:

"But of course—only if it is your majesty's wish." And turning to Miloradovitch he gave the order to attack.

The ranks moved on; two battalions of the Novgorod Regiment and one of the Apcheron Regiment marched past; as the last was passing Miloradovitch galloped forward, his cloak flying open and displaying his uniform covered with medals and stars. With his cocked hat and immense waving plume stuck on one side he jauntily saluted the czar, pulling up short just in front of him.

"By God's help, general!" said the czar.

"We will do our best," he gaily retorted, and the staff-officers smiled at his queer French accent. Miloradovitch, cleverly turning his horse, fell back a few paces behind the czar, and the soldiers, excited by the presence of their sovereign, marched forward with a steady, brisk step.

"Lads!" cried Miloradovitch suddenly, himself forgetful of the emperor's presence and sharing the excitement of his men with whom he had served under Souvorow. "Mind, lads—this is not the first village you take!"

"Ready, aye, ready!" said the men, and at the chorus of voices the emperor's horse—the same that he had ridden at reviews in Russia—shied at the unexpected shout. Here, on the field of battle of Austerlitz, startled by the vicinity of the Austrian emperor's stallion, he pricked his ears at the unaccustomed noise of volleys of which he could not discern the meaning, while he could not guess the thoughts and feelings of his august rider. The czar smiled and pointed out the advancing battalions to one of his more immediate friends.

CHAPTER LXVI

KOUTOUZOW, followed by his staff, slowly rode after the carabineers. After going about half a verst he halted near a solitary house, probably an abandoned inn, which stood at the meeting of two roads, each coming down from the mountain and crowded with Russian soldiers. The fog was lifting, and the indistinct masses of the hostile force were becoming visible on the opposite heights. A brisk fire could be heard in the valley to the left. Koutouzow was talking to the Austrian general, to whom Prince Andrew turned, requesting the loan of his field-glass.

"Look, look!" said the Austrian, "there are the French!" and he pointed, not to the distance, but to the base of the hill just in front of them.

Two generals and the aides-de-camp eagerly looked through the field-glass. An involuntary panic was visible on their faces; the French, who were supposed to be two versts away, had suddenly started into life close to them.

"The enemy! No! Yes, undoubtedly! But how is it possible?" said several voices. And Prince Andrew watched a formidable body of French troops marching up on the right to meet the Apcheron Regiment, at about 500 yards from the spot where they were standing.

"Now this is the great moment! This is where I distinguish myself," thought Prince Andrew and spurring his horse, rode up to Koutouzow. Your excellency, the regiment must be stopped!" But at this moment a thick smoke shrouded the scene, a loud explosion of musketry rattled in their ears, and a voice, breathless with terror, said quite close to them: "It is all over, boys—all over with us! . . ." Then, as though this exclamation were an order, great mobs of soldiers driven back, pushing and hustling each other, fled past the spot where, five minutes before, they had filed off in front of the emperors. Any attempt to check this crowd would have been madness, for it bore down everything in its way. Bolkonsky had the

285

greatest difficulty in making a stand against the torrent, and only vaguely understood what was happening. Nesvitsky, heated and half crazy, cried out to Koutouzow that he would be made prisoner if he did not retreat. Koutouzow, without stirring, pulled out his handkerchief and pressed it to his cheek, from which blood was flowing. Prince Andrew forced his way to him: "You are wounded?" he said with deep anxiety.

"The real wound is not here but there," said Koutouzow, keeping the handkerchief over his cheek and pointing to the fugitives.

"Stop them!" he cried. But understanding at once how useless his appeal was, he set spurs in his horse and taking the right, straight into the midst of a party of fugitives, was swept away with it into chaos.

The mass was so closely packed that escape was impossible; in the midst of the confusion, some were shouting, others looking back and firing in the air. Another was belabouring the horse ridden by Koutouzow himself. Koutouzow, having succeeded in cutting across the stream, rode off with his sadly diminished staff towards the spot where the firing was going on. Prince Andrew, while making superhuman efforts to join him, detected through the smoke, on the slope, a Russian battery, which was not yet silenced, and which the French were rushing up to assault. A little higher up the Russian infantry stood motionless. A general came forward to speak to Koutouzow, whose escort was reduced to four persons. These four, pale and agitated, looked at each other in silence.

"Stop those miserable cowards!" said Koutouzow to the commanding officer; and, as if in revenge, a shower of bullets, like a flock of little birds, flew singing over the regiment and over his head. The French who were firing on the battery, perceiving Koutouzow, now aimed at him. At this fresh attack the colonel of the regiment clapped his hand to his leg; some privates fell, and the ensign let the flag drop. It tottered and then caught on the men's bayonets; they, without waiting for the word of command, began to return the fire.

Koutouzow groaned in despair.

"Bolkonsky," he murmured in a weak, old man's voice, as he pointed to the battalion of which half the men had fallen, "what is the meaning of that?"

The words were hardly spoken when Prince Andrew, choking with tears of rage and shame, leaped from his horse and rushed forward to seize the flag.

286

"Come, lads! Come on!" he shouted at the top of his voice. "My time has come!" he said to himself seizing the standard and exulting as he heard the bullets whistling round him. Some more men fell by his side.

"Hurrah!" he shouted, lifting the flagstaff with difficulty.

He ran forward, firmly convinced that the men would follow him; he went a few steps, and then one soldier—a second—the whole detachment rushed after him and outstripped him. A sergeant relieved Bolkonsky of his burden which was so heavy that his arm shook, but he was shot down that instant. Prince Andrew again seized the flag, and dragging it along by the pole ran after the battalion. In front of him he now saw the Russian artillery, some fighting, some deserting their guns and running to meet the infantry—he saw the French foot pouncing on the horses in the battery and turning the cannon against the Russians. He was within twenty yards of it, the shot were pelting and mowing down the ranks near him, but he never took his eyes off the battery. A red-haired artilleryman, with his shako crushed in, was struggling with a Frenchman for the possession of a ramrod; he could distinguish the furious and vindictive expression of their faces; it was quite clear that they were hardly conscious of what they were doing.

"What are they about?" said Prince Andrew to himself. "Why does not our man take to his heels, as he has no arms, and why does not the Frenchman make an end of him? He will not have time to be off before the Frenchman gets a shot at him!" And just then a second Frenchman came up, and the fate of the red-haired Russian, who had wrenched the ramrod out of his adversary's hand, was sealed.

But Prince Andrew did not see the end. He felt a tremendous blow on the head, dealt, as it seemed to him, by someone close to him. The pain was sickening rather than acute, but it changed the current of this thoughts.

"What has come over me? I cannot stand—my legs have given way. . . ." And he fell on his back.

Presently he opened his eyes to see the end of the struggle between the gunner and the Frenchman, and whether the guns had been rescued or captured. But he saw nothing but the deep, far-away sky above him, with light grey clouds lazily sailing across it.

"What peace! what rest!" he thought. "It was not so just now when I was running! we were all running and shouting; it was not so when those two scared creatures were struggling

287

for the ramrod—the clouds were not floating so then, in that infinite space! How is it that I never noticed those endless depths before? How glad I am to have seen them now—at last. Everything is a hollow delusion excepting that. . . . Thank God for this peace—this silent rest. . . ."

CHAPTER LXVII

AT nine o'clock the right wing under Bagration had not yet begun to fight. In spite of Dolgoroukow's urgency, he was so anxious to escape responsibility that he wished to send for orders to the commander-in-chief. As the distance between the two wings of the army was not less than ten versts the messenger—if he escaped being killed, which was highly improbable, and if he found the commander-in-chief, which would be a difficult matter—could not be back again before evening; of this he was quite sure. Glancing round at his retinue, Bagration's sleepy, expressionless eyes fell on Rostow's eager, almost childish face. He selected him.

"And if I should meet his majesty before I find the commander-in-chief, excellency?" asked Rostow.

"You can take his majesty's orders," said Dolgoroukow, anticipating Bagration's reply.

After being relieved at the outposts, Rostow had had some hours' sleep, and was full of life, spirits, and confidence in himself and his guiding star; he was ready to attempt impossibilities. His highest hope was fulfilled; a great battle was being fought; he had a part to play in it; nay, he was attached to the person of one of the bravest of the generals; and now he was sent on a mission to Koutouzow with the chance of meeting the emperor, The morning was bright, and he was well mounted. His spirit rose with jubilant delight. He first rode along the motionless ranks of Bagration's division to the position occupied by Ouvarow's cavalry; there he saw the preliminary signs of the proposed attack. Once past these he heard the growl of cannon and the rattle of musketry, louder and louder as he went further. It was not now an occasional shot, ringing at regular intervals through the fresh morning air, but a steady thunder—the roar of artillery mingling with the volleys of small arms and echoed from the heights fronting Pratzen. Light whiffs of smoke curling and catching each other floated off from the muskets, while heavy swathes rolled up from the batteries like clouds that hung and spread in mid-air. The bayonets of endless lines of infantry glittered through the smoke, and in the distance the artillery train with its green caissons wound along like a narrow riband.

Rostow halted to see what was happening: where were they going? Why were they marching in such various directions—forwards, backwards? He could not make it out; but the scene, instead of alarming him or depressing him, only fired his zeal.

"I do not know what will come of it," said he to himself, "but it is sure to be all right."

Having ridden past the Austrian troops, he came on the line of attack. It was the Guards about to charge.

"So much the better, I shall see it closer."

Several horsemen came cantering towards him, and he recognised them as the Uhlan Guards, whose ranks had been broken, and who were retiring from the *mêlée*. Rostow noticed blood on one of the men.

"Much I care!" thought he. About a hundred paces farther on he observed, on his left, a large body of cavalry coming on at full trot, so as to cross his path; their uniforms were white and glittering, their chargers black. He set spurs to his horse so as to get out of their way and would have succeeded but that the troop increased their pace; he saw that they were gaining ground, and heard the tramp of hoofs and the clatter of arms coming nearer and nearer. In less than a minute they were close enough for him to distinguish their faces; they were the Horse Guards about to charge the French infantry; they were going at top speed, but with their horses well in hand. Rostow heard the word of command given by an officer who was spurring his thoroughbred to his utmost pace. Fearing lest he should be either borne on or crushed, Rostow flew along in front of them, hoping to get across before they were down on him.

Still, he thought he could not escape collision with the last man in the line, whose heavy build was a striking contrast to his own slight frame. He must inevitably have been overthrown and ridden down, and his horse with him, if he had not been happily inspired to wave his whip close to the eyes of the guardsman's fine and powerful charger; it shied and pricked its ears, but, at a touch of his rider's spurs, whisked his tail and stretched his neck, and flew on faster than ever.

Rostow had scarcely cleared the line when he heard a loud cheer, and, looking back, he saw the first ranks of horse-soldiers swallowed up as it were in a regiment of French cavalry with red epaulettes. Then the dense smoke from invisible cannon hid them from view. Rostow wavered whether to follow them or to go on where he had been sent. This was the splendid and famous charge of the Horse Guards which even the French admired and praised. How his heart tightened as he afterwards heard that of all this mass of fine men, this flower of wealthy and splendid youth, mounted on noble beasts, who had rushed past him at such a furious pace but eighteen had come out alive!

"My turn will come; I need not envy them," said Rostow, as he turned away. "Perhaps I may see the emperor."

When he at last reached the Regiment of Foot Guards he found he was in the midst of the fire; this he guessed at rather than heard, from seeing the uneasy looks of the privates, and the grave, stern expression of the officers.

A voice—it was Boris's—suddenly addressed him:

"Hallo, Rostow; we have front places. What do you think of it? Our regiment has had a sharp tussle!" And he smiled with the reckless smile of youth, fresh from the baptism of fire.

Rostow stopped: "Well, and what came of it?"

"Repulsed," said Boris, who was ready to talk. And he went on to tell him that the Guards, having seen the troops in front of them and taken them for Austrians, had soon discovered, by the whistling of the bullets, that they were themselves in front and must begin the attack.

"Where are you going?" asked Boris.

"To his majesty."

"There he is," said Boris, pointing at the Grand Duke Constantine, about a hundred yards away, in the uniform of the Horse Guards, his head sunk between his shoulders, and knitting his brows while he gesticulated and shouted at a pale and trembling Austrian officer.

"But that is the grand duke, and I am looking for the commander-in-chief or the czar," said Rostow, riding away.

"Count, Count Rostow," cried Berg, holding up his hand, wrapped in a blood-stained handkerchief. "I have been wounded in the right wrist and have not left my post! You see, I am obliged to hold my sword in my left hand! In my family all the Von Bergs were knights." And he went on talking when Rostow was already some way off.

After crossing a vacant space he rode along the line of the

reserve force in order to find shelter from the enemy's fire, and so went farther away from the scene of action. But suddenly, in front of him and behind the Russians, in a place where it was impossible to suspect the presence of the French, he heard brisk firing close at hand.

"What can that be?" he thought. "The enemy in our rear? It is impossible. . . ." And blank terror overwhelmed him as he thought of the possible issue of the battle. "Well, come what may, there is no escape now; I must try to find the commander-in-chief, and if all is lost I can but die with them!"

His darkest presentiments were confirmed at every step he took on the ground occupied by the various corps behind the village of Pratzen.

"What is the meaning of this? Who is firing, and at whom?" said Rostow, as he met Russians and Austrians alike flying in utter disorder.

"The devil alone knows what is doing.—He has beaten every one.—All is lost! . . ." replied the fugitives in Russian, German, Czech, understanding no more of what was going on than he himself did. "Down with the Germans!" cried one. "Oh, let them them go to the devil, the traitors!"

"Devil take the Russians, I say!" growled a German.

A few wounded were dragging themselves along, and oaths, shouts, and groans mingled in one long and dismal chorus. The firing had ceased, but Rostow heard later that the German and Russian fugitives had fired on each other.

"Good God!" thought Rostow, "and the emperor may come past at any moment and see this rout. It is only a handful of cowards of course. It is impossible—impossible; I must get past them as fast as I can."

The idea of a total defeat could not enter his brain, in spite of his seeing the French batteries and men on the Pratzen plateau, on the very spot whither he had been sent to find the czar and the commander-in-chief.

CHAPTER LXVIII

ROSTOW was directed to look for Koutouzow and the emperor at Pratzen village, but all round the village of Pratzen not an officer was to be seen. Rostow met no one but the rank and file flying in disorder; on the high-road officers' carriages and waggons of every kind with Russians and Austrians of every corps, wounded and whole, ran past him. The crowd was crushing, pushing, buzzing, swarming, and mingling its cries with the ominous roar of the shell thrown by the French batteries from the heights of Pratzen.

"Where is the emperor? Where is Koutouzow?" he asked one and another, but got no reply. At length he caught a private by the collar, and forced him to attend.

"Why, my good man; they have all been down there a long time; they have made their way forward," said the man with a laugh.

Letting go of the man, who was evidently drunk, Rostow stopped an officer's servant, whom he supposed to be the groom of someone of high rank. This man told him that the czar had passed along this road an hour since, as fast as he could go in a carriage, and that he was dangerously wounded.

"Oh! impossible. It cannot have been he!" said Rostow.

"But I saw him with my own eyes," said the man with a knowing smile. "I have known him long enough; why, how often have I seen him at St. Petersburg. He was very pale, leaning back in the carriage. And what a pace Ilia Ivanitch was going with his four black horses! Do you suppose that I don't know those horses, or that anyone could drive the czar but Ilia Ivanitch?"

"For whom are you looking?" asked a wounded officer, a little way on. "The commander-in-chief? He was killed by a shot in the breast in front of our regiment."

"He was not killed, only wounded," said another.

"Who, Koutouzow?" asked Rostow.

"No, not Koutouzow—what's his name? After all, what does it matter? There are not many left alive. If you go down there you will find all the commanders together at the village of Gostieradek."

Rostow went on, walking his horse, not knowing what to do or to whom to turn. The emperor wounded! The battle lost! Following the road pointed out to him, he saw at a distance the spire and belfry of a church. What was the hurry? He had nothing now to ask the czar and Koutouzow, even if they were safe and sound.

"Turn to the left, highness; if you go straight on you will be killed."

Rostow considered for a moment, and then took the path he was warned against. "It is all the same to me! If the czar is wounded, what have I to live for?" And he came out on the ground which was most thickly strewed with dead and fugitives. The French had not yet reached it, and the few Russians who had escaped had fled from it. On this spot the killed and wounded lay in heaps of ten, fifteen—like piled-up shocks of corn; the wounded were crawling along to get closer to each other, with cries of pain that seemed to Rostow often forced and unnatural; he put his horse to a gallop to escape this scene of human suffering. He was afraid—not for his life, but of losing the balance of mind which was indispensable, and which had almost failed him at the sight of these hapless wretches.

The French had ceased to fire on the field where none remained but the dead and dying, but as they caught sight of the aide-de-camp riding across they sent a few balls after him. The sharp, ominous sound, and the sight of the dead scattered around him, gave him an impulse of terror and self-pity. He remembered his mother's last letter, and said to himself: "What would her feelings be if she could see me here, exposed to the fire of cannon?"

In the village of Gostieradek, which was out of range of the guns, he found the Russian forces retiring in good order, though the regiments had got mixed. The battle was talked of with defeat as an accepted fact, but no one could tell Rostow where to find the czar and Koutouzow. Some said Alexander was really wounded; others contradicted this rumour, accounting for it by the flight of Tolstoï, the steward of the household, who had been seen pale and panic-stricken in the emperor's carriage. Hearing that some persons of importance were under shelter of a hamlet to the left, Rostow went thither, not with any hope of finding those he sought, but to satisfy his conscience. About three versts further he outstripped the front ranks of the Russians, and then he saw two horsemen near an orchard divided from the road by a wide ditch. He thought he recognised one of them, with a white feather; the other

293

riding a splendid chestnut, which he also had seen before, came to the ditch, spurred his horse, and giving him his head, leaped it easily; a few clods of earth were kicked up by the horse's hoofs, but turning him round, the officer leaped the trench back again, and went respectfully up to his companion, evidently urging him to follow his example. But the rider he addressed shook his head and hand, and Rostow recognised him as his czar, his adored sovereign, whose defeat he deplored.

"But he cannot stay there, alone, in this deserted spot!" said he to himself. Alexander looked round, and he could clearly see the features that were graven on his heart. The czar was pale; his cheeks were hollow, and his eyes sunk; but the gentleness and sweetness of his expression were all the more striking. Rostow was the happier for seeing him, happy to be assured that his wound was an unfounded fiction; and he said to himself that it was his duty to deliver Prince Dolgoroukow's message without a moment's delay. But just as a tremulous and anxious young lover dares not give utterance to his most passionate dreams and timidly seeks any excuse for delaying the meeting he pines for, Rostow, seeing the realisation of his desires, could not make up his mind whether he ought to go up to the emperor, or whether the proceeding would not be ill-timed and presumptuous.

"I might perhaps seem to be taking advantage of his solitude and overthrow. An unknown face might strike him un-pleasantly; and besides, what could I say to him, when his mere glance is enough to strike me dumb?"

The words he had prepared seemed to die on his lips; all the more so because he had framed them to suit the triumphant mood of victory, or the event of his being stretched on his bed with the czar thanking him for his heroic exploits, while he, with his dying breath, should give utterance to his devotion to that beloved sovereign—a devotion so nobly sealed by death.

"And after all, what can I ask him? It is four o'clock, and the battle is lost! No, I will not speak to him; I have no right to interrupt his reflections. I would rather die a thousand deaths than meet an angry glance from him." And he sadly rode away, with despair in his soul, looking back many times to watch the czar's movements.

He saw Captain von Toll go up to the emperor and help him across the ditch on foot; then he sat down under an apple-tree. Toll stood by his side talking eagerly. The little scene stirred Rostow's envy and regret, especially when he saw the emperor cover his eyes with one hand, and hold out the other to Toll.

"I might have been in his place," he said to himself; and, barely restraining his tears, he rode on, away from the czar, but not knowing which way to go. His despair was all the deeper because he felt guilty of weakness. He might, he ought to have approached the sovereign. This, or never, was the moment for giving proof of his devotion, and he had missed it. He turned round and rode back to the spot where he had seen the emperor; there was no one there. A long train of carts and waggons was slowly passing, and Rostow learnt from one of the drivers that Koutouzow's staff were not far from the village, and they were going to join them. Rostow followed.

Ahead of him was Koutouzow's groom leading some horses covered with cloths. Behind the groom was a waggon and behind the waggon an old man with bandy legs, dressed in a sheepskin coat; this was Titus, and every few minutes the groom made some joke at his expense.

By five in the evening the defeat was total. More than a hundred field-pieces had fallen into the hands of the French. All Przcbichewsky's corps had laid down their arms; the others having lost more than half their number, retired in disorder. The remains of the divisions under Langeron and Dokhtourow were crowded in confusion round the pools and sluices of the village of Auguest. By six the enemy's fire was directed on this point only; they had posted their batteries half-way up the heights of Pratzen, and were firing on the allies as they retreated.

Dokhtourow and some others of the rear pulled their regiments together, reformed their battalions, and turned against the French cavalry, who were pursuing them.

It was now dusk. The narrow mill dam of Auguest—where for a long course of peaceful years the good old miller had dropped his fishing-line into the pool, while his grandchild, with his shirt-sleeves rolled up, plunged his bare arms into the water-can among the wriggling silver fish—where the Moravian farmer in his fur cap and dark-blue coat had followed the huge, slow waggons carrying heavy sheaves of wheat to the mill, and returning with full sacks of fine white flour, filling the air with light dust—was now packed with a scared and bewildered crowd, pushing, falling, to be crushed by the hoofs of horses, or the wheels of waggons and gun-carriages, or trampling the dead under foot merely to be killed in their turn a little further on.

Every few seconds a ball or a shell came hurtling and bursting in the midst of this compact mass of human beings, killing and bespattering all within range. Dologhow, who had already gained his promotion, himself wounded in the hand, with ten men and his colonel, were the sole survivors of their regiment. Carried on by the stream, they had forced their way to the end of the mill dam, where they were stopped by a horse in a gun-carriage, which had been killed, and which had to be cut from the harness. A ball killed a man behind them, and another fell in front and sprinkled Dologhow over with blood. Then the mass rushed forward desperately a few paces, and had to stop again.

"A hundred yards farther, and there is safety! To stop here another two minutes is death!" This was what everyone was saying.

Dologhow, who had been shoved back into the middle, got as far as the edge of the mill-pool, and ran across the thin ice that coated the water.

"Look here, come this way!" he cried to the gunner. "The ice will bear."

The ice in fact did not break under his weight, but it cracked and yielded, and it was quite evident that even without the weight of the gun and of the mass of men it would give way under him. The men looked at him, and crowded on the bank, but could not make up their minds to follow him. The general in command, who was on horseback, raised his arm, and had just opened his lips to speak, when a ball crashed past, so low down over the terrified heads, that all bent low—and something fell. It was the general, who sank in a pool of blood. No one looked round at him; no one could think of picking him up.

"On the ice! Don't you hear? On the ice! Turn round, turn!" shouted several; most of the men had no idea themselves why they shouted this.

One of the gun-carriages made the venture; the crowd rushed on to the ice, which cracked under one of the fugitives; his foot was in the water, and in trying to get it out, he fell in to the waist. The men who were nearest to him held back; the gunner stopped his horse, while behind them the shouts rose louder than ever: "Get on to the ice; go on, push on!" and shrieks of terror sounded on every side.

The soldiers gathered round the cannon, tugging and beating

Dokhtourow and some others of the rear pulled their regiments together

the horses to get them on. The poor beasts started, the ice gave way in one sheet, and forty men sank. The cannon-balls did not cease whistling and pelting with hideous steadiness, falling sometimes on the ice, and sometimes in the water, decimating the living mass that swarmed on the dyke, on the pools, and on the shore.

CHAPTER LXIX

ALL this time Prince Andrew was lying on the same spot on the hill of Pratzen, clenching his hand over a fragment of the staff of the flag, losing blood, and unconsciously uttering feeble and plaintive moans, like a child. Towards the evening he ceased to moan; he lay quite senseless. Suddenly he opened his eyes. He had no idea of the lapse of time, and feeling himself alive, with an acute pain from a burning wound in the head, his first thought was:

"Where is the infinite sky I saw this morning, and had never seen before? This pain, too, is new to me! I have never known anything—anything at all till now. But where am I?"

He listened, and heard the noise of several horses and voices coming towards him. They were speaking French. He did not turn his head; he lay gazing at the sky so high above him, whose fathomless blue could be seen between the floating clouds. The horsemen were Napoleon and two of his aides-de-camp. Bonaparte had been all over the field of battle, and giving orders for the reinforcement of the batteries that were firing on the dyke at Auguest; now he was examining the wounded and dead who had been left on the field. "Fine men!" he exclaimed, as he saw a Russian grenadier lying, face downwards, on the ground; his neck was livid, and his arms already rigid in death.

"The ammunition for the field-guns is exhausted, sire," said an aide-de-camp, who had been sent up from the batteries directed on Auguest.

"Bring up the reserve," ordered Napoleon, going on a few steps; but he stopped by Prince Andrew, who still clutched the broken staff of the flag which had been seized as a trophy by the French.

"A splendid death!" exclaimed the emperor.

Prince Andrew understood that it was Napoleon who spoke and himself of whom he was speaking; but the words buzzed in his ears without his paying any heed to them, and he forgot them immediately. His head was burning; his strength was ebbing with his blood, and he could see nothing but that remote, eternal blue. He had recognised Napoleon—his hero—but at this moment how small, how insignificant the hero seemed in comparison with the message to his soul from that immeasurable heaven. What was said, and who it was that halted close to him, were matters of indifference; but he was glad they had stopped; for he felt vaguely that they would help him to return to that life which seemed to him so well worth living since he had begun to understand it. He collected all his strength to make some movement, to utter some sound—he stirred one foot, and moaned feebly.

"Ah! he is not dead!" exclaimed Napoleon. "Pick up this young man, and carry him to the ambulance."

And then the emperor rode forward to meet Marshal Lannes, who smiled, and took off his hat, and congratulated him on the victory.

Prince Andrew remembered nothing after this; under the pain caused by the mere fact of being lifted, by the jolting of the litter, and the probing of his wound, he again became unconscious. He did not come to himself till the evening, while he was being carried to the hospital with several other Russians, wounded or prisoners. During the transfer he revived once more, and could look about him, and even speak. The first words he heard were spoken by the French officer in charge of the wounded:

"We must stop here. The emperor will ride past, and we must give him the pleasure of seeing these gentlemen."

"Pooh! There are so many prisoners this time—a large part of the Russian army. He must have had enough of it," said another.

"Yes, but that one," said the first speaker, pointing to a wounded Russian officer in the uniform of the Horse Guards, "was, they say, the commander-in-chief of all the Emperor Alexander's Life Guards."

Bolkonsky recognised Prince Repnine, whom he had met in society at St. Petersburg. By his side was a young horse-guardsman of about nineteen, also wounded.

Napoleon rode up at a gallop, and pulled his horse up short, just in front of them.

"Who is highest in rank here?" he asked, seeing the wounded officers. Colonel Prince Repnine was named to him.

You are the commander-in-chief of the Imperial Horse Guards."

"Only in command of a squadron."

"Your regiment did its duty with great honour "

"Praise from a great general is the soldier's best reward," replied Repnine.

"I give it with great pleasure," said Napoleon. "Who is this young man with you?"

Repnine mentioned him as Lieutenant Suchtelen, and Napoleon looked at him with a smile.

"He is very young to try odds with us."

"Youth is no bar to courage," murmured Suchtelen, in a choking voice.

"Nobly answered, young man; you will do!"

Prince Andrew had also been placed in the front rank to swell the triumph; he could not fail to attract the emperor's eye, and Napoleon remembered having seen him lying on the field.

"And you, young man; how are you feeling, my gallant fellow?"

Bolkonsky fixed his eyes on him, but did not speak. Only five minutes before he had said a few words to the men who were carrying him, and now he only looked at the emperor, and was silent. What, after all, were the interests, the pride, the elation of Napoleon? What was the hero himself when compared with that glorious heaven of justice and mercy which his soul had felt and apprehended? To him everything seemed sordid, petty; so unlike those stern and solemn thoughts that had been borne in upon him by his utter exhaustion and expectation of death. Even with his eyes fixed on the emperor, he was reflecting on the insignificance of greatness—the insignificance of life, of which no one knew the aim and end—the still greater insignificance of death, whose purpose is inscrutably hidden from the living.

"Let these gentlemen be cared for," said Napoleon, without waiting for Prince Andrew's reply. "Take them to the tents, and let Dr. Larrey attend to their wounds. We shall meet again, Prince Repnine!" and he left them, his face beaming with satisfaction. The soldiers who were carrying Bolkonsky, seeing the emperor's benevolent feeling towards the prisoners, hastened to return to him the little image which his sister had hung about his neck, and which they had stolen from him; he suddenly felt it laid on his breast outside his uniform, without knowing how, or by whom, it had been replaced.

"What a happy thing it would be," thought he, as he

remembered Maria's deep feeling of pious veneration, "a happy thing if everything were as simple and as clear as Maria believes it to be! It would be good, indeed, to know where to seek help and comfort in this life, and what awaits us after death. I could be so happy, so calm, if only I could say: 'Saviour have mercy on me . . .' But to whom could I say it? The great immeasurable, incomprehensible Power, to whom I cannot turn or express my feelings, is either the great All, or it is nothingness; or else it is the God enclosed in this image of Maria's! Nothing on earth is certain excepting the worthlessness of everything within the compass of my intelligence, and the Majesty of the fathomless Unknown—the only Reality, perhaps, and the only Great Power."

The litter was lifted, and at every jolt he felt the acutest pain, now increased by the fever and delirium that were coming upon him. He fancied he saw his father, his sister, his wife, the son that was to be born to him, Napoleon's stunted and insignificant figure—and all these images passed and repassed against the blue background of that vaultless sky, which was present through all his fevered dreams. He seemed to be living happily again at Lissy-Gory in domestic peace and quiet, when, suddenly, a little figure of Napoleon stood close before him, and his cold gaze, his satisfaction at the misfortunes of others, filled him with doubts and anguish . . . but he turned away to that beatific sky which alone promised any relief.

Towards morning all these visions were blurred and lost in the chaotic gloom of utter delirium, which would be more likely to end in death than in recovery—so said Dr. Larrey, Napoleon's private physician.

"A nervous and bilious subject," said the doctor, "he will not get over it." And the prince, with some other hopeless cases, was entrusted to the care of the natives of the district.

BOOK FOUR

CHAPTER LXX

At the beginning of the year 1806, Nicholas Rostow and
Denissow went home on leave. As Denissow was going to
Voronège, Rostow proposed that they should travel together
as far as Moscow, and that his friend should spend a few days
in his father's house. At the last halting-place but one on the
road, Denissow met an old comrade, and with him emptied
three bottles of wine; thus in spite of the fearful jolting of the
sleigh, in which he lay at full length, he never woke for an
instant. The nearer they got, the more impatient Rostow
became:

"Faster, faster! oh! these endless streets, shops, kalatch-
sellers,[1] lanterns!" he said to himself, after they had passed
the city gates, and their names had been entered as arriving
on leave. "Denissow, here we are! He is asleep!" and he
leaned forward, as if the see-saw action would accelerate their
progress. "There is the cross-road where Zakhar used to
stand—and there is Zakhar with his old horse! And there is
the shop where I used to buy gingerbread! Oh, when shall we
be there? Go on, go on!"

"Where am I to go?" asked the driver.

"There, down there, out there. What, don't you see? that
big house—you know our house? Denissow, Denissow, we
are just there!"

Denissow raised his head and coughed, but did not reply.
"Dmitri," Nicholas went on to the servant sitting on the box,
"is that light in our house."

"Certainly it is—in your father's room."

"They are not in bed then? What do you think? . . .
By the way, do not forget to unpack my new uniform"—and he
passed his hand over his downy moustache. . . . "Well, well,
get on! Vaska, wake up!" But Denissow was asleep again.

"Go on, get on—three roubles to drink!" cried Rostow, who,

[1] Kalatch is a sort of white bread or cake peculiar to Moscow.

301

though only a few yards from home, thought he should never reach it. The sleigh turned to the right, and drew up in front of the steps; Rostow recognised the dilapidated cornice, and the corner stone of the footway, and leaped out before the sleigh had fairly stopped; he was up the steps with one bound. The outside of the house was as cold and calm as he remembered it. What did those stone walls care for coming and going? There was no one in the hall. "Good God! Has anything happened?" thought Rostow with a tightening about the heart; for a minute he paused; then on he went again, up the worn stairs he knew so well. "And the handle of the door, still askew, though its untidiness always worried the countess—and the ante-room!" At this moment it was only lightened by a tallow candle.

Old Michael was alseep on a bench, and Procopius, the man-servant, whose strength was proverbial—he could lift the hind wheels of a carriage—sat in a corner plaiting bark-shoes. He looked up at the sound of the door which opened noisily, and his sleepy indifferent face suddenly assumed an expression of joy not unmingled with alarm.

"Mercy! Our Heavenly Father and all the archangels! The young count! Is it possible!" he cried; and trembling with excitement, he rushed towards the door, but he returned at once, and bending over his young master's shoulder he kissed it.

"They are all well?" asked Rostow, drawing away his hand.

"Thank God, thank God! Yes, they have but just done dinner. Let me look at you, highness."

"All is well, then?"

"Thank God! Thank God!"

Nicholas, forgetting Denissow, would not allow the servant to announce his arrival; he tossed off his pelisse, and went quickly, but on tiptoe, into the great dark drawing-room; the card-tables were in the same places, and the chandelier still wrapped in brown holland. But hardly had he entered the room when a perfect whirlwind swept down upon him from a side door, and he was covered with kisses. A second and a third fell upon him in turn. It was a scene of kissing, exclamations and tears of joy. He hardly knew which of the three was his father, Natacha, or Pétia; they were all talking and embracing him at once; but he observed that his mother was absent.

"And I knew nothing about it—Nicolouchka—my dear boy!"

"Here he is—just his old self—Kolia, my darling—but how he has altered! And there are no lights! Bring tea at once."

"Kiss me, kiss me!"

"Dear, sweet soul!"

Sonia, Natacha, Pétia, Anna Mikhaïlovna, Vera, and the old count, all hugged him in turn, and the servants and maids, coming in behind them, were exclaiming in surprise.

Pétia clung to his legs, saying: "And me too, me too!"

Natacha, after smothering him with kisses, had caught hold of his coat, and was jumping up and down like a kid, and uttering little shrieks of delight. Her eyes shone through tears of joy and affection, and again their lips met to kiss once more.

Sonia, as red as *koumatch*,[1] held his hand and gazed at him in radiant delight. She was now sixteen, very pretty, and her excitement added to her beauty. Panting with agitation she stood smiling and never taking her eyes off him. He responded with a grateful look, but he was evidently waiting—looking for someone: his mother, who had not yet made her appearance. Suddenly outside the door they heard a hurried step, so hasty and eager that it could be no one but the countess. The rest stood aside and he threw himself into her arms. She clung to him sobbing, and had not strength enough to raise her head; her face was pressed against the cold lace braiding of his uniform. Denissow, who had come in unobserved, was looking on and wiping his eyes.

"Vassili Denissow, a friend of your son," he said introducing himself to the count, who stared at him in astonishment.

"To be sure, I know, I know," said the count embracing him. "Nicolouchka wrote about you. . . . Natacha, Vera—this is Denissow."

All the happy faces turned at once on Denissow, and crowded round him till he felt quite shy.

"What, my dear little Denissow!" exclaimed Natacha, whose head was turned with joy; she rushed up to him and kissed him. Denissow, somewhat embarrassed, coloured, and taking her hand kissed it politely. A room was ready to which he was conducted, while the Rostows gathered round Nicholas in the large drawing-room.

The countess still held her son's hand and raised it every minute to her lips; his brother and sisters vied with each other in watching his every movement—word—glance; disputing as

___
[1] A red cotton stuff worn by the peasants.

to which should sit next to him, and rushing at his teacup, handkerchief, pipe, to have the pleasure of handing it to him. The first emotion of his return had been to Rostow so exquisitely happy that he thought the impression must inevitably grow weaker, and in his excitement he craved more and yet more.

Next morning he slept on till ten o'clock. The adjoining room, which smelt strongly of tobacco, was littered with knap-sacks, open trunks, swords, cartridge-pouches, and dirty boots side by side with other boots, well cleaned and with spurs on, in a row by the wall. The servants were carrying in washing-basins, hot water for shaving, and the clothes they had just brushed.

"Here, Grichka, my pipe!" cried Denissow in a hoarse voice. "Rostow, get up."

Rostow, rubbing his eyes, lifted his unkempt head from his pillow. "It is late?" he said.

"Certainly it is late," answered Natacha's voice. "It is ten o'clock!" And outside the door there was a crackling of starched petticoats mingling with girls' whispering and laughter, and whenever it was opened there was a glimpse of blue ribands, black eyes, and bright faces. Natacha, Sonia, and Pétia had come to know whether he were up.

"Nicolouchka, do get up," said Natacha.

"Directly."

Pétia, having spied a sword, at once seized upon it. Carried away by the warlike enthusiasm which is infallibly stirred in a little boy by an older soldier-brother, and forgetting that it was hardly correct that his sisters should see the two men before they were dressed, he flung open the door.

"Is it your sword, Nicholas?" he asked, while the two girls shrunk aside. Denissow, quite abashed, threw the counterpane over his hairy feet, and his eyes appealed for help to his com-panion. The door at once closed behind Pétia.

"Nicholas," Natacha called out, "come here; put on your dressing-gown."

"Is the sword his or yours?" asked Pétia, addressing Denissow, whose long black moustache commanded his respect.

Rostow hastily slipped on his shoes and dressing-gown, and went into the next room, where he found that Natacha had put on one of his spurred boots and was getting her foot into the other. Sonia was spinning round to make a balloon of her skirts. Both the girls were fresh and eager and they were dressed alike in new, blue frocks. Sonia escaped at once, and

Natacha, taking possession of her brother, dragged him down so as to talk more at her ease. A brisk fire of question and answer was at once begun, though dealing only with trifles of personal interest. Natacha laughed at every word, not that he said anything funny, but because the exuberant joy of her heart could find no outlet but laughter.

"How nice this is! Quite delightful!" she kept saying.

And Rostow, under the spell of this warm effusiveness, insensibly smiled once more with the childlike smile, which, since his departure, had never once lighted up his features.

"But do you know you are a man now, quite a man?—and I am proud to have you for a brother!" She stroked his moustache. "I should like to know what men are really like. Are you like us? No—I suppose not."

"Why did Sonia run away?" asked her brother.

"Oh! that is a long story. How will you address Sonia? Quite familiarly? Will you call her thou?"

"I really don't know. Just as it may happen."

"Well, then; do call her you. I beg you—and you will know why afterwards. Well, I will tell you: Sonia is my particular friend—so much my friend that I have burnt my arm for her—" and turning up her muslin sleeve she showed a red spot on her thin, white arm, a little below the shoulder, where even a short sleeve would hide it; "I burnt it myself, to prove how much I love her. I took a ruler and made it red hot in the fire, and burnt myself there."

The room was their old schoolroom, and Rostow, stretched on the sofa, piled with cushions, and looking into Natacha's bright eyes, threw himself completely into this world of his childhood, this familiar home circle, whose incidents and gossip had meaning and value for him alone, while they renewed one of the keenest joys of life. This burn, as a token of affection, was to him quite natural; he understood it, and it did not surprise him.

"Well," he said, "and what next? Is that all?"

"We are such close friends that this is nothing—mere nonsense . . . we are friends for ever and ever. When she loves anyone it is for all her life; but as for me—I do not understand her. I always forget so soon."

"Well, but what then?"

"Well, she loves you as she loves me," said Natacha, blushing. "You must remember—you know—before you went away. . . . Well, she says that you will have forgotten it all . . . and she

305

says: 'I shall always love him, but he must be quite free.' Now, that is fine and noble—very noble, is it not?"

Natacha asked the question with so much gravity and feeling that it was evident that the mere thought of Sonia's abnegation had touched her often before. Rostow sat silent for a few seconds.

"I shall not take back my word," he said. "Besides, Sonia is so charming that a man must be a double-distilled idiot to refuse such happiness."

"No, no," cried Natacha. "We have discussed the matter, and we were quite sure, she and I, that you would say that. But it is impossible, don't you understand; because, if you think yourself bound only by your word, it makes it seem as if she had said it on purpose. You marry her as a point of honour, and that would not be at all the same thing."

Rostow found no reply; Sonia's beauty had struck him the night before, and this morning he had thought her prettier still. She was sixteen, she loved him devotedly, and he knew it. Why should he not love her, even if the idea of marriage had to be postponed? "I have still so many untried pleasures before me," he said to himself. "It is best so—I will not pledge myself."

"All right," he said, "we will talk it over by-and-by. But oh! how glad I am to see you again. And you—are you faithful to Boris?"

"Oh! what nonsense!" cried Natacha, laughing. "I never think of him—nor of anyone else. I do not want to hear anything about him."

"Bravo! But then . . ."

"I!" said Natacha, with a beaming smile on her little face. "Have you seen Duport, the great dancer? No? then you cannot understand — but look," and bending her arms and lifting one corner of her skirt, she flew off, spun round, cut a caper and a double caper, then, lifting herself up, she walked a few steps on tiptoe. "I can stand, you see, on the very tips of my toes! Do you see? Well—I do not mean to marry; I mean to be a dancer. Only mind you don't tell."

Rostow laughed so loudly and heartily that Denissow quite envied him, and Natacha could not help joining in.

"What do you say to that? Well done, don't you think?"

"Well done? What do you mean? Then you will not marry Boris?"

She coloured crimson.

"I will not marry anyone, and I will tell him so when I see him."

"Will you?" said Rostow.

"Pooh! this is all nonsense," she went on, laughing again. "And your Denissow—is he nice?"

"Very nice."

"Very well then, good-bye. Get dressed. . . . And he is not alarming?"

"Alarming! why? Vaska is a very good fellow."

"And you call him Vaska? How odd! Then he really is nice?"

"To be sure he is. . . ."

"Good-bye. Make haste and come down; we shall be all together."

Natacha left the room on the tips of her toes, like an opera-dancer, with a smile like the child she was. Nicholas soon made his way to the drawing-room, where he found Sonia; he coloured, and did not know how to address her. The day before, in the first impulse of gladness, they had embraced, but to-day they felt that this was impossible; he, too, felt the inquiring glances of his mother and sisters, who were trying to fancy what he would do. He kissed her hand, and said "you," though their eyes met and seemed to speak the more tender "thou;" Sonia's seemed indeed to crave his forgiveness for having ventured to remind him, through Natacha, of his promise, and they thanked him for his affection. His, on the other hand, were thanking her for releasing him from his word, and telling her that he would always love her, for to see her was to love her.

"What an odd thing," said Vera, when presently there was a silence. "Sonia and Nicholas speak to each other as formally as strangers."

She had hit the mark as usual, but—also as usual—she had said the wrong thing, and everybody—including the countess, who regarded this attachment as standing in the way of a good marriage for her son—coloured and looked awkward. At this instant, however, Denissow came into the room in his new uniform, oiled, scented and curled as if he were going forth to battle; and his unwonted gallantry to the ladies greatly amazed Rostow.

CHAPTER LXXI

NICHOLAS ROSTOW, on his return from the army, was welcomed as a hero by his family; by his distant relations, as a young man of elegance and distinction; by his acquaintances, as a dashing young hussar, a capital dancer, and one of the first "eligibles" of Moscow.

All Moscow visited the Rostows. The count, having renewed the mortgage on his estates, was quite flush of money this year; and Nicholas, having acquired a splendid horse, carried his dandyism to the point of wearing a pair of trousers such as had not yet been seen in the town, and fashionable boots with pointed toes and little silver spurs. He spent his time, much to his satisfaction, with that sense of recovered ease which comes to us so keenly when we have for some time been deprived of it. He had grown, and was now a man in his own eyes; the memories of his despair when he failed in his examination on the catechism, of the money he had borrowed from Gavrilo, the *isvostchik*, of the kisses he had given Sonia in secret—these were all puerilities lost in a remote past. Now, he was a lieutenant of hussars, with a silver-embroidered jacket and the cross of St. George on his breast; he had a fine trotter which he backed for amateur racing in the company of other well-known connoisseurs, older than himself and highly respectable; he had struck up an acquaintance with a lady living on the Boulevard, with whom he spent his evenings; he led the mazourka at Arkharows' balls, talked of war with Field-Marshal Kamenski, dined at the English Club, and called a colonel of forty "thou"—a friend of Denissow's.

As he had not seen the czar for a long time, the passion he had felt for him had cooled a little; still, he liked to talk about him, and give an impression that his loyalty was based on a feeling quite unknown to ordinary mortals, while he heartily shared the devotion which all Moscow felt for the adored sovereign, to whom they had given the name of the "Angel on Earth."

During his short stay at home Nicholas had grown apart from Sonia rather than closer to her, in spite of her beauty and charms, and her passion for him. He was going through a phase of youth when every minute is so filled up that a young man has no time to think of love. He was afraid of pledging himself; he was jealous of the independence which alone entitled him to live as he pleased, and as he looked at Sonia he said to himself: "I shall find plenty more like her, plenty whom I have not yet seen! I shall have time enough to fall in love and think of such things by-and-by." His manliness scorned to live among the women of his family circle, and he affected a great dislike to balls and general society; but races, the English Club, gay evenings with Denissow, and so forth, were quite another matter; that was what suited the handsome young hussar.

At the beginning of March the old count was very busy with the arrangements for a dinner to be given at the English Club to Prince Bagration. He was walking up and down his big drawing-room, giving his orders to the steward and the famous Theoctiste, the head chef of the English Club, about early vegetables, of fish, the veal, asparagus, cucumbers, strawberries! . . . The count had been on the committee from the foundation of the club. He was entrusted with the arrangements of the banquet to Bagration because no one knew better than he did how to organise a banquet on a grand scale, all the more because he was always ready to pay any excess of expense out of his own pocket. The steward and the head cook listened to his instructions with evident satisfaction, knowing by experience the profits that would accrue to them out of a dinner costing several thousand roubles.

"Now, do not forget the cock's combs in the turtle-soup."

"Then we must have three cold dishes?" asked the cook.

"I do not see how we can do with less," said the count, after a short pause.

"And we are to buy the large sterlet?" asked the steward.

"Certainly. What can we do if they will not reduce the price . . . Dear me, dear me! I had forgotten that we must have another entrée! Where is my head?"

"And where am I to get flowers?"

"Mitenka, Mitenka," called the count to his own steward. "Go at once and tell the gardener to set all hands to work to send up everything in the houses. We must have two hundred shrubs by Friday. Tell him to pack them carefully and cover them with felt."

Having finished all his arrangements, he was about to withdraw to his "little countess's" room and rest a while, but remembering a number of details he had forgotten, he sent for the steward and the cook once more and repeated his instructions. Just then the door opened, and Nicholas came in with a light confident step, his spurs jingling as he walked. The happy results of an easy, jolly life, were visible in his blooming complexion.

"My dear boy, I am half-distracted," said the old man, a little ashamed of his important occupations. "Come and help me. We must have the singers of the regiment, and there will be an orchestra . . . how, as to gipsy musicians, what do you say? You military like them?"

"My dear father, I would bet anything that Prince Bagration himself, when he was preparing for the battle of Schöngraben, was not in such a fuss as you are in to-day."

"Do you try to do it, I advise you!" exclaimed the old count, pretending to be angry; then, turning to the steward, who was eyeing them with good-humoured amusement: "This is the way with the young ones, Theoctiste: always laughing at us old fellows."

"Very true, excellency; they only ask for good food and good liquor; as to how it is found or served, that is all the same to them."

"That's it, that's it!" cried the count, grasping both his son's hands. "Now, I have got you, you rascal, and you are going to do me the favour to take my sleigh and a pair of horses, and go to ask Bésoukhow to spare me some fresh strawberries and pineapples. He is the only man who has any. If he is away, ask the princesses. Then go on to Rasgoulaï; Ipatka, the coachman, knows the way. There you will find Illiouchka, the gipsy—the man who danced at Count Orlow's in a white jacket—bring him back with you."

"And the girls, too?" said Nicholas, laughing.

"Come, come!" said his father.

The count had got thus far with his instructions, when Anna Mikhaïlovna, who had come in with her usual cat-like step, suddenly appeared at his elbow, with the expression she always wore—a mixture of the busybody and the hypocritical humble Christian. The count, thus discovered in his dressing-gown, though it was a daily incident, poured forth his apologies.

"It is of no importance, dear count," said she, gently closing her eyes. "With regard to your commission—I will undertake it. Young Bésoukhow has just arrived in Moscow, and we will get him to give us whatever you want. I have to see him. He has sent me a letter from Boris, who, thank God! is now on the staff."

The count, delighted at her obliging offer, ordered the horses to be put in.

"And tell him to come; I will put his name down. Is his wife with him?"

Anna Mikhaïlovna turned up her eyes with an expression of deep suffering.

"Indeed, my dear friend, he is in great trouble; if all I hear is true, it is a terrible business. But who could have foreseen it? And he is such a noble, generous soul! I pity him with all my heart, and will do all I can, humanly speaking, to comfort him."

"Why, what has happened?" asked father and son in a breath.

"But do you not know? Dologhow, Maria Ivanovna's son has quite compromised her—" said the lady, with a sigh, and speaking in an undertone; she half swallowed her words, as if she were afraid of compromising herself. "Well, it is he who was so kind to him, who invited him to his house at St. Petersburg—and now she has come here with that wrong-head at her heels, and poor Peter is broken-hearted, they say."

Notwithstanding her wish to display her pity for Bésoukhow, Anna Mikhaïlovna's accent and meaning smiles revealed a stronger interest perhaps in the "wrong-head," as she called Dologhow.

"That is all very well, but he must come to the club-dinner; it will occupy his mind. It will be a colossal banquet."

On the 3rd of March, at two in the afternoon, two hundred and fifty members of the club, and fifty others, met to entertain their illustrious guest, Prince Bagration, the hero of the campaign in Austria.

The news of the defeat of Austerlitz had confounded Moscow. Till then, victory had so faithfully attended the Russians that the report was not believed, and everyone tried to find some extraordinary cause for it. When, in the course of the month of December, the fact was established beyond dispute, it became an understood thing at the English Club—which was a rendezvous for all the aristocracy of the city and the best-informed officials—that no allusion was ever to be made to the war or to the last battle. The most influential men, who were apt to give the key of the conversation—Count Rostopchine, Prince Youry Vladimirovitch Dolgoroukow, Valouïew, Count Markow, Prince Viazemsky—never came to the club, but met privately; and the rest of the world, who, like the Count Rostow, expressed only other people's views, had remained for some time without a guide of any accurate data of the progress of the war. Feeling

311

instinctively that the news was bad, and that it was difficult to get it with any exactness, they kept a prudent silence, till the bigwigs, like a jury returning to pronounce their verdict, came back to the club and gave their opinion; to them everything now was as clear as day, and they promptly discovered a thousand and one reasons to account for so incredible, so impossible a catastrophe as the defeat of Russian troops. Thenceforth, in every corner of Moscow, nothing else was discussed: the bad supplies of food, the treachery of Austria, of Przebichevsky the Pole, of Langeron the Frenchman, Koutouzow's incapacity, and (in quite a whisper) the czar's youth, inexperience, and misplaced confidence. On the other hand, the army had achieved prodigies of valour, on that point all agreed; privates, officers, and generals, all had fought like heroes. But the hero of heroes was Prince Bagration, who had covered himself with glory at Schöngraben and at Austerlitz, where he alone had succeeded in keeping his division in good order, while he retreated, fighting every inch of ground, from an enemy twice as strong as himself. The fact that he had no relations at Moscow, where he was a stranger, had greatly facilitated his promotion as a hero. He was haled as a soldier of fortune, devoid of interest and unaided by intrigues, whose sole aim was to do battle for his country, and whose name was already remembered in connection with memories of the campaign in Italy, and of Souvorow. The ill-will and disapprobation which were loaded on Koutouzow were all the more marked by contrast with the honours done to Bagration—the man "who if he had not existed would have had to be invented," said Schinchine spitefully, in parody of Voltaire. Koutouzow was only mentioned to be abused, and called a Court time-server and an old satyr.

Dolgoroukow's witticism: "If you hammer iron long enough you become a blacksmith" was in everybody's mouth; it was a consolation for this defeat to remember former victories; and Rostopchine's aphorisms were no less popular: "The French soldier," he said, "must be stirred up to fight by high-sounding phrases; the German must be convinced by argument that it is safer to fight than to fly; but as to the Russian, you have to hold him back and entreat him to keep quiet."

Every day some new feats of courage transpired on the part of the Russian troops at Austerlitz: such a one had saved a standard, had killed five Frenchmen, such another had loaded five guns. Berg was not forgotten, and even men who did not know him told how, after being wounded in the right hand, he held his sword in his left and marched bravely forward. As to Bolkonsky, no one spoke of him; only his relations bewailed his early death, and pitied his poor little wife and his queer old father.

CHAPTER LXXII

ON the 3rd of March a hum of voices, like a swarm of early bees, buzzed in all the rooms of the English Club. The members and their guests, some in uniform and some in dress-coats, even some in powder and long coats, were coming and going, sitting, rising, and talking in eager groups. The powdered footmen in silk stockings and knee-breeches stood by the door, ready for duty. The larger number of the company were men of advancing years, respectable and contented-looking, with heavy figures and a confident manner and voice. This class of members had their own accustomed places reserved for them, and formed a little knot of intimates. The minority consisted of guests chosen rather haphazard, most of them young, and among them Nesvitsky, an old member of the club, Denissow, Rostow, Dologhow, who was now again an officer in the Séménovsky Regiment, and several more. This youthful party gave themselves airs of slightly contemptuous deference to the elder generation, and seemed to imply: "We are very ready to respect you, but the future is ours, remember."

Peter, who, to oblige his wife, had let his hair grow, left off wearing spectacles, and taken to dressing in the latest fashion, aired his melancholy and ennui first in one room and then in another. Here, as everywhere, he was surrounded by men who worshipped him as a Golden Calf, but he was used to this incense and treated it with scornful indifference. In years he belonged to the youthful faction, but his fortune and position gave him a place among the senior and more influential men, and he joined them all in turn.

The conversation of the more distinguished elders—Rostopchine, Valouïew and Narischkine—attracted the attention of many more or less conspicuous members of the club, who stood round them listening devoutly. Rostopchine was narrating how the Russians, being driven back by the Austrian fugitives, had to force their way through at the point of the bayonet;

313

Valouïew was telling his neighbours, under seal of secrecy, that Ouvarow's mission to Moscow was solely to learn the feeling of the Muscovites as to the battle of Austerlitz; and Narischkine was repeating an old story of Souvorow, who at an Austrian Council of War had begun to crow like a cock in contempt of the utter ineptitude of the members of it. Schinchine, who always tried to find an opportunity for some ill-natured jest, added sadly that Koutouzow had not succeeded in learning from Souvorow even how to crow like a cock. But the stern eyes of the seniors showed that it was not the thing to speak thus of Koutouzow on the present occasion.

Count Rostow bustled backwards and forwards between the dining-room and the drawing-room in constant anxiety, bowing with his usual good-humour to great and small alike, looking round now and then for the fine young fellow who was his son, and winking and blinking at him gaily. Nicholas stood by the window, talking to Dologhow, whose acquaintance he had lately made, and to whom he had taken a fancy. The old count came up to shake hands with Dologhow:

"You will come to see us, I hope—since you are acquainted with this warrior; you were a pair of heroes down there . . . Ah! Vassili Ignatieïtch, how are you, old friend? . . ."

But he had not time to finish his sentence, for a breathless and excited servant announced: "He is come!"

A bell on the staircase rang loudly, the committee rushed down, and all the club members, scattered in various corners like wheat in the winnowing, came together in a group and stood at the door of the great drawing-room. Bagration came in; he had left his sword and cocked hat in the vestibule in accordance with the custom of the club. He wore a perfectly new uniform, covered with Russian and foreign orders, the Star of St. George on his breast; this was not as Rostow had seen him at Austerlitz, in his fur cap, and with a Cossack's heavy whip through his belt. He had even had his hair and whiskers cut a little, and this did not improve him. His smartened appearance, which did not suit his strongly-marked features, gave a rather comical look to his face. Béklechow and Fédor Pétrovitch Ouvarow came in at the same time, but they stopped at the doorway to allow the more illustrious guest to pass first; he, abashed by their politeness, paused, and, after exchanging a few civil phrases, made up his mind to go on. The awkwardness of his gait, and the way in which he slipped on the polished floor, were enough to show that he was far more accustomed to tramp across a ploughed field under a hail of bullets, as he had done at Schöngraben at the head of the Koursk Regiment.

The committee, who had gone forward to meet him, expressed, in a few words, their pleasure in welcoming him, and without waiting for his answer, gathered round him and seized on him to lead him into the drawing-room. But the crowd in the doorway made it almost impossible to get in; everyone was trying to see Bagration over his neighbour's shoulder, as if he had been some strange beast. Count Rostow, pushing with his elbows and saying: "Allow me, my dear fellow—pray make room," made way for the new-comer to reach the grand divan, where at length he found a seat. The bigwigs of the club formed a circle round him, while the old count slipped out of the room and returned in a few minutes, in company with another member of the committee, to present to Bagration an ode composed in his honour and laid on an immense silver salver.

At the sight of this salver Bagration looked about him uneasily, as if looking for some invisible rescuer; however, submitting to the inevitable, and feeling himself at the mercy of all these eyes centred on him, he took the tray in both hands, not without casting a reproachful glance at the count, who held it out to him with extreme deference. Happily a member of the club came to his assistance and politely relieved him of the salver, which he seemed to think he could not relinquish, recommending the verses to his attention.

"Well, if I must!" he seemed to express, as he took the scroll; then looking down at it with his sleepy eyes, he began to read it with a look of grave concentration.

But the author of the verses proposed to read them aloud, and Prince Bagration, resigned to his fate, bent his head and listened.

> "Be thou the pride of Alexander's reign,
> Be thou the buckler of our sovereign's throne,
> As worthy as a man, as thou art brave!
> Be thou the bulwark of our native land,
> Since thou art Cæsar in the battle-field.
> The deed is done! Triumphant Bonaparte
> Has learnt ere now what man Bagration is,
> And will no more defy great Russia's sons."

He had got no further when the steward announced in stentorian tones:

"Dinner is served."

The doors were thrown open, and from the dining-room came

the sound of music; the band was playing the famous Polonaise: "Loud may the thunder of Victory roll, Long may brave Russia rejoice!"

Count Rostow, out of all patience with the hapless author, went up to Bagration with a low bow, and as, at the moment, dinner was more interesting than poetry, everyone rose, and Bagration led the way into the dining-room. He filled the place of honour between Béklechow and Narischkine, both of whom happened to be named Alexander, so this was intended as a delicate allusion to the czar's name. Three hundred persons sat down at the long table, in order of their rank and dignities, the most important nearest to the guest of honour. A little while before dinner Count Rostow had brought up his son to introduce to the prince, and had looked about him with proud satisfaction while Bagration, who recognised Nicholas, stammered out a few inarticulate words.

Denissow, Rostow, and Dologhow were placed about the middle of the table, and opposite to Peter and Nesvitsky. The old count, facing Bagration, did the honours with the rest of the committee as representing the genial hospitality of the city of Moscow. The pains he had taken were crowned with success. Still, though the two dinners (as they were in fact; one *gras*, of meat, and one *maigre*, of fish, for those who chose to fast) were both served to perfection, to the very end he could not get over an involuntary anxiety, which expressed itself in a sign to the butler or a whispered word to the servant who stood behind him. He coloured with modest pride at the sight of the enormous sterlet, and no sooner was it brought in than bottles were uncorked all along the line and champagne flowed in rivers. When the excitement caused by the big fish had somewhat subsided, Count Ilia Andréïévitch consulted with his colleagues; "It is high time to propose our first toast," he said. There are a great many to follow . . ." And he rose, glass in hand. Everyone was silent.

"To the health of his majesty the czar!" he exclaimed, his eyes sparkling with tears of joy and enthusiasm, and the orchestra sounded a flourish of triumph.

They got up, they shouted hurrah, and Bagration responded with a cheer as loud as that he had given at Schöngraben, while Rostow's voice was audible above those of the three hundred guests. Agitated to the verge of tears, he went on repeating: "His majesty the czar!" and after emptying his glass at a gulp, he flung it behind him on the floor. Several others did the same, and cheers rang out once more. When silence at last was restored the servants swept up the broken glass, and everyone sat down again, quite pleased with himself for making so much noise. Then the count, glancing at a list that lay by his plate, rose once more and proposed the health "of the hero of our last campaign, Prince Peter Ivanovitch Bagration." Again emotional tears were in his eyes, and again a cheer from three hundred voices answered his toast; but instead of the orchestra, a chorus of singers struck up a song composed by Paul Ivanovitch Koutouzow:

> "The Russian fears no obstacle,
> For conquest crowns his bravery.
> Bagration leads the foremost van,
> And foes shall cringe in slavery."

And no sooner was this ended than the litany of toasts began again. The count was constantly moved to tears; more and more glasses and plates were broken, and everyone shouted till he was hoarse. They had drunk the health of Béklechow, Narischkine, Ouvarow, Dolgoroukow, Apraxine, Valouïew—of the committee, the club members, and the guests; and at length the health was proposed of Count Ilia Andréïévitch, himself the responsible organiser of the dinner; but at the first words he was overcome by his emotion, and pulling out his handkerchief, he hid his face, and melted into a flood of tears.

CHAPTER LXXIII

PETER ate and drank a great deal with his usual avidity. But he was silent, gloomy, and downcast, and looked about him with a wandering gaze, not seeming to hear anything that was going on around him. Seeing him so absent-minded, his friends easily understood that he was absorbed in considering some crushing and unanswerable question. This question, which tortured his heart and his mind, arose from the hints thrown out by his cousin, Princess Catherine, with reference to the intimacy between Dologhow and his wife.

That very morning he had received an anonymous letter, written in the vein of coarse mockery, which is common to such letters, in which he was told that his spectacles were of very little use to him, since his wife's connection with Dologhow

317

was no longer a secret to anyone but himself. He had not believed in the letter, nor in his cousin's insinuations; still, the sight of Dologhow, sitting opposite to him at table, made him singularly uncomfortable. Every time those fine audacious eyes met his own, Peter felt a horrible, monstrous thrill of revulsion, and turned away hastily. Remembering certain rumours as to Helen's early life, and her familiarity with Dologhow, he admitted that, if she had not been his wife, there might have been some truth in the anonymous letter. He involuntarily remembered Dologhow's first visit to his house, and how, in remembrance of their past follies, he had lent him money; how he had invited him to stay in his house, and Helen, with that everlasting smile, had spoken of the arrangement as a bore; and then how Dologhow, who was always singing the praises of his wife's beauty in a cynical key, had never stirred an inch since.

"And he is very handsome, no doubt," said Peter to himself. "And I know that it would give him particular pleasure to dishonour me and play me a foul trick on account of my having done him so many services; I quite understand how smart he would think it to betray me in that way—but I do not believe it, I have no right to believe it of him."

Dologhow's evil expression had often struck him as it had done on the occasion of his flinging the bear and the police officer into the river; and on others, when, without any cause, he would insult a man, or when he had once shot an *isvostchik's* horse dead; and now, whenever their eyes met, he read the same look in them.

"Yes, he is a bully; he does not care a straw about killing a man; he flatters himself that everyone is afraid of him—I most of all; and that must be a pleasure to him. . . . It is true too! I am afraid of him." Thus thought Peter, while Nicholas was chatting gaily with his two friends, Denissow and Dologhow —one an honest hussar, and the other an undisguised blackguard. The noisy trio formed a strange contrast to Peter— burly, grave and preoccupied; nor had Rostow any prejudice in his favour. In the first place he was a civilian and a millionaire, the husband of a fashionable beauty, and a milksop—three unpardonable crimes in the young hussar's eyes: in the second place, Peter, lost in thought, had not returned his bow; and when the czar's health was drunk, Peter, in utter absence of mind, had remained sitting.

"You!" Rostow shouted to him. "I say, are you deaf?

BEFORE TILSIT

To the czar's health!" Peter sighed, rose resignedly, emptied his glass, and then, when they were all seated again, he said to Nicholas with his honest pleasant smile: "Dear me! I declare I did not recognise you!"

Rostow, who was cracking his throat with cheering, did not hear.

"Do you not mean to renew the acquaintance?" said Dologhow.

"Bless the man for a gaby!" said Rostow.

"You should always be civil to a pretty woman's husband," observed Denissow in a low voice.

Peter guessed they must be talking of him; he could not hear what they were saying, but he looked away and coloured.

"Now let us drink to the health of all pretty women," said Dologhow, half-seriously but half-smiling. "Pétroucha—to the health of all pretty women, and their lovers!"

Peter did not raise his eyes; he drank without answering or even looking at Dologhow. At this moment the manservant who was handing round copies of the words of the chorus, offered one to Peter as being one of the leading members of the club. He was about to take it when Dologhow leaned across the table, and snatched it away. Peter suddenly raised his head, and carried away by an irresistible spasm of anger, he said as loud as he could:

"I forbid you!"

At these words, and seeing to whom they were addressed, Nesvitsky and the man on his right were alarmed; they tried to soothe Bésoukhow, while Dologhow, fixing on his face a pair of eyes as bright and as cold as steel, said to him with deliberate emphasis: "I shall keep it."

Peter turned pale and snatched it from his hand, saying with a quivering lip: "You are a blackguard—you will answer to me for this!" He rose from table, and it flashed upon him suddenly, that the question of his wife's guilt—the question which had been maddening him for the past twenty-four hours —was settled beyond a doubt. At this moment he hated her, and felt the breach between them could never be healed.

In spite of Denissow's remonstrances, Rostow agreed to be Dologhow's second, and when dinner was over he discussed the arrangements for the duel with Nesvitsky, who was Peter's second. Peter went home, while Rostow, Dologhow, and Denissow stayed at the club till a late hour, listening to the gipsies and the singers of the regiment.

"To-morrow, then, at Sokolniki," said Dologhow, as he parted from Rostow on the steps.

"And you are quite cool?" said Nicholas.

"Look here," said Dologhow, "I will tell you the secret in two words. If, on the eve of a duel, you set to work to make your will, and write pathetic letters to your relations, above all if you think of the probability that you may be killed, you are a simpleton, a doomed man. If, on the contrary, it is your firm intention to kill your adversary, and to do it as quickly as possible, everything goes on wheels. What did our bear-hunter say to me the other day? 'How can you help being afraid of a bear?' said he. 'And yet, when you see him, the only thing you are afraid of is, that he will escape.'—Well, my dear fellow, this is the very same thing. Good-bye till to-morrow."

Next morning, at eight o'clock, when Peter and Nesvitsky reached the wood of Sokolniki, they found Dologhow, Denissow and Rostow already on the ground. Peter seemed to be absolutely indifferent to the impending event. His weary face showed that he had not slept all night, and his eyes involuntarily shrank from a full light. In fact, two questions wholly filled his mind: his wife's guilt—of which he no longer had a doubt, and Dologhow's innocence—since he recognised his right to be indifferent to the feelings of a man who, after all, was but a stranger: "Perhaps," thought he, "I might have done the same—yes, no doubt, I should have done the same! . . . but then this duel is sheer murder? Either I shall kill him, or he will send a bullet through my head—or my elbow, foot, knee. . . . Cannot I hide myself and escape somewhere?" And even while he was thinking this, he was asking, with a coolness which commanded the respect of the bystanders: "Shall we soon be ready?"

Nesvitsky stuck two swords into the snow, marked out the spot where each was to stand, and loaded the pistols; then he went up to Peter:

"I shall fail in my duty, count," and he spoke timidly, "I should be unworthy of the confidence you have shown me, and the honour you have done me in choosing me for your second, if at this solemn moment I did not tell you the whole truth. . . . I do not think that the ground of quarrel is serious enough to justify bloodshed. You were in the wrong, for you were in a passion. . . ."

"Yes, it was very foolish," said Peter.

320

"Well, then, allow me to be the bearer of your apologies, and I am sure our opponents will accept them," said Nesvitsky, who, like all men who get entangled in an affair of honour, had not taken the meeting seriously till the last moment. "It is more dignified, count, to acknowledge an error than to commit an irreparable wrong. There was no serious harm done on either side. Allow me. . . ."

"Waste of words!" said Peter. "It matters not to me . . . You need only tell me where I am to stand and when I am to fire."

He took the pistol, and never having held one in his life before, and not caring to confess it, he asked his second how he was to press the trigger: "To be sure—-like that—I had forgotten."

"No apology—none; that is positive," said Dologhow to Rostow, who on his part had tried to effect a reconciliation.

The spot selected was a little clearing in a pine-wood, covered with half-melted snow, and about eighty yards distant from the road where they had left their sleighs. All the way from where the seconds were standing to where the two swords were stuck in the ground to mark the limit to which the combatants might advance, Nesvitsky and Rostow had trampled the soft, deep snow, in measuring off the forty paces from which they were to start. It was thawing, and heavy mists veiled everything beyond. Though all had been ready some three minutes, no one had given the signal: no one spoke.

CHAPTER LXXIV

"Well, let us begin!" cried Dologhow.

"Very well," said Peter smiling.

The situation was really frightful. The quarrel, so trivial in its beginning, could not now be stopped. It was going its deadly way, irrespective of human volition; it must go on to the end. Denissow went forward to the limiting point.

"The adversaries having positively refused to come to any agreement," he said, "we may proceed. Each take his pistol. At the word 'three' advance and fire."

"One—two—three—" spoke Denissow in a hollow voice, and he stood back. The antagonists went forward on the trodden path, each seeing his opponent's figure gradually emerge from the fog. They had the option of firing if they chose before stopping at the line. Dologhow walked forward coolly and without raising his weapon; his blue eyes glittered and were fixed on Peter; there was something like a smile on his lips.

At the word "three," Peter started quickly; he got off the track and into the snow. He held the pistol at arm's length in front of him for fear of wounding himself. His left hand he carefully held behind his back, because he wanted to prop up his right with it, and knew that this was not allowed. After walking six paces off the trodden path into the snow, he looked down at his feet, and glancing swiftly up at Dologhow pulled the trigger as he had been taught. The recoil was so much stronger than he expected that he staggered, stood still, and smiled at the novelty of the experience. The smoke, which was made heavy by the fog, at first prevented his seeing anything, and he stood, vainly waiting for the return shot, when he heard hasty steps, and through the smoke he made out Dologhow, pressing one hand to his left side while the other convulsively clutched his pistol, though he did not raise it, Rostow had hurried to his side.

"No. . . ." hissed Dologhow, between his teeth. "No, no—this is not the end. . . ." He tottered forward a few steps and fell on the snow, close to one of the swords. His left hand was covered with blood; he wiped it on his uniform and leaned upon it; his pale, sinister face quivered with a nervous spasm.

"I beg. . . ." he began, and went on with difficulty: "Pray. . . ."

Peter, choking with a sob, was going towards him when he cried out. "Go—keep the distance!"

Peter understood and stood still. They were now only ten paces apart.

Dologhow buried his head in the snow, filling his mouth with it; then sitting up he tried to recover his balance while he still sucked and swallowed the frozen snow. His lips trembled, but his eyes shone with the light of hatred; collecting all his strength for a final effort, he raised his weapon and slowly took aim.

"Don't expose yourself—stand sideways!" cried Nesvitsky.

"Don't face him!" even Denissow shouted in spite of himself, though he was Dologhow's second.

Peter, with a pathetic smile of pity and regret, had remained defenceless, and his broad chest was a good mark for Dologhow's fire, while he stood looking sadly at his adversary. The three seconds shut their eyes; Dologhow fired, and then, with a furious howl of "missed!" he fell face downwards.

Peter clutched his head in his hands, and turning on his heel, walked away among the trees, striding along.

"What folly! What folly!" he said to himself. "Death! Falsehood!"

Nesvitsky followed him and took him home.

Rostow and Denissow took charge of Dologhow, who was badly wounded. They laid him at full length in a sleigh and he did not move; his eyes were shut and he answered none of their questions. No sooner, however, had they got into the town than he recovered himself, and lifting his head with great difficulty, he took Rostow's hand; Rostow was struck by the complete change in the expression of his face; it was softened and mournful.

"How are you feeling?"

"Badly. But that is not the point. My dear boy," he went on in broken sentences, "where are we? In Moscow? I thought so. . . . Listen. . . . I have killed her—she will never bear it—never live through it."

"Who; what do you mean?" asked Rostow in surprise.

"My mother, my dear, dear mother," and Dologhow broke into sobs. He explained to Rostow that he lived with his mother, and that if she were to see him dying she would die too, of grief; so he implored Rostow to go and break it to her. This Rostow at once did, and so learnt that this rascal, this bully, lived with his old mother and a humpbacked sister, and was the tenderest of sons and kindest of brothers.

CHAPTER LXXV

PETER'S *tête-à-tête* meetings with his wife had become rarer and rarer, particularly during the last few weeks. At Moscow, as at St. Petersburg, their house was full of company. The night after the duel, instead of joining his wife, he retired to his father's study—as indeed he often did—the very room where the old count had died. Throwing himself on the sofa he tried to sleep and forget all that had happened; but such a storm of feelings and recollections tossed his soul, that not only could he not sleep, but he could not even lie still. He got up and walked about the room with a short, angry step, thinking sometimes of the early days of their married life, of her beautiful shoulders, her languishing, passionate gaze, sometimes he pictured Dologhow standing by her side, handsome and impudent, with his diabolical smile, just as he had seen him at the club dinner; sometimes he saw him pale and shivering, undone and sinking on the snow.

"But after all I have killed her lover—yes, my wife's lover! How could such a thing come about?"—"It came of your marrying her," said an inward voice.—"But how was I to blame?"—"You were to blame for marrying her without loving her," the voice went on. "And you cheated her by wilfully blinding yourself." And the moment when he said with so much effort: "I love you," came back vividly to his mind. "Yes, that is where I was wrong. I felt at the time that I had no right to say it." He coloured as he recalled the days of his honeymoon. Particularly vivid, insulting and shameful was the recollection of how once, at after eleven o'clock at night, dressed in a silk dressing-gown, he had come from the bedroom to his study, and in the study found his head steward, who bowed respectfully, looked at Peter, at his dressing-gown and smiled slightly, as if by this smile, he expressed his respectful sympathy in his employer's happiness. "And yet," he thought, "how often I have felt proud of her, of her admirable tact, of our handsome home where she received all the town; proud above all of her unapproachableness and beauty. And this is what I was proud of! I fancied I did not appreciate her, and wondered why I did not love her. As I studied her character I thought it was my own fault that I did not understand that total impassivity, that absence of all interest, all wifely feeling—and now I know the dreadful answer to the riddle. . . . She is a depraved woman.

"When Anatole wanted to borrow money of her and kissed her shoulders, she would not lend him the money, but she let him kiss her. When her father tried in jest to make her jealous, she replied with her calm smile that 'she was not such a fool as to be jealous. He may do just what he likes,' she said of me. Nay, did she say she did not want to have any children, much less to be the mother of mine?"

All the coarseness of her mind, the vulgarity of her familiar expressions, in spite of her aristocratic education, recurred to his mind: "I'm not such a silly fool . . . try it yourself . . . *allez vous promener* . . ." she used to say, and often watching her success in the eyes of old and young men and women, he could not understand why he did not love her. "No—I never loved her! And now, here is Dologhow lying in the snow, trying to smile, dying perhaps, and mocking my repentance with affected bravado."

Peter was one of those men who, in spite of a weak nature, never want a confidant in their troubles. He fought them down in silence.

"She is guilty of it all, she alone, but why did I tie myself to her, why did I say 'I love you' which was a lie and worse than a lie . . . I am guilty—and what is it I am to bear? The disgrace to my name, the misery of my life. All that is nonsense. Name and honour are mere conventional phrases; my real self is independent of them. Louis XVI was decapitated because he was guilty, and his executioners were quite as much in the right as those who, after calling him a saint, died for him as martyrs. Was not Robespierre guillotined, too, for being a despot? Who was right, and who was wrong? Neither. —Live while you live: to-morrow, perhaps, you may die—as I might have died a few hours since. Why torment yourself, when you reflect what life is, after all, as compared with eternity?"

And then, when he fancied he had argued himself into indifference, she again rose before him, and the wild fever of his transient passion; he paced the room once more, smashing everything that came under his hand, till, for the tenth time, he asked himself why he had said: "I love you?" And he caught himself smiling as Molière's phrase occurred to him: "*Que diable allait-il faire dans cette galère ?*"

It was not yet daylight when he rang for his man and ordered him to pack for his departure. Feeling it impossible to have anything more to say to his wife, he was going back to St. Petersburg, and he meant to leave a letter to her, announcing his intention of living apart from her henceforth and for ever. A few hours later, when the man came in with his coffee, he found him lying on the sofa, a book in his hand, but fast asleep. He woke with a start, and could not at first remember why he was here.

"The countess wishes to know if your excellency is at home?"

Peter had not time to reply when the countess came into the room, in a loose gown of white satin embroidered in silver, and with the two heavy plaits of her hair bound round her beautiful head—as calm and imposing as ever, though on her marble forehead—a slightly prominent forehead—a deep line of fury was visible. She contained herself till the servant had

left the room, though she stood in front of her husband and
her lips parted in a contemptuous smile. She knew all the
history of the duel, and had come to speak of it. Peter timidly
glanced up at her over his spectacles, and pretended to take up
his book again, as a hare at bay lays back its ears and remains
motionless, face to face with the foe.

"What now? What have you been doing—I ask you?"
she said severely, as the door closed after the man.

"How . . . I . . .?" said Peter.

"What is the meaning of this fit of valour? What is the
history of this duel? Come, answer."

Peter turned heavily on the sofa; he opened his mouth, but
found nothing to say.

"Well, I can answer, then. You believe everything you
hear, and you have been told that Dologhow is my lover,"—
and she said "*amant*," in French, with her habitual cynical
precision, in as matter-of-course a way as she might have said
anything else. . . . "You believed it! And what have you
proved by fighting him? That you are a fool, an idiot—
though for that matter all the world knew it. And what is
the consequence? That I shall be the laughing-stock of all
Moscow. Everyone will say that you were drunk, that you
called out a man of whom you were jealous without a cause—a
man who is immeasurably your superior in every way. . . ."
And as she talked her voice rose with her excitement.

Peter did not stir; he murmured a few inaudible words
without looking up.

"And why did you believe that he was my lover? Because
I found his society pleasant? Well, if you had been less stupid
and more agreeable I should have preferred yours."

"Do not talk to me—I entreat you," said Peter hoarsely.

"Why not? I have a right to talk to you, for I can boldly
declare that the woman who, with a husband like you, has not
lovers is an exception—and I have none."

Peter scowled at her with a dark look which she did not
understand, and flung himself back on the couch. He was in
physical pain; his chest laboured, he could scarcely breathe . . .
he could put an end to this torment he knew, but he knew, too,
that what he wanted to do was horrible.

"We had better part," he said, in a choked voice.

"Part! By all means," said Helen, "on condition that you
give me enough money. Parting! And you think to frighten
me by that word?"

BEFORE TILSIT

Peter sprang to his feet and flew at her.

"I shall kill you!" he cried. He seized a piece of marble that was lying on the table, brandishing it with a degree of strength that he felt was appalling. Her face was terrible to see; she yelled like some wild beast, and shrank back. The nature of his father came out in him. Peter was rapt, drunk with rage. He flung the marble on the floor, and following her up with outstretched arms:

"Go!" he said, in a thundering tone that sent terror through the house. God knows what he would have done at that moment if Helen had not fled.

A week after Peter left for St. Petersburg, after making over to his wife the entire control over all his property in Greater Russia, which amounted to quite half of his fortune.

CHAPTER LXXVI

About two months had gone by since the news of the battle of Austerlitz had reached Lissy-Gory, and since Prince Andrew had disappeared; in spite of letters to ambassadors, and of every inquiry, his body had not been found, and his name was not on any list of prisoners. The most painful alternative for his family was to think that he might have been picked up on the field by some of the country-people, and be ill or dying, alone among strangers, and unable to send them any token of his existence. The newspapers, from which the old prince had first learnt the defeat of Austerlitz, simply stated in brief and vague terms that the Russians, after a brave struggle, had been forced to retreat and had accomplished it in good order. From the official bulletin, however, the prince could plainly infer that the defeat had been complete. Ten days later a letter from Koutouzow announced the mysterious disappearance of his son:

"Your son," he wrote, "fell like a hero in the front of the regiment, grasping the standard—worthy of his father and his country. He is universally lamented, and to this hour no one knows whether he is numbered with the dead or the living. All hope is not, however, lost, for if he were dead, his name would have been inserted in the lists of officers found dead on the field, which have been sent to me under flag of truce."

It was very late one evening when this letter reached the old prince, and next morning he went out as usual to take his walk; but he was gloomy and morose, and did not speak a word to his man of business, his builder, or his gardener.

When Maria went into his room she found him busy at his lathe, but he did not look round as usual.

"Ah! Princess Maria!" he said suddenly, with a push on the treadle. The wheel went on whirling from the impetus, and the whirr of this wheel as it died away remained associated in his daughter's mind with the whole scene. She went up to him, and at the sight of his face an indescribable feeling clutched her heart; her eyes grew dim. The old man's features were pinched with an expression of vindictiveness rather than of sorrow or dejection; they betrayed the violent struggle that was going on within him, and showed that a terrible grief was hanging over her head—the most terrible of all—one which she had not yet known: the irreparable loss of one of those she held dearest.

"Father! Andrew?" The poor girl, awkward and ungainly as she was, spoke the words with such a potent charm of self-devotion and sacrifice that the old man, under the influence of her gaze, gave a sob and turned away.

"Yes, I have had news. He is nowhere to be found, neither among the prisoners nor among the dead. Koutouzow writes . . . He is killed!—" he added, suddenly, in a piercing voice, as if to scare his daughter from him.

But the princess did not stir, she did not faint; she was pale, but her face seemed transfigured as he spoke, and her fine eyes lighted up suddenly. It seemed as though an ineffable unction from above, independent of the joys and sorrows of earth, had fallen like a balm over the wound that had just been dealt them. Forgetting her habitual dread of her father, she took his hand, drew it to her, and kissed his dry, parchment cheek.

"Father," she said, "do not turn away from me. Let us mourn together."

"Those wretches, those villains!" cried the prince, pushing her aside. "To lose an army, to lose men! And what for? —Go and tell Lisa." Princess Maria dropped into an armchair and burst into tears. She could see her brother as she had seen him taking leave, when he had come to her and his wife; she could see his look—touched, but slightly disdainful— as she slipped the image round his neck. Had he learnt to believe? Had he repented of his scepticism? Was he now in the realms above, the Heaven of peace and bliss?

"Father," she said, "how did it happen?"

"Why, why—he was killed in this battle, where the best men of Russia were led to the slaughter and Russian honour was sacrificed! Go, Princess Maria, go and tell Lisa."

Maria went to her sister-in-law, whom she found at work and who looked up at her with a calm, self-contained happiness.

"Maria," she said, pushing away her embroidery-frame, "give me your hand." Her eyes were bright and her lips parted in a childlike smile. Maria knelt down at her feet and hid her face in the skirt of her dress; she could not look up, for she was crying.

"What is the matter, Maria dear?"

"Nothing—I was thinking of Andrew, and that made me melancholy," she said, wiping away her tears.

In the course of the day Princess Maria several times attempted to prepare her sister-in-law for the catastrophe, but each time she began to cry, and her tears, though Lisa could not understand them, alarmed her in spite of her unobservant nature. She asked nothing, but fidgeted with anxiety, as if she were seeking for something close at hand. The old prince, of whom she was still afraid, came into her room before dinner; he looked vicious and agitated, but he went out again without speaking. Lisa looked at Maria and burst into sobs.

"Have you any news of Andrew?" she asked.

"No, you know the thing is impossible; but my father is anxious, and I am frightened."

"There is nothing then?"

"Nothing," replied Princess Maria, looking at her frankly. She had decided, and had persuaded her father, to tell her nothing till after the birth of her child, which was now imminent.

Father and daughter bore the heavy burthen each after a different fashion. Though the prince sent a messenger to Austria to seek some trace of his son, he was convinced that Andrew was dead, and had already ordered a monument to be made at Moscow and erected in the garden. He made no change in his habits of life, but his strength was failing him; he walked and ate less, slept less, and was visibly more feeble. Princess Maria did not abandon hope; she prayed for her brother as if he were alive, and expected every hour to be told of his return.

CHAPTER LXXVII

"My dear Maria . . ." said the little princess on the morning of March 19th, and her short upper lip curled up as it always did, but with a saddened expression, for, since the day when the terrible news had reached them, the smiles, voices, the step even of everyone about the house wore a tinge of grief, and the little princess, half unconsciously, had yielded to the influence. . . . "My dear Maria, I am afraid my *frühstück*,[1] as Phoca the cook calls it, must have disagreed with me this morning."

"What is the matter, my dear little soul? You are pale, very pale . . ." cried Maria, hurrying towards her.

"Had we not better send for Maria Bogdanovna, excellency?" said a maidservant who happened to be present. Maria Bogdanovna was the midwife of the country town, and had been living in the house at Lissy-Gory for the past fortnight.

"To be sure, you are right; perhaps it is that. I will go for her. Be brave, my darling. . . ." Maria kissed her sister-in-law and was about to leave the room.

"No, no," cried Lisa, whose white face betrayed not only physical suffering but a childish dread of the anguish she foresaw. "No—it is indigestion—say it is indigestion, Maria—say so . . ." and she wrung her hands in despair, crying as a sick child cries in its impatience: "Oh dear—oh dear!"

Princess Maria hurried away to fetch the midwife, whom she met in the passage.

"Maria Bogdanovna! It is beginning, I think," she exclaimed, her eyes dilated with terror.

"Well, well. So much the better, princess," said the woman, not hurrying herself. "You young ladies need know nothing about such things."

"And the doctor is not come from Moscow!" said the princess, for in obedience to Prince Andrew's wish, and his wife's, a doctor had been sent for.

"That does not matter. Do not worry yourself, princess. We shall do very well without the doctor."

Five minutes later Princess Maria heard some very heavy object being carried past her room; it was a leather couch out of Prince Andrew's room, which was being taken into the bedroom; and she noticed that even the men's faces wore an

[1] *Frühstück*, German for breakfast.

330

unwonted look of softness and gravity. Princess Maria listened to the sounds in the house, opened her door and looked out anxiously at what was going on in the passage. Some women-servants were coming and going, and turned away when they saw her. Not daring to question them, she withdrew into her bedroom, where she first threw herself into an arm-chair, with a prayer-book in her hand, and then knelt down in front of the Holy Images; but to her surprise and distress she found that prayer was ineffectual to calm her agitation. Suddenly the door was thrown open and Princess Maria's old nurse, with a large kerchief tied over her head, appeared on the threshold, Prascovia Savischna very seldom came into the princess's rooms; it was against the prince's orders.

"It is I, Machinka," said the old woman with a sigh. "I have brought their wedding tapers, my angel, to light in front of the Images."

"Oh; nurse, I am glad of that."

"The Lord is merciful, my little dove"—and the old nurse lighted the tapers at the lamp in front of the Images; then she sat down by the door, and pulling a stocking out of her pocket, she began to knit. Princess Maria took up a book and pretended to read, but at every step, at every sound, she looked up at her nurse in terrified inquiry, and the old woman glanced at her reassuringly. The feeling which was agitating Maria was shared, indeed, by every inhabitant of this enormous house. It is an old superstition in Russia, that the less notice is taken of the sufferings of a woman in labour, the less she feels them; so everyone pretended ignorance. No one said a word about what was going forward; still, irrespective of the solemn and respectful manner which was habitual with the old prince's household, a certain tender anxiety was evident in all, and an intuitive sense that some great and mysterious event was about to take place.

There was not a sound of laughter in the part of the house where the waiting-women and girls lived; the menservants and footmen sat silent and watchful in the ante-room. Not a soul could sleep in the houses on the estate; fires and lights were kept burning. The old prince was pacing his study, treading on his heels, and he sent Tikhon every two minutes to inquire of Maria Bogdanovna how matters were going on, saying each time:

"Say, 'the prince sends to inquire' . . . and come back and tell me."

"Tell the prince," said Maria Bogdanovna with emphasis, "that labour has begun."

"Very good," said the prince, shutting his door, and Tikhon heard not another sound in the study.

A few minutes later, however, he stole in under pretence of carrying in fresh candles, and he saw the prince was lying on the sofa. At the sight of his anxious face the old servant shook his head, and going up to his master he kissed his shoulder; then he hastily quitted the room, forgetting the candles and his excuse.

The most solemn mystery on earth was in process of accomplishment.

Thus the evening passed slowly; night came on, and this feeling of agitated expectation, instead of diminishing, seemed to intensify every minute.

It was one of those nights in March when winter seems to resume its empire and lets loose a last desperate onslaught of howling winds and squalls of snow. A relay of horses had been sent forward on the high road for the German doctor, sent for to the little princess; and men with lanterns were posted at the turning to guide him safely past the ruts and holes of the road to Lissy-Gory.

Princess Maria had a book in her hand, but she had ceased to read it. She sat gazing at her old nurse, whose little shrivelled face, with a lock of grey hair straggling from under her head-kerchief, and a wrinkled double chin, was so familiar an object. The old woman sat knitting and babbling of old-world gossip of the Princess Maria's birth in Kischineff with nobody but an old Moldavian peasant-woman as midwife. "If God is merciful no doctors are necessary."

A violent gust of wind shook the window frame; the ill-fitting bolt sprang, and a sharp draught of icy, damp air fluttered the stiff curtains and blew the candle out. Princess Maria shuddered. The old nurse laid down her knitting and went to the window, leaning out to pull it to again.

"Princess, little mother," said she, as she closed the window, "they are coming up the road with the lanterns. It must be the doctor."

"Oh, thank God!" cried Maria. "I must go to meet him! He does not understand Russian."

She threw a shawl over her shoulders, and as she passed through the ante-room she noticed that the carriage had already drawn up at the steps. She went forward on the landing; on one of the columns of the balustrade a candle was standing, guttering in the draught. On the landing below stood a man-servant, looking very much scared, with another candle in his hand; and lower still, at the turn of the stairs, she heard the tread of heavy furred boots, and a well-known voice struck her ear:

"Thank God!" said the voice. "And my father?"

"The prince is in bed," replied Démiane, the house-steward.

"It is Andrew!" said Princess Maria—and the steps came nearer. "But it is impossible! It would be too extraordinary!"

At this moment Prince Andrew, wrapped in a pelisse with the collar white with snow, came into sight on the landing below. . . . It was certainly he, but pale, thin and altered, with an expression, very rare in him, of anxious and tender softness. He mounted the last steps and took his sister in his arms; she was speechless with emotion.

"And you have not had my letter?" he said, kissing her again, while the doctor, who had come the last stage with him in the carriage, went upstairs.

"Maria, what a strange coincidence!" and pulling off his fur boots, he went to his wife's room.

CHAPTER LXXVIII

THE little princess, with a white cap tied over her head, was lying on the pillows; her long dark hair fell over her flushed cheeks, and her rosy lips wore a smile. Her husband went in and stood at the foot of the couch. Her eyes glittered with the restless look of an over-excited child; she fixed them on him, but their expression did not alter: "I love everybody," they seemed to say, "I have done no one any harm; why should I be punished?" She saw her husband without realising that it was he. He bent down and kissed her forehead.

"My little soul," he said—he had never called her so before— "God is merciful!" Then he made way for the doctor, and left the room. He met Princess Maria, and they talked together in a low voice, pausing every now and then in fevered expecta-tion. Finally he sat down in the room next his wife's. A maidservant came out and started on seeing him there; he, with his face hidden in his hands, did not stir. Presently he went to the door and tried to open it; someone held it on the inside. "No one can come in—impossible!" said a frightened voice.

He tried walking about; a dead silence had fallen; then, after a few minutes, he heard a shriek of horror.

"That was not Lisa—she cannot have the strength . . ." said Prince Andrew to himself. He ran to the door; all was quiet, and then he heard the cry of an infant.

"Why have they brought a child here?" he exclaimed impatiently in the first surprise. "What business has it here? —or is it the new-born baby?"

With a sudden comprehension of the happiness that cry announced, tears choked him; he bent his head on the window-sill and sobbed aloud. The door opened. The doctor came out in his shirt-sleeves, pale and tremulous. Prince Andrew turned round, but the doctor, looking wildly at him, went on without speaking. A woman came rushing by, but stopped short, speechless too, at the sight of Prince Andrew.

He went into the room. His wife was dead, lying just as he had seen her a few minutes since; her sweet young face wore just the same expression, though her eyes were fixed and her cheeks were white:

"I love everybody, and I have done no one any harm. . . . Why should I be punished?" said the lovely, lifeless face.

In one corner of the room a small, red object was wailing in the trembling hands of the nurse.

Two hours later Prince Andrew slowly went towards his father's room. The old prince had been told everything, and as his son opened the door he found himself face to face with him. The old man did not speak, but threw his withered arms, like iron tongs, round his son's neck, and melted into tears.

The little princess was buried three days after, and Prince Andrew went up the steps to the catafalque to bid her a last farewell. Her eyes were closed, but her small features had not altered, and still she seemed to ask: "What have you done to me?" Prince Andrew did not weep, but his heart was torn with the thought that he had wronged her, and that now all wrongs were irreparable and unforgettable. The old prince in his turn kissed one of the slender waxlike hands lying crossed upon her breast, and he could have fancied that the poor little face asked him too: "What have you done to me?" He turned hastily away.

Five days later the infant was christened; the nurse held up the swaddling clothes, tucking them under her chin, while the priest, with the end of a feather, dropped holy oil on the palms and the soles of the feet of tiny Prince Nicholas Andréïévitch.

The grandfather, as sponsor, carried him round the baptistery, and then hastened to surrender him to his godmother, Princess Maria. The father, greatly agitated, and fearing lest the priest should drop the child into the water, waited anxiously in the adjoining vestibule till the ceremony was over. He looked at his son with extreme satisfaction when the old nurse brought him out, and nodded with friendly pleasure when she told him the good news that the scrap of wax placed in the water with a few of the infant's hairs on it had floated.[1]

CHAPTER LXXIX

THANKS to his father, Rostow's share in the duel between Dologhow and Bésoukhow escaped notice; instead of being degraded, as he fully expected, he was appointed to the staff of the general, who was governor of Moscow; this, however, prevented his spending the summer in the country with his family, and obliged him to remain in town.

Dologhow recovered from his wound and during his convalescence Rostow became very intimate with him. His old mother, Maria Ivanovna, was passionately fond of her son, and would say to Rostow, to whom she had taken a great fancy in return for his liking for her Fédia:

"Yes, count, he is too good and too noble for this corrupt world. No one values goodness as they ought, for everyone feels it a reproach to himself. Now, I ask you, is it just or handsome in Bésoukhow? . . . And my boy has never said a word against him. All their St. Petersburg follies were laid at his door—Bésoukhow never suffered for them. My boy has just been promoted, to be sure; but then where in the world will you find another as brave as he is? . . . As to this duel! . . . Have men like that a shade of honourable feeling? He knew he was an only son; he insults him, and then fires at him point-blank! However, God in his mercy has pulled him

[1] The priest cut the infant's hair as part of the baptismal ceremony, and a custom obtained of putting some hairs on a little wax and throwing it into the water in the font. If the wax floats it is a good omen, if it sinks, it is unlucky.

through! . . . And what was it all about? Who in these days has not some intrigue on hand, and whose fault is it if Bésoukhow chooses to be jealous? He might have shown it a little sooner, I should think, but now it has been going on for a year; and he thought Fédia would refuse to fight because he owes him money! How mean! How cowardly! I like you with all my heart, for you have been able to appreciate my Fédia, and so few people do him justice, though he has such a noble soul."

Dologhow, again, would drop expressions which Nicholas would never have expected from him.

"People think me wicked," he said to Rostow, "but I do not care. I only care to be sure of those who are attached to me, and for them I would lay down my life; as for all the rest, if they stand in my way I tread them under foot; I am devoted to my mother, and I have two or three friends, you above all. As for the rest of the world, I never think of them, excepting as they may be useful to me or mischievous—and most are mischievous, especially women . . . Yes, my dear fellow, I have known noble men, tender, high-minded—but the women! Countess or cook, everyone has her price, without exception. That heavenly purity and devotion which I have looked for in woman I have never seen. If I had only met the woman I have dreamed of I would have sacrificed everything for her—but the rest! . . ." and he snapped his fingers. "And I will confess to you that I only care for life because I hope one day to meet with that ideal, who will raise me, purify me, regenerate me—but you do not understand me?"

"On the contrary, I understand it perfectly," said Rostow, altogether bewitched by his new friend.

The Rostow family returned to Moscow in the autumn. Denissow was not long in coming back to town, too, and settled himself under their roof. The first months of this winter, 1806–07, were full of life and amusement for the Rostow party. Nicholas brought a great many young men into the house, who were much attracted by Vera, now twenty, by Sonia, whose sixteen summers gave her the charm of a half-opened flower, and by Natacha who, with the saucy fun of a child, had the added fascinations of a young girl. Each felt, more or less, the charm of these smiling young faces, radiant with happiness and susceptible to every impression. Living among their gay, inconsequent chatter, sparkling with originality and buoyant

The Rostow family returned to Moscow in the autumn

with life and hope—mingling with the stream of idle bustle broken by the sudden gushes of music and song, taken up and laid aside under the impulse of the moment—the men were fascinated, intoxicated by an atmosphere that seemed saturated with love, and which predisposed them, as well as the girls, to grasp at some vaguely imagined happiness.

These magnetic currents were stirring, naturally enough, amid all these young creatures, when Dologhow was brought to the house by Nicholas. Everyone was pleased with him, excepting Natacha, who almost quarrelled with her brother about him; for she maintained that he was a bad man, and that in the matter of the duel, Peter had been right and Dologhow to blame, and that besides, he was disagreeable and affected.

"There is nothing to understand in the matter," Natacha insisted, with determined obstinacy, "he is horrid; he has no heart at all! Your Denissow now, I like him! He may be a scamp, very likely, but I like him all the same! . . . I say it just to show you that I do understand! In the other everything is done with an object, and that I hate!"

"Oh! Denissow! that is quite another matter," said Nicholas, in a tone that implied that he was not to be compared with Dologhow: "You should see him with his mother. He is such a noble fellow—so tender!"

"Of that I cannot judge; I know that I am never at my ease with him. . . . And he is in love with Sonia. Do you know that?"

"What nonsense!"

"I am perfectly certain he is. You will see."

Natacha was right. Dologhow, who did not like ladies' society was, nevertheless, a frequent visitor, and it was soon discovered, though no one said a word about it, that Sonia was the attraction. She never would have owned it, though she had in fact guessed it, and blushed as red as a cherry whenever he came in; he came to dinner almost every day, and whether at the play, or at the balls given to his pupils by Ioghel, Dologhow never failed to make his appearance when the Rostows were present. He paid marked attention to Sonia, and there was that in the expression of his eyes, that not only could Sonia not bear to meet them, but the countess and Natacha coloured if they happened to do so. It was very evident that this strange and vehement man was yielding and submitting to the irresistible influence of this graceful little brunette, while she, all the time, loved another. Rostow noticed the conditions of their acquaintance, but failed to understand them: "They are all in love with one or another of the girls," he said to himself; and feeling uncomfortable under all this high pressure, he often was to be found elsewhere than in his father's house.

During these autumn months, war with Napoleon again became a subject of conversation, and it was more eagerly discussed than ever. A conscription of ten men in every thousand for the regular army, and nine in every thousand for the militia was now talked of; anathemas on the French emperor were uttered on every side, and Moscow was full of rumours of war. The only share taken by the Rostow family in these anticipations centred in Nicholas, who was only waiting till Denissow's leave was out to join his regiment after Christmas. Their approaching departure did not interfere with their amusements; on the contrary, it spurred them to enjoyment, and Nicholas spent the chief part of his time at dinners, evening parties, and balls.

CHAPTER LXXX

On the third day after Christmas the Rostows gave a semi-ceremonial dinner in honour of Denissow and Rostow, who were to start the day after Twelfth-night. Among the score or so of guests was Dologhow. The electric and fevered currents which haunted the household had been more perceptible than ever during the last few days. "Seize the swift lightnings of joy as they fly!" this mysterious stir seemed to whisper to the young creatures. "Love and be loved! that is the only thing worth aiming at, for it is the only great truth in life!"

In spite of having two pairs of horses in the stable, Nicholas had not done more than half his errands, and only came in just before dinner. He, too, at once felt the oppression which, that day, weighted the stormy and passion-laden atmosphere they all breathed; a strange embarrassment seemed to hover between some of the persons present—especially between Sonia and Dologhow, the old countess, and to a certain extent Natacha. He understood that something must have occurred, and in the goodness of his heart his behaviour to them was full of tender tact and delicacy. There was to be a ball that evening at Ioghel's—Ioghel was a famous dancing master, who often on fête days issued invitations for a dance to his pupils of both sexes.

338

"Nicholas, will you come to the dance at Ioghel's? Do come, he particularly begged that you would, and Vassili Dmitritch has promised to come."

"Where would I not go in obedience to Countess Natacha?" said Denissow, who, half in fun and half in earnest, had declared himself Natacha's knight. "I am ready even to dance the shawl dance."

"Yes, I will if I have time; but I promised to go to the Arkharows' this evening. And you?" he asked, turning to Dologhow. But he at once saw that the question was indiscreet, from the short: "Yes, perhaps," of Dologhow's reply, and his scowl at Sonia.

"There is something in the air between those two," he thought; and Dologhow's departure as soon as dinner was over confirmed him in the idea. He called Natacha, intending to question her.

"I was just looking for you," she cried, running after him. "Did not I tell you?—and you would not believe me!" she added, triumphantly. "He has proposed."

Now, though Sonia did not at that time largely occupy his thoughts, Nicholas felt a slight pang at this announcement. Dologhow was a suitable match, nay, in some ways a very good match for an orphan who had no fortune. The old countess and the world about them had a right to expect her to accept him. So Nicholas's first impulse was one of annoyance, and he was about to give vent to it in satirical observations on Sonia's forgotten promises and easy surrender, when Natacha went on:

"And only fancy, she has refused him, positively refused him! She says she loves someone else."

"Of course, my Sonia could not have done otherwise," said Nicholas to himself.

"Mamma entreated her in vain; she refused, and I know she will never change her mind."

"Mamma entreated her?" said Nicholas reproachfully.

"Yes, and do not be vexed, Nicholas. I am quite sure— though I do not know why I am so sure—you will never marry her. I am quite sure."

"Come, come; you cannot know anything about it . . . But I must go and speak to her. What a sweet creature she is, Sonia!" he added, with a smile.

"Sweet! I should think so! I will send her to you . . ." and she kissed her brother and ran away.

A few minutes later Sonia came into the room alarmed and confused, like a criminal. Nicholas went to meet her and kissed her hand; it was the first time since he came home that they had been together *tête-à-tête*.

"Sonia," he began shyly, but he soon recovered confidence, "you have refused a very good, a very advantageous offer . . . He is a very excellent fellow; high-minded—a great friend of mine . . ."

"But the thing is at an end; I have refused him," interrupted Sonia.

"If you have refused him for my sake, I am afraid . . ."

"Do not say that, Nicholas," she interrupted again, with an imploring look.

"But it is my duty to say it. Perhaps it is conceit on my part, but I would rather speak, for come what may, I am bound to tell you the truth. I love you, I think more than anything in the world . . ."

"That is all I want," she said, blushing deeply.

"But I have often been in love, and I shall fall in love again; still, I have not for anyone else the feeling of confidence, friendship and love that I have for you. I am young; mamma, as you know, does not like the idea of our marrying. So I can make you no promise, and I implore you to give full consideration to Dologhow's proposal,"—he hesitated as he spoke his friend's name.

"Do not say such things. I ask for nothing. I love you, as a brother—I shall always love you, and that is enough for me."

"You are an angel, and I am not worthy of you; I am afraid of deceiving you . . ." And again Nicholas kissed her hand.

CHAPTER LXXXI

"Ioghel's balls are the nicest in Moscow!" said the mammas, as they watched their daughters performing their new steps and figures; and the girls and young men were of the same opinion, and danced till they were exhausted, as happy as kings, though some of them came out of pure condescension. The two pretty Princesses Gortchakow had even found husbands there in the course of the winter, and this added to Ioghel's success. The great charm was the absence of any host and hostess; there was no one to preside but the worthy dancing-master skipping about as light as a feather; and one and all, down to the young girls of thirteen and fourteen who there appeared in their first long gowns, had but one aim and end: to dance and be amused. All, with very few exceptions, were —or at any rate looked—pretty; eyes sparkled, and smiles were happy and bright. The best pupils, among whom Natacha was prominent for grace, sometimes danced the shawl dance; but, this evening, quadrilles and the caledonians were more in favour, and the mazurka, which was just coming into fashion. Iohgel gave his dance in one of the great rooms in the hotel Bésoukhow, and everyone agreed that it was a complete success. There were pretty faces by the dozen, and the Rostow girls, even brighter and happier than usual, were the queens of the ball. Sonia, equally proud of Dologhow's proposal, of her refusal, and of her explanation with Nicholas, waltzed round her room with joy, and in the effervescent delight that trans-figured and irradiated her she hardly gave the maid time to plait her fine, dark hair.

Natacha, not less happy, and particularly proud of a long frock which she was to wear for the first time, was dressed like Sonia, in white muslin with pink ribbons. They had hardly entered the ball-room when she got into such a state of excite-ment that every possible partner on whom her eyes fell filled her with a passion of admiration.

"Oh! Sonia, Sonia! how lovely!" she exclaimed.

Nicholas and Denissow took stock of the young ladies with a glance of protecting tenderness.

"She is perfectly charming!" said Denissow, with an air.

"Who, who?"

"Countess Natacha," said Denissow. "And how she dances! What grace!"

"Who?" repeated Rostow.

"Why your sister!" said Denissow, out of patience. Rostow smiled.

"My dear count, you are one of my best pupils; you really must dance," said little Ioghel to Nicholas. "Look what a choice of fair partners!" and he repeated the request to Denissow, who had also learnt of him.

"No, my good friend, I will stand among the wallflowers. Do you forget how little credit I did to your teaching?"

"Not at all, quite the contrary," Ioghel hastened to assure

341

him for consolation. "You were not very attentive, to be sure —but you had a taste for it, you certainly had."

The first notes of the mazurka were now heard, and Nicholas led out Sonia. Denissow, seated among the mammas and leaning on his sword, watched the swaying crowd of dancers, beating time with his foot while he sent his neighbours into fits of laughter by telling them stories. Ioghel led the mazurka with Natacha, who was his best pupil, and the pride of his heart. Placing his little feet, shod with pumps, in position, he started lightly, carrying Natacha with him; and she, though greatly alarmed, performed her steps with the greatest care. Denissow never took his eyes off her, and his look plainly said that if he did not dance it was only because he did not care about it, but that at a pinch he could acquit himself creditably. In the middle of the figure he stopped Rostow, who was passing him:

"That is not the real thing at all," he said. "Is that like a mazurka? But she dances well all the same."

Now, Denissow had in Poland acquired a great reputation as a dancer of the mazurka; so Nicholas went up to Natacha: "Choose Denissow," he said. "He dances perfectly."

When it came to her turn she rose and went the whole length of the room on her light little feet straight up to Denissow; she felt that everyone was looking at her and wondering what she was going to do. Nicholas saw that there was some little discussion between them, and that Denissow refused with a gay smile.

"Do, pray, Vassili Dmitrich, come, when I ask you."

"No, no, countess, really and truly. Do not insist."

"Come, Vassa," said Nicholas, coming to the rescue. "It is like a kitten coaxing a big cat!"

"I will sing for you a whole evening," said Natacha.

"Ah! little enchantress, you can do whatever you please with me," replied Denissow, and he took off his belt. He made his way through the barricade of chairs, took firm hold of his partner's hand, drew up his head, lifted one foot behind him, put himself in an attitude, and waited for the music. When he was on horseback or dancing his small stature was quite forgotten, and he made the most of all its advantages. At the first note he rapped his heel on the floor, with a satisfied and triumphant glance at his partner, and bounding forward with the elasticity of a ball, he flew into the circle carrying her with him. He went half across on one foot, hardly touching the ground, and going straight at the row of chairs which he did not seem to see; then suddenly, with a clank of his spurs, he pulled up with a short slide; jingled his spurs again, paused on his heels, turned without moving from the spot, and with a lift of his left heel was off again to the other end of the room. Natacha followed every movement almost unconsciously, giving herself up unresistingly to his guidance. Now and then he put one or the other hand behind her waist and spun round with her; again, dropping on one knee, he turned her round himself; then rising to his feet he flew off at such a pace that it seemed as though the impetus would carry them through the wall, till he suddenly bent and repeated the graceful figure. Finally, he brought his lady back to her place, pirouetted her with elegant ease, jingled his spurs, and made her a bow, while Natacha, quite bewildered, forgot to make the usual courtesy. Her smiling eyes looked into his face in astonishment; she seemed not to know him: "What has come over him?" she thought.

Though Ioghel refused to recognise this mazurka as a classic dance, every one was enthusiastic about Denissow's performance; the young ladies chose him again and again, and the old folks, looking at him out of the corner of an eye, talked of Poland and the good old times. Denissow, quite hot with his exertions, wiped his brow and sat down by Natacha, whom he did not quit again all the rest of the evening.

CHAPTER LXXXII

IT was two days after this that Rostow, who had seen nothing more of Dologhow, either at his father's house or in his own home, received the following few lines:

"As I do not intend to call at your house again, for reasons which are no doubt known to you, and as I am off to join the army very soon, I have asked my friends to say good-bye to me this evening. You will find a party of us at the Hotel d'Angleterre."

On leaving the theatre with Denissow and his own family, at about ten o'clock, Nicholas went as he was bidden, and was shown into the best room, which Dologhow had engaged for the occasion. There was a party of about twenty, gathered round a table at which, between two wax candles, Dologhow was sitting. In front of Dologhow was a pile of gold and small notes; they were at cards and Dologhow held the bank. Nicholas had not seen him since Sonia had refused him and felt a little awkward over the meeting. As Rostow came in Dologhow looked up with a cold, hard glance, as if he had been sure that he would come.

"I have not seen you for a long time," he said. "Thank you for coming. Let me finish this deal. Illiouchka and the gypsy choir are coming presently."

"I have called at your house," said Rostow, colouring a little.

"Take a card if you will," said Dologhow, not answering him.

At this instant a strange conversation they had had one day recurred to Rostow's memory: "None but an idiot would trust to chance," Dologhow had said.

"Or perhaps you are afraid to play with me?" said Dologhow with a smile—and in fact he had read his thought.

Now, as he saw Dologhow's smile, Rostow perceived that he was in a mood, as he had been at the club-dinner, when, simply to escape from the weary monotony of life, he let himself be carried away to commit a crime. Nicholas muttered a few words, trying to find some jest wherewith to answer him, when Dologhow, looking him full in the face, said very slowly and distinctly, so that everyone could hear him:

"Do you recollect our talking of cards one day, and my saying: 'None but an idiot would trust to chance; if you really must play let it be a safe game . . .?' Well, I am going to try, nevertheless!'"

"Try what? Luck or certainty?'' thought Rostow.

He cracked the pack of cards with his thumb, and exclaimed: "Now, gentlemen, we begin."

He pushed aside the money that lay in front of him and prepared to cut. Rostow sat down next to him, but not to play.

"Do not play, it is better not," said Dologhow. But Nicholas, oddly enough, now felt as if he must take a card; still, he staked but a trifling sum on it. "I have no money," he said.

"Name your stakes then," said Dologhow.

Rostow lost his five roubles; he staked, and lost again. Ten times Dologhow won.

"Gentlemen," he said, "please to lay your stakes on your cards or I shall make some mistake."

One of the players expressed his opinion that he was to be trusted.

"Certainly! but I am afraid of getting confused—pray lay

your money on the cards. As for you, don't let it worry you," he added, turning to Rostow, "we can settle our accounts another time."

The game went on, and the champagne flowed freely. Rostow had already lost eight hundred roubles and was going to stake it all on a card, when a glass of champagne was offered him and that stopped him; so he only put down twenty roubles, as before.

"Leave it," said Dologhow, who nevertheless did not seem to be watching him, "you will recover yourself all the sooner. It is very odd, the others are winning and you lose every time. Is it because you are afraid of me?"

Rostow complied. He picked up a dog-eared card, a seven of hearts which he remembered only too well afterwards, wrote 800 on it very plainly, swallowed his champagne, and smiling at Dologhow he watched his fingers as he dealt the cards, looking for a seven to turn up. The loss or gain that this card might bring him was of great importance to him, for, on the previous Sunday, his father, while giving him 2000 roubles, had confessed to him that he was in considerable difficulties, and had begged him to make that money last him till May. Nicholas had assured him that it was plenty and to spare, and now he had only 1200 roubles left; so if he were to lose on this seven of hearts, he not only would have to pay 1600 roubles, but he would have broken his word to his father.

"Only let him turn up the right card and make haste about it," he said to himself, "and I will be off home to sup with Denissow, Sonia, and Natacha, and never touch a card again as long as I live." All the details of his family life—his romps with Pétia, his duets with Natacha, games at piquet with his father—all these domestic pleasures rose before him with the vivid clearness and charm of lost and inestimable joys. He could not believe that blind chance, by making a seven of hearts fall to the right hand or the left should shut him out from these sacred pleasures, and cast him into an abyss of endless and unknown disaster. It could not be—and he fixed his eyes in fevered anxiety on Dologhow's large, hairy, red hands with thick joints, as he paused before dealing, and laid down the cards to take a glass and a pipe.

"Then you are not afraid to play with me?" Dologhow said to him; he threw himself back in his chair as if he had something very amusing to tell his friends, and went on: "Yes, gentlemen, I have been told that there is a report in Moscow that I cheat at cards! If so, I can only advise you to be on your guard."

"Come, deal away," said Rostow.

"Oh! those wicked old Moscow gossips!" he exclaimed, and he took up the pack.

At the same time Rostow, hardly able to check a loud exclamation, clasped his hands to his head. The seven of hearts on which his all depended was the top card, and he had lost more than he could pay.

"Look here," said Dologhow, "don't give in," and he went on dealing.

CHAPTER LXXXIII

An hour and a half later all the interest of the game centred on Rostow. Instead of the first 1600 roubles, he had before him as set down against him a column of figures of which the sum total might, as he guessed, reach 15,000 roubles, but which in fact came to more than 20,000. Dologhow had ceased to tell stories; he watched Rostow's every movement, and determined to continue playing till he had won 43,000 roubles; he had fixed on this figure because forty-three was the sum of his age and Sonia's. Rostow, with his elbows on the table and his head between his hands, in front of the green cloth all smeared with chalk and stained with wine and strewed with heaps of cards, sat, with death in his soul, watching those fingers which had their clutch on him:

"Six hundred roubles—ace, nine—impossible to recover it. —And they are happy there, at home! . . . Knave on five. . . . Why does he treat me so?"

Now and then he raised his stake, but Dologhow would not allow it and named a lower figure. Rostow yielded and prayed, —prayed as he had prayed on the field, at the bridge at Amstetten. Sometimes he defied fate, and picking up a card that had dropped by chance on the table, hoped it might change his luck, or again, he counted the rows of braid on his jacket and put the sum of the tags on the card before him; and sometimes, after glancing round at the other players as if to appeal to them for advice, he fixed his eyes on his opponent's stony face, and tried to read what was passing in his mind.

"He knows, too, how important this money is to me, and he is my friend, and I was fond of him. . . . But it is no fault of his since the luck is on his side; and it is no fault of mine either. . . . What harm have I done him? . . . Have I killed or insulted anyone? . . . Why am I to be the victim of such a disaster? It seems only a minute since I came to this table hoping to win a hundred roubles to buy mamma a present for her birthday, and then to go home again. . . . I was happy, free. . . . When did this dreadful change come over me? . . . And yet I am the same—and in the same place. . . . Oh! this is impossible, it cannot go on so!"

His face was burning, he was bathed in sweat, and it was dreadful to see the superhuman efforts he made to keep calm.

The long column of losses had reached the critical sum of 43,000 roubles, and Rostow had already turned down the corner of a card to stake double 3000 roubles which he had just won, when Dologhow, sweeping the cards together, hastily added up the figures and wrote down the total in a neat row:

"Come to supper," he said, "it is high time. Here are the gypsies." And ten or more copper-skinned men and women came into the room, bringing with them a cold gust of outer air. Nicholas saw that all was over.

"What! is that the end? and I had such a pretty little card ready for you," said he to Dologhow, affecting to be indifferent and to care for nothing but the chances of the game.

"This is the end of all things!" he thought to himself. "A bullet in my skull—that is the only thing left to me!"

"Come—one more!" he said.

"If you like," said Dologhow, finishing his sum; it came to 43,021 roubles. "Make it 21 roubles." Rostow had written 6000 on the card, he scratched it through and made it 21.

"All right, I don't care," he said. "What I want to see is whether you will give me this ten." Dologhow dealt gravely. Oh how Rostow hated him at this moment! . . . The ten fell to Nicholas.

"Then you owe me 43,000 roubles, count," said Dologhow, rising and stretching himself. "How tired one gets with sitting so long."

"I am tired of it too," said Nicholas.

"When can I have the money, count?" said Dologhow, as if to suggest that any jesting was out of place.

Nicholas coloured up to his eyebrows, and taking him aside

he said: "I cannot pay you the whole of it, you must take an IOU."

"Listen," said Dologhow with an icy smile. "You know the proverb: 'Lucky in love, unlucky at play,'—your cousin loves you, I know."

"Oh, it is intolerable to be at this man's mercy," said Nicholas to himself. He thought of the blow this must be to his mother, to his father; he realised what a happiness it would be to him not to have to confess this dreadful thing; he felt that Dologhow, too, understood that, and that he might save him this anguish and disgrace, but that he was playing with him as a cat plays with a mouse.

"Your cousin. . . ." Dologhow began again.

"My cousin has nothing to do with this," Rostow fiercely interrupted: "it is quite unnecessary to name her even."

"When can I have the money then?"

"To-morrow," said Rostow, and he left the room.

CHAPTER LXXXIV

NOTHING could be easier than to say "To-morrow" with suitable dignity, but what was dreadful was to have to go home, to meet his sisters, his father and mother, to tell them everything, or to fail to keep his pledge.

No one was gone to bed. The young people had supped after coming from the theatre, and were standing round the piano. When Nicholas went into the music-room he was again struck by the hot-house atmosphere of poetry that seemed to pervade the house; and now, since Dologhow's proposal and the ball at Ioghel's, it had gathered as if in portent of a storm, over the heads of Sonia and Natacha. They were dressed alike in blue, as they had gone to the theatre, looked wonderfully fresh and pretty, and were very well aware of it as they chatted and laughed by the instrument. Vera was playing at chess in the next room with Schinchine and the countess was busy with "a patience" till her husband should come in, while an old lady—noble, but poor, to whom they had given a home—watched her game. Denissow, seated at the piano with his hair on end and one foot under his chair, was feeling for chords on the keys with his heavy fingers, rolling his eyes and trying in a husky but true voice to find an air to some lines he had just written to the enchantress:

> "Enchantress, tell me: Whence the sweet dominion
> That stirs the sleeping music in my heart,
> That bids it soar on melody's free pinion?—
> Reveal the secret of thy mystic art."

His voice thrilled with passion, and he fixed his dark eyes on Natacha, who was tremulous but happy.

"Charming, delightful!" she exclaimed. "Another verse!"

"Nothing is different here," said Nicholas to himself.

"Ah! here he is!" cried Natacha.

"Is my father in?" he asked.

"I am so glad you have come home," she went on, without replying. "We are having such a nice evening—and Vassili Dmitritch is going to stay a day longer to please me."

"No, papa is still out," Sonia answered.

"Nicholas, my dear, come here," said his mother from the adjoining room. Nicholas went; he kissed her hand and sat down by her in silence, watching her lay out the cards on the table for her "patience," and the laughter and chatter reached their ears from the piano.

"Very well, very well," said Denissow, "there is no resisting you; but sing the barcarole, pray."

The countess looked round at her son, who had not spoken a word.

"What is the matter?" she said.

"Nothing," he replied, as if she had asked him several times already. "Will my father come in soon?"

"I think so."

"Nothing is altered. They know nothing. Where can I hide myself?" he thought to himself; he went back into the music-room, where Sonia was now seated at the piano and was playing the introduction of the song Natacha was going to sing, and Denissow was gazing at her with glowing eyes. Nicholas walked up and down the room.

"What possesses them to make her sing! . . . What can she sing? What is it that they can find so amusing?"

Sonia struck a chord.

"Good God!" he thought, "I am a ruined wretch, lost, disgraced. There is nothing for it but a bullet in my brain. Oh! why do they sing? Can I get away? Pooh! Let them go on; after all, what does it matter to me!" and Nicholas, gloomy and scowling, continued his walk, avoiding the girls' questioning eyes.

"Nicholas, what is the matter?" Sonia seemed to be asking him, and she had been the first to observe how melancholy he was.

Natacha, with her unfailing keenness, had noticed it too; but all thought of sadness, care, pain, or repentance, was so far from her present mood, her spirits were so exuberant that, being but a young thing, she soon forgot it again: "I am much too happy," was her feeling, "to spoil my own pleasure for a grief that does not directly concern me. Besides, very likely it is only my fancy, and he is really as cheerful as I am."

"Now, Sonia," she exclaimed, and she danced into the middle of the room, where she thought the voice sounded better. Raising her head and letting her arms hang simply by her side, she flashed a look at Denissow, as much as to say: "Yes, I am just as you see me."

"What can she have to be happy about," wondered Nicholas. "How is it that he is not bored to death."

Natacha began; her bosom rose and her eyes assumed a rapt expression. She was thinking of nothing now, of no one; her lips parted in a smile and the notes came out—those sounds which may proceed from any throat in the world, at any hour, and with the very same intonation, but which leave us untouched a thousand times, and make us thrill and cry with emotion the thousand and first. Natacha had been working steadily at her singing during the winter, chiefly with a thought of Denissow, knowing that her voice lifted him to the seventh heaven. She no longer sang like a child or with the effort of a schoolgirl. Her voice was of unusual compass, but—connoisseurs said—not yet sufficiently trained; nevertheless—and though she had not yet learned to take breath at the right places or to laugh at difficulties—even connoisseurs, in spite of their criticisms, involuntarily gave themselves up to the charm of that voice, and after it had ceased asked nothing better than to hear it again and yet again. It was so frank a revelation of that sweet maidenhood whose bloom no touch had yet marked, and of its unconscious sway, that any change, as it seemed, must diminish the charm.

"What has come over her?" thought her brother, opening his eyes at hearing her sing like this. "What is it? How she sings!" Forgetting all his woes, he waited eagerly for each succeeding note, and for a few minutes there was nothing in the world to him but the triple time air of the song.

"What a mad world we live in!" thought he. "Ill-luck, money, Dologhow, hatred, honour—what are they all? Nothing. This is the real thing! Natacha, sweet little bird! . . . Will she take that upper B? She has hit it, thank God!" And to support the high B he threw in the third below:

"Lovely! I hit the right note too!" he exclaimed, and the harmony of that third filled him with a strange sense of all that was best and purest. As compared with this supreme and heavenly pleasure what were losses at cards and his promise to pay? Mere folly! Why a man might kill and rob and yet be happy!

CHAPTER LXXXV

It was many a day since Rostow had been so excited and charmed by any music; but Natacha had no sooner finished her barcarole than he recovered his sense of reality, and made his escape to his room without saying a word. A quarter of an hour later the count came in from his club in the best spirits; his son went to his room.

"Well, have you enjoyed yourself?" asked the father, with a proud smile as he looked up at him. Nicholas vainly tried to answer; he was choking. His father lighted his pipe without noticing his discomfort.

"Well, it has to be done," thought he, and assuming an airy tone, of which he was utterly ashamed, as though he were only asking his father to let him have a carriage out for a drive: "I came to speak to you about business," he said. "I had forgotten, almost—I want some money."

"Indeed!" said the count, who was in the best possible humour this evening. "I was sure that would not be enough. Do you want much?"

"Yes, a great deal," he said, affecting stolid indifference. "Yes, I have lost a little—not to say a great deal—43,000 roubles."

"What? To whom? But you are in jest!" cried the count, and the blood mounted to his neck.

"And I have promised to pay to-morrow."

His father gave a groan of despair and fell back helplessly on the sofa.

"What can I do?" Nicholas went on in a hard, bold voice. "It is the sort of thing that happens to everyone. . . ." But while he spoke he felt what a wretch, what a cur, he was; his conscience told him that his whole life would not be long enough to expiate his sin; and as he declared to his father with rough audacity that this "happened to everyone," he longed to fall at his feet and kiss his hands and beg his forgiveness.

At these words the old count looked down and began to fidget distressfully.

"Yes, yes. . . ." he said. "Only . . . I am afraid . . . I shall find a difficulty. It happens to everyone of course—it happens to everyone. . . ." He looked at his son, and then made his way to the door. Nicholas, who had expected him to be very angry, could bear it no longer.

"Father, father, forgive me!" he exclaimed with a sob; he seized his father's hand and pressed it to his lips, bursting into tears like a child.

While the father and son were having this explanation, a no less serious conversation was passing between the mother and daughter.

"Mamma, mamma, he has done it."

"What do you mean?"

"He has told me—he has proposed!"

The countess could hardly believe her ears. What! Denissow had been making love to this little chit of a Natacha, who only the other day was playing with her doll, and was still doing her lessons.

"Come, Natacha, no nonsense!" said the countess persuasively, hoping to make her confess that it was a trick.

"What, mamma! nonsense! It is a very serious matter," said Natacha, stung to the quick. "I came to ask you what I ought to do and you tell me it is nonsense."

The countess shrugged her shoulders.

"If it is true that Mr. Denissow has made you an offer, you may tell him from me that he is a simpleton."

"Certainly not; he is not a simpleton."

"Well, what do you want then? All you children have had your heads turned. If you are in love with him, marry him, and God be with you!"

"But, mamma, I am not in love with him! On my honour I do not think I am."

"Very well, then, go and tell him so yourself."

"Now you are vexed. Do not be vexed, dear little mother. . . . Now, is it any fault of mine?"

"No, my darling, but what is it you want? Shall I go and tell him?"

"No. I will tell him myself, only explain to me how. You laugh, but if you had seen him when he said it. . . . He did not mean to say it, I know—but it came out."

"But then at any rate you must refuse him."

"Oh, no. I must not refuse him; I should be so sorry—he is so kind. . . ."

"Then you had better accept him. Indeed, it is high time you should get married!" said her mother, half laughing and half annoyed.

"No, mamma, I cannot do that. Still, I really am very sorry. How ought I to say it?"

"Well, you need not say it at all; I will go and talk to him," said the countess, who was beginning to feel it altogether unfitting that anyone should think of little Natacha as a grown-up person.

"Not for worlds! I will speak myself, and you may listen at the door if you like. . . ." And Natacha flew back to the music-room, where Denissow was sitting at the piano with his face hidden in his hands, just where she had left him. At the sound of her footstep he raised his head:

"Natacha," he said, going forward to meet her, "my fate is in your hands, speak the word."

"Vassili Dmitritch, I am so very sorry . . . but it cannot be, and you are so kind; but it cannot be . . . but I will always, always love you!"

Denissow bent low to kiss her hand, and could not choke down a smothered sob as he felt the girl's kiss on his black, stubborn, wavy hair. At this moment the rustle of the countess's dress was heard:

"Vassili Dmitritch, I thank you for the honour you have done us," she said, not without emotion, though he thought her stern, "but my daughter is so young. . . . And I should have thought you would have spoken to me before addressing her."

"Countess," he began, looking down like a criminal, and struggling in vain to find words in reply. Natacha, seeing him so crushed, began to cry convulsively.

"Countess, I was in the wrong," Denissow began again in a broken voice, "but I worship your daughter—and I love you all so much, that I would give my life twice over for any of your family!" Then he saw that the countess was looking very grave. "Good-bye, then," he added hastily; he kissed her hand without looking again at Natacha, and left the room with a firm step.

Rostow spent the next day with Denissow, whose one idea was to quit Moscow as soon as possible. His friends gave him a farewell supper with a gypsy concert, and he never could remember how they had got him packed into his sleigh, or anything about the three first stages of his journey. After he had left, Nicholas, for whom his father had not been able to raise so large a sum, remained a fortnight in Moscow, without ever stirring out of the house; he spent nearly all his time with the girls, filling their albums with copies of verse and music. Sonia was more gentle and affectionate than ever, as if she wanted to prove to him that this loss at cards was quite an exploit, and that she could only love him the better for it; while Nicholas, on his part, could only feel that henceforth he was unworthy of her.

Having at last sent the 43,000 roubles to Dologhow, who gave him a receipt in due form, he got away without taking leave of any of his acquaintance, and went to join his regiment which was now in Poland.

BOOK FIVE

CHAPTER LXXXVI

AFTER the scene with his wife, Peter had set out for St. Petersburg. When he reached Torjok, a post-town not half-way from Moscow, he found no horses — or else the post-master did not choose to let him have them; being obliged to wait, without undressing, or even taking off his heavy furred boots, he threw himself on a large divan, with a round table in front of it, and was soon lost in thought.

"Shall I bring in the luggage, and make up a bed? Will your excellency have some tea?"

Peter made no reply: he saw, heard, cared for nothing; his mind was wholly absorbed in the reflections which had occupied it for some hours; in the face of the serious questions which were troubling him it mattered little to him whether he reached St. Petersburg a few hours earlier or later, or slept here or there. The post-master, and his wife, the servant, the woman who sold gold and silver embroidery—a speciality of the town— all came in to offer their services. Peter did not move; he looked at them over his spectacles, not fully understanding what they wanted of him. How could these folks live easy without having solved any of the crucial problems that had never ceased to haunt him since the duel and the terrible night that had followed it? In the solitude of his journey he could not help recurring to them incessantly, and still he could not solve them. It was as though the main cog-wheel of his existence had had a wrench, but could not stop, and still turned on without catching any corresponding notch. Presently the post-master came in very humbly, to say that if his excellency would only wait "two little hours," he could let him have mail post-horses to the next stage. He was lying, that was quite evident; his only object was to fleece his customer: "Now is he doing right or wrong?" said Peter to himself. "It is doing good to me, for I get the benefit, but it is wronging the traveller who may happen to come after me. He, poor wretch, cannot help himself, for he has not enough to put between his teeth. He told me the officer had beaten him—well, it must have been because the officer himself was in a hurry, and was kept waiting. And I shot Dologhow, because I thought myself insulted; and Louis XVI. was guillotined, because they thought him guilty; and a year later his judges were executed! What is wrong, and what is right? Who is to be loved or hated? What is the end of life—nay, what is life, what is death? What is the mysterious power which governs it all?" But there was no reply to these questions or only one, which was not really an answer: "Death! and then either you will know everything, or you will cease to ask . . ." But death was terrible to him.

The woman who sold embroidered leather goods praised her merchandise with shrill vehemence, particularly some kid slippers. "I have hundreds of roubles that I do not know what to do with," thought Peter, "and this woman in her ragged pelisse looks at me so humbly. Now, what would she do with the money? Would it give her the value of a hair more in happiness or peace of mind? Can anything on earth save her, any more than me, from the ills of life or death? Death, which may come to either of us to-day or to-morrow, makes everything seem worthless in comparison with eternity . . ." And so, again and again he started the mechanical train of thoughts which kept whirling round in vacuity.

His man brought him in a book—a half-cut novel, by Madame de Souza, and he began to read the history of the woes and virtuous struggles of one Amélie de Mansfield. "Why on earth did she resist her lover if she really loved him?" he asked himself. "It is impossible that God should have given her desires opposed to her will. My wife—she that was my wife— fought no battle; and perhaps she was right. Nothing really worth knowing has ever been discovered or invented; 'we know nothing save that we know nothing?' That is the sum total of human wisdom."

Everything, within and without, was confusion and doubt; he felt a sort of general disgust, and yet that sense of disgust gave him a fractious satisfaction.

"Might I ask your excellency to make a little room for this gentleman," said the post-master, showing in another traveller, who, like Peter, was obliged to wait for lack of horses.

He was a little old man, very wrinkled and yellow, with long

At Torjok he found no horses—or else the post-master did not choose to let him have them

grey eyebrows that overhung bright eyes of a doubtful colour. Peter had thrown his legs up on the table; but he now rose and went to lie down on a bed that had been arranged for him; he lay watching the new-comer, who seemed very tired, and allowed his servant to take off his outer garments, leaving him in a short fur-lined jacket with felt boots on his thin bony feet. He took a seat on the sofa, and leaned his head, which was large in proportion to his figure, against the back of it. His forehead was high, and he wore his hair cut very close. Then he looked at Peter, and his grave, intelligent, piercing gaze struck the younger man; he was about to make some commonplace remark, when he observed that the stranger had already closed his eyes and folded his withered hands—he wore on one finger a leaden ring, with Adam's head—and seemed to be either asleep, or lost in meditation.

His servant, like himself, was old, wrinkled, yellow, and absolutely beardless; the smooth parchment-like skin showed that no razor had ever touched it. He briskly unpacked a basket of provisions, laid the table for tea, and fetched a samovar. When all was ready the traveller opened his eyes, drew up to the table, poured out two glasses of tea, and gave one to his old servant. Peter was beginning to feel embarrassed; it was evident that he must speak to the new-comer. The man presently brought back his glass turned upside down on the saucer with the lump of sugar half eaten, and asked his master if he needed anything.

"Give me my book," he said, and he began to read with absorbed attention.

Peter thought by the look of the book that it was a religious work, and he watched the reader till he laid the book down and leaned back again. Peter was still studying his appearance when the old man, turning towards him, looked at him with a steady, stern gaze which disturbed while it attracted him.

CHAPTER LXXXVII

"If I am not mistaken I have the honour of addressing Count Bésoukhow," said the stranger, in strong deliberate tones. Peter looked at him inquiringly over his spectacles. "I have heard of you," the old man went on, "and of the misfortune that has occurred;"—he emphasised the word "misfortune," as much as to say: "you may call it what you please, but it is a misfortune—I feel for you deeply."

Peter coloured, sat up with his feet on the ground, and bowed to the old man with a shy smile.

"A better reason than mere curiosity induces me to remind you of it," the stranger added after a brief silence, during which he still looked at Bésoukhow, and he made room on the sofa, as if to invite him to come and sit there. Little as Peter felt inclined to talk, he submitted, and sat down by his side.

"You are unhappy, sir—and you are young, while I am old; I should be glad to help you so far as lies in my power."

"Yes?" said Peter with a doubtful smile. "I am sincerely grateful. . . . Have you come from a distance, sir?"

"If for any reason it is disagreeable to you that I should talk to you, do not hesitate to say so . . ." And though there was nothing gentle in his face, rather it was cold and severe, Peter felt himself unaccountably drawn to this new acquaintance.

"By no means—I am most happy to make your acquaintance . . ." and Peter's eye fell on the head of Adam on the ring; a token of Freemasonry. "May I ask if you are a Freemason?"

"Yes, sir, I belong to the craft—and in its name and in my own, I offer you the right hand of brotherhood."

"I fear," said Peter, hesitating between the sympathetic liking he felt for the old man, and the recollection of the mockery of which freemasons were commonly the butt, "I fear that we may not understand each other. I am afraid that my views of creation generally will be diametrically opposed to yours."

"I know what your views are. You think—and most men think with you—that they are the outcome of the labour of your intelligence? No. They are the outcome of pride, indolence, and ignorance. You are cherishing a sad error—it is to combat that error that I have entered on this conversation."

"And why should I not believe the mistake to be on your side?"

"I do not venture to say that I know the truth," said the freemason, whose decision and clearness of speech astonished Peter more and more. "No one can attain to the truth; stone by stone, by the efforts of many successive generations from the time of Adam till our own day, the structure is being raised which, some day, will be the worthy temple of the Omnipotent God."

"I ought perhaps to confess at once that I do not believe in God," said Peter, not without an effort, but he felt it his duty not to conceal his opinions. The stranger looked at him with the deep, pitying gaze of a kind-hearted millionaire who can enrich the poverty-stricken man who owns his misery:

"Because you do not know Him; you cannot know Him; and you are unhappy for that very reason."

"Very true—I know that I am unhappy—but how can I help it?"

"You do not know Him. And He is here, in me, in my words," the Freemason went on in a stern voice. "Nay, He is in you—even in the blasphemous denial you have just now uttered."

He ceased and sighed, trying to recover his usual calmness. "If He did not exist," he went on in a lower tone, "we could not talk about Him. Of whom were you speaking? Whom have you denied?" he suddenly exclaimed with excited enthusiasm and in an imperious tone. "If He had not existed who could have invented Him? Whence did you—you and the whole of mankind—derive the idea of a Being whose very attribute is bound up with Incomprehensibility, Omnipotence, and Eternity? He is!" he added after a long silence which Peter was careful not to break. "To comprehend Him is impossible." The stranger fidgeted nervously with the pages of his book. "If you had told me that you doubted the existence of a man I might have taken you to see the man; but how can I, a miserable mortal, prove His omnipotence, His eternity, His infinite mercy to the blind, even to those who shut their eyes that they may not see Him and understand Him, who will not perceive their own baseness and worthlessness? You! who are you? You think yourself wise in your blasphemy no doubt," he added with a scornful smile, "and you are as helpless, as silly as a child that trifles with the complicated works of a watch. He does not understand it, and he does not believe in the existence of the maker. It is hard indeed to know Him. We have toiled at it for ages, from the days of Adam until now, and the infinite still divides us from Him! . . . In that we see our weakness and His greatness."

Peter, with a melting at his heart and shining eyes fixed on the face of the Mason, listened and dared not interrupt, but without questioning himself believed with all his soul what this stranger was telling him. Did he believe in the reasonable deductions which were in the man's speech, or did he believe, as children believe, the intonation, the certainty, the sincerity that was heard in it, the trembling of the voice which at times broke his sentences, or did he believe those brilliant aged eyes, grown old in this certainty, or that calm firmness and knowledge of his mission, which showed itself in the whole being of the Mason and which particularly impressed itself when compared to his own despondency and hopelessness—but he longed with all his heart and soul to believe, and believed, and felt a happy peace, a renewal of his life.

"It is not the mind that understands God; it is life that makes us understand Him.

Peter, fearing to detect in his new friend's arguments some obscurity or weakness which might shake his growing confidence, interrupted him:

"But why is it that the human intellect cannot rise to the comprehension of which you speak?"

"Supreme wisdom and truth," replied the Freemason with his gentle, paternal smile, "may be compared to a heavenly dew which we long to feel falling into our souls. And can I, an unclean vessel, absorb this dew and set myself up as a judge of its spirit? Nothing but an inward purification can render me fit to receive even a small portion of it."

"Yes, yes, that is the truth," cried Peter with eager effusiveness.

"Supreme wisdom is founded on a basis different from that of human knowledge and human experience—history, physics, and chemistry, into which it is divided. Supreme wisdom is one. It knows of but one science: the universal science, which explains all creation and man's place in it. To understand it you must purify and regenerate the inner man; hence, before you can know you must believe, and become righteous. The divine light that shines in our souls is called conscience. Turn your spiritual gaze on your inmost being and ask yourself if you are satisfied with yourself, and the results you have achieved with no guide but your intelligence. You are young, rich and intelligent—what have you done with the gifts that have been poured upon you? Are you satisfied with yourself and your life?"

"No—I hold it in horror!"

"If you hold it in horror, alter it, purify yourself and by degrees, as you yourself change, you will learn to discern wisdom. How have you spent your life? In orgies and depravity, taking everything from society and giving nothing in return. How have you used the fortune that was bestowed on you? What have you done for your fellow men? Have you ever given a thought to your tens of hundreds of serfs? Have you done anything to help them morally or physically? No. You have benefited by their toil to lead a worthless life. That is what you have done. Have you tried to employ yourself for the good of others? No—you have eaten the bread of idleness. Then you married; you undertook the responsibility of guiding a young woman through life. How did you do it? Instead of helping her to find the right path you flung her into a gulf of falsehood and misery. A man offended you, and you shot him; and then you say that you do not know God, and that you hold your life in horror! How should it be otherwise?"

The stranger, evidently fatigued by his own vehemence, leaned against the back of the sofa and closed his eyes in extreme exhaustion. His lips moved but gave no sound. Peter watched him. His heart was full but he dared not break the silence.

The Freemason roused himself with a little, old man's cough, and called his servant.

"The horses?" he asked.

"Some have just come in. But will you not rest a little?"

"No—have them put to."

"Will he really leave me without divulging his mind to me, without starting me in the right path?" thought Peter, who had risen and was walking up and down the room with his head bent low. "Yes, I have led a contemptible life; but I did not like it, I never wished it! . . . And this man knows the truth and could teach it to me."

The stranger, having arranged his luggage, turned to Bésoukhow and said in a tone of cool politeness: "And which road are you travelling, sir?"

"I am going to St. Petersburg," said Peter; with some hesitation he added: "And I am very much obliged to you. I quite agree with you; do not think me altogether wicked. I sincerely wish I were just such as you desire to see me, but no one has ever advised or helped me. . . . I acknowledge my guilt—help me, teach me, and some day perhaps . . ." a sob choked his voice. The Freemason was silent for a space, meditating. Then he said:

"God alone can help you, but such advice as our Brotherhood can give will be afforded you. Since you are going to St. Petersburg, carry this to Count Villarsky—" and taking out a pocket-book he wrote a few words on a large sheet of letter-paper folded in four. "Now, I will give you a word of good counsel: give up the first weeks of your solitude to self-study; do not return to your former mode of life. *Bon voyage*," he added as his servant came in, "and good-luck to you!"

Peter saw in the post-master's book that the stranger's name was Ossip Alexéiévitch Basdéiew. He was a Freemason well known in Novikow's time. Long after he had left, Peter still paced the room without thinking of going to bed or even of proceeding on his journey, looking back on his past evil life, and depicting, with the excited fancy of a man who longs to be regenerate, the future of faultless virtue which looked to him so easy. He fancied he had gone wrong only because he had unconsciously forgotten how pleasant it was to do right. All his doubts had vanished; he believed firmly in the brother-hood of all men whose only task was to help each other along the path of life. This was what he understood as the order and rule of Freemasonry.

CHAPTER LXXXVIII

When he reached St. Petersburg Peter did not announce his arrival to anyone; he retired into solitude, and spent his days in reading Thomas à Kempis, which had been sent to him, by whom he knew not. He found in his study of it only one thing: the possibility, which till then had never dawned upon him, of attaining to perfection and of believing in that active, brotherly love of man to man of which Basdéiew had spoken. About a week after his return home Count Villarsky, a young Pole whom he knew but slightly, called upon him one evening with a solemn and official manner which reminded Peter of that of Dologhow's second. He closed the door, and having carefully ascertained that there was no one else in the room, he said:

"I have waited on you to lay a proposal before you. A man high in the craft of our Brotherhood has been exerting himself to procure your admission before the usual time, and he has begged me to be your sponsor. I have no more sacred duty than to do what he wishes. Do you desire to join the fraternity under my sponsorship?"

The cold, severe tone in which he spoke—a man whom he had never seen excepting in a ball-room, flirting and smiling with fashionable ladies—struck Peter strangely.

"Yes, I do desire it," he replied.

Villarsky bowed. "One more question, count, I must ask you, and beg you to answer, not with a view to becoming a member of our society, but in all honesty and as a man of honour: Have you renounced your former opinions? Do you believe in God?"

Peter paused: "Yes," he said, "I do believe in God."

"Very well, in that case. . . ."

"Yes," interrupted Peter, "I believe in God."

"Come then; my carriage is at your service."

During their drive Villarsky sat in silence, and when Peter presently asked him what he would have to say or do, he told him that one of the brethren, more worthy than himself, would test him, and that he had only to speak the truth.

They drove into the courtyard of a large house where the lodge was being held, went up a dark staircase and into a well-lighted ante-room where they took off their wraps before going into the adjoining room. A man, strangely dressed, held the door. Villarsky went forward, spoke a few words in French in his ear, and then opened a small wardrobe in which lay various articles of wear such as Peter had never seen before; he took out a handkerchief with which he bandaged Peter's eyes, tying the knot in such a way as that some of his hairs were caught up in it. Then he drew him to him, embraced him and led him forward by the hand. Burly, tall Peter, very uncomfortable under this bandage which pulled his hair, smiling shyly, and with his arms swinging by his side, followed him with hesitating steps.

"Whatever happens," said Villarsky when they stopped, "face it bravely if you are determined to be one of us. . . ." Peter nodded. "When you hear a knock at the door you may take off the bandage." He wrung his hand and left him.

Peter, left alone, involuntarily put up his hand to raise the bandage, but he recollected himself and let it drop. Five minutes went by, which to him seemed hours; his legs trembled under him, his hands turned numb; he felt extremely tired and went through a variety of sensations; he was at once afraid of what might await him, and afraid of failing in courage; his curiosity was excited, but what really reassured him was his conviction that he had indeed started on the way to regeneration, and taken the first steps in that useful and virtuous life of which he had never ceased dreaming since his meeting with the stranger. He presently heard a violent rapping. He pulled off the bandage and looked about him. The room was very dark; a small lamp shed a tiny light out of a white object on a table covered with black, on which lay a book, in one corner of the room. The book was the Gospels; the white object was a skull with its teeth. He read the first verse of the Gospel of St. John: "In the beginning was the Word, and the Word was with God,"—and even while he read he wandered round the table and found a coffin full of bones: he was not surprised; he expected to meet with strange things. The skull, the coffin, the book were not enough for his overheated imagination. He wanted more, something more; and peering round him he said: "God — Death — brotherly love. . . ." Vague words enough, but epitomising to him a new life.

The door opened and a little man came in; the sudden transition from light to gloom made him pause a moment; then he came cautiously up to the table on which he laid his gloved hands. This little man wore an apron of white leather which fell from his breast to his feet, and over it, round his neck, a sort of necklace or collar, while his long chin was framed in a deep ruff.

"Why are you here?" asked the new-comer, addressing Peter. "Why have you, who do not believe in truth, and who are blind to the light, come here, and what do you want of us? Is it wisdom, virtue, and progress that you seek?"

At the moment when the door opened Peter had felt a qualm of religious awe such as he remembered feeling in his childhood at confession, face to face with a man who, in the routine of daily life, was a total stranger to him, and who now was his nearest kin by the tie of human brotherhood. He was greatly agitated; however, he went to meet this second steward (as the brother was called, whose duty it was to prepare the candidate for initiation), and recognised him as a friend, a man named Smolianinow. This jarred upon him; he would rather have met him simply as a brother, an unknown but friendly guide. He was so long finding an answer that the steward repeated his question.

"Yes, I seek . . . I seek . . . regeneration."

"That is well," said Smolianinow; and he went on; "Have you any idea of the means at our disposal to assist you in attaining your end?"

"I hope for guidance—for help. . . ." replied Peter, in a tremulous voice, which prevented his speaking distinctly.

"What is your notion of Freemasonry?"

"I take it to be a fraternity of equality among men who aim at virtue."

"Very good," said the other, satisfied with the answer. "Did you ever try to attain virtue through religion?"

"No, for I thought religion contrary to truth," said Peter, so low that his companion could scarcely hear his answer and made him repeat it. "I was an atheist."

"Then you seek truth with a view to obeying the laws of life; consequently you seek virtue and wisdom?"

"Yes."

The steward folded his gloved hands on his breast and went on:

"It is my duty to initiate you into the chief aim of our Order; if it harmonises with the end you have in view, you will become a useful member. The foundations on which it rests are such that no human effort can overthrow it; they are the preservation and transmission to posterity of certain important mysteries which have been handed down to us from the remotest past—from the time even of the first man, and on which the fate of humanity depends; but no man can fully understand them or profit by them till after a long preparation and purification. Our next object is to help and comfort the brethren; to help them to grow better, to purify themselves; to learn, by means of the methods discovered by the sages and handed down by tradition, and to prepare themselves to become worthy of their initiation. By thus purifying and encouraging the brethren we strive to purify and encourage all men, setting the initiated before them as examples of righteousness and virtue, and exerting all our efforts in the struggle with the evil that is in the world. Reflect on what I have said to you. . . ." And he left the room.

"Fight against the evil that is in the world!" repeated Peter; and this course of action, so new to him, spread itself out before his imagination. He pictured himself exhorting those who have erred—such as he had been a week or two since —perverted or wretched souls whom he rescued by word and deed—or again, oppressors, from whom he snatched their victims. Of the three purposes suggested to him by the steward, the third—the regeneration of humanity, attracted him most strongly; mystical secrets only appealed to his curiosity, and he could not think of them as essential; and even the second, self-purification, did not greatly interest him, for he already felt the secret joy of having completely renounced every vice, and being ready for all that was good.

Half an hour later the steward came back to initiate the candidate into the seven virtues that were symbolised by the seven steps of the Temple of Solomon, and which every free-mason is pledged to exercise in his own person: I. Discretion: never to betray the secrets of the order; II. Obedience to the masters of the order; III. Virtuous living; IV. The love of mankind; V. Courage; VI. Liberality; VII. The love of death.

"And to school yourself to the seventh precept think often of death, that it may lose its terrors for you and cease to seem an enemy; it will, on the contrary, appear as a friend, to deliver the soul wearied out by works of virtue from this life of misery, and to guide it to the realm of reward and peace."

"Yes, so it should be, no doubt," said Peter to himself, when his instructor had again left him to his meditations. "But I am so weak that I still love life; and it is only now and by degrees that I am beginning to understand its end and purpose." As to the other five virtues, which he counted off on his fingers, he felt them within him: Courage, liberality, virtuous living, the love of mankind, and, above all, obedience, which he did not regard as a virtue, but as a solace and happiness, for nothing suited him better than to be quit of all responsibility and submit to guides who knew the truth; and as for the seventh virtue, he had forgotten what it was and could not remember it.

For the third time his mentor appeared, and asked him if his determination was immovable, and if he would submit to whatever might be required of him.

"I am ready for anything," said Peter.

"I ought to tell you that our Brotherhood is not satisfied to diffuse truth by words alone, but makes use of other means, more cogent perhaps than words, to convince those who seek wisdom and truth. The objects you have seen in this ' chamber of reflection' must, if your heart is sincere, have told you more than any speech, and, in the course of your advancement, you will often have occasion to consider similar symbols. Our Order, like those of antiquity, imparts instruction by means of hieroglyphics, which are the images of abstract ideas, and which embody the properties of the things they symbolise."

Peter knew quite well what was meant by a hieroglyphic; but foreseeing the pressure of some test he said nothing.

"If you are fully resolved, I will proceed to the initiation: In proof of liberality, I must ask you to give me everything of value that you possess."

"But I have nothing with me," said Peter, imagining that he was expected to surrender all his fortune.

"Whatever you have about you—your watch, money, rings. . . ."

Peter hastily took out his watch and purse, and with great difficulty drew off his wedding-ring, which was tight on his thick finger.

"Now, in sign of obedience, proceed to undress." Peter took off his coat and waistcoat, and his left boot; then the steward opened his shirt over the left breast, and rolled up the left leg of his trousers above the knee. Peter was about to do the same with the right leg to save the brother the trouble, but Smoliani-now stayed his hand and gave him a slipper for his left foot. Feeling awkward, and ashamed of his awkwardness, he stood like a shy child, his arms hanging by his sides, waiting for further instructions.

"Finally, in token of sincerity, I ask you to tell me what is your greatest fault?"

"My greatest? I had so many!"

"The sin that has most frequently led you astray from the path of virtue?"

Peter considered.

"Is it gluttony, drunkenness, laziness, anger, hatred, women. . . ." He thought over the list, not knowing which to choose.

"Women," he presently said, hardly audibly.

The brother did not reply, and there was a long silence; at last he took the handkerchief from the table and bound it over Peter's eyes.

"For the last time," he said, "I entreat you to examine yourself thoroughly. Put a bridle on your passions; seek happiness, not in them but in your own heart, for the source of happiness is in ourselves." And already Peter felt the fount unsealed, filling his soul with joy and soft emotion.

CHAPTER LXXXIX

His sponsor Villarsky now came back into the room; Peter recognised his voice. In answer to their repeated inquiries as to the firmness of his resolve, he answered: "Yes, yes—I consent, I am ready. . . ." and he followed his guides with a beaming face, his broad and brawny chest now quite bare, while Villarsky held a naked sword across it; but his step was timid and unequal, and his left foot still shod with the slipper. In this way they went along several corridors, turning sometimes to the right and sometimes to the left, and at length reached the door of the room where the lodge was held. Villarsky coughed; a rap with a mallet was the reply, and the door was opened. A deep voice asked Peter whence he came, and where he was born; then, still blindfold, he was led forward, while all the time he was exhorted in allegorical figures of speech, as to the difficulties of his journey, the sacred brotherhood, the Great Architect of the Universe, and the courage he would need in his perils and his labours. He noticed, too, that he was designated by different names: "The Seeker," "The Sufferer," "The Inquirer;" and that at each new appellation the swords and mallets sounded with a different ring. While he was thus being led about there was a short confusion of opinion among his guides; he heard a discussion in low tones, one of them insisting that he was to cross a certain carpet. Then his right hand was laid on an object which he could not distinguish; a pair of compasses was placed in his left, and he was directed to point them against his breast while he took the oath of obedience to the Order. The lights were extinguished, some spirit of wine was burnt, as Peter guessed from the smell, and he was told that he was to be made the recipient of the lesser light. His bandage was removed, and by the faint blue glimmer he could dimly see, as in a dream, a number of men, all wearing masonic aprons, standing round in front of him, and each holding a drawn sword pointed at him. One, he perceived, had a bloodstained shirt. Seeing this, Peter bent forward, as if he only wished to be pierced by the blades; but the swords were withdrawn and his bandage replaced.

"Now, you have seen the lesser light," said a voice, "you will receive the greater light." The candles were lighted again, the handkerchief removed, and a choir of ten or more voices chanted: "*Sic transit gloria mundi.*"

368

When he had got over the first bewilderment, Peter saw twelve brethren sitting round a large table covered with black; some of them he recognised, having met them in society. The president was a young man whom he did not know; and he wore a different badge round his neck. On his right hand sat the Italian Abbé we have met at Anna Schérer's, a high St. Petersburg official, and a Swiss who had been tutor to the Kouraguines, were also among the number. All listened in solemn silence to the Worshipful Master, who held the mallet. A blazing star glittered on the wall; on one end of the table lay a little cloth with various attributes worked into it, and at the other there was a sort of altar, on which were a book of the Gospels and a skull. Seven large candlesticks, like those used in churches, stood round the table.

Peter was led up to the altar by two of the brethren; he was made to stand with his feet square, and desired to lie down at full length, as though he were laying his body at the foot of the Temple.

"Give him the trowel," said one of the bystanders.

"No need for that," said another.

Peter, somewhat confused, looked about him with his short-sighted eyes, wondering for a moment where he was, and whether they were making fun of him; whether at a future time he might not feel ashamed of this experience; but as he looked in the grave faces of the group his doubts vanished. He saw that he could not now withdraw, and summoning once more a spirit of humble and pathetic submissiveness, he threw himself on the ground at the gate of the Temple.

In a few minutes he was bidden to rise; he was invested with a white leather apron like those of the other brethren, and received a trowel and three pairs of gloves. The Worshipful Master then explained to him that he was to keep the apron immaculately white as an emblem of strength and purity; that the trowel was to eradicate vice from his own heart, and to lay the foundation of virtue with charity in the hearts of his fellow-men; the first pair of gloves he was to keep without knowing what they signified; the second pair he was to wear at the meetings of the order; the third pair were a woman's gloves.

"These, my dear brother, are to be given to the lady whom you will reverence above all others. This gift will be to her a pledge of the purity of your heart; only beware lest they are worn by unworthy hands. . . ."

As the Worshipful Master spoke, Peter fancied he seemed

uneasy, and he himself, glancing uncomfortably round at the brethren, blushed till his cheeks tingled and his eyes filled with tears, as a child blushes.

There was an awkward silence, but one of the brethren broke it. He led Peter to look at the table-cover, and read to him out of a manuscript book, an explanation of the symbols figured upon it: The sun, the moon, the mallet, the plumb-line, the trowel, the cube of building stone, the pillar, the three windows, and so on. His place was pointed out to him, he was shown the masonic signs, they told him their password, and at last he was allowed to sit down.

Then the Worshipful Master read the statutes of the Order. They were very long, and Peter was too much agitated to listen attentively; he could remember nothing but the last paragraph:

"In our Temple there are no differences of rank but those which separate vice from virtue. Beware of showing any feeling which may tend to destroy this equality. Fly to succour your brother be he what he may; guide the erring, raise the fallen; never give place to any impulse of hatred or aversion. Be kind and benevolent; strive to light the fire of virtue in every heart; share your joys with your neighbour, and never let envy trouble your happiness. Forgive your enemies, and take no vengeance but by returning good for evil. In the fulfilment of these supreme laws you will find the traces of your primal and lost greatness."

He rose as he ceased speaking, and embraced Peter, who, with his eyes full of tears, did not know how to respond to the congratulations of the brethren—those whom he had never seen till this hour as well as those who now renewed a former acquaintance with him. He made no distinction between old friends and new brethren; his one desire was to be associated with them in carrying out their great work.

The Worshipful Master rapped with the mallet, and all sat down again: he spoke a short address on the subject of humility, and then proposed to proceed to the last ceremony. The treasurer, the high dignitary, went round to each. Peter would willingly have put his name on the list for everything he possessed, but the fear of being thought ostentatious checked him, and he put down the same sum as the others.

The meeting over he went home, feeling as if he were returning, another man in every respect, from a long journey of many years' duration, and with nothing left in common with his former life and habits.

BEFORE TILSIT

CHAPTER XC

THE day after his initiation Peter spent the morning in reading the book that had been put into his hands and trying to apprehend the meaning of the figure of which one side represented the Divinity, the second the spiritual world, the third the world of sense, and the fourth the union of the two worlds. From time to time he interrupted his reading and study of the squares to sketch a plan of future life; for he had been informed at the masonic meeting that the story of his duel had reached the czar's ears, and that he would be wise to quit St. Petersburg. He proposed therefore to go and reside on his estates in the south, and devote himself to caring for his peasants.

Suddenly Prince Basil walked into the room.

"My dear fellow, what have you been doing at Moscow? What is the meaning of this quarrel with Helen? You are labouring under a complete mistake; I know everything, and I declare to you she is as innocent with regard to you as Christ with regard to the Jews. And why," he went on, not allowing Peter to put a word in, "why did you not refer at once to me as your friend? I quite understand, you behaved like a man who cares above all things for his honour; perhaps you were over-hasty, but we will talk that over by and by. Only think of the difficult position you have placed us in—my daughter and me—in the eyes of the world, and in the eyes of the Court," he added in a lower tone. "She at Moscow, and you here! You must see, my dear fellow, that it can be nothing more than a misunderstanding; I fondly believe that you must see it in that light. Write to her; she will come to you; everything will be cleared up. If you don't, my dear fellow, I am afraid you will live to repent . . ." and Prince Basil gazed at him very significantly. "I know for certain that the empress-dowager takes a great interest in the matter; she has always been extremely kind to Helen."

Peter, who had tried more than once to stem this flood of words, did not know how to express a point-blank refusal; he got confused, turned red, got up, sat down again—reminded himself of the masonic precepts of charity, while at the same time he felt he must make himself unpleasant by saying the very reverse of what he was expected to say. He was so much accustomed to give way to this tone of dictatorial recklessness that he feared he should not know how to resist it, though he knew that his whole future depended on the next word he might utter. Should he follow the old groove, or should he resolutely start on the new path, so full of allurements, that had been laid down for him—the path that he was sure would lead to the renewal of his whole being?

"Well, my good friend," Prince Basil went on in an airy way, "you have only to say 'Yes, I will write,' and we will kill the fatted calf."

But before he had finished his sentence, Peter, with a flash of rage that made him look like his father, answered in a choking voice, and without looking at Prince Basil:

"Prince, I did not send for you. Go! . . ." and he rushed forward and opened the door. "Go," he repeated to his father-in-law, whose face was quite terror-stricken.

"What ails you? Are you ill?"

"Go away, I tell you!" Peter said once more, and his voice trembled; and Prince Basil was forced to go without getting the answer he required.

Within a week Peter, after taking leave of his new friends and leaving a considerable sum in their hands to be distributed in charity, set out for his estates. He carried with him numerous letters of introduction to members of the Order at Kiew and at Odessa, and promises that they would write to him and advise him in his new way of life.

CHAPTER XCI

NOTWITHSTANDING the czar's severity in cases of duelling the meeting of Peter and Dologhow was hushed up; neither the principals nor the seconds were prosecuted; but the story of the quarrel—which was confirmed by the separation of Peter and his wife—was repeated everywhere. Peter, who had been received with condescending affability when he was only a bastard, and who had been overwhelmed with attentions and flattery while he was the most eligible match in Russia, had lost much of his importance in the eyes of society by his marriage. It had left the mothers of marriageable daughters bereft of all hope, besides which he had never been able, or even tried, to insinuate himself into the good graces of the fashionable and

372

select few. Consequently he alone was pronounced guilty and regarded as a jealous and raging monomaniac, exactly like his father. After his departure Helen returned to St. Petersburg, and was received by all her friends with the respectful consideration due to her misfortunes. If by any chance her husband's name was mentioned in her presence she put on a dignified expression, which her native tact had led her to adopt without fully understanding its value; her face conveyed that she would bear her abandonment with resignation, and that her husband was the cross which God had thought fit to send her. As to Prince Basil, he expressed his views more openly; he would tap his forehead and say whenever the opportunity offered:

"Cracked, cracked—I always said so."

"Pardon me," replied Anna Schérer, "I said so, and before others, before witnesses"—and she always insisted on the priority of her opinion. "The unfortunate young man is perverted by the corrupt notions of the day. I saw it at once when he came back from abroad, and set up for being a second-hand Marat—do you remember? Well, and this is the result. I never liked the marriage; I foretold everything."

Anna Paulovna still gave evenings "at home," which she had the gift of arranging with particular success, collecting, as she herself said, "the cream of the best society," and "the flower of the intellectual spirit of St. Petersburg." Her parties had another attraction; every time she managed to introduce to this select circle some new and interesting personage. Nowhere in St. Petersburg could the political thermometer be more accurately studied than in her drawing-room, as it rose and fell with the state of the conservative atmosphere of Court society.

She was giving such a party one evening at the end of the year 1806, after the arrival of the melancholy news of the defeat of the Prussians at Jena, and at Auerstedt, of the reduction of the greater number of the Prussian fortresses, and just as the Russian army had crossed the frontier to prepare for a second campaign. "The cream of the best society" consisted of the unfortunate and deserted Helen, of Mortemart, of fascinating Prince Hippolyte, who had just returned from Vienna, two diplomats, "*la tante*," a gentleman known to the circle as "the very promising young man," a lately-promoted maid of honour with her mother, and some less conspicuous figures. The choice morsel of the evening on this occasion was

Prince Boris Droubetzkoï, who had come to St. Petersburg as a special messenger from the Prussian army, and was attached as aide-de-camp to a man of distinguished rank.

The reading of the political thermometer that day amounted to this: "The rulers of Europe and their generals may bow to Napoleon if they please, and do what they will to cause *me*— and to cause *us*—every possible annoyance and humiliation; our opinion about him is unchangeable. We shall never cease to express our views on the subject in the plainest terms, and we say, once for all, to the King of Prussia, and the rest of them, 'So much the worse for you. You made your bed, and must lie in it.'"

When Boris, the lion of the entertainment, came into the room all the other guests had arrived; the conversation, led by Anna Paulovna, had turned on the Russian negotiations with Austria, and the probabilities of an alliance. Boris, whose appearance was more manly than of yore, wore an elegant aide-de-camp's uniform; he came in with an easy manner, and after paying his respects to "*la tante*," he joined the chief circle. Anna Paulovna gave him her dry little hand to kiss, and introduced him to those of the party who were unknown to him, naming them one by one:

"Prince Hippolyte Kouraguine—a delightful young man— M. Krouq, chargé d'affaires from Copenhagen, a man of great acumen—M. Schittrow, a young man of great promise."

Thanks to his mother's efforts, and to his own taste and self-control, Boris had succeeded in making a very snug place for himself: an important mission to Prussia had been entrusted to him, and he had returned as special messenger. He had soon mastered the unwritten code which had struck him for the first time at Olmütz—the social code, which gave a lieutenant precedence over a general, which made no demands on labour, courage, or tenacity to ensure success, but required only tact and skill in dealing with the dispensers of places and promotion. He was surprised sometimes at his own rapid advancement, and at finding that so few men understood how easy it was to climb by this road. As a result of his discovery, his mode of life, his relations to his old acquaintances, his projects for the future, all were completely changed. In spite of his narrow circumstances, he would spend his last rouble to be better dressed than other men, not to wear a shabby uniform, or be seen in the streets in a cheap carriage; but he was capable of denying himself many comforts. He frequented the society only of those who were above him in position and who could be useful to him; he liked St. Petersburg, and scorned Moscow. The memories of the Rostows, and of his boyish love for Natacha, were odious to him, and he had not once set foot in their house since his return from the army. But being invited to Anna Paulovna's soirée, he regarded it as a step forward in his career, and understood his part at once. He left it to her to make the most of all that was interesting in himself, devoting his attention to studying the rest of the guests, and considering what advantage he might derive from establishing an intimacy with any of them, and how this was to be achieved.

He took the seat pointed out to him next to the fair Helen, and listened to the conversation. The Danish chargé d'affaires was speaking.

"Austria regards the basis of the negotiations as utterly inadmissible, and cannot consent to accept them—not even if they were led up to by the most splendid successes; and she doubts there being any means of gaining them for Russia. That is the reply from the Vienna Cabinet, word for word. The doubt is flattering," added the "man of great acumen," with an ironical smile.

"But you must make a distinction between the Vienna Cabinet and the Emperor of Austria," said Mortemart. "The Emperor of Austria would never have thought of such a thing; it is the dictum of the Cabinet alone."

"Oh! my dear vicomte," said Anna Paulovna, "Yurope" —she said Yurope, perhaps, as a subtle proof of good taste in speaking to a foreigner—"Yurope will never be the honest ally of Russia . . ." and she went off into a rhapsody on the King of Prussia's heroic courage and firmness, with a view to giving Boris an opening. Boris patiently waited for his turn, listening to what the others had to say, while, from time to time he sent a glance in the direction of his fair neighbour, who responded by a smile at the handsome young aide-de-camp. Anna Paulovna appealed to him, as a matter of course, to describe the expedition to Glogau, and the present position of the Prussian army. Boris, without any fuss or hurry, gave a few interesting details with regard to the Russian troops and the Court of St. Petersburg, speaking correctly in very good French, and taking care not to express any personal views on the facts he related.

For some little time he absorbed the attention of the whole party, and Anna Schérer noted with pride that her company fully appreciated the treat she had set before them. Helen, above all, displayed the greatest interest in Boris and his narrative, and making a show of much anxiety as to the condition of the Prussian army, she questioned him about his journey.

"You must really come to see me," she said with that perpetual smile, and in a voice which seemed to imply that circumstances of which he knew nothing made it indispensable that he could call on her. "On Tuesday, between eight and nine? I shall be so pleased to see you."

Boris promised eagerly and was about to say more to her when Anna Paulovna interrupted their personal talk by calling Boris to speak to her aunt.

"You knew her husband, I think?" said "*la tante*," closing her eyes, and indicating Helen by a pathetic gesture. "What an unhappy, what an enchanting woman! But never mention him in her presence, I entreat you! It is too much for her feelings."

CHAPTER XCII

DURING their brief *tête-à-tête* Prince Hippolyte had taken possession of the lead in the conversation. He had been leaning at his ease in an arm-chair, and now sat bolt upright and suddenly exclaimed: "The King of Prussia!" Then he began to laugh and said no more. Everyone turned to look at him, and Hippolyte, still laughing, settled into his chair again, and repeated: "The King of Prussia!"

Anna Paulovna, seeing that he did not intend to say anything more important, broke out in a violent attack on Napoleon, and to justify her virulence went on to tell the story of how, at Potsdam, that thief Bonaparte had stolen the sword of Frederick the Great.

"The sword of Frederic the Great, that . . ." she was saying; but just then Hippolyte interrupted her by repeating: "The King of Prussia!" and nothing more. Anna Schérer made a face, and Mortemart, who was Hippolyte's friend, said:

"Well, what have you to say, with your King of Prussia?"

"Oh, nothing! I only meant to imply that we are making a mistake in making war for the King of Prussia." He had heard the little pleasantry at Vienna, and had kept it simmering all the evening, in the hope of introducing it. Boris smiled discreetly, in such a way that he might be supposed to approve or to be laughing at the speaker.

"Your joke is a bad one," said Anna Paulovna, shaking a threatening finger. "Extremely witty, but quite unjust. We are not making war for the King of Prussia but for the right principles. Oh! naughty, naughty, Prince Hippolyte!"

The conversation still dwelt on politics, and presently became more eager when it turned on the subject of the rewards distributed by the emperor.

"Last year N. had a snuff-box given him with the czar's portrait," said the "man of great acumen." "Why should not S. have the same?"

"But excuse me," said the attaché, "a snuff-box with the czar's portrait is a reward no doubt but not an official distinction; it is more in the nature of a present."

"There are precedents—Schwarzenberg for instance."

"Impossible!" said another.

"I am prepared to bet: a ribbon, of course, is quite a different thing."

When the party broke up, Helen, who had hardly opened her lips the whole evening, repeated her invitation, or rather her command to Boris with pressing significance, bidding him not forget next Tuesday. In her sudden interest in the army Helen had discovered an all-important reason for asking Boris to call; and her manner seemed to convey that she would inform him of it when he came.

Boris, as he was desired, kept the appointment. Helen's handsome drawing-room was full of people, and he was about to withdraw without having had any particular explanation, when the countess, who had only spoken a few words to him, suddenly said in his ear as he bent to kiss her hand—and for once she was not smiling.:

"Come to dine with me to-morrow—to-morrow evening. You must come—do not fail."

And this was how Boris became intimate in the countess' house during his first stay in St. Petersburg.

WAR AND PEACE

CHAPTER XCIII

WAR had broken out again and was fast approaching the Russian frontier. On all sides nothing was to be heard but anathemas against Napoleon, "the enemy of the human race." In all the villages soldiers and recruits were being called out, while the most improbable and contradictory intelligence was brought in from the seat of war.

At Lissy-Gory things had altered in everyone's life since the previous year. The old prince had been chosen as one of the eight heads of the militia appointed for the whole of Russia. Notwithstanding his feeble health, which had suffered severely by the suspense in which he had lived for so many months as to his son's fate, he thought it his duty to accept the post conferred on him by the czar's personal desire, and his renewed activity restored all his former strength. He spent all his time in riding about the three governments which came under his jurisdiction. Sternly punctual himself in the fulfilment of his duties, he was strict almost to cruelty with his subordinates, and went into the minutest details. His daughter had no more lessons in mathematics, but she went to see her father in his study every morning, followed by the nurse carrying little Prince Nicholas, as his grandfather called him. The child lived in what had been his mother's rooms with his wet nurse and old Savichnia, and there Princess Maria, taking the place of his mother, spent the chief part of her day. Mademoiselle Bourrienne seemed equally devoted to the little boy, and Princess Maria would sometimes leave it to her to watch and amuse their darling. A shrine had been erected in the church over the Princess Lisa's grave, and on the tomb an angel in white marble spread its wings. The angel's upper lip curled a little, and it really looked as if it were going to smile; Prince Andrew and his sister both had been struck with its resemblance to the little princess, and strangely enough—though Prince Andrew took care not to point it out to his sister—the artist had unconsciously given it the same expression of gentle reproach that he had observed on the rigid features of the dead princess: "What have you done to me?"

Soon after his return home the old prince had made him master by deed of gift of his estate of Bogoutcharovo, about forty versts distant from Lissy-Gory, and he took advantage of his father's generosity to quit the scene of so many painful associations and betake himself to solitude, all the more as he found it difficult to accommodate himself to his father's vexatious temper. He made himself a new home, intending to spend most of his time there. He had quite made up his mind after the battle of Austerlitz, to retire from military life; so, to escape active service when the war broke out again, he was obliged to place himself under his father's orders and occupy himself in helping to organise the militia. Father and son seemed to have changed parts: The elder man, excited by his own energy, foretold a happy issue to the campaign, while the younger lamented it with all his heart, and saw none but black prospects.

On the 26th of February, 1807, the old prince started on a tour of inspection, Prince Andrew remaining at Lissy-Gory—as he commonly did when his father was absent. The coachman who had driven the prince to the next town brought back some letters and papers for Prince Andrew. The manservant not finding him in his own room made his way to Princess Maria's, but he did not find him there; the child had been ailing for the last four days and his father was with him.

"Pétroucha wants to speak to your excellency; he has brought some papers," said a maid to Prince Andrew, who was sitting on a low stool, and dropping some medicine with a trembling hand into a glass half full of water, counting the drops with the greatest care.

"What is it?" he said sharply, and the sudden movement made him put in a few drops too much. He threw away the contents of the glass and began again. There was no furniture in the room besides the cradle and two arm-chairs and a few nursery accessories; the curtains were closely drawn; a taper was burning on the table, and a large sheet of music placed as a screen kept the light out of the little sick child's eyes.

"My dear," said Princess Maria, who was standing by the side of the bed, "wait a little while; I assure you it will be better to wait."

"Leave me alone; you do not know what you are talking about. You have waited and waited, and you see the consequences," he answered bitterly in a low voice.

"But indeed, dear, I would wait a little while. He is asleep."

Prince Andrew rose and stood doubtful, and the medicine in his hand.

"Do you think I really had better wait?" he said.

"Well, you must judge for yourself, but I think so," said his sister, somewhat embarrassed by his making this slight concession to her opinion.

This was the second night they had sat up with the child, who was suffering from a sharp attack of fever. Their confidence in the doctor who attended the household was very limited, and they had sent for the medical man from a neighbouring town; meanwhile they were trying various remedies. Tired, anxious, and overwrought, their fears betrayed themselves in unconscious irritability.

"Pétroucha is waiting," the girl said presently.

Prince Andrew went out to receive his father's verbal instructions by message, and came in again with his hands full of papers.

"Well?" he said.

"No change, but do not be disheartened. Carl Ivanitch assured me that sleep was a good sign."

Prince Andrew felt the child's hot dry skin.

"You have no sense at all, you and your Carl Ivanitch." And taking the medicine he had mixed he bent over the cradle, while Princess Maria held him back, entreating him.

"Let me alone," said the prince impatiently. "Well, then, do you give it him."

Princess Maria took the glass, and calling the old nurse to help her, tried to make the child drink, but it struggled, and cried, and choked. Prince Andrew clasped his head in his hands and walked away. He went into the next room and sat down on the sofa. There he mechanically tore open his father's letter and read as follows, in the old prince's scrawl on a sheet of blue paper:

"Unless the good news that has just come to hand by special messenger is a disgraceful hoax, Bennigsen has won a victory over Napoleon at Eylau. St. Petersburg is wild with joy, and it rains rewards and honours. He is a German, but I congratulate him all the same. I cannot imagine what that fellow Handrikow is doing at Kortchew: neither supplies nor reinforcements have arrived yet. Set out at once, and tell him that I will have his head cut off if everything does not come to hand in the course of the week. A letter has come from Pétia from the field of Eylau; he was engaged in the fight—and it is all true. When those whom it does not concern keep out of the way even a German can beat Napoleon. They say he is retreating and severely damaged. So be off at once to Kortchew and carry out my orders."

The second letter he opened was an interminable effusion from Bilibine; he put it aside to read later.

"Go to Kortchew! Certainly not at this juncture. I cannot leave my child ill." He glanced into the adjoining room and saw his sister standing by the cradle, which she was rocking.

"And what is the other disagreeable news in his letter? To be sure, the victory—now that I have left the army! Oh, yes! he can always laugh at me—so much the better, if it amuses him." And he proceeded to read Bilibine's letter, not half understanding what he read, to divert his mind from the matter that so exclusively occupied and worried him.

CHAPTER XCIV

BILIBINE, who was diplomatic attaché to the staff corps, had written him a long letter in French and full of quips and jests; but he gave a thoroughly patriotic picture of the campaign with bold frankness, and not hesitating to pronounce an opinion, even a satirical one, on the acts and deeds of his fellow-countrymen. It was easy to perceive in reading it that he was weary of the guarded discretion which a diplomat is bound to observe, and glad of an opportunity to pour out his bile to so safe a correspondent as Prince Andrew. The letter was already some days old, having been written before the battle of Eylau:

"Since our grand success at Austerlitz, my dear prince, I, as you know, have been inseparable from the staff of the generals in command. Certainly I have acquired quite a taste for war, and it is a lucky thing that I have! What I have seen these three months is beyond belief.

"I begin at the beginning. The 'enemy of the human race,' has, as you know, turned on the Prussians. The Prussians are our faithful friends and have deceived us no more than three times in three years. So we take up the cause. But, as it turns out, the 'enemy of the human race' pays no heed to our eloquent defence; and in his horrid rude way he

381

flies at the Prussians, and without giving them time to finish their review even, he gives them a sound thrashing and makes himself at home in the palace of Potsdam.

"'My greatest wish,' writes the King of Prussia to Napoleon, 'is that your majesty should be received and treated to your entire satisfaction in my palace, and I have hastened to take every step in my power under the circumstances to secure that end. I only hope I have succeeded.' The Prussian generals are on their politest behaviour to the French, and lay down their arms at the first word.

"The colonel of the garrison of Glogau, with ten thousand men under his command, asks the King of Prussia what he is to do if he is called upon to surrender!—this is a fact.

"The long and the short of the matter is that after trying to impress the foe by our military attitude we are fairly in for war, and what is more, war on our own frontier, for and with the King of Prussia. Everything is complete, only one thing is wanting: a commander-in-chief. As it is now thought that our success at Austerlitz might have been more decisive if the general had been a little older, our octogenarians are to have a chance, and between Prosorofsky and Kamensky, the choice is in favour of the second. So the general comes in a kibitka, in imitation of Souvorow, and is hailed with acclamations of delight and triumph.

"On the 4th behold the first courier from St. Petersburg. The mailbags are taken straight to the marshal, who likes to do everything himself. I am sent for to help sort the letters and set aside those addressed to headquarters. The marshal sits looking on and waiting for any addressed to him. We hunt them all through—not one. The marshal waxes impatient and sets to work himself; he finds letters from the czar addressed to Count T., to Prince V., and others. He goes into one of his livid rages. Fire and flame are flung right and left; he seizes the letters, tears open and reads those written by the czar to other people: 'So this is the way I am treated! No confidence! Other people are set to watch me! Leave the room!' And he writes the famous order of the day to General Bennigsen: 'I am hurt, and I cannot ride, consequently I cannot command the army. You have taken your defeated division to Poultousk where it lies exposed without wood or forage; this must be remedied according to your report to Count Bouxhoevden. You must retire towards our frontier; proceed to do so this day.'

"'From constantly riding about,' he wrote to the czar, 'I

have been galled by the saddle and this prevents my sitting on horseback and taking the command of so important an army. I have placed the command in the hands of Count Bouxhoevden, the senior general; advising him, if he is short of bread, to retire into Prussia, for we have not more than enough for one day's rations, and some regiments have none at all, as reported by the generals in command, Ostermann and Sedmoretzki; the peasants, too, have none. I shall remain in hospital at Ostrolenko till I am well. In laying before your majesty this report up to date I have the honour of adding that if the army remains in camp here another fortnight there will not be a single man capable of fighting in the spring.

"'Allow me as an old man to retire to the country with the deepest regret at finding myself unable to carry out the great and glorious duties which were required of me. I shall await your majesty's gracious permission in hospital here, so as not to take up the part of letter-writer instead of that of commander. My retirement will make no more difference than that of a blind man might. There are hundreds like me to be found in Russia.'

"So the marshal is angry with the emperor and punishes us! Highly logical.

"Thus ends the first act. In the following scenes the interest, and the absurdity, increase in due proportion. When the marshal is fairly gone we find that we are face to face with the foe and must fight, whether or no. Bouxhoevden is the commander by seniority, but Bennigsen does not see it—all the more because he and his division are within sight of the enemy and he is dying to fight on his own account '*auf eigene Hand*' as the Germans say. So he fights. This is the battle of Poultousk which we are told was a great victory, but in my opinion was nothing of the kind. We civilians, as you know, have a bad habit of making up our minds as to whether a battle is lost or won. The side that retires after the fight, has been beaten we say; and that being so, we lost the battle of Poultousk. After fighting we retire; but we send off a courier to St. Petersburg with a report of a victory, and meanwhile the general does not make way for Bouxhoevden, hoping, as the reward of his success (!) to get his appointment from St. Petersburg as commander-in-chief.

"During this interregnum we perform a remarkably interesting and original series of manœuvres. Our object, in point of fact, is neither to avoid nor to attack the enemy—as it should be— but simply and solely to avoid General Bouxhoevden, who, by right of seniority, would give us his orders. Nay, we put so much energy into this endeavour, that having crossed a river which is not fordable we burn the bridge to cut off the enemy —not Bonaparte, but Bouxhoevden. And General Bouxhoevden was within an ace of being attacked and beaten by a superior French force in consequence of one of our clever manœuvres for escaping from him. Bouxhoevden follows us; we sneak off. No sooner does he cross to our side of the river than we cross back again. At last the enemy—Bouxhoevden—catches us up and turns upon us. The two generals get angry; nay, Bouxhoevden even sends a challenge, and Bennigsen has an epileptic fit. However, at the most critical moment the courier who carried the news of our victory to St. Petersburg, returns with our appointment as general-in-chief, and Bouxhoevden, foe No. 1, being disposed of, we can turn our attention to foe No. 2— Napoleon. But at this juncture behold a third rises up before us—this is the orthodox army clamouring for bread, for meat, for *soukharyi*,[1] for hay—and what not! the stores are empty and the roads impassable.

"The 'orthodox' take to pillage, and in a way of which the last campaign can give you not the faintest notion. Half the regiments form themselves into companies of freebooters, devastating the country and putting everything to fire and sword. The inhabitants are utterly and totally ruined, the hospitals overflow with sick, and famine stalks abroad. Twice have the marauders attacked us at headquarters, and the commander-in-chief has been obliged to get a battalion to drive them off. In one of these raids my empty portmanteau and my dressing-gown were stolen. The czar has just issued a document authorising us to shoot the freebooters, but I am very much afraid that that would mean setting one half of the army to shoot the other half."

Prince Andrew had read without much attention at first, but by degrees he was carried away by his interest in the subject, while he took care not to overrate the importance of information coming through Bilibine; as he read the last sentence he crumpled up the letter and tossed it aside, vexed with himself to find that this life, now so remote from him, could occasion him any emotion. He shut his eyes and passed his hand across his forehead as if to efface the impression, listening to what was going on in the child's room. He fancied he heard

[1] *Soukharyi* is a coarse kind of biscuit.

a strange sound. Fearing lest the child might have become worse while he was reading the letter, he went in on tiptoe. As he entered he fancied from the expression of the old nurse's face that she was hiding something, and that his sister had left the room.

"My dear old boy!' said his sister, coming up behind him.

As often happens after a sleepless night or acute anxiety, a dumb terror seized him; he thought her words conveyed a desperate appeal—the announcement that his child was dead which indeed seemed only too probable.

"It is all over," he thought to himself, and a cold sweat broke out on his forehead. He went up to the cradle, fully convinced that he should find it empty and that the old woman was hiding the dead child; he drew aside the curtain, but his eyes were dim with alarm and for a moment he could distinguish nothing. Then he saw the little boy lying with rosy cheeks across the crib, with his head lower than the pillow and sucking in his dreams. He was breathing softly and regularly.

Comforted and happy Prince Andrew bent down and put his lips to the baby's face, as he had seen his sister do, to feel how hot he was. He felt the moisture of the little forehead and damp, downy head, and understood that, not only was he not dead, but that this favourable turn meant rapid recovery. He longed to snatch up the little creature and clasp it to his breast; he dared not, but his eyes rested fondly on the little head, the tiny hands, and the small limbs under the coverlet. Then he heard a gown rustle, and a shadow stood by his. It was Princess Maria, who had raised the curtain and let it fall behind her. Her brother, while listening to his baby's breathing, did not turn round, but he put out his hand and she grasped it fervently.

"He is in a perspiration. . . ."

"I was going to tell you. . . ." she replied.

The child turned in his sleep, smiled and rubbed his face against the pillow.

Prince Andrew looked up at his sister, whose bright eyes sparkled with tears in the shadow of the curtain. She drew her brother to her across the cradle to kiss him, having accidentally caught the edge of the curtain they were afraid of disturbing the baby, and stood so for a minute or two in the dim light—those three apart from all the world besides. Prince Andrew was the first to move, and as he felt his way through the folds of the curtain he said with a sigh: "Yes, this is all I have left!"

CHAPTER XCV

PETER carried with him from St. Petersburg full instructions, written out by his new brothers, for his guidance in the different projects he was meditating for the benefit of his serfs. When he reached Kiew he sent for the stewards of all his estates in that government, and informed them of his wishes. He explained to them that he was about to take steps immediately to emancipate the peasants from serfdom; meanwhile they must do their best to second him, and not overwork them. Women and children were to be exempt from hard labour; no punishments were to be inflicted, only reprimands; and on every estate, hospitals, schools, and almshouses were to be erected. Some of the stewards—and some could hardly read—listened in horror, lending a wholly personal meaning to his words: He was dissatisfied with their management they supposed, and knew that they robbed him. Others, after the first shock of alarm, were amused by their master's embarrassment and hesitation, and by notions to them so new and strange. The third group listened as a matter of duty and without any dissatisfaction. The fourth set, consisting of the sharpest wits among them, and at their head the chief steward, perceived at once the line they should take to gain their own ends. Indeed, Peter's philanthropic schemes met with their hearty concurrence: "But first," said they, "the state of the land itself must be looked into, seeing what a mess your affairs are in."

In spite of the immense fortune left by Count Bésoukhow, Peter had in fact been richer with the allowance of 10,000 roubles made to him by his father than with the 500,000 a year he was supposed to have inherited. His expenses were pretty much as follows: 80,000 roubles was the annual interest due to the Land-Mortgage Bank of Russia; 30,000 for the maintenance of the country-house close to Moscow, of the house in Moscow and the pension to the three princesses; 15,000 in other pensions and as much in charities; 150,000 to his wife; 70,000 in interest on debts; about 10,000 had been laid out during the last two years in building a church; and the 100,000 left went, he knew not how, but so effectually that he had been obliged to borrow; without counting the cost of fires, short crops, and necessary rebuilding of factories and houses. So now, at the very outset, Peter was forced to devote himself to inquiring into his own affairs, and for this he had neither the taste nor the capacity.

However, he gave some hours daily to the task; still, matters seemed no forwarder. He felt that things were going on in the old way, and that his efforts had not the slightest influence on their steady flow in the old grooves. His chief steward, on his part, represented everything in the gloomiest light; insisting on the necessity for paying off his debts and undertaking fresh enterprises with forced labour, which Peter resisted, and gave orders that steps were to be taken as soon as possible for the emancipation of his serfs; and, as it was impossible to do this till the debts were cancelled, the whole thing was put off till the Greek calends. The stewards had no hesitation in telling him so plainly, and proposed to raise the money by selling some timber forests in the government of Kostroma, some valuable lands irrigated by a river, and an estate in the Crimea. But all this business was complicated and entailed such elaborate proceedings—paying off of mortgages, taking legal possession, getting authority to sell, etc., that Peter lost himself in the labyrinth and confined himself to saying: "yes, yes—let it be done."

He was devoid of that practical spirit which makes work easy, and he did not like it: he did his best to seem to take an interest in it in the steward's presence, and the man pretended that everything was for his master's ultimate benefit, though entailing a great deal of trouble to himself.

Peter found a few acquaintances at Kiew, and strangers rushed forward to offer hospitality to the millionaire who was the largest landowner in the government. The temptations which consequently offered themselves on all sides were too great to be resisted. Days, weeks, months slipped by in the same round of breakfasts, dinners and balls as he had known during his stay in St. Petersburg; and, instead of living the new life of which he had dreamed, he lived the old one, only amid new scenery.

He could not persuade himself that, of the three obligations considered binding on Freemasons, he was fulfilling that which could conduce to make him an example of moral purity; or, that of the seven virtues, pure living and the love of death found any echo in his soul. He comforted himself with the belief that he was fulfilling the other half of his mission: the regeneration of humanity; and that he was possessed of other virtues: the love of his neighbour, and liberality.

387

In the spring of 1807 he made up his mind to return to St. Petersburg, visiting his estates on the way, so as to know from personal inspection how far his scheme was prospering, and in what way the human beings entrusted to him by God, and whom he intended to load with benefits, were now living.

The chief steward—in whose eyes the young count's projects were purely extravagant, and as much to his own disadvantage as to that of his master and the peasants themselves—condescended to his whims. While he represented that emancipation was an impossibility, he began building on a large scale on all the estates—hospitals, asylums, and schools. He had not the pompous receptions organised for him on every estate, feeling very sure that would displease his master; but processions, patriarchal and semi-religious in character, with bread and salt, and the Holy Images borne at their head, the very things to act on Peter's imagination and to keep up his illusions.

The southern spring and the journey home by himself, in a comfortable carriage of Vienna build, caused him real enjoyment. These estates, which he had never before seen, were each more beautiful than the last. The peasants looked happy and prosperous, and grateful for his beneficence. The receptions that had been everywhere prepared for him embarrassed him a little, to be sure, but in his heart he was deeply touched by them. In one of the villages a deputation offered him, with the bread and salt, images of St. Peter and St. Paul, and begged his permission to add a chapel to the church at the cost of the commune in honour of his patron saint, St. Peter. In another, the women, with their babies in their arms, came to thank him for having delivered them from hard labour. In a third, the priest, with a cross in his hand, presented to him the young children to whom, thanks to their lord's generosity, he was giving elementary instruction. Wherever he went he saw infirmaries, almshouses, and schools being built, or finished, or ready to open, according to the plans he had laid down. Wherever he looked through the stewards' accounts he found that forced labour had been reduced by half, and his peasants, in their loose blue coats, came to thank him for the remission. But unfortunately Peter did not know that the village where bread and salt had been offered with the petition to be allowed to build a chapel, was a very flourishing parish, that the chapel had in fact been long since begun by the rich people in the neighbourhood, and that it was they who had come to meet him while nine-tenths of the peasants were destitute. He did not know that, in consequence of his order that the women with babies at the breast were not to be sent out to forced labour of any kind, very much harder work in their own fields fell to their lot. He did not know that the priest who had met him, cross in hand, weighed cruelly on the poor people, extorting heavy tithes in kind, and that the pupils he brought in his train were placed with him very unwillingly, and often ransomed back by their parents at a heavy price. He did not know that these new stone buildings, erected by his plans, were the work of his peasants whose forced labour they greatly increased, that the "corvée," in short, was only reduced on paper. Nor could he know that when his head steward entered the peasants' money payments as diminished by a third, that third was made up by an increase in forced toil.

So Peter, delighted with the results of his tour of inspection, felt his heart warm with philanthropic ardour, and wrote enthusiastic letters to his brother instructor, as he chose to call the Worshipful Master.

"How easy it is to be good; how little effort it costs, and how little we think about it," thought Peter.

The gratitude with which he was met made him happy, but that very gratitude also made him feel ashamed to think how much more good he might have done. The head steward, an inferior but cunning man, had soon taken the measure of the intelligent but simple-minded young count, and fooled him in every way. He took advantage of the demonstrations which he himself had organised, to find fresh arguments against emancipation, and to persuade his master that the peasants were perfectly happy. Peter sincerely believed that he was right; he could not fancy folks better content, and quite pitied their fate if they should be set free; but still his sense of justice prompted him not to give up his project at any cost.

The steward promised to do his utmost to carry out the count's wishes, being fully convinced that his master would never thoroughly inquire into his proceedings to assure himself that he had done his best to dispose of so much of the estates and timber as would release the remainder from debt; that he would never ask any questions, or discover that the buildings raised for benevolent ends would remain useless, and that the serfs would still be made to pay in money and in labour the same taxes as on every other great property—that is to say the uttermost farthing that human effort could produce.

CHAPTER XCVI

On his way home from the south, Peter, in the happiest possible frame of mind, carried out his intention of going to see his friend, Bolkonsky; they had not met for two years. Bogoutcharovo lay in the midst of a plain varied by forests and fields, some of the timber having been felled, and the country was not particularly picturesque. The house and adjoining premises were at one end of a village of which the *isbas*[1] stood in a row on each side of the high-road. In front of it was a pond so recently dug and filled with water that the grass had not yet had time to grow green on the banks; a young plantation, with a few tall fir trees rising above it, screened the residence. The outbuildings consisted of a granary, stables, and a bath-house; the house which was a large one with two wings, was built of stone; the semicircular façade was as yet unfinished; a garden was laid out round it. The fencing and gates were new and well made; under a shed stood two fire-engines, and a water-tub painted green. The roads, laid out in straight lines, were carried over bridges with handsome balustrades. Everything bore the stamp of care and good order.

To the question: "Where is the prince?" the servants replied by pointing to a small new house on the edge of the pond. Prince Andrew's old body-servant, Antony, helped Peter out of his travelling-carriage and showed him into a waiting-room recently redecorated. He was struck by the simplicity of this dwelling, which was in marked contrast to the brilliant conditions of existence under which he had last met his friend. He hastily went forward into the next room which smelt of pine-wood and was not even whitewashed yet. Antony hurried past him and went on tiptoe to knock at a door opposite.

"What is it?" asked a harsh, cross voice.

"A visitor," said Antony.

"Beg him to wait." Then there was a noise of a chair being pushed back. Peter went quickly forward and on the threshold ran up against Prince Andrew. He raised his spectacles to embrace him and looked at him closely.

"This is a surprise—I am delighted!" said the prince; but Peter said nothing; he could not take his eyes off his friend, he was so much struck by the change in his appearance. In

[1] Russian peasants' cottages.

spite of the warmth of his greeting, the smile on his lips and his effort to put some brightness into his gaze, his eyes were dim and lightless. He had grown thin, pale, and old; everything in his appearance, from the expression of his glance to the deep lines on his forehead, bore witness to his preoccupation by one single thought. This unwonted look in the prince's face troubled Peter beyond words.

As is always the case after a long separation, the conversation consisted of fragmentary and miscellaneous questions and answers, and hardly touched on those more interesting subjects which they felt would demand longer discussion. By degrees it became more steady, and incoherent sentences gave way to long stories of the past and plans for the future. Peter's journey was spoken of, his undertakings, and the war; and Prince Andrew's expression grew gloomier and more depressed as he listened to Peter, who talked with feverish eagerness of his past and of his future. It really seemed that the prince could not take any interest in all this even if he wished it, and Peter began to feel that it was in bad taste to give vent in his presence to all the dreams of happiness and benevolence which he allowed his fancy to cherish. He dared not, for fear of being laughed at, dilate on the new masonic theories that his tour had revived in all their force; at the same time he was dying to prove to his friend that he was no longer the same man that he had known in St. Petersburg, but another Peter, better, and regenerate.

"I cannot tell you all that I have gone through during the last few months; I hardly know myself."

"Yes, we have changed a great deal, in many things," said Prince Andrew.

"And you? What are your plans for the future?"

"My plans?" he retorted ironically. "My plans?" he repeated, as if the question astonished him. "You see—I am building; I expect to live here altogether next year."

"Not that—I meant to ask . . ." Peter began.

"But what is the use of talking about me?" interrupted the prince. "Tell me about your journey. What did you see? What did you do on your different estates?"

Peter began his story, passing as lightly as he could over his own share in the improvements in the management of his property. The prince now and then threw in a finishing touch to Peter's description, and laughed at him for his enthusiasm over various old and time-worn things which to him had been novelties. At length Peter, feeling ill at ease, let the conversation drop altogether.

"Look here, my dear fellow," said Prince Andrew, evidently sharing his feeling. "I am here only on a flying visit as you see; I came to see how things were going on, and I am going back to Lissy-Gory this evening. Come with me and I will introduce you to my sister. By the way, do you not know her already?" he added, for the sake of saying something to an old friend from whom he felt that he had drifted apart. "We will set out after dinner—now, come and see my new house."

They went out, talking only of politics and subjects of general interest, like mere acquaintances. Prince Andrew showed no care for anything beyond doing the honours of his new building; and even then, as they made their way among the scaffolding, he stopped suddenly in the midst of his explanations and said shortly: "Come to dinner—this is not particularly interesting." During the dinner—the conversation turned on Bésoukhow's marriage.

"I was very much surprised to hear of it," said his friend. Peter coloured and hesitated; then he said hastily:

"I will tell you some day how it all came about. But it is at an end now, and for ever."

"For ever? There is no for ever."

"But you must have heard how the matter ended. You heard of the duel?"

"Yes, I know you had to submit to that too!"

"Well, I can thank God for one thing, at any rate, and that is that I did not kill that man," said Peter.

"Why? There is no harm, there is even much good in killing a mad dog."

"Yes, but to kill a man! That is not good, it is unjust."

"Why unjust? It is not given to us to know what is just or unjust. Humanity has always been, and will always be deceived on that point."

"Injustice lies in any wrong we may do our fellow-creatures," said Peter, pleased to see his friend's interest in the conversation reviving, and to think that he would presently discover what had so completely changed his demeanour towards him.

"And who has told you what is wrong to your fellow-creatures?"

"Why," said Peter, "do we not know of ourselves what is wrong?"

"Yes, we know it; but what would be wrong in one might

not be wrong in another," said Prince Andrew eagerly. "I know of only two real evils: remorse and sickness; and there is no good but in the absence of these evils: live for yourself and avoid those, is all my love of life."

"And love of your neighbour, and self-sacrifice?" cried Peter. "No, I cannot agree with you! To live avoiding evil that we may not have to repent is not enough; I have lived so, and my existence was wasted and useless; it is only now that I really live—now that I try to live for others, that I understand the happiness of it. No, I cannot agree with you —and you yourself, you do not believe what you say."

Prince Andrew, gazing at him with a satirical smile, sat listening.

"You will make acquaintance with my sister, Princess Maria, and you and she will suit each other to perfection, I am sure. After all, perhaps you are right, for yourself; and each man must live his own life. You talk of having wasted your existence in living thus, and of having found happiness only in living for others; well, with me it is just the reverse; I lived for glory, and what is glory if it is not love of one's neighbour too; a wish to serve him and to deserve his applause? So I have lived for others; still my existence is wasted, gone, irrevocably gone. But since I have lived for myself I have been quieter."

"But how is it possible to live for oneself?" exclaimed Peter warmly. "Besides, your boy, your sister, your father . . .?"

"They are part of myself, they are not other people—and your neighbour means other people; your neighbour, as you and Princess Maria say—the source of all evil and mischief! Your neighbour, you know, means your Kiew peasants whom you dream of loading with benefits."

"But you are not in earnest!" exclaimed Peter, much excited by this invective. "What harm, what injustice can there be in my wish—still so far from fulfilment—to do them good? What is wrong in trying to teach these poor creatures, these peasants—who are our brothers after all, and who are born and die without ever knowing anything of God or of truth, beyond the mere external services of religion, and prayers devoid of meaning to them? What harm can there be in teaching them to believe in a future life, where they will have the consolation of finding compensation and reward? What wrong, what harm is there in keeping them from dying without advice or help, when it is so easy to give them material comforts: a hospital, a doctor, a refuge. Is it not a distinct and substantial benefit to give a labouring man, a woman with children, worn day and night with anxiety, a few minutes' rest? I have done this—on a very small scale to be sure, still I have done it, and you want to persuade me that I have done wrong, and that you do not agree with me. However, I have myself acquired another conviction which is that the good we do is the only joy of life."

"Yes; and if you put the matter in that way it is quite another thing," said Prince Andrew. "I build a house and plant a garden while you establish hospitals; two different modes of pastime. But we may leave it to Him who knows all things to decide the balance of good and evil. You wish to carry on the discussion I see. Well, come out then. . . ."

And they went out on the balcony at the top of the flight of steps, which formed a sort of terrace.

"You talk of schools, and teaching," the prince went on, pointing to a peasant who raised his hat as he went by. "That is to say you want to drag that man out of his mire, to give him moral needs, when, in my opinion, animal joys are the only joys within his reach—and you would deprive him of them! I envy him as he is, and you want to give him the conscious *I* without giving him the means of satisfaction which I have at my command? You want to lighten his toil when, in my opinion, bodily labour is as indispensable to him as intellectual labour is to us? You cannot keep yourself from thought and reflection; I, for my part, go to bed at three in the morning, and cannot sleep then: thoughts crowd upon me, I turn and toss, and think and think again; it is as much a necessity of my existence as digging and mowing are of his! otherwise he would only go to the tavern and drink, and make himself ill. A week of his toil would kill me, while he would get fat if he spent a week in physical idleness like mine. What else was there? To be sure, hospitals and doctors! Well, he has a fit of apoplexy and he dies. You would bleed him and cure him; and he lives on, helpless for ten years, a burden on his family. It would have been much easier for him if you had let him die, for there are always plenty born to take his place. Of course it would be different if you thought of him as an able-bodied worker the less; that, I own, is my way of viewing the matter; but you cure him out of brotherly love, and he does not want it. Not to speak of the delusion that makes you believe that medicine ever cured anyone! It is great at killing, on the contrary!" he added, with virulence.

It was evident from Prince Andrew's clear and positive way

"Your neighbour means your Kiew peasants whom you dream of loading with benefits"

of expressing his views, that he had thought them over more than once; he spoke readily and eagerly, like a man who has long been debarred from such a satisfaction; his eye brightened by degrees as his opinions became more and more gloomy.

"But that is horrible, quite horrible!" said Peter. "I cannot conceive how you can bear to live thinking as you do. I myself, I own, have had such fits of despair, at Moscow and abroad; but then I cease to live; I go down so low—so low that everything is loathsome to me, including myself. . . . I do not eat, I do not wash. . . ."

"But why not wash? That's not clean! No, we must do all we can on the contrary to make life as pleasant as possible. It is no fault of mine that I live at all, and I try to vegetate till I die—without interfering with other people."

"But what makes you think such things? Do you really wish and purpose to do nothing, to undertake nothing?"

"You talk as if life had really left you in peace! I should have liked nothing better than to do nothing; but the nobility in the neighbourhood did me the honour to elect me their marshal, and I had no small difficulty in getting out of it. They failed to see that I am quite devoid of that fidgety, good-natured dullness that they look for and would have liked to find in me. Then I am busy fitting up a nook here where I may live in quiet, when the militia are called out and I am bound to get into harness again, whether I will or no."

"Why do you not join again?"

"What! After Austerlitz?" said Prince Andrew gloomily. "No. I have vowed never to go on active service again; and I will keep my vow, even if Napoleon were to come and to occupy the government of Smolensk. He might threaten Lissy-Gory itself, and I would not take up arms. As regards the militia, as my father is now commander-in-chief of the third district I had no way of avoiding active service but by taking work under him."

"Well then, you see you are in service."

"Oh! yes, I am in service."

"But why?"

"Why? That is very plain: My father is one of the most extraordinary men of the day. He is growing old, and without being precisely hard he has a too restless temper. The long habit of unlimited power makes him really terrible, particularly now that he holds his authority from the czar himself. Only a fortnight ago, if I had been two hours later he would have hung a miserable clerk at Youknow. No one but myself has any influence over him, so I am obliged to take service to prevent his doing things which by and by would leave him a prey to remorse."

"You see!"

"Yes, but it is not what you think. It was not that I felt, or ever could feel kindly to the rascally clerk who had been robbing the militia-men of their boots; in fact, I should have been delighted to see him swing. It was for my father that I felt, and my father and myself are one and the same thing."

Prince Andrew's eyes sparkled with a feverish light as he tried to make Peter understand that he never took any interest in doing good to his fellow-men: "You want to set your peasants free? It is a good action; but, take my word for it, it will be neither to your advantage—for I suppose you never either flogged or exiled a soul—nor to that of your serfs, who would be none the worse for being flogged and sent to Siberia, for out there their scars have time to heal and they soon begin to live the same animal round of life as they have led before and are every whit as happy. The men whom it really would benefit are those whose moral nature is depraved by their abuse of power to inflict punishments, and who, under the pangs of remorse, end by stifling their conscience to harden their hearts. You, perhaps, have never seen, as I have, men by nature sound but brought up in the traditions of unlimited power, who, in the course of years, have become irascible, cruel, incapable of self-control, and thus, day by day, add to the sum of their own wrongdoing. Those are the men I pity; those are the men to whose serfs freedom would be a boon. It is man's dignity that I lament over, his peace of conscience and purity of impulse—but as to the backs and heads of the others, they will still be backs and heads to be flogged or shaved!"

From Prince Andrew's vehemence Peter could not but suspect that these views were suggested to him by his experience of his father.

"No—a thousand times no, I shall never agree with you."

BEFORE TILSIT

CHAPTER XCVII

THEY set out for Lissy-Gory in the evening. Prince Andrew occasionally broke the silence with a few words which bore witness to the perfect amiability of his temper; but it was in vain that he pointed out his fields to Peter, and enlarged on the great agricultural improvements that he was introducing— Peter was lost in thought, and only replied in monosyllables. He told himself that his friend was most unhappy; that he was wrong, that he did not know the true light; that it was his own duty to help him, to enlighten him, and to elevate his mind. But he felt, too, that, at his very first word, Prince Andrew would upset all his theories, and he was afraid to begin; afraid above all of exposing the sacred ark of his beliefs to the prince's irony.

"What makes you think so?" he suddenly asked, putting down his head like a bull about to thrust at his opponent. "You have no right to think so."

"To think what?" said Prince Andrew, startled.

"To think so of life, and of man's destiny. I had the same ideas; and do you know what saved me? Freemasonry. Do not smile; it is not, as I thought and believed, a religious sect confined to empty ceremonial; it is the sole expression of all that is best, all that is eternal in the human race," and he explained to him that Freemasonry, as he understood it, was the doctrine of Christianity freed from the encumbrances of social and religious dogma; the simple, practical exercise of equality, fraternity, and charity.

"Our holy association is the only one which really understands the true aim and end of life—all else is mere mirage; outside of it all is falsehood and iniquity—so much so, that outside of it a good and intelligent man has no alternative but to vegetate as you do, with no higher care than to avoid doing ill to his neighbour. But when once you accept our fundamental principles, if you join our Order, if you give yourself up to it, and allow yourself to be guided, you will feel at once—as I felt—that you are a link of the invisible and eternal chain of which one end is hidden in the heavens."

Prince Andrew sat looking fixedly before him, and listening without saying a syllable, excepting to ask for the repetition, now and then, of something he had lost in the noise of the carriage-wheels. The light in his eyes, and even his silence, made Peter hope that his words were not in vain, and would not be met with mockery. In this way they presently reached a river that had overflowed, and which had to be crossed in a ferry-barge; they got out while the carriage and horses were taken across. Prince Andrew, leaning against a balustrade, gazed in silence at the rolling mass of water as it sparkled in the setting sun.

"Well," said Peter, "what do you think of it all? Why do you not speak?"

"What do I think? Well, I am listening to you. That is all very well! You say to me: 'Join our Order, and we will teach you the aim and end of life, the destiny of man, and the laws that govern the world.' But, after all, who are you? Men. How then does it come to pass that you know everything, and that I do not see as you see? In your eyes virtue and truth ought to reign on earth; but I, I do not see them!"

"Do you believe in a future life?" asked Peter, abruptly.

"In a future life?" murmured Prince Andrew. Peter inferred a negation from his friend's answer, and having long known him to be an atheist, he went on:

"You say that you cannot see the reign of virtue and truth on earth? I do not see it either; and it is impossible to see it if you accept this life as the end of all things. On this earth there is no truth, no virtue; all is a lie; but in the universal scheme of creation it is truth that rules. We are of course the children of this world, but in eternity we are the children of the Universe. I cannot help feeling that I am an integral atom in this immense and harmonious whole. In the numberless myriads of beings who are the manifestations of the Divinity— or, if you prefer it, of that supreme force—I feel that I am a link, that I mark a degree in the ascending scale. Seeing, as I do, that this scale, beginning at the plant, rises till it comes to me, why should I suppose that it stops at me, and rises no higher? Just as nothing in this world can ever be lost or destroyed, so can I never be lost in nothingness! I know what I have been, and shall become! I know that outside and beyond me spirits dwell, and that Truth inhabits that realm!"

"Yes, that is Herder's doctrine," said Prince Andrew. "But that cannot convince me. Life and death—they indeed are convincing! When we see a creature that we love, that is bound up with our life, to whom we have done wrongs that we hoped to atone for . . ." and his voice was unsteady . . .

"when that being suddenly is a victim to pain, struggles with suffering, and ceases to breathe—we wonder why! It is impossible that there should be no reply to that query, and I believe that there is one! That is what can convince a man, and it convinced me."

"But," said Peter, "is not that precisely what I said?"

"No. What I mean to say is that no arguments would lead me to believe in the certainty of a future life; but that when we go through life, a pair hand in hand, and suddenly our companion vanishes—drops into the void—we stand on the edge of the gulf, and look in . . . then conviction comes upon us! And I have looked in."

"Well, then! You know that there is something else and Some One; that is to say another life and God!"

Prince Andrew made no reply. The carriage and horses had long since crossed the river, the sun was half set, and the evening chill was frosting the pools that lay at the foot of the slopes leading down to the river, while Peter and Andrew, to the great astonishment of the servants, coachmen, and passers-by, were still arguing on the ferry-steps: "If there is a God, there must be a future life; consequently truth and virtue must exist; man's chief happiness must lie in his efforts to reach them. We must live, love, and believe that we do not exist only for the present on this speck of earth, but that we have lived, and shall live for ever in that infinitude"—and Peter pointed to the sky.

Prince Andrew listened, still leaning against the railing, and his eye lingered on the darkening waters, lighted only by a purple gleam from the dying sunset. Peter said no more. All was still, not a sound to be heard but a soft lapping against the keel of the boat which lay moored, a murmur that seemed to say, "It is true—believe!"

Bolkonsky sighed; he turned with a tender and softened gaze to look at Peter's excited and enthusiastic face; while Peter, us usual, felt shy before the superiority he recognised in his friend.

"Ah! if only that were so!" said Prince Andrew. "But let us be going."

As they left the landing stage he glanced once more at the sky that Peter had pointed to, and, for the first time since Austerlitz, he saw it again, deep and restful—the heaven of his dreams, as he had seen it bending over him on the field of battle. A feeling that had long been downcast, the better part of himself, woke up in the depths of his soul: a revival of his youth, of his craving for happiness. He drifted back into the routine of life, and this feeling by degrees grew weaker and paler; still, ever after this conversation, though his life remained unchanged, he was conscious at the bottom of his heart of the living germ of a quite different moral existence.

CHAPTER XCVIII

It was already dark when they reached the principal entrance of the house at Lissy-Gory, and Prince Andrew drew Peter's attention, with a smile, to the commotion produced by their appearance, at a low side door. A little old woman, bending under the weight of a sack, and a short, square man, with long hair, dressed in black, fled at their approach; two other women hurried after them, and all four, after turning round to look at the carriage in evident alarm, disappeared up a back staircase.

"Those are the 'Men of God' that Maria allows to come here," said Prince Andrew. "They took me for my father, who always has them turned out, while she makes them welcome. It is the only point on which she dares to disobey him."

"And what are the 'Men of God'?" asked Peter.

But there was no time to explain; the servants came out to meet them; the prince inquired of them as to his father's return—he was expected at any moment from the neighbouring town.

Leaving Peter in his own room, which was always ready for him, Prince Andrew went to see his boy, and then came back to introduce Peter to his sister:

"I have not seen her myself yet; she is hidden away with the 'Men of God'; we shall take them by surprise, and she will be very much abashed no doubt; but you will see them—a strange sight, I can tell you."

"What are they?" asked Peter.

"Wait, and you will see."

Princess Maria was greatly discomposed, and blushed up to the eyes as she saw them come into her little room, where the gilt images gleamed in the light of the votive lamps. By her side, on the sofa, sat a lad in the habit of a lay friar, with a long nose and long hair; and close beside her, in a deep arm-chair, was a wrinkled and furrowed old woman whose face was expressive of the utmost humility and gentleness.

"Andrew! Why did you not send for me?" said his sister reproachfully, and standing in front of her pilgrims like a hen trying to hide her chickens. "But I am delighted to see you," she added to Peter, who kissed her hand. She had known him as a child; his devotion to Andrew, his recent misfortunes, but above all his kind, honest face prejudiced her in his favour. She looked at him with her deep sweet eyes as if to say: "I like you very much; only I implore you not to laugh at my people."

When the first civilities were over she begged him to be seated.

"Ah! Here is Ivanouchka," said Prince Andrew, with a smile at the young neophyte.

"Andrew!" murmured the princess beseechingly.

"He is a girl you must know," Prince Andrew went on.

"Andrew, for pity's sake! . . ."

It was evident that Maria's vain entreaties and Andrew's teasing jests about the pilgrims were a matter of course between them.

"But my dear child, you ought to be grateful to me on the contrary, for giving Peter some explanation of your familiarity with the young man."

"Indeed!" said Peter, with some curiosity, but with no suspicion of laughter, which finished his conquest of Maria's good graces.

Her uneasiness on behalf of her flock was quite superfluous; they themselves were not in the least embarrassed. The little old woman, after turning her cup upside down on her saucer by the side of the mumbled remains of her lump of sugar, sat quite still with downcast eyes, stealing sly glances to right and left waiting to be offered a second cup of tea. Ivanouchka was sipping his out of the saucer, and looking from under his brows at the two gentlemen, with a glance of womanish cunning.

"And where have you been? To Kiew?" asked Prince Andrew.

"I have been there, father," said the old woman. "At Kiew I was esteemed worthy to receive the blessed and heavenly communion with the saints; I have just come from Koliasine. A great and gracious dispensation has been vouchsafed there."

"And Ivanouchka is with you?"

"No; I am alone," said Ivanouchka, trying to make his

401

voice sound deep. "We only met Pélaguéïouchka at You-know . . ." But the old woman could not restrain her anxiety to tell her story and she broke in:

"Yes, father. Grace was revealed at Koliasine!"

"What happened? Some more relics found?" asked Prince Andrew.

"Come, come, Andrew. Do not tell him anything, Pélaguéïouchka."

"But why not tell him, good little mother? I love him, he is a good man, one of the elect of God; he is my benefactor. I have not forgotten that he gave me ten roubles. Well, when I was at Kiew, Kirioucha said to me—you know Kirioucha, the innocent,[1] a real 'Man of God' he is, and goes barefoot all the winter through—Kirioucha said to me: 'Why are you wandering about in unknown places? Go to Koliasine; a miraculous image of our Holy Mother Mary is to be seen there.' So I said good-bye to the saints and I went there. When I got there," the old woman went on in a monotone, "the saints I met there said to me: 'A great grace is vouchsafed to us. Holy oil trickles from the cheek of our Holy Mother the Virgin . . .'"

"That will do, that will do," said Princess Maria colouring; "you can tell us the rest another time."

"Excuse me," said Peter; "let me ask her one question: Did you see it with your own eyes?"

"Certainly, father, to be sure I did. I was found worthy of such mercy. The Virgin's face was bright with heavenly glory, and the oil trickled and dropped from her cheek."

"But it is a trick!" exclaimed Peter who had heard her attentively.

"Oh! father, what are you saying!" exclaimed the old woman, turning to Maria as if appealing to her for help.

"That is how they deceive the people!" he went on.

"Merciful Lord!" cried the old pilgrim, crossing herself. "Oh, do not say that again, father! I knew a general who was a disbeliever, and who used to say: 'The monks are cheats.' Yes, he did, and he went blind. Well, and then he dreamed that he saw the Holy Virgin of Petchersk, who said to him: 'Believe in me and you shall be healed.' And then he begged and prayed to be taken to her. I am telling you the gospel truth, for I saw him when they led him in blind and he fell on his knees before her and said: 'Heal me, and I will give you the present I had from the czar.' I saw it, and I have seen

[1] Idiot, half-witted.

402

the star, for she gave him back his sight! . . . It is very wicked to talk so, and God will punish you for it."

"What star?" asked Peter.

"The Holy Virgin was promoted to the rank of general, no doubt," said Prince Andrew smiling. The old woman turned pale and clasped her hands in despair.

"Good God! how wicked!" she cried, turning very red again. "And you have a son! What have you said? God forgive you!" and she crossed herself. "God forgive him," she repeated to the princess, as she gathered her poor clothes together to go. She was ready to cry, for she was afraid and ashamed to benefit by the charity of a house where such things were said, while at the same time, no doubt, she was grieved to forgo it.

"What pleasure can it be to you to disturb them in their faith?" said Princess Maria. "Why did you come here?"

"But my dear, it was only my fun, only a jest. On my word I did not mean to hurt Pélaguéïouchka. It was not in earnest, I assure you."

The old woman paused, looking doubtful, but the sincere repentance in Peter's face, and Prince Andrew's look of kindness by degrees reconciled her.

CHAPTER XCIX

HAVING recovered from her annoyance, she turned to her favourite theme, and talked to them of Father Amphilochus, of his saintly life, and of how his hands smelt of incense; how that at Kiew, when she was last there, a monk she knew had given her the key of the catacombs where she had spent forty-eight hours among the saints, with nothing to eat but a piece of dry bread.

"I prayed before one and another; I slept a little and I kissed a third; and what peace, mother! What heavenly peace! I did not want to come up to God's earth again."

Peter watched her and listened to her eagerly; Prince Andrew presently left the room, and his sister, leaving the "Men of God" to themselves, led Peter into the drawing-room.

"You are most kind," she said.

"I did not wish to offend her, believe me; I sympathise with her feelings."

403

Princess Maria answered him with a smile.

"I have known you a long time and think of you as a brother. —How do you find Andrew? I am uneasy about him. His health was better last winter but in the spring his wound reopened, and the doctor recommends his going through some cure abroad. His state of mind worries me too: he cannot cry his grief out as we women can, but he carries it buried within himself; to-day he is lively and in good spirits, thanks to your visit—but he so seldom is! Try and persuade him to travel; he wants change and stir, this monotonous life is killing him. No one notices it, but I see it."

At ten o'clock at night the tinkling of harness-bells made all the servants rush out to the front steps to receive the old prince. Andrew and Peter went out to meet him.

"Who is it?" he asked as he got out of the carriage. "Ah! to be sure! Very glad!" he added, recognising the young man. "Kiss me—there!"

He was in a very good humour, and loaded Peter with friendly civilities, so that an hour later Prince Andrew found them in a warm discussion. Peter was proving that the day would come when there would be no more war, while the old man, without any temper, but laughing at him all the time, maintained the contrary.

"Bleed your men, and pour in water instead of blood, and then war will cease! All mere women's talk, mere women's dreams!" he added, patting his adversary kindly on the shoulder, and going up to the table where his son, who would take no part in the discussion, was looking over the papers he had brought.

"The *Maréchal de la Noblesse*," he said, "Count Rostow, has furnished scarcely half his contingent, and when I arrived in the town he actually took it into his head to ask me to dinner! I gave him an answer . . . to dinner, indeed! Just look at this paper. Do you know I like your friend; he wakes me up. Other people come and make intelligent observations and I do not want to listen to them, while this fellow pelts me with cock and bull stories which amuse my old brain. Now, go, go to supper; I will come presently perhaps, and have another argument . . . You will do me the favour of talking to my silly little Princess Maria, I hope?"

During this stay at Lissy-Gory Peter learnt to appreciate the charm of the affection that bound him to Prince Andrew. The old prince, and Princess Maria, who hardly knew him when he arrived, already treated him as an old friend. He felt himself warmly liked, not only by Princess Maria whom he had won by his gentleness to her protégés, but by the little man of a year old—Prince Nicholas, as his grandfather always called him; the child would smile at him and let him carry him. Mademoiselle Bourrienne and the architect listened in delight to his discussions with the old prince. The prince himself had come down to supper—this was a signal honour to Peter, and his good humour never failed him for an instant during the two days his guest spent under his roof.

When the family met together after his departure, and, as a natural consequence of his visit there, proceeded to dissect his character, they all, for a wonder, agreed in singing his praises, and in expressing the sympathy they felt for him.

CHAPTER C

ROSTOW on rejoining his regiment understood for the first time, how strong the ties were that bound him to Denissow and his fellow-soldiers. At the first sight of a hussar with his jacket unbuttoned, in whom he recognised the red-headed Denissow, of the chestnut horses picketed out, and, finally, at the sight of Lavrouchka shouting triumphantly to his master: "The count has come!"—at finding himself embraced by Denissow as he rushed out of his hut all tousled and sleepy, and at feeling the hearty clasp of his comrades' hands on his shoulder, Rostow felt just as he had felt on going home when his parents and sisters had smothered him with kisses; tears of joy rose to his throat and choked his speech. The regiment was also "home," a "home" as unchangeably dear as that of his parent's house.

After reporting himself to the colonel in command, and being appointed by him to his old duties in the same squadron, after making every inquiry into the minutest details, he felt in taking leave of his liberty and in fulfilling his duty in his narrow sphere the same sense of support and moral strength that he would have had in his own family. There was not indeed the mad whirl of the outer world which had so often led him into miserable wrongdoings; there was no Sonia, with

405

the perpetual doubt as to whether he ought or not to come to some explanation with her; here there was no possibility of rushing off ten ways at once, nor those twenty-four hours to be killed in various ways, nor that crowd of acquaintance, for the most part indifferent, nor those perpetual, unpleasant and embarrassing demands for money, nor such terrible losses at play as that to Dologhow; here everything was clear and precise. To him the whole world was divided into two unequal portions: one was *ours*, the Pavlograd Regiment; the other was everyone else, for whom he cared not a straw. Here everyone was known: they knew who the lieutenant was, who the captain—who was a rascal and who a good fellow; while the most important person in the world was the comrade, the *chum*. The purveyors gave credit, and a man drew his pay every third; hence there was no choice, no calculation was needed; nothing to do but to behave well and obey orders promptly and exactly.

Rostow, restored to these military habits of bondage, was as glad as a weary man is to go to bed and rest. This mode of life was all the more satisfactory because he had vowed after his losses at cards—which he could never forgive himself, in spite of the forgiveness of his parents—to atone for his wrongdoing, he would be irreproachable in the service, a good comrade and a blameless officer—that is to say, that he would be a thoroughly gallant gentleman, which in the wider world was far from easy, though in the regiment nothing could be easier. Finally, he had determined to repay the money to his father in the course of five years, by never spending more than two thousand roubles out of the ten thousand he received, and leaving the remainder at his father's disposal.

After various retreats and advances, and battles fought at Poultousk and at Preussisch-Eylau, the Russian forces were finally concentrated at Bartenstein. The czar was expected to open the campaign. The Pavlograd Regiment, which had fought in that of 1805, and which had just joined the main corps after recruiting its numbers in Russia, had not been present at those earlier engagements. As soon as it joined it was told off to serve with Platow, independently of the rest of the army. The hussars had had several skirmishes with the enemy, and on one occasion had even taken some prisoners and carried off Marshal Oudinot's baggage.

The month of April was spent in camp close to a deserted

and ruined German village. It was beginning to thaw; the weather was cold and dirty, the rivers drifted down blocks of ice, and the roads were impracticable, thus hindering the carriage of forage for the horses and victuals for the men; the soldiers wandered about the abandoned villages in search of a few wretched potatoes. Nothing was left; the inhabitants had fled, and the few that remained behind had sunk to the lowest depths of wretchedness, and were objects of compassion to the soldiers, who, rather than rob them of their last mouthful, gave them what little they could spare.

The regiment had lost but two men in their late skirmishes, but sickness and famine had reduced them to half their number. The mortality in the hospitals was so great that the soldier, reduced by fever and swellings produced by bad food, would remain at his post and drag himself in the ranks with his aching feet, rather than go into hospital. In the early days of spring the soldiers unearthed from the soil a plant somewhat resembling asparagus, which they named "sweet-root"—why, no one knew, since it was in fact very bitter. They hunted for it in every direction, dug it up and ate it, though this was expressly forbidden. A new form of disease—swelling of the face, hands and feet—which the doctors ascribed to the use of this noxious plant, carried off numerous victims, and yet Denissow's squadron continued to feed principally on this root. For a fortnight they had been kept on short rations of biscuit, and the last supplies of potatoes sent to the front had been found sprouting and frost-bitten.

The horses, quite appallingly lean, had nothing to eat but the straw of old thatch, and their winter coats were staring and knotted.

But in spite of all this misery, officers and soldiers alike lived on in the same routine. With pale and swollen faces, dressed in ragged uniforms, the hussars drew up in line as usual, fetched forage, groomed their horses, cleaned their arms and accoutrements, tore the thatch off the roofs, sat round their kettles to dine and got up famishing, laughing all the while at their meagre fare and hunger. In leisure moments they lighted their fires as usual, stripped to warm themselves, smoked, sorted and roasted their frost-bitten potatoes, telling stories all the while of the wars under Potemkin and Souvorow, or wonderful legends about Alëcha the spendthrift, or Mikolka the artisan.

The officers sat in twos and threes in their tumble-down huts; the older ones took thought for straw, for potatoes—

money was plentiful, but nothing to eat—and most of them spent their time in playing cards or the more innocent games of knuckle-bones or *svaïka*.[1] As a rule affairs in general were not much discussed, partly because nothing definite was known, and partly because they had a feeling that the war was not going well.

Rostow lodged with Denissow, and quite understood that, though his friend never mentioned the family, it was to Denissow's unfortunate attachment to Natacha that he owed his revived warmth of affection; their friendship was all the closer. Denissow sent Nicholas as rarely as possible on a service of danger, and welcomed him with enthusiastic delight when he returned safe and sound. In an expedition on which Rostow had been sent in search of supplies, he found, in a neighbouring village, an old Pole with his daughter, who had an infant at the breast. Only half clothed, perishing of cold and hunger, they had no means of quitting the place. Rostow brought them to the camp, took them into his own lodgings, and helped and fed them till the old man was well again. A fellow-officer, happening to speak of women, declared with a laugh, that Rostow was the sly one of them all, and that he might at least have introduced them to the pretty young Pole he had rescued. Rostow, hurt and indignant, replied with a torrent of abuse, and Denissow had the greatest difficulty to prevent their fighting. When the officer had left them Denissow, who himself was not fully aware of his friend's position with regard to the Polish lady, reproved him for his violence.

"But how could I help it? I regard her as my sister, and I cannot tell you how deeply I was hurt and offended—for it is just as if. . . ."

Denissow slapped him on the shoulder and took to walking up and down the room, a sign in him of very unusual excitement.

"What a devilish good sort these Rostows are!" he muttered; and Nicholas saw tears in his eyes.

[1] A game played with a ring and a nail with a large head.

The soldiers wandered about the abandoned villages in search of a few wretched
potatoes

BEFORE TILSIT

CHAPTER CI

At last, in April, the troops heard with delight that the czar had arrived. The Pavlograd Corps being quite to the front, beyond the outposts near Bartenstein, Rostow had not the pleasure of figuring at the imperial review.

He and Denissow were housed in a sort of underground hovel, dug out, and roofed in with branches and sods in a way that had recently been introduced. A trench was made more than twice as long as it was wide, with steps hewn out at one end to form an entrance; the trench was the abode; the richer officers had a wide plank, serving as a table, which rested on props, and occupied the end opposite to the entrance. A ledge left lengthwise formed the bed-place and sofa; the roof was sufficiently arched to allow of a man standing upright in the middle, and by squeezing past the table it was possible to sit up even on the bed. Denissow, whose men were devoted to him, always had everything in style; the front of his hovel was formed of a board with a pane of glass in it—the glass, to be sure, was broken, and mended with paper and glue. When the cold was severe, a sheet of metal was placed on the steps— Denissow styled that end "the drawing-room"—and on it was piled burning charcoal brought from the soldiers' fire; this gave out such a comfortable heat that the officers who met under his roof could sit in their shirt-sleeves.

Rostow on his return from duty one day, wet and weary after a night on horseback, had a heap of this live charcoal brought in, changed his clothes, said his prayers, swallowed his tea, arranged his belongings in his own corner, and stretched himself, well warmed, on his bed, his head resting on his arms while he dreamed, very much at his ease, of the promotion he might hope for, for his last reconnoitring expedition. Suddenly he heard his friend speaking outside in angry tones, and leaning over to the window to see what was wrong, he recognised Toptchenko, the quartermaster:

"I particularly desired you to forbid their eating that root!" cried Denissow, "and I saw a man carrying some."

"I have forbidden it, highness, but they will not listen to me."

Rostow lay down again, saying to himself with great satisfaction: "Faith! I have done my day's work; now it is his turn to see to his own!"

Lavrouchka, the crafty servant, threw his word into the

conversation that was going on outside; he declared that as he was going down to take the rations, he had seen strings of oxen and loads of biscuit.

"Saddle and mount at once, second company," cried Denissow, moving away.

"Where can they be going?" thought Rostow.

Five minutes later Denissow came in and threw himself on his bed, without taking off his muddy boots, lighted his pipe with evident ill-humour, rummaged through his baggage which he turned topsy-turvy, took up his sword and disappeared.

"Where are you off to?" cried Rostow; but Denissow, after muttering that he had something to do, rushed out exclaiming: "God and the czar be my judges!"

Rostow heard the trampling of horses in the slush, and then went to sleep very contentedly without troubling himself any further about Denissow. When he woke towards evening he was surprised to find that his comrade had not yet returned. The weather was fine; two officers and a *junker* were playing at *svaïka,* and he joined them. In the midst of their game they saw some waggons coming with an escort of hussars, about fifteen men on their haggard chargers. As soon as they reached the outposts they were surrounded by others.

"Here are supplies!" cried Rostow . . . "And Denissow was grumbling . . ."

"What a good time for the men!" said the officers.

Denissow arrived the last, riding with two infantry officers; they were wrangling vehemently.

"I tell you plainly, captain . . ." said one of them—a short, lean man, and very indignant.

"And I tell you plainly, I will give nothing back."

"You will have to answer for it, captain. It is pillage—seizing waggons under escort! And our men have had nothing to eat these two days."

"And mine have had nothing these two weeks."

"It is highway robbery, and you will be called to account for it," repeated the infantryman, raising his voice.

"Let me alone, will you?" exclaimed Denissow, suddenly firing up. "All right—I will account for it; it is my doing and not yours. What are you talking about? Look out there —Clear the way."

"Very good!" exclaimed the little man, without flinching or stirring from the spot.

"Go to the devil! Clear out, and mind what you are about . . ." and Denissow turned the head of his antagonist's horse.

"Very good, very good!" said the other, in threatening wrath, and he set off at a trot that shook him in the saddle.

"A dog, a hound! A dog riding a gate-post. . .!" This was the bitterest form of insult a cavalryman could offer to an infantryman on horseback. "I carried off all their baggage train by force!" added Denissow, going towards Rostow. "I could not leave my men to die of starvation!"

The waggons he had captured belonged to a detachment of foot, but having ascertained from Lavrouchka that they had no escort, Denissow had fallen upon them with his hussars. Double rations of biscuit were at once served out, and the other squadrons had a share.

Next day, the colonel of the regiment sent for Denissow, and looking at him through his spread-out fingers, he said:

"Now this is my view of the matter; I do not want to know anything about it, and I ask no questions; but I advise you to go straight to headquarters and make matters right with the commissary. Do your best to persuade him to take your receipt for such and such supplies furnished to you; otherwise it will all be entered to the credit of the infantry regiment, and an inquiry once started might come to no good."

Denissow went off at once, fully prepared to act on this advice but on his return he was in such a state that Rostow, who had never seen him like this, was terrified. He could hardly speak or breathe, and made no reply to his friend's questions but by volleys of husky and gasping abuse. Rostow persuaded him to undress, to drink a little water and send for the doctor.

"Would you believe it?—they are going to try me for pillage! . . . Give me some water. Well, let them, but I will punish them, the cowards. I will appeal to the emperor. Give me some ice."

The doctor came and bled him, and the dark blood filled a plate. When this had relieved him he was able to tell Rostow what had happened.

"I got there—'Where is the chief?' They showed me . . . 'You must wait.'—'Impossible; my duty is waiting, I have ridden thirty versts, I have no time to wait—show me in.' At length the robber-in-chief condescends to make his appearance; he gives me a lecture—'It is highway robbery!'—'A robber,' say I, 'is not the man who seizes victuals to feed his soldiers, but the man who fills his own pockets.'—Very good; he tells me I must sign a receipt in the commissary's office, and then the matter must take its course. I am shown into the room; the commissary is sitting at his table. Who is it do you think? Guess—guess who it is that is starving us," cried Denissow, striking the table with his crippled arm with such force that the board danced and the glasses rattled.—"Télianine!—'What,' said I, 'so it is you who stop our supplies? You have had your face slapped once already, and got off only too cheaply.' And I gave it him; how I enjoyed it!" he went on, with ferocious satisfaction, showing his white teeth under his black moustache.

"Come, come, don't shout, keep quiet; here is your arm bleeding again; wait while I bandage it."

They got him to bed and when he woke he was himself again.

The next day, before dusk, an aide-de-camp came in looking grave and regretful, showed him the official paper sent in to the colonel, and asked him several questions as to his yesterday's exploit. He did not conceal from him that the matter looked ugly, that a military commission had been appointed, and that, seeing how severely cases of rapine and breach of discipline were generally treated, he might think himself lucky if he were only degraded.

This was the aspect given to the affair by the plaintiffs: "Major Denissow, after pouncing on the baggage train, had come, unbidden and the worse for liquor, into the presence of the chief of the commissariat, had called him a thief, had threatened to thrash him, and then, when he was dragged away, had rushed into the office and beaten two clerks, one of whom had had his arm sprained."

Denissow laughed, and said it was a fancy-picture, devoid of sense; that he was not afraid of any trial, and that if those wretches attacked him he had means of shutting their mouths as they would very well remember.

Nicholas, however, was not to be taken in by the light way in which he affected to treat the business; he knew him too well not to guess at his uneasiness about a matter which might lead to serious issues. Every day someone came to worry him with fresh questions and fresh explanations, and on the first of May he was ordered to give up his command to the officer next in seniority, and to present himself at headquarters to give an account of his acts of violence in the Food-Supply Commission.

The day before, Platow had been reconnoitring with two regiments of Cossacks and two squadrons of hussars. Denissow proved his unfailing courage by advancing to the very lines of

"It is highway robbery!"

the enemy's sharpshooters. A French bullet hit him in the leg. Under ordinary circumstances he would have made nothing of so slight a wound and would not have quitted his duty, but it now served as an excuse for avoiding appearing at headquarters and for being sent to hospital.

CHAPTER CII

IN the month of June the battle of Friedland was fought; in this the Pavlograd Hussars bore no part; it was followed by an armistice. Rostow, feeling very deserted without his friend, and having had no news of him since his departure, was uneasy as to the possible results of his wound, and took advantage of the truce to go to the hospital, which had been established in a hamlet twice sacked by Russian and by French troops. It looked doubly dismal because the season was a fine one, and the sight of the fields gladdened the eyes, while nothing was to be seen in the ruined streets but a few natives in rags, or drunk and invalided soldiers. A stone house with the window panes for the most part broken, was dignified by the name of hospital. A few soldiers with limbs wrapped in bandages, pale and puffy, sat or walked up and down to warm themselves in the sun.

Rostow had hardly crossed the threshold when he felt choked and sickened by the mingled stench of drugs and decomposition that pervaded the place. On the stairs he met a Russian army-doctor with a cigar in his mouth, and with him a surgeon.

"I cannot be in two places at once," the doctor was saying. "I will meet you this evening at Makar Alexéïévitch's lodgings. Do the best you can. Is it not all the same in the end?"

"Whom are you wanting, highness?" said the doctor to Rostow. "Why do you come here to take typhus fever when you have escaped the French bullets? It is a plague-stricken spot."

"What?" said Rostow.

"The typhus is fearful; it is death to come within these walls. We have not succumbed to it, Makéïew and I," he added, pointing to his companion, "but five of our colleagues have been carried off. A week after a man comes in . . . and it is all over with him. They sent us some Prussians, but it did not suit our allies at all."

413

Rostow explained that he wished to see Major Denissow.

"I do not know, I do not remember him. That is not to be wondered at: I have three hospitals on my hands and four hundred sick, more or less. And we think ourselves lucky when the charitable German ladies send us two pounds of coffee and some lint every month; without it we could not hold out. . . . Four hundred, think of that, without counting the fresh cases to come in."

The surgeon's worn and weary expression betrayed his impatience of the loquacious doctor's delay.

"Major Denissow," repeated Rostow. "Wounded at Molliten?"

"To be sure. He is dead I think—is not he, Makéïew?" said the doctor with the utmost indifference; but the surgeon thought not.

"A red-haired man, tall?" asked the doctor; and then when Rostow described his friend, he added quite joyfully: "To be sure; I remember. He must be dead. However, I will look through my lists. Are they in your rooms, Makéïew?"

"Makar Alexéïévitch has them. Would you take the trouble to go yourself into the officers' room?" added Makéïew, turning to Rostow.

"I strongly advise you not, my dear fellow, you run the very greatest risk," said the doctor; but Rostow took leave of him and begged the surgeon to show him the way.

"You have no one but yourself to blame, remember, if mischief comes of it," cried the doctor from the bottom of the stairs.

The smell in the hospital was so revolting in the narrow passage they went through, that Rostow held his nose and even staggered for a moment. A door opened on the right, and out of it came a living skeleton—pale, emaciated, and barefoot, dragging himself on crutches and looking with envious eyes at the new-comer. Our hussar glanced into the room and saw the patients lying on the floor, some on straw, some on their cloaks.

"May I go in?" he asked.

"There is nothing to see," said the surgeon, but this reply only piqued his curiosity, and Rostow went in. The stench here was even worse and more penetrating.

In a long room, exposed to a broiling sun, lay two rows of sick and wounded, their heads towards the wall, leaving a passage down the middle; most of them were delirious, and took no notice of the intruders. The others, raising their heads as the two visitors came in, turned their wax-like faces to gaze at them with a look of expecting some providential rescue, and of involuntary jealousy of Rostow's fresh health. Rostow went forward as far as the middle of the room, and looking beyond, through half-open doors into the adjoining wards, he saw only a repetition of the same terrible sight which he stood silently contemplating. Close to his feet, almost across the passage, lay a man, a Cossack no doubt, as was easily seen by the way his hair was cut. With his arms and legs flung out, a burning face, and eyes turned up till only the whites were visible, the veins in his hands and feet swelled almost to bursting, he beat his head against the floor, saying some word again and again in a hoarse voice. Rostow bent over him to hear: "Drink, drink!" said the poor wretch.

Rostow looked about him wondering whither he could carry the dying man to give him some water.

"Who looks after them?" he asked the surgeon.

At this moment a soldier attached to the ambulance came out of the next room, and taking Rostow for one of the hospital inspectors touched his cap as he passed.

"Carry this man away and give him some water."

"Certainly, highness," said the soldier, but he did not move.

"Nothing will be done," thought Rostow, and he was about to leave the room when a gaze resolutely fixed on his face impelled him instinctively to look into one corner. An old soldier, yellow, gloomy-looking, with an unkempt grizzly beard, seemed to wish to speak to him. Rostow went up to him, and saw that one of his legs had been amputated above the knee. Next to him lay a young man quite motionless; his head thrown back, his colourless face and fixed gaze with half-shut eyelids attracted Rostow's notice. He shuddered: "But this man, it seems to me . . ."

"Yes, highness; and we have begged and prayed," said the old soldier, with a tremulous quiver of his jaw. "He died at daybreak. . . . And they are men after all, and not dogs. . . ."

"He shall be removed this minute," the surgeon hastened to throw in. "Come, highness."

"Yes, come, come—" said Rostow no less hurriedly; he cast down his eyes, trying to pass unobserved through the cross-fire of all these anxious eyes fixed on him with reproach and envy.

CHAPTER CIII

THEY crossed the corridor and went into the officers' ward, consisting of three rooms opening into each other; here there were beds, on which the patients were lying or sitting. Some of them were walking up and down, wrapped in their dressing-gowns. The first man Rostow observed was a lean little officer who had lost an arm, in a cotton night-cap with a pipe in his mouth, who was pacing the first of the three rooms. He tried to remember where he had seen him before.

"This is how we meet again!" exclaimed the little man. "I am Touschine who got you back safe at Schöngraben, and as you see," and he waved his empty sleeve, "I am minus a small portion. You want to find Denissow; he is my neighbour here. Come this way," and he led him into the next room, where loud laughter was audible.

"How can they find anything to laugh at here?" said Rostow to himself; he could not get rid of the deathlike smell, nor forget the eyes that had followed him out of the other room.

Denissow, with his head under the coverlet, was still fast asleep, though it was now noonday.

"Oh, Rostow! how do you do, how do you do?" he exclaimed in his usual voice, but Rostow perceived with pain that an unwonted asperity betrayed itself in his face and in his words, through all his vivacity and light-heartedness.

His wound, though trifling, had not healed through six weeks spent in the hospital; his face was white and swollen like those of his fellow sufferers; still, it was not that which struck Rostow; it was his friend's forced smile—he seemed to find no pleasure in his visit, and asked him no questions as to the regiment or what was happening; he merely listened when Nicholas spoke of it.

He took no interest in anything; he seemed to have made up his mind to forget the past, and to have one sole predominating thought: his quarrel with the commissariat. When Rostow asked him how matters were progressing, he pulled a number of papers out from under his pillow, among them the last document he had received at the close of the inquiry and the rough copy of his own reply, with which he was evidently much pleased, for he pointed out to Rostow, the various sharp insinuations with which it was spiced. His companions, who at first had crowded round a new-comer freighted with news from out-

416

side, dropped away one by one as soon as Denissow began to read, and their faces plainly betrayed that they had long since had more than enough of the story. His neighbour in the next bed, a burly Uhlan, who was gloomily smoking, and little Touschine, shaking his head disapprovingly, were the only two who remained to listen.

"It seems to me," said the Uhlan, interrupting him in the middle of his reading, "that there is but one thing to be done, and that is to petition the emperor for pardon. They say that rewards and honours will be rained upon us, and he will be sure to grant it . . ."

"I! ask pardon of the emperor!" exclaimed Denissow, indignantly, though he tried in vain to give his voice its old energy. "Why? If I had been a robber I could have done no more than crave pardon; and because I attack these wretches? . . . They may try me, I am not afraid: I have served the czar and my country with honour; I did not steal! And I am to be degraded because . . . What next! . . . But listen to what I go on to say: 'If indeed, I had robbed the government . . .'"

"It is capitally written, as anyone can see," said Touschine, "but that is not the point, Vassili Dmitritch. You must give in. And that is what he will not do," he added, addressing Rostow; "though the presiding officer told him it was a bad business."

"Well, so much the worse!" said Denissow.

"But the president drew up a petition for you," Touschine went on. "You had better sign it and entrust it to Rostow; he is sure to have some acquaintance on the staff, and you will not have a better opportunity."

"I have told you that I will stoop to no mean trick," said Denissow, and he went on with his reading.

Rostow was quite of Touschine's opinion, as were the other officers; he felt instinctively that this was the only possible issue, and he would gladly have done his friend this service; but knowing his stubborn will, and that his wrath was well founded, he dared not urge him.

When this wearisome reading, which lasted more than an hour, was at an end, the others gathered round them again, and Rostow, very painfully impressed, spent the rest of the day talking of one thing and another, and listening to the tales of these poor wounded men; while Denissow, depressed and morose, said no more. At length, late in the evening, Rostow felt he must be going, and at the last moment asked Denissow if he had no commissions.

"Yes," he said. "Wait a moment," and pulling out his papers again, he went to the window-ledge, where an inkstand stood, and dipped a pen.

"There is nothing for it, a switch cannot break an axe," he said, as he gave an envelope into Rostow's hands.

It was his petition to the czar, in which, without a word as to his grievances against the commissariat, he merely and simply craved pardon.

"Give it to the right person; it is quite clear . . ." but he could say no more; he forced his lips to a melancholy and painful smile.

CHAPTER CIV

On his return Rostow put the colonel in possession of the facts as to Denissow's position, and then set out for Tilsit with the petition in his pocket.

On the 13th of June the two emperors, Alexander and Napoleon, met; Boris Droubetzkoï obtained permission to form part of the suite of an officer of high rank on this grand occasion.

"I should like to see the great man," he had said, speaking of Napoleon, whom, till now, he, like everyone else, had called Bonaparte.

"You mean Bonaparte?" said the general with a smile.

Boris perceived at once that this was a sort of test of his tact.

"I mean the Emperor Napoleon, prince . . ." And his patron patted him kindly on the shoulder.

"You will get on," he said; and he took him with him.

Thus it came to pass that Boris was one of the elect who were present at the interview on the banks of the Niemen. He saw the tents and rafts displaying the interlaced initials of the two sovereigns; the arrival of Napoleon and his driving past his Guards. Napoleon on the further shore; Alexander, grave and thoughtful, awaiting the arrival of his future ally in a tavern. He saw the two monarchs get into boats, and saw Napoleon, who reached the raft first, hasten forward to meet the czar and give him his hand; then they disappeared into the marquee. Since his introduction to the upper circles, Boris had made a practice of attentively watching all that went on around him, and making notes: he inquired the names of the various members of Napoleon's suite, examined their uniforms, listened to what the more important dignitaries were saying, looked at his watch to ascertain the exact hour at which the emperors had withdrawn into the tent, and again when Alexander reappeared. The interview lasted one hour and fifty-three minutes, and he recorded it among other facts of historical importance. The czar's suite was not numerous; hence it was a matter of mark to have been at Tilsit on this occasion, and Boris was not slow in finding this out. His position was secured; his presence was an accepted fact; thenceforth he was one of this select "set," and twice he was sent on a mission to the czar. Nay, the czar himself recognised him, and the Court circle, ceasing to regard him as an interloper, would, indeed, have been surprised by his absence.

He shared the lodgings of another aide-de-camp, Count Gelinski, a Pole, who had been educated in Paris, immensely rich, and an enthusiastic admirer of the French, whose tent, during the few days spent at Tilsit, was the centre where the French officers of the Guard and the imperial staff constantly met at breakfast and at dinner.

On the 27th Count Gelinski gave a supper; one of Napoleon's aides-de-camp filled the place of honour, and among the guests were several officers of the French Imperial Guard, and a young lad, of an old and distinguished family, who was Napoleon's page. That very evening Rostow took advantage of the darkness to pass unrecognised in mufti, and went to call on Boris.

The troops with whom he was serving were not yet by any means tuned up to the pitch of the harmony so recently established at headquarters with Napoleon and the French—their old foes now recognised as friends: a state of affairs which inevitably followed on the change that had come over the political attitude of the two nations. In the army Bonaparte was still regarded by all with feelings of hatred, contempt, and terror. Rostow, a few days previously, when discussing the matter with an officer of Platow's division, had done his utmost to prove that if only they had had the luck to take Napoleon prisoner, he would have been treated as a criminal, and not as a crowned head. On another occasion he was talking with a French officer, who had been wounded, and allowed himself to be so far heated as to say that there could be no question of peace between a legitimate emperor and a rascal. Hence, the sight of the French officers, and of the uniforms he had been accustomed to see only at outposts, startled him strangely. He had hardly caught sight of them when the natural feelings of a soldier—the hostility that they always roused in him, fired up in his soul.

He stopped at Droubetzkoï's lodgings, and asked in Russian if he were within. Boris, hearing a strange voice, came out to meet him, and could not conceal an impulse of annoyance.

"It is you?" he said. "I am very glad to see you," he added, however; but not so soon but that Rostow had become aware of his first impression.

"I have come at a wrong time," he said, coldly. "I came on business; otherwise . . ."

"Not at all; I was only astonished to see you here. I will be with you in a moment," replied Boris, to someone who was calling him from within.

"I see—I am intruding," Nicholas repeated; but Boris had by this time made up his mind as to his conduct, and drew Rostow in along with him. His calm and sober gaze seemed to have disappeared, hidden behind the "blue spectacles" of worldly ease and wisdom.

"You are quite wrong in thinking so. Come in here!" The table was laid; he introduced Nicholas to his guests, and explained to them that he was not a civilian, but an officer, and one of his oldest friends. Rostow looked hard at the Frenchmen, and bowed ungraciously.

Gelinski, ill pleased at the advent of this Russian, said nothing: Boris, on his part, pretended not to be aware of the awkward lull in the circle, and did his best to revive the conversation. One of the company turned to Rostow with true French politeness, and, to break his obstinate silence, asked him if he had come intending to see the Emperor Napoleon.

"No, I came on business," said Rostow, sullenly.

His ill-temper, reinforced by the evident discomposure of his friend, made him believe that everyone was eyeing him with ill-will; though, for that matter, this was true enough: his presence fettered them, and in consequence of his being there, the conversation began to flag.

"And why does he go on sitting there?" questioned the glances of the guests. "I feel that I am in the way," he said to Boris. "Let me tell you my business, and be off again."

"Not at all: stay here; or if you are tired, go and rest a little while in my room."

They went into the little room where Boris slept. Nicholas, without even sitting down, explained to him in a tone of great irritation all Denissow's business, and asked him, in so many words, whether he could and would place his petition in the hands of the general to be laid before the czar. For the first time in his life Boris's expression struck him unpleasantly; in fact, Boris, sitting with his legs crossed, was looking about him and round the room, and paying the vaguest attention to his friend. He listened to his story, much as a general listens to a report by one of his subalterns:

"Yes," he said, "I have heard of many such cases; the czar is extremely rigid on these points. It would be better, I believe, to give up the idea of presenting it to his majesty, and to address it simply to the general commanding the division; after that I believe. . . ."

"Which all means that you will do nothing: Say it out!" exclaimed Rostow, greatly provoked.

"On the contrary; I will do everything I can."

Gelinski, on the other side of the door, was calling Boris.

"Go, go to them," said Nicholas; but he declined to join the supper party, and remained in the little bedroom, which he paced in all directions to the lively sound of French voices.

CHAPTER CV

THE day in fact was ill chosen for any proceedings of this character. Rostow could not present himself before the general on duty without either uniform or leave; and Boris, even with the best will in the world, could do nothing next day—the 27th June—(9th July)—when the preliminaries of peace were to be signed. The emperors exchanged orders on the occasion, Alexander accepting the ribbon of the Legion of Honour, and Napoleon that of the Russian Order of St. Andrew. A splendid banquet, at which the emperors were present by invitation, was to be given by the French Imperial Guard to the Préobrajensky Regiment.

The more Rostow reflected on Boris's line of conduct, the more it disgusted him. He pretended to be asleep when Boris came, and next morning he vanished at an early hour to run about the town in his civilian's dress and top hat, to stare at the French and their uniforms, and at the houses where the two sovereigns were lodged. On the main square men were already employed in setting out the tables for the great entertainment, and in hanging the fronts of the houses with Russian and French flags embroidered with the letters A. and N.

"It is perfectly clear that Boris will do nothing," said Nicholas to himself, "it is an end to our friendship! But I will not quit the place and leave a stone unturned in Denissow's cause. His letter must reach the czar . . . and the czar is in there!" he added, meditatively, as he involuntarily went up to the imperial quarters. Two horses, ready saddled, were waiting at the door, and the suite were assembled to escort Alexander.

"I shall see him, but how can I present the petition myself? How can I tell him everything? Shall I be arrested, I wonder, because I am not in uniform? No, no; *he* will understand, for *he* understands everything. And if they should arrest me? there would be no great harm in that. . . . Ah! they are assembling! Well, I shall go forward and present it: so much the worse for Droubetzkoï, who compels me to it. . . ."

And he went towards the door of the imperial residence with more decision than he could have expected in himself. "I will not miss my chance this time, as I did at Austerlitz; I will fall at his feet, I will entreat him, beseech him . . ." his heart beat high at the mere thought of seeing him: "He will listen to me, bid me rise and say: "I am glad to be able to do good, and right injustice. . . ." And he went in, taking no notice of the inquiring eyes that followed him.

A wide staircase led up to the first floor; to the right was a closed door, and under the slope of the stairs another door.

"Whom do you want?" asked someone.

"I have a petition to present to his majesty," said Nicholas wtih a tremulous voice.

"Then be so good as to go to the officer on duty (and the lower door was pointed out to him), else it will not be accepted."

At this bidding, so calmly given, Rostow took fright; the mere idea of suddenly finding himself face to face with the czar was at once so delightful and so appalling, that he was on the point of flying, but the sergeant in waiting opened a door and showed him into the presence of the officer on duty. A man of middle height and of about thirty years of age, in white breeches and high boots, who had just got himself into his fine cambric shirt, was standing to have his braces buttoned by his valet.

"A good figure and very bewitching!" he was saying to some-one in an inner room. Seeing Rostow he frowned and said no more.

"What do you want? A petition?"

"What is it?" asked a voice from within.

"Another petitioner," replied the one who was dressing.

"Tell him to wait; put him off till later. He is going out now, and we have to attend him."

"To-morrow, to-morrow; it is too late now."

Rostow withdrew a few steps towards the door. "Who is the petitioner."

"Major Denissow."

"And you, who are you? An officer?"

"Count Rostow, lieutenant."

"How rash! The petition should have come through your colonel's hands. Go—be off—as quick as you can." And he went on with his interrupted toilet.

Rostow went. The terrace outside was crowded with generals in full dress, and he had no choice but to pass by them. Dying of terror at the mere thought that he might possibly meet the emperor, he was afraid lest he should be put to confusion before him, perhaps even arrested; he now saw and repented of his injudicious conduct, and was stealing with downcast eyes through the splendid crowd, when a familiar bass voice called him by his name, and a hand was laid on his shoulder: "What are you doing here, my dear fellow—and in mufti too?"

It was a cavalry officer, formerly in command of Rostow's division, who, during this campaign, had succeeded in gaining the czar's good graces. The younger man in his alarm hastily justified himself; but his superior's good-humoured tone of raillery reassured him; he took him aside, explained the position of affairs with eager pathos, and implored his assistance. The general shook his head. "A hard case for a brave fellow," he said. "Give me the petition."

Hardly had he obeyed when a sound of spurs was heard on the steps and the general rejoined the rest. The suite all came down and immediately mounted. An equerry named Heine, the same who had attended the czar at the battle of Austerlitz, was leading the emperor's charger; then a slight creaking of boots was heard on the stairs within, and Nicholas guessed who was coming. Forgetting all his fears of being recognised, he made his way among the curious bystanders, and once more, after an interval of two years, could gaze on those features, that mien, that dignified figure, that fascinating union of sweetness and majesty which was so dear to him. His loyalty and devotion revived with new force. The czar wore the uniform of the Préobrajensky Guards: tightly-fitting breeches and high boots, and on his breast blazed a foreign order—the Legion of Honour—which Rostow did not recognise. He held his hat under his arm while he pulled on his gloves, and his brilliant glance seemed to light up all he looked on. He spoke a word or two as he passed to a few privileged beings, and recognising the cavalry general, he smiled and signed to him to approach. Everyone else made way, and Rostow saw that they held a rather long conversation.

The czar took a step towards his horse; the suite and the crowd pressed forward, and Alexander, laying his hand on the saddle, turned once more to the general and said in a distinct voice, as if he wished to be heard by all:

"Impossible, general. Impossible, because the law is greater than I." He put his foot in the stirrup; the general bowed submissively.

As the czar rode off at a gallop, Rostow, forgetting everything but his enthusiasm, ran after him with the crowd.

CHAPTER CVI

The Préobrajensky Guards and the French Imperial Guard, with their tall fur caps, were drawn up in line; the Russians on the right, the French on the left.

Just as the czar rode up, and they were presenting arms, another party of horsemen, in front of which rode a personage whom Rostow easily guessed to be Napoleon, made their appearance on the other side of the square. He galloped forward on a thoroughbred grey Arab, covered with a purple housing, embroidered with gold. He wore the well-known little cocked hat, the ribbon of St. Andrew on a dark blue uniform, which was unbuttoned over a white waistcoat. As he came up with the czar he raised his hat, and Rostow's practised eye at once detected that his seat was not good. The soldiers shouted "Hurrah;" and "Vive l'empereur!" After exchanging a few words, the allied sovereigns dismounted and shook hands. Napoleon's smile was artificial and unpleasing, while Alexander's was conspicuous for its expression of natural benevolence.

Rostow never took his eyes off them, in spite of the pushing of the French mounted guard, who had been charged to keep the crowd in order; he was amazed to see the czar treat Napoleon in every respect as an equal, and Napoleon do the same with perfect ease of manner.

The two emperors, followed by their suites, went towards the Préobrajensky Regiment; Rostow, who was in the foremost rank of a great crowd collected just at this spot, was so near his adored sovereign that he was afraid he might be identified.

"Sire, I would ask your leave to give the Legion of Honour to the bravest man in the ranks," said a clear voice, pronouncing every syllable distinctly. It was little Bonaparte's; as he spoke he looked up from below, straight into the czar's eyes and Alexander, listening attentively, smiled and bowed assent.

"To the man who behaved with the greatest courage in the late war," added Napoleon, with a cool precision that provoked Rostow; and he looked along the Russian ranks, who had presented arms, and never took their eyes off the czar's face.

"Your majesty will allow me to take counsel of the colonel?" said Alexander, going forward a few steps towards Kozlovsky, in command of the battalion. Napoleon, with some difficulty, drew his glove off his small white hand; it tore, and he threw it away. And aide-de-camp rushed forward to pick it up.

"To whom is it to be given?" asked Alexander, in a low tone, and in Russian.

"To the soldier your majesty may designate."

The czar frowned involuntarily: "I must give him an answer," he said.

Kozlovsky's eye ran down the ranks and rested for an instant on Rostow.

"What—me, by any chance?" thought Nicholas.

"Lazarew," said the colonel, decisively; the first man in the front rank stepped forward, his face quivering with excitement—as a man's face always does at being suddenly called to the front.

"Where are you going? Stand still!" muttered several voices; and Lazarew not knowing what to do, stood still in alarm.

Napoleon slightly turned his head and held out his plump little hand as if to take something. The officers of his suite, understanding his wish, whispered and stirred, and handed a

small object from one to another, till the page whom Rostow
had seen at Boris's rooms came forward, and with a low bow,
placed a cross with a red ribbon in the waiting hand. Napoleon
took it without looking at it, and went up to Lazarew, who still
stared wide-eyed at the czar. With a glance at Alexander,
intended to convey that this proceeding was a courtesy to
him, Napoleon laid his hand holding the cross on the soldier's
breast, as if his mere touch was enough to make the brave
fellow for ever happy to wear the cross that distinguished him
above the rest. His hand graciously rested on the private's
breast, and the cross was immediately pinned into the place
where he had held it by eager officers, Russian and French.
Lazarew watched the little man's proceeding with gloomy
gravity, and then, without moving a muscle, looked once
more at his sovereign as if to ask him what he was to do;
but receiving no orders he remained where he was for some
minutes, as motionless as a statue.

The emperors remounted and rode away. The Préobrajensky
Guards dispersed, mingled with the French Grenadiers, and
took their places at the tables. Lazarew was placed in a seat
of honour; he was embraced and congratulated by all, French
and Russians; officers shook hands with him, and crowded
round him; and the confused buzz of languages, with laughter
and singing, was to be heard on every side of the square. Two
officers with heated and jolly faces passed just in front of
Rostow:

"What a feast, my dear fellow! and all served on silver
plate! . . . Did you see Lazarew?"

"Yes, I saw him!"

"To-morrow, they say, the Préobrajensky are going to return
the dinner."

"A lucky rascal that Lazarew! 1200 francs a year for life."

"What a headpiece!" exclaimed a Préobrajensky, putting
on a grenadier's bearskin cap.

"Most becoming!"

"Have you heard the password?" asked an officer of the
Guards of his companion. "The day before yesterday it was
'Napoleon, France and courage'—yesterday 'Alexander, Russia
and glory.' One day the czar gives the words and the next
day Napoleon—and to-morrow he will send the Cross of St.
George to the bravest man in the French Guards. He can do
no less than return the compliment!"

Boris and his friend Gelinski had come out to admire the

banquet scene, and they discovered Rostow leaning against a house-corner.

"Nicholas! How are you? What have you been about? I lost you. What ails you?" he added, seeing that Rostow looked fierce and morose.

"Nothing, nothing."

"You will join us by and by?"

"Yes, I will come."

But Rostow stood a long time leaning against the wall, watching the heroes of the entertainment, while a painful process was going on within him. His soul was torn by agonising doubts, and he could find no satisfactory answer to them. He thought of Denissow, of his embittered indifference, and unexpected surrender; he could see the hospital and its dirt, the horrible diseases, the missing arms and legs,—he almost fancied he smelt the dead man lying there. Indeed, the impression was so strong that he looked about him to see what it was that sickened him. He thought of Bonaparte, and his self-satisfied air; of Bonaparte, an emperor, welcomed and respected by his own adored czar. But then what reason was there for all these lost limbs? For all these men killed?— Lazarew with an order on one side, Denissow disgraced and hopeless on the other—till he himself was frightened at the turn his reflections were taking.

Hunger, and the smell of the food roused him from his reverie; and as, after all, he must get something to eat before going home, he went into an inn that was at hand. A large number of officers were assembled there, who, like him, had come in mufti to look on, and he had much difficulty in getting himself served with dinner. Two of his own fellow-officers joined him: they began discussing the peace, and all, like most of the army indeed, expressed their dissatisfaction. They declared that if only they had stood their ground after Friedland, Napoleon must have been defeated, for that he had neither supplies nor ammunition. Nicholas ate his dinner in silence, and drank more than he ate; he had got through two bottles of wine already, and yet the confusion in his brain weighed on him more and more and grew no clearer; he was afraid to give way to his thoughts, and yet he could not shake them off. Suddenly, hearing an officer observe that the presence of the French was humiliating, he broke out with a violence which there was no excuse for, and which amazed his neighbour. His face grew crimson:

427

"How dare you criticise the czar's actions?" he said. "What right have we to judge? We cannot know either his purpose or his motive!"

"But I have not said a word about the emperor," replied the officer, unable to attribute this strange burst of temper to anything but drink.

"We are not diplomatic bureaucrats, we are soldiers and nothing more," Rostow went on. "We are ordered to die, and we die, . . . and if we are punished there is no help for it—it is because we have deserved it—it is not our place to judge! If our sovereign chooses to recognise Napoleon as emperor, and to conclude an alliance with him, it must be right for some reason, and if we once begin to criticise and judge, there will soon be nothing sacred. We shall end by denying the existence of God—of anything!—" and he struck the table with his fist; his ideas, though they could not but seem incoherent to his audience, were the logical outcome of his meditations.

"There is but one thing for us to do: Our Duty—to fight and never think; that is the whole story!" he exclaimed in conclusion.

"And drink," added one of his companions, anxious to avoid a quarrel.

"Aye, and drink," echoed Nicholas eagerly. "Waiter, another bottle!"

*This book was designed by William B. Taylor
and printed on wood-free paper,
made by Papeteries de Belmont
by Klausfelder S. A., Vevey
The binding was executed
by H. Weber AG., Winterthur*

Printed in Switzerland